Three Kingdoms

三國演義

Three Kingdoms
China's Epic Drama

by Lo Kuan-chung

Translated from the Chinese and edited by
MOSS ROBERTS

PANTHEON BOOKS
New York

Designed by Irva Mandelbaum

Library of Congress Cataloging in Publication Data
Lo, Kuan-chung, ca. 1330–ca. 1400.
  Three Kingdoms.

  Abridged translation of *San kuo chih yen i.*
  1. China—History—Three kingdoms, 220–265—Fiction. I. Roberts, Moss, 1937–   II. Title.
PL2690.S3E53   1976   895.1'3'4   76–9607
ISBN 0—394—73393—2

Manufactured in the United States of America

98765432

To the memory of
Peter A. Boodberg
Edna Luftig
Eugene Roberts

ACKNOWLEDGMENTS

The translator wishes to express his gratitude first of all to those under whom he studied Chinese language and culture: the late Professor Peter A. Boodberg, Professor W. T. de Bary, Liu Yü-yün, Mr. Charles Lo, Mr. K. H. Lu, and Professor C. N. Tay.

The translator wishes to thank the editor, James Peck, and the copy editor, Mary Barnett, for the care and sensitivity with which they worked on the manuscript; David Horowitz for his help and encouragement; and Jung May Lee for her exquisite maps.

The translator also wishes to express his appreciation to the students in the Chinese studies program at New York University.

Finally, the translator wishes to thank his mother, Helen, and his wife, Florence, and E. A. M., for more than can be expressed in words.

CONTENTS

ILLUSTRATIONS

These illustrations have been taken from three books: an early Ch'ing woodblock edition of *Three Kingdoms (Ssu ta ch'i shu ti i chung)* * in the Gest Oriental Library at Princeton University; Lu Chan's *Illustrated Record of the Saintly Career of Lord Kuan* (1829); and an 1894 edition of *Three Kingdoms.* The translator is indebted to Mr. James T'ung, Curator, and Ms. Maureen Donovan, Reference Librarian, of the Gest Oriental Library at Princeton University for their assistance in locating and identifying the illustrative material.

An [a] after the caption denotes that the illustration is from the 1644 edition.

A [b] denotes that the illustration is from the 1829 edition.

A [c] denotes that the illustration is from the 1894 edition.

* Although the preface is dated 1644, the text is possibly later.

MAPS

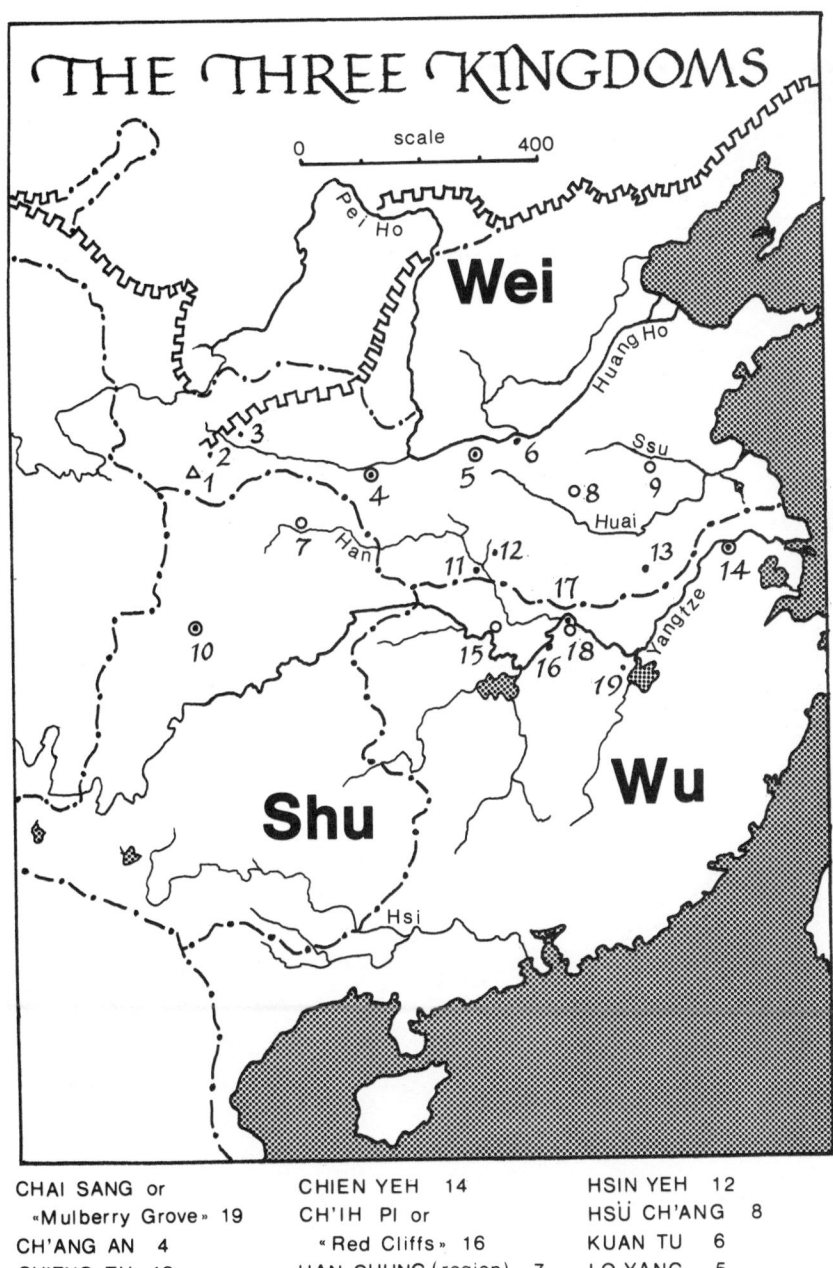

THE THREE KINGDOMS

scale
0 ———————— 400

Pei Ho

Wei

Huang Ho

Ssu

△2 ·3

△1 4 5 6 8 9

Huai

7 Han 11 ·12· 13

17 14

10 15 16 18

19 Yangtze

Shu

Wu

Hsi

CHAI SANG or	CHIEN YEH 14	HSIN YEH 12
«Mulberry Grove» 19	CH'IH PI or	HSÜ CH'ANG 8
CH'ANG AN 4	«Red Cliffs» 16	KUAN TU 6
CH'ENG TU 10	HAN CHUNG (region) 7	LO YANG 5
CH'I MOUNTAINS 1	HO FEI 13	NAN CHÜN 15
CHIANG HSIA 18	HSIA K'OU 17	P'ENG 9
CHIEH T'ING 3	HSIANG YANG 11	SHANG FANG KU 2

The three kingdoms. Though somewhat altered, the provincial lines were still recognized.

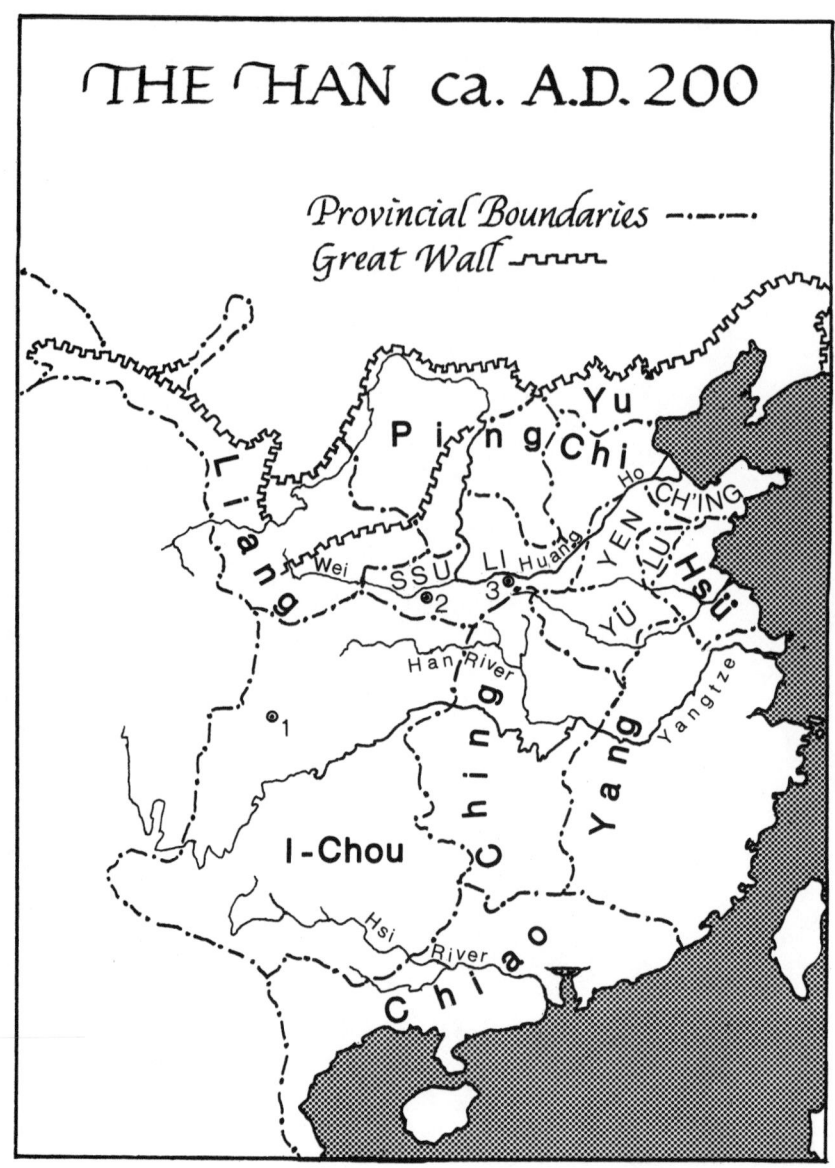

THE HAN ca. A.D. 200

Provincial Boundaries —·—·
Great Wall ~~~~

I-Chou

CH'ENG TU 1   CH'ANG AN 2   LO YANG 3

The Han ca. A.D. *200.* Shows the provinces of China during the period A.D. 194–213. Ts'ao Ts'ao reorganized the northeast provinces in 213.

INTRODUCTION

From the ruins of the Han (206 B.C.–A.D. 220), longest and mightiest of China's dynasties, three smaller states emerged and began warring for sovereignty. Lo Kuan-chung's *Three Kingdoms* portrays this fateful moment in Chinese history, when it was uncertain whether the empire could be made whole again. The book is a popular classic, the foremost work of semifictional history in China, and one of the greatest Chinese literary master-pieces. Though it was written six centuries ago, its heroes and legends are still vivid for the Chinese, whose intense consciousness of their history has always been central to their culture. Mao Tsetung has said:

> What I enjoyed were the romances of old China, and especially stories of rebellions. I read . . . the *San Kuo* [*Three Kingdoms*] while still very young and . . . so did most of my schoolmates. . . . We learned many of the stories almost by heart, and discussed and rediscussed them many times. We knew more of them than the old men of the village, who also loved them and used to exchange stories with us.*

The vast canvas of *Three Kingdoms* is crowded with stories and peopled with kings and courtiers, peasants, soldiers, sorcerers, scholars. Its themes of power, loyalty, and social obligation ap-pear and vanish, only to surface again in a different context and with ironically altered significance. Its scale of time is dynastic rather than individual: men's acts overtake them, but then run beyond their personal destinies until the flow of history absorbs

* Edgar Snow, *Red Star over China*, 1937, p. 127.

them all. In much the way that Shakespeare fashioned the English
chronicles into drama, Lo Kuan-chung collected tales that had
been treasured for centuries by the Chinese people and then transformed them into a sophisticated and panoramic work of art.

Three Kingdoms is not only a complex book but a very long
one. For the reader who is unfamiliar with Chinese culture this
translation presents the essential dramatic narrative while reducing
the multiplicity of historical detail. The abridgment aims at a
clarity of focus which, it is hoped, reveals the story's vivid life as
a work of art, a masterpiece from a high civilization.

The action of *Three Kingdoms* opens in the last decades of the
four-hundred-year Han dynasty. Having secured a larger territory
and developed a more complex economy than any of its prede-
cessors, the Han had given new historic form to China. Now,
however, the Emperor's ruling circle has become corrupt and
oppressive, and a secret society known as the Yellow Scarves initiates a major rebellion. The Emperor's appeal goes out for loyal
subjects to join the army and fight the rebels.

Among the young men who respond to the appeal are Liu Pei,
a remote relation of the ruling clan; Kuan Yü, a fugitive; and
Chang Fei, a pig butcher. The three meet, become friends, and
swear brotherhood, promising to live and die as one in the service
of their country and its people. This is the famous Peach Garden
Oath, from which all the story's consequences, positive and negative, will flow.

The three sworn brothers distinguish themselves in the loyalist
cause, and Liu Pei is presented to the Emperor Tributor by
Ts'ao Ts'ao, the Chancellor.

Liu Pei is the "dark horse" of the imperial clan. He bears the
dynastic patronym, and his formal name of Hsüan-te means "obscured virtue." When he realizes that the Chancellor Ts'ao Ts'ao
is plotting to overthrow the Emperor, Liu Pei breaks with him
and strikes out on his own with his brothers. Ts'ao Ts'ao, considering Liu Pei a serious rival, manages to capture one of his sworn
brothers, Kuan Yü, and Liu Pei's family.

Ts'ao Ts'ao treats Kuan Yü with exaggerated generosity, hoping to win him from his allegiance to Liu Pei. Kuan Yü remains
steadfast, accepts nothing, and eventually rejoins his lord. But he
feels obliged to Ts'ao Ts'ao for his own life and the lives of Liu
Pei's family.

Now at the nadir of his fortunes, hunted by Ts'ao Ts'ao, lacking a base for his small army, Liu Pei wins to his service a genius of diplomatic intrigue and military strategy: Chuko Liang, formally named K'ung-ming ("vast wisdom"), also known as Sleeping Dragon. Liu Pei's two brothers are mighty warriors, but K'ung-ming is the architect of the long-range strategy to recover the north from Ts'ao Ts'ao and revive the failing Han dynasty.

K'ung-ming's first move is to arrange an alliance between Liu Pei and Sun Ch'üan, patriarch of a quasi-independent territory called the Southland. Ts'ao Ts'ao attempts to invade the Southland and is defeated by the combined forces of Liu Pei and Sun Ch'üan in the famous battle at the Red Cliffs. This battle is the dramatic pivot of *Three Kingdoms*.

His army decimated, Ts'ao Ts'ao retreats northward. K'ung-ming, anticipating Ts'ao's escape route, has posted Kuan Yü to intercept him. But when Kuan Yü confronts the broken Chancellor he is torn between his allegiance to his brother and his lord, Liu Pei, and his obligation to Ts'ao Ts'ao. It is an obligation of which Ts'ao Ts'ao delicately reminds him in an appeal for mercy: "You have been well, I trust, since your departure?" Kuan Yü wavers and turns aside to let his lord's mortal enemy pass. The Chancellor escapes northward to regroup.

Amid the fluidity of circumstance in the wake of Ts'ao Ts'ao's retreat, K'ung-ming wins for Liu Pei the pivotal province of Chingchou—around which, north, east, and west, the three kingdoms are beginning to take shape. But Chingchou's strategic location makes it precious, and Liu Pei's ally, the Southland, claims it as the rightful spoils of war. K'ung-ming, whose long-range plan to recover the north depends on the alliance with the Southland, promises to return Chingchou to the Southland once he can relocate Liu Pei in the third kingdom, the Riverlands to the west.

The three kingdoms are thus forming: in the north, Wei, ruled by the Ts'ao clan; in the southeast, the Southland, located below the Yangtze and ruled by the Sun clan; in the west, the Riverlands, ruled by Liu Pei, the imperial Han kinsman and the last hope for the restoration of the Han.

Kuan Yü is left alone as an anchor in Chingchou as Liu Pei takes over the Riverlands. But the Southlanders cannot wait. Frustrated by the delays in gaining Chingchou, they agree to Ts'ao Ts'ao's proposal to make a coordinated strike against Kuan Yü.

North and south they attack Chingchou, seize it, and divide the territory between them. The consequences of letting Ts'ao Ts'ao pass after the battle at Red Cliffs are now visited upon Kuan Yü. He is captured and executed by Sun Ch'üan, who delivers his head to Ts'ao Ts'ao.

The execution of Kuan Yü invokes the Peach Garden Oath. To K'ung-ming's dismay, Liu Pei abandons the alliance with the Southland, key to his imperial cause, to honor his sworn commitment to avenge his brother. Together with the third brother, Chang Fei, Liu Pei mobilizes the Riverlands for an invasion of the Southland. The cause of the Han is doomed by the very brotherhood which almost saved it.

Three Kingdoms comes to a tragic close as Liu Pei fails to restore the Han. A four-hundred-year period of division and instability will follow, during which the northern homeland falls more often than not under the control of non-Chinese.

The lessons were large, terrible, and capable of many interpretations, and over the centuries the Chinese developed them into a lively popular tradition of stories and legends. Liu Pei came to symbolize Chinese resistance to foreign invasion, and public feeling was strong in his favor and fiercely against Ts'ao Ts'ao.

Among the primary questions posed by *Three Kingdoms* is the basic issue of government: What is the source of political legitimacy? Is it geographic advantage—possession of the sacred northern heartlands? Is it genetic right, sanctioned by the principle of continuity within the dynastic patronym? Or is it some higher virtue—a moral charisma that affects both the inner circle of advisers, officers, and officials, as well as the people at large?

At first, *Three Kingdoms* appears to counterpose the first two types of legitimacy through the conflict between the Emperor Tributor and his Chancellor Ts'ao Ts'ao. But in the course of the action Liu Pei validates himself as a contender because he is a moral force, becoming true heir to the Han by his virtue rather than his blood right.

Confucius had sought to idealize clan right by projecting a potential brotherhood of men, although of "noble" men rather than men in general. The Peach Garden Oath, by making strangers brothers in a cause, poses a similar challenge to clan rules for the transmission of position and property. These rules were the mainstays of feudal order. In one episode not included in this translation, Chang Fei, the third brother, presents himself to Liu Pei to atone with his life, thinking he has lost Liu Pei's land and family. Liu Pei comforts him: "A brother is a limb. Wives and children are but clothes, which torn can be mended. But who can restore a broken limb? We linked our destinies in the Peach Garden when we vowed to die as one. My land, my family, I can spare, but not you, midway in our course."

Liu Pei's moral virtue is at full strength when, in flight, with neither land nor titles to bestow, his brothers, advisers, and a human sea all follow him into adversity. By contrast, after he has taken power in his kingdom of the Riverlands, he attempts to reward his followers with choice estates in the newly conquered land. But a loyal general, Chao Yün, stops him: "Military disaster has befallen these people again and again. The deserted fields and homesteads should revert to the local people and not be appropriated for your personal bounty." Liu Pei is dissuaded, but the danger of his ultimate corruptibility should he reign over a restored Han is suggested.

Liu Pei is established as a model, however flawed, against which any Emperor could be tested. Lo Kuan-chung probes the relation between kinship and kingship and the ethics pertaining to each sphere. When the two spheres are in harmony, social order is assured. When they conflict, the consequences may be tragic.

The tragedy of Lo's epic arises from Kuan Yü's imperfect commitment to the brotherhood, followed by Liu Pei's too-perfect commitment. Liu Pei will be brother before king. Breaking with K'ung-ming to fulfill the oath and avenge Kuan Yü, Liu Pei shows the same noble ardor and generosity of spirit that ruined Kuan Yü when he reciprocated the kindness of Ts'ao Ts'ao.

But at his crucial moment Kuan Yü meets with no reciprocity from Ts'ao Ts'ao. When the Southland sends Kuan Yü's head north, Ts'ao Ts'ao mocks the dead visage with the very words he used to beg for mercy after the battle of the Red Cliffs: "You have been well, I trust, general, since we parted?" Unlike Liu Pei, Ts'ao Ts'ao has ambition unrestrained by conscience.

One Chinese scholar has said: "The artful chessplayer in a casual move [ten moves ago] gains the desired response ten moves ahead. The method of narration in *Three Kingdoms* is like this."*

---

* Mao Tsung-kang of the early Ch'ing dynasty, principal editor of the text.

But in the course of the epic a larger theme is asserted. Through the accumulation of ironies a karmic pattern of retribution develops—history's "law of obligations." In the ever-lengthening perspective of historical movement, the major events and characters are canceled out.

The flow of history, like the flow of the mighty Yangtze, sweeps heroes off the stage and clears the way for their successors. The effect of individual purpose on the future is small and uncertain.

The law of retribution that flickers through the narrative as irony (the faint indication of retribution's ultimate force) is not something metaphysical or independent. It arises dialectically from the concrete character or event. This is the dramatic reality of *Three Kingdoms*. The ultimate ground of the law of retribution is the will and the judgment of the people. This is the historical reality of *Three Kingdoms*. In the first chapter the popular rebellion that initiates the fall of the Han is described as the result of corruption in the Court. And when Liu Pei is fleeing Ts'ao Ts'ao, he refuses to abandon the human sea following him, remarking: "Any undertaking must be based on the people."

However, the retributive power of the people is rarely manifested overtly in feudal China; it is shown through charms, cures, jingles, omens, and the like. However potent, mass sentiment is largely latent and may manifest itself as a supernatural force. This crucial theme is established in the case of the magician Yü Chi. Executed by a feudal lord for "seducing" the masses, Yü Chi returns to haunt the murderer and eventually drives him to his death. Magic, retribution, and the moral force of the masses are intertwined, preparing the way for the exploits of K'ung-ming, Liu Pei's principal adviser and architect of his restorationist cause. K'ung-ming's phenomenal powers of insight and natural magic rise to apparently supernatural heights, but only when based on the moral force of Liu Pei's virtue. The taproot of that virtue is Liu Pei's link to the masses and to the transcendence of clan right. The ultimate power of history is the people.

In presenting the nucleus of the epic as economically as possible, this translation concentrates on chapters 20 to 85 of the original one hundred and twenty. Thus a little over half of the text is covered. However, many of these inner sixty-five chapters are only partially translated, with many summary bridges, condensations, and splices. Thus the bulk of the translation amounts to about one-fourth of the original. By number the chapters translated are: 1,* 20 to 29, 34 to 44, 46 to 52, 60, 63, 65, 73 to 78, 80 to 81, 83 to 85, 95, 103 to 104. The edition of *Three Kingdoms* used was published by the People's Publishing House (Jen min ch'u pan she) in Peking in 1972.

---

* Except for chapter 1, the translation preserves the order in which events were originally presented.

Three Kingdoms

The Oath of
Fraternity in the Peach Garden;
Three Heroes Establish Their Name

The Long River passes east away,
Surge over surge,
Whiteblooming waves sweep all heroes on
As right and wrong, triumph and defeat all turn unreal.
But ever the green hills stay
To blush in the west-waning day.

The woodcutters and the fishermen,
Whiteheaded, they've seen enough
Spring air and autumn moon
To make good company over the winejars,
Where many a famed event
Provides their merriment.

They say the momentum of history was ever thus: the empire, long divided, must unite; long united, must divide. Thus the House of Chou reached its end and the empire was partitioned into seven warring kingdoms in 403 B.C. Thus these seven were absorbed into the House of Ch'in, the first imperial dynasty, in 221 B.C. Then Han and Ch'u destroyed the Ch'in and waged war on each other until the empire was reunited under the House of Han in 202 B.C. Four centuries later, in A.D. 189, the succession reached the Emperor Tributor,* last of the Han, after whose generation the land was partitioned into the three kingdoms in A.D. 220.

In the second month of the second year of his reign, A.D. 169, the Emperor Interlocutor,† father of Tributor, entered the Hall of

* In Chinese his name is Hsien, meaning "a worthy offering." This refers to his eventual abdication.
† Ling, meaning "able to summon the dead or the forces of nature."

Balming Virtue. As he ascended, a violent wind sprang up from a corner of the hall. Out of it came a giant green serpent that glided down from a beam and coiled itself on a seat. The Emperor fainted and was rushed to the inner chambers. The assembly of officials bolted. In a moment the serpent was gone. Then, without warning, rain and hailstones laced through the air, pelting down for half the night and wrecking countless buildings.

Two years later earthquakes struck Lo Yang, the capital. The ocean inundated the shoreline, sweeping those who lived on the coast out to sea. Eight years later hens suddenly became transformed into roosters. And in the middle of that same year, on the first day of the sixth month, a trail of black mist one hundred feet long floated into the Hall of Balming Virtue. The next month a rainbow was observed in the Chamber of the Concubines. And there was an avalanche on the bluffs of the Wu Yüan Mountains.* A variety of evil portents appeared—too many to be dismissed as isolated signs.

The Emperor Interlocutor called on his officials to explain these disasters and prodigies. Some claimed that the rainbow in the Chamber of the Concubines and the transformation of the hens were a consequence of the eunuchs' interference in the government and the denial of office to men of high caliber. But no reforms were made. Court administration continued to worsen until across the land men's thoughts turned to rebellion, and thieves and traitors swarmed like bees. The Court issued a call for warriors loyal to the throne.

The call was posted in Cho county,† where it was seen by a young man of the district who, though no scholar, was broadminded and even-tempered, taciturn yet ambitious, a man of character who was himself attracted to outstanding men. His height was considerable, his ears long-lobed, his arms strikingly long, his eyes wide-set and almost able to see behind him, his face like flawless jade, his lips like dabs of rouge. A remote descendant of a son of the fourth Han Emperor, High Brilliance, he bore the dynastic patronym of Liu. His given name was Pei ("prepared"), his formal name Hsüan-te ("obscured virtue").

Many generations ago this branch of the Liu clan had held a landed estate in Cho county, but their holding had been confiscated by the Court on charges that they had evaded payments

* Implies danger from non-Chinese tribes to the north.
† In Yu, a northeast border province.

of tribute. Liu Pei's father, a government official, was cited by the Court for integrity and filial devotion. He died early, however, and Liu Pei remained with his mother, serving her with unstinting filial piety. He supported their poor household by selling sandals and weaving mats.

The family lived in a village of Cho county called Double Mulberry because of the giant mulberry tree near their home. It was over fifty feet high. Tall and proud, the tree seemed from afar like the canopy of a chariot. A fortune-teller had seen in it a sign that the family would produce a man of destiny. As a youth Liu Pei had played under the mulberry, saying, "I'll be the Emperor and take my seat on this chariot." An uncle, struck by the figure of speech, had remarked, "This is no ordinary child."

Liu Pei was already twenty-eight when the provincial authorities issued the call for volunteers to fight the rebellions. The rebels were known as the Yellow Scarves. Their leader was Chang Chüeh, a man who had failed the official examinations and retired to the hills to gather healing herbs. There he had met an ancient mystic, emerald-eyed and young of face, leaning on a staff of goosefoot wood. The mystic led Chang Chüeh into a cavern and handed him three sacred texts.

"These are called the *Essential Arts for the Age of Equality*," the old man had said. "Now that you have them, propagate their teachings as Heaven's messenger to promote universal salvation. Use them for any other purpose and retribution will follow." With that, the old man transformed himself into a breath of crystal air and vanished.

Chang Chüeh had attacked the text. He learned to summon the winds and invoke the rain and came to be called Tao-Master for the Age of Equality. When pestilence spread through the land, he traveled far and wide curing the afflicted with charms and potions. He styled himself Great Worthy and Good Doctor, and his followers, numbering over five hundred, bound up their heads with yellow scarves. They were as mobile as the clouds, and all could write the charms and recite the spells.

As his following grew, Chang Chüeh set up thirty-six commands under his chieftains and began to prepare an insurrection against the Han. He and his two brothers assumed patriarchal titles and told their people: "The Han's fated end is near. A mighty sage emerges. Let one and all, in obedience to Heaven, in true allegiance, strive for the Age of Equality." And in the four

張桓侯

智敗張郃定中州
義釋嚴顏出蜀境
長坂橋邊水逆流
寇中關上歇先聲

閬渠
閬渠

Chang Fei

quarters of the realm the common folk bound their heads with yellow scarves and followed Chang Chüeh in such numbers that the armies of the Court would flee at the rumor of their approach. The Court ordered all districts mobilized.

Reading the order posted in Cho county, Liu Pei sighed with indignation that traitors would attack the throne. Someone spoke roughly behind him: "What are the long sighs for? A hardy fellow like you should be giving his all for home and country."

Liu Pei turned to see a man even taller than he, with a blunt head like a panther's, huge round eyes, a swallow's cheek, a tiger's whiskers, a thunderous voice, and a stance like a horse in stride. To Liu Pei, who asked his name, he said, "My surname is Chang, my given name Fei ['flying'], and my formal name Yi-te ['wings to virtue']. We've been in this county for generations and farm a bit of land, sell wine, and slaughter pigs. I was looking for men of adventure and, coming upon you reading the recruitment call, took the liberty of addressing you."

"Actually," Liu Pei replied, "I am an imperial relation, and I want to raise troops to destroy the Yellow Scarves and defend the people. I was reflecting on my limitations when you heard me sigh."

Chang Fei said, "I have resources that could be used to outfit some local youths. What if you were to join with me in serving this great cause?" Liu Pei was elated, and together they went to a nearby inn. As they drank, they noticed a striking fellow stop at the inn's entrance to rest.

"Some wine, and quickly," the stranger said. "I'm off to the town to volunteer." Liu Pei observed him: gleaming skin, glistening lips, eyes like the crimson phoenix, brows like nestling silkworms. His appearance was stately, his bearing awesome. Liu Pei invited him to share their table and asked who he was.

"My surname is Kuan," the man replied, "my given name Yü ['plume'], my formal name Yün-ch'ang ['cloud-lasting']. One of the notables in our district was using his position to exploit people. I killed him and had to flee. I have been on the move these past five or six years. When I heard of the mobilization I came to answer the call."

Liu Pei then told of his own ambitions, to Kuan Yü's great excitement. Together the three men went to Chang Fei's farm to talk further. Chang Fei proposed: "Behind the farm is a peach garden. The flowers are at their fullest. Tomorrow we must make

避難至涿

Escaping his past, Kuan Yü arrives in Cho county

offerings there to Heaven and Earth, declaring that we three join together as brothers, combining strength and purpose." To this Liu Pei and Kuan Yü agreed.

The next day they prepared their offerings, which included a black bull and a white horse. Amid burning incense the three men performed obeisance and spoke their vow:

"We three, Liu Pei, Kuan Yü, and Chang Fei, though of separate birth, now bind ourselves in brotherhood, combining our strength and purpose to relieve the present crisis. Thus we may fulfill our duty to home and country and defend the common folk of the land. We could not help our separate births, but on the self-same day we mean to die! Shining imperial Heaven, fruitful Queen Earth, witness our determination, and may god and man jointly scourge whichever of us fails his duty or forgets his obligation."

The oath sworn, Liu Pei became the eldest brother, Kuan Yü the second, and Chang Fei the youngest. When the sacrificial ceremony was concluded, they butchered the bull and spread forth the wine, gathering three hundred youths in the peach garden, where they drank themselves to sleep.

Equipped by wealthy merchants with weapons, horses, and cash, the three brothers distinguished themselves in the field, winning several engagements with the Yellow Scarves. Liu Pei and his followers then joined a loyalist force that had driven the rebels into defensive positions at Ch'ang She.

There the rebels had fortified their camp with brambles, and the loyalists decided to attack with fire. Each soldier gathered a handful of dry grass and hid near the perimeter of the enemy camp. That night a strong wind arose. After the second watch the loyalists fired the brambles and fell upon the enemy. Flames stretched across the sky as the rebels scattered and fled, leaving shields and saddles.

The massacre continued until morning. Then the rebels forced an exit for their battered units and bolted, but as if from nowhere came caparisoned war horses surrounded by red flags to cut off their retreat.

The leader of this cavalry flashed into sight—tall, narrow-eyed, with a long beard—the Chief Commandant. His surname was Ts'ao, given name Ts'ao,* formal name Meng-te ("first-born

---

* A different word from the surname, meaning either "integrity" or "manipulator." The names Ah-man and Chi-li are not Chinese.

Sacrifice and vow in the Peach Garden

virtue"). Originally a Hsia-hou, he was adopted into the Ts'ao
clan. At birth his milk-name was Ah-man; another was Chi-li.

In adolescence Ts'ao Ts'ao had loved the hunt, and delighted
in song and dance. He was a boy with ingenious ideas for any occasion—a regular storehouse of mischief and machinations. He
had an uncle who complained to his father about his excesses, and

the father in turn reproved Ts'ao Ts'ao. So the next time the boy saw his uncle, he fell to the ground and pretended to have a fit. The uncle fetched the father, who rushed to his son's side only to find him perfectly sound. "Your uncle told me you had a fit," Ts'ao's father said. "Has it passed?"

"I have never suffered from fits," replied Ts'ao Ts'ao. "He accuses me of everything simply because I have lost favor with him." The father believed his son and thereafter ignored the uncle's complaints, so that Ts'ao Ts'ao was free to indulge his whims.

Once a friend said to Ts'ao Ts'ao, "The empire is on the verge of civil war and can be preserved only by a man capable of dominating the age. You may be the one." On another occasion Ts'ao Ts'ao asked for an assessment of his character from a sage renowned for his insight into human nature. The answer was given reluctantly: "You could be a statesman capable of bringing order to the age, or a traitor in an age of sedition." This appraisal elated Ts'ao Ts'ao.

At twenty Ts'ao Ts'ao was made a yeoman of the Court and promoted to command of security at the capital, Lo Yang. When he took office he had a dozen multicolored bludgeons hung at the gates of his area of jurisdiction. They were a sign that any violator of the laws, however powerful or high-born, was subject to correction by bludgeon. One night a relative of a Court eunuch was apprehended for walking through the streets with drawn sword, and the bludgeon was applied. Thereafter no one dared break the laws, and Ts'ao Ts'ao's prestige spread far. Later, during the rebellion of the Yellow Scarves, he was advanced to the rank of chief commandant.

Now Ts'ao was approaching the fleeing rebels at the head of five thousand men. When he intercepted them, ten thousand fell and countless flags, gongs, and horses were seized. Liu Pei, Kuan Yü, and Chang Fei were bringing up reinforcements when they heard the sounds of slaughter and in the distance saw spears of fire enkindling the heavens. Since the rebel force was decimated, Liu Pei's troop was ordered back to Cho county.

*   *   *   *

This campaign against the Yellow Scarves took place in A.D. *184. The uprising was largely suppressed, but the forces called into being to suppress it were to prove more dangerous*

The brothers establish their merit serving the Han

to the Han than the rebellion itself. Many loyalists who had rallied to the Han began to act as independent warlords or to interfere in Court politics.

In the summer of 189 the Emperor Interlocutor died. His preference for his younger son, Hsieh, was ignored; Pien, the elder son, was enthroned. But in the fall of 189 Pien was *forced to abdicate, and at the age of nine, Hsieh became Tributor, the last Emperor of the Han.*

In the course of the battles that crisscrossed north China, the two capitals—Ch'ang An in the west and Lo Yang in the east—were laid waste. Tributor lost his geographic base, and various local strongmen warred with one another to serve as his protector.

In 199, fifteen years after he had routed the Yellow Scarves at Ch'ang She, Ts'ao Ts'ao succeeded in bringing the Emperor Tributor under his own wing and establishing him in the city of Hsü, which became the capital by virtue of the Emperor's presence. Since the great battles of 184, Liu Pei too had joined forces with Ts'ao Ts'ao and rendered distinguished service to the Han Emperor.

The Imperial Hunt;
The Secret Decree

Ts'ao Ts'ao, who was now Chancellor, told the Emperor Tributor of Liu Pei's achievements in the wars against the Yellow Scarves. Then he presented Liu Pei, who paid homage at the royal vermilion steps.

The Emperor beckoned him and inquired about his ancestry. "Your servant," said Liu Pei, "can trace his lineage to Prince Ching, a son of the fourth Han Emperor. My father was Liu Hung, my grandfather Liu Hsiung."

The Emperor ordered the royal clan registry brought forth and had the recorder recite: "Of the fourteen sons of the fourth Han Emperor, the seventh was Prince Ching." The recorder then read out the fourteen generations down to Liu Pei's grandfather. According to the genealogy, Liu Pei was indeed an uncle of the Emperor. Elated, the Emperor summoned him to an adjoining chamber, where they enacted the formalities befitting uncle and nephew.

The Emperor thought: "Ts'ao Ts'ao so abuses his authority that state affairs are no longer in my control. But now that we have a valiant warrior in the person of my uncle, he may provide a remedy!" Tributor conferred on Liu Pei a general's rank and the title of precinct master, and he was thereafter known as the Imperial Uncle.

Returning to his quarters, Ts'ao Ts'ao was confronted by his adviser Hsun Yü, who said, "I wonder if you have much to gain, sire, when the Son of Heaven acknowledges Liu Pei his uncle."

曹操

圖此世之雄也耶
令央牡然

Ts'ao Ts'ao

"Since the Emperor is under my protection and Liu Pei's actions are subject to his approval," replied Ts'ao, "he is unlikely to defy us. Besides, by detaining him here in Hsü, where nominally he is close to the Emperor, I can in fact better keep him under my hand."

Another adviser, Ch'eng Yü, appealed to Ts'ao Ts'ao: "Sire,

The imperial hunt in the fields at Hsü

your prestige now increases daily. Why not seize the opportunity to put your supremacy into effect?"

But Ts'ao Ts'ao replied: "There are too many loyal ministers at Court for us to move imprudently, though we might invite the Son of Heaven to a hunt to see what develops."

They selected prime horses, falcons, and champion hounds. The bows and arrows were all made ready. Assembling his soldiers outside the city, Ts'ao Ts'ao entered to extend the invitation.

"This appears somewhat unorthodox," said the Emperor.*

Ts'ao Ts'ao replied, "The kings and emperors of ancient times held four hunts, one at each season, when they would ride out of the city to show the world their martial prowess. Now, when the land is in commotion, is the very time to use the hunt to exercise our arms."

The Emperor complied. Mounting his easy-gaited horse, belting on his jeweled bow, he led the ranked procession of chariots, their bells jingling, out of the city walls. Liu Pei, Kuan Yü, and Chang Fei, bows and blades at the ready, shields under their dress, led several dozen horsemen in the cavalcade. Ts'ao Ts'ao, riding his horse Winged Lightning, led one hundred thousand of his followers to join the Son of Heaven in the fields of Hsü. His men fanned out to enclose the field in a ring some two hundred leagues across. Ts'ao Ts'ao kept his horse parallel with the Emperor's—never more than a head away—while his trusted lieutenants massed behind him. The regular imperial officials, whether civil or military, trailed far in the rear, none daring to advance.

As the Emperor rode to the fields of Hsü, Liu Pei saluted him from the roadside. The Emperor said, "I shall look forward to admiring your marksmanship today." As if hearing a command, Liu Pei took to his horse. A hare sprang out from the bushes, and Liu Pei felled it with a single arrow. The Emperor shouted praise and rode on. The procession turned and crossed a low hill. A stag charged out of the brush.† The Emperor shot three arrows but missed.

"Try for it, my companion," he said to Ts'ao Ts'ao, who impudently snatched the Emperor's jeweled bow and barbed arrows. Ts'ao drew the bow to the full and released an arrow that pierced the deer's spine and toppled it in the brush. Seeing the royal ar-

---

* In fact it was *lèse majesté*, since such an invitation implied the subordination of king to minister (after a story in the Confucian classic *Spring and Autumn*).
† "A deer is loose" means "The kingship is open to contention."

row, the assembly assumed that the Emperor had scored the hit and surged forward to congratulate him. But Ts'ao Ts'ao guided his horse past the Son of Heaven to acknowledge the cheers. The assembly blanched. Behind Liu Pei, Kuan Yü seethed. Brows arching, eyes glaring, he raised his sword and rode forward to cut Ts'ao Ts'ao down. Liu Pei motioned him back with a severe look, and seeing his elder brother's inclination, Kuan Yü reined his horse.

Liu Pei bowed to Ts'ao Ts'ao and offered his congratulations: "The Chancellor shoots like a god! Few in this age can equal you."

"It was the largess of the Emperor, really," Ts'ao Ts'ao laughed, as he brought his horse round to face Tributor and express his compliments. But instead of returning the jeweled bow, he simply hung it at his waist.

Later, Kuan Yü asked Liu Pei, "Why did you stop me? That traitor has abused the sovereign and ensnared the government, and I meant to rid the state of him."

Liu Pei said, " 'If you aim for the mouse, don't bring down the house.' Ts'ao Ts'ao was only a head away from the Emperor, and his lieutenants were thick around him. Dear brother, suppose you had vented your moment's anger in a hasty act and had hurt the Emperor. Then *we* would be the ones standing trial for the very crimes you denounce!"

"By not dispatching him today we assure future disaster," Kuan Yü replied.

"No more," Liu Pei said. "We cannot speak freely here."

In the palace the Emperor said tearfully to his queen: "Since I assumed the throne treacherous pretenders have multiplied, and we have faced griefs that the common man does not know. Then came Ts'ao Ts'ao, whom we thought of as a loyal servant of our dynasty's shrines, never dreaming he would usurp the government and abuse his authority by arbitrary exercise of fear and favor. How it nettles me to see him! Such is his impudence that today in the hunting field, he took it upon himself to accept the acclamation for the royal shot. Before long there will be a coup, and you and I will lie in unmarked graves."

The Empress, Lady Fu, replied, "In this courtful of lords and peers, not a one of whom but eats by the generosity of the Han, is there really none to assist the nation in distress?"

The queen's father, Fu Wan, entered and said, "Who did not see the incident at the deer hunt? But the whole Court consists of either Ts'ao's clansmen or his followers. Except for the queen's family, who will demonstrate the loyalty to bring the traitor to justice? I lack the power, but what about the Senior State Uncle, Tung Ch'eng, general of the chariots and cavalry?"

"He has stepped into the breach more than once," the Emperor agreed. "Have him summoned for consultation."

Fu Wan said, "Your majesty's closest attendants are Ts'ao Ts'ao's lieutenants. If they discover anything, the consequences will be serious."

"Then what?" queried the Emperor.

Fu Wan: "I have an idea. Fashion a garment and obtain a jade sash, both of which you can privately present to Tung Ch'eng. Sew a secret decree into the sash lining. When he reaches home and sees the decree, he will devote himself to devising a strategy. Not even the spirits will know."

The Emperor approved, and composed the decree himself. Biting open his finger, he transcribed it in blood. The queen sewed it into the purple embroidered lining of the sash. Then the Emperor slipped into the garment, tied the sash tightly, and summoned Tung Ch'eng.

The formalities of audience concluded, the Emperor said, "Last night the queen and I were recalling your loyal service in times of tribulation and decided to send for you to express our gratitude for the hardships you have suffered." Tung Ch'eng bowed low and disclaimed the honor.

The Emperor led him to the main ancestral temple and then to the gallery devoted to meritorious servants. The Emperor completed the incense ceremony and led Tung Ch'eng on to admire the portraits. Among them was one of the Supreme Ancestor, the founder of the Han dynasty.

"Tell me," the Emperor said, "where did the sacred Supreme Ancestor commence his career, and how did he come to found the heritage we enjoy?"

Tung Ch'eng was stunned. "You must be mocking me! How could I forget the deeds of our sacred Supreme Ancestor? He began as a precinct master. From there he took up the three-foot sword and slew the serpent to mark the rising against the Ch'in. Crisscrossing the land, he annihilated Ch'in in the third year and Ch'u in the fifth, whereupon he took possession of the empire and established this immortal patrimony."

The Emperor: "So splendidly valiant the forefather, so fainthearted and feeble the progeny! One can't help sighing." He directed Tung Ch'eng's attention to the portraits of the founder's ministers.

"Indeed, the Supreme Ancestor relied considerably on these two," commented Tung Ch'eng.

The Emperor checked to see that no one was near and whispered to Tung Ch'eng, "So should you, good companion, stand at our side."

The Emperor Tributor confers the sash

"I have no merit," replied Tung Ch'eng. "How could I deserve this honor?"

"We remember well your past service, though we have been unable to confer a reward," said the Emperor. "But won't you wear this garment of mine, and tie it with this sash, so that you will always seem to be in my presence?"

Tung Ch'eng bowed and declined. The Emperor slipped off the robe and sash and gave them to Tung Ch'eng, murmuring, "Examine these thoroughly when you get home. Do not fail me." Tung Ch'eng perceived his intent, put on the garment and, taking leave, quit the gallery.

Ts'ao Ts'ao, who had already been informed of this audience with the Emperor, rushed to the palace and intercepted Tung Ch'eng. With no place to conceal himself, the Emperor's kinsman could only stand at the roadside and offer a ritual greeting.

"Where has the Senior State Uncle been?" asked Ts'ao Ts'ao.

"The Son of Heaven summoned me and presented me with this brocade robe and jade sash."

"For what reason were you so honored?"

"In recognition of past services."

"Take off the sash and let me see it."

Tung Ch'eng was convinced that somewhere in the clothing there was a secret edict, and, anxious lest Ts'ao Ts'ao discover it, procrastinated until the Chancellor barked to his attendants, "Take it off him at once."

But after examining the sash closely, Ts'ao Ts'ao simply expressed his admiration for the workmanship and asked Tung Ch'eng to remove the robe. Tung Ch'eng was too alarmed not to comply. Ts'ao Ts'ao held it against the light and inspected it minutely. Then he slipped it on and tied the sash. Turning to his men he said, "Do you find it becoming?"

"Perfect!" they exclaimed, left and right.

Ts'ao Ts'ao said to Tung Ch'eng: "Would Senior State Uncle consider ceding this to me as a gift?"

"What the sovereign bestows of his generosity can never be given away. Let me have another fashioned to present to you."

"These clothes you have received must be linked with some intrigue?"

Tung Ch'eng said tensely: "How could one dare? If the Chancellor insists, of course, I shall leave them with you."

"My lord," Ts'ao Ts'ao replied, "how could I appropriate what the sovereign vouchsafes? Bear with my facetiousness." He removed the garments and returned them to Tung Ch'eng.

That night, alone in his library, Tung Ch'eng went over the robe inch by inch. Finding nothing, he mused, "When the Son of Heaven gave me these clothes and instructed me to examine them, he had to have something in mind, but now I see no trace. Why?" He scrutinized the sash, its white jade tesserae formed into a miniature dragon snaking through a floral design, the underside lined with purple brocade, the hemming flawless. There was simply nothing to be seen. He laid it on his desk and puzzled over it until he grew tired.

Tung Ch'eng was on the verge of falling asleep on his bench when a spark from his smoldering snuff leaped onto the sash and burned into the lining. He brushed it out, but the spark had already eaten away a spot, revealing a glimpse of the white silk and traces of blood showing from the hiding place. He took a knife and slit the sash open. There was the secret decree, bloodscript of the Emperor's hand. The decree read:

> We believe that in the human order the bond of father and son is the foremost, and that in the social order the obligation between sovereign and servant is paramount. Of late the treasonous Ts'ao Ts'ao, abusing his authority, deceives his sovereign and abases his sire, contriving liaison with factions and units to the detriment of our dynasty's rule. Instructions, land grants, rewards, and punishments are now outside the imperial jurisdiction. Day and night we brood on this, dreading the peril to the realm. Good friend, you are a great public servant and our nearest kinsman. Think of the obstacles and hardships the Supreme Ancestor faced when he founded this dynasty. Forge a union of distinguished leaders—men of unimpaired integrity and unimpeachable loyalty—to restore the security of our holy shrines. Exterminate this unscrupulous faction for the greater felicity of the ancestral clan. I slit my finger to shed this blood and compose this decree confided to you. Remain vigilant. Fail not our hopes. A.D. 199, 3rd month.

Tung Ch'eng read it through tears. He was unable to sleep that night, and in the morning he returned to the library to read and reread the document. But he could think of no concrete plan. Finally he fell asleep against his taboret, pondering ways to kill Ts'ao Ts'ao.

A Court officer, Wang Tzu-fu, arrived. Recognizing him as an intimate friend, the gateman ushered him into the library. He entered and saw Tung Ch'eng motionless, a silk scroll in his sleeve, the imperial "We" just visible on it. Wang Tzu-fu could not believe what he saw. Silently he took up the document, read it through, and stowed it in his sleeve.

"Senior State Uncle!" he cried. "Are you not ashamed? How self-indulgent to be sleeping so!"

Tung Ch'eng leaped to his senses. Missing the decree, he felt his body and soul separate and lost the composure of his limbs.

Wang Tzu-fu: "You are preparing to murder the Chancellor, then! I shall have to denounce you!"

Tung Ch'eng wept. "Brother, if that is your intention, the House of Han expires."

"I did not mean it seriously," replied Wang Tzu-fu. "Our clan has enjoyed the fruits of service to the Han for many generations. Far from failing in loyalty, I mean to lend the strength of my arm and join you in disposing of the traitor. Let us draw up our righteous charge and prepare to die, forsaking our clans if necessary, for the sovereign of the Han."

Ts'ao Ts'ao Judges the Contenders

Seeking additional support for the loyalist cause, Tung Ch'eng went to Ma T'eng, governor of the northwestern province of Liang.

Ma T'eng: "Liu Pei is one who might support us. Can we draw him in?"

Tung Ch'eng: "Though 'uncle' to the Emperor, he is now an adherent of Ts'ao's. How could he allow himself to get involved in this business?"

Ma T'eng: "I witnessed the incident in the hunting field, when Ts'ao Ts'ao accepted the public's accolade. Lord Kuan was behind Liu Pei with his sword poised to strike Ts'ao Ts'ao. But Liu Pei restrained him with a glance. Liu Pei is willing enough to organize against Ts'ao, but he feels thwarted, unequal to Ts'ao's legion claws and teeth. Try to enlist him. I am sure he will respond eagerly."

The next night Tung Ch'eng hid the decree in his robe and took a side street to Liu Pei's quarters. Flanked by Kuan Yü and Chang Fei, Liu Pei received him. "The Senior State Uncle would not come in the dead of night," Pei said, "but for some issue of consequence."

Ch'eng: "To come in daylight might have made Ts'ao suspicious. The other day at the hunt Lord Kuan was on the verge of killing Ts'ao Ts'ao. He pulled back only after you motioned him off. Why? Mind you, no one else saw it."

Liu Pei could not dissemble. "My brother was outraged to see Ts'ao so ambitiously exceed his place. It was not premeditated."

Ch'eng hid his face and cried out: "If only the sons and servants at court measured up to Lord Kuan! There would be no fear for the tranquillity of the nation."

Liu Pei cautiously framed his reply: "With Chancellor Ts'ao in power, *need* there be any 'fear for the tranquillity of the nation'?"

Ch'eng's face stiffened. "It was, after all, only because you are the Imperial Uncle that I risked exposing my innermost feelings. Why have you taken advantage of me?"

Liu Pei: "Lest *you* play *me* false, I had to put you to a test."

Tung Ch'eng produced the secret decree for Pei, who, reading it, could not master his dismay and indignation. Next Ch'eng brought out an accusation against Ts'ao Ts'ao which the loyalist conspirators had written. Only six names were signed to it.

Liu Pei said: "Since you have received a charge to bring a traitor to justice, I will serve this cause as the ox toils and the horse labors."

*   *   *   *

To avoid arousing Ts'ao Ts'ao's suspicions, Liu Pei took to his back garden, planting vegetables and watering them, keeping his purposes hidden. Kuan Yü and Chang Fei said: "Brother, you seem to have lost interest in the great issues of the commonwealth and given yourself to a commoner's toil. Why?"

Liu Pei: "This is not something you would appreciate at this time." It was not mentioned again.

One day when Chang Fei and Kuan Yü were away and Liu Pei was tending his vegetables, two of Ts'ao's officers led a score of men into the garden. "The Chancellor orders my lordship to come with us at once." Liu Pei could not but follow them.

Smiling, Ts'ao greeted Liu Pei. Then he said, "That's quite a project you have at home!" in a tone so menacing that Liu Pei's face turned pale as dust. Taking Pei's hand, Ts'ao led him to his own garden. Only when Ts'ao remarked: "You have taken up a most difficult subject—horticulture," did Liu Pei feel safe. He replied, "To while away the time when there is nothing to occupy me—"

Ts'ao Ts'ao: "I just saw the plumlets on the branch. The new green called to mind last year's campaign against the rebels when we ran short of water on the march. The men were so parched!

But I conceived a plan. 'There's a plum tree grove ahead,' I cried, and pretended to locate it with my whip. When the troops heard me, their mouths watered and their thirst was gone. Seeing these plums now, I can't help feeling a sense of appreciation. And now the plum wine we brew is at the peak of its ripeness, so I decided to invite you for a gathering at the Little Pavilion."

Steadier now, Liu Pei followed Ts'ao. The cups and delicacies were already set forth. New green plums adorned the plates. The two men sat opposite one another, loosened their shirts, and drank freely.

The wine had made them cheerful when dark clouds appeared and overspread the heavens. A flash storm was threatening. Someone pointed to a distant dragon suspended on the horizon. The two men leaned against the balcony and watched it.

Ts'ao: "Does my lordship understand the dragon's multiform manifestations?"*

Pei: "Not in any great detail."

Ts'ao: "Dragons can enlarge and diminish themselves, surge aloft or lie beneath the surface. Enlarged, they create clouds and spew mist. Diminished, they can fit themselves into a granule. Aloft, they prance triumphant in the upper realm of space. Under the surface they lurk among the surging breakers. Now in the fullness of spring they mount the season, like men who would fulfill an ambition to dominate the length and breadth of the land. In this respect they can well be compared to the heroes of the age. You yourself have traveled widely and surely must be familiar with the great warriors of our time. Please try to describe them for me."

Pei: "How can these eyes of mine sight heroes?"

Ts'ao: "Set your modesty aside."

Pei: "Thanks to your gracious protection, Chancellor, I have succeeded in serving the dynasty. But as for the heroes of this lower realm, such things are more than I know of."

Ts'ao: "Even if you do not know any personally, you should at least have heard of some."

Pei: "Yüan Shu of Huai Nan? His weapons are first-rate, his provisions abundant. Would he be one?"

Ts'ao laughed. "Dry bones, rattling for the grave. Sooner or later I will have him."

* The dragon was a symbol of political sovereignty as well as of the cyclical force that dominates nature.

Liu Pei: "What about Yüan Shao, then? For four generations the Yüans have held the highest office, and many established officials are of his party. He has a firm grip on Chi Chou, where he is supported by capable men. Would you count him?"

Ts'ao: "His expression is fierce, but his courage is thin. He is fond of conniving but lacks decision. He plays for high stakes but begrudges personal sacrifice. He spots a minor gain and forgets his destiny. No hero he!"

And each name that Liu Pei raised—Liu Piao, Sun Ts'e—Ts'ao dismissed derisively. At last he said, "Now, what I mean by a hero is this: He cherishes an ambition for grandeur, a mine of marvelous schemes, the ability to encompass the realm or disappear within it, and the will to swallow this world of men or spit it out!"

Pei: "Who merits such a description?"

Ts'ao pointed first to Liu Pei, then to himself. "Heroes of the present day number but two—you, my lordship, and myself."

Liu Pei swallowed his fright, but before he realized it his chopsticks had fallen to the ground. Then the storm came on. A peal of thunder gave him the chance to bend down casually and retrieve them. "See what a clap of thunder has made me do."

Ts'ao laughed: "A grown man afraid of thunder?"

Liu Pei: "Confucius himself became agitated in thunderstorms; why should I not fear them?" In this way he sought to hide the cause of his anxiety, and in the end Ts'ao did not suspect.

Of the warriors whom Ts'ao Ts'ao derided, Yüan Shao was the most formidable. But he was estranged from his brother, Yüan Shu, who had come into possession of the imperial signet when the Emperor was in flight, and who had imperial ambitions of his own. The following day Liu Pei and Ts'ao Ts'ao were again together when it was reported that Yüan Shao had conquered and assimilated the forces of Kung-sun Tsan, and that his brother Shu was now reconciled with him and planned to deliver the imperial signet. Combined, the forces of Yüan Shao and Yüan Shu could overwhelm Ts'ao Ts'ao.

Hearing this news, Liu Pei thought, "What better time for me to make my break?" He said to Ts'ao Ts'ao: "If Yüan Shu makes common cause wtih his brother Shao, he will have to pass through

Hsü province.* But with troops to intercept him, I could stop his army."

"Submit this proposal to the Emperor," Ts'ao Ts'ao said. "We can easily muster the forces."

After formal appeal had been made to the Emperor, Ts'ao Ts'ao gave Liu Pei command of fifty thousand horse and foot soldiers and sent two generals to serve with him. Liu Pei took leave of the Emperor, who escorted him tearfully out of the palace. Then Tung Ch'eng accompanied Liu Pei beyond the city wall.

Liu Pei said, "Senior State Uncle must content himself and bear with this. I will find a way to fulfill the secret decree."

"Let it be your abiding concern," said Tung Ch'eng. "Do not turn away from the Emperor's purpose."

Later, when his brothers questioned his haste in commencing this campaign, Liu Pei replied, "Here, I am like a caged bird, a trapped fish. With this move I gain the sea, the lofty space."

Liu Pei defeated Yüan Shu, enabling Ts'ao Ts'ao to hold his own against Yüan Shao and to recover the imperial signet. Then Ts'ao Ts'ao sought to dispose of Liu Pei. Pei's adviser, Ch'en Teng, suggested the following plan to foil Ts'ao's attempts to have Pei assassinated.

* Hsüchou—not the same word as Hsü the capital, which is properly titled Hsü Ch'ang. *Chou* means "province."

Yüan Shao and Liu Pei
in the Field Against Ts'ao Ts'ao

"Who alarms Ts'ao Ts'ao more than Yüan Shao?" said Ch'en Teng. "Shao, with his predatory hold on four provinces and a million men who are fully equipped and well led? Why not send to him for help?"

"Yüan Shao and I have had no dealings with one another," said Liu Pei. "And now I have just defeated his younger brother, Shu. How could he possibly aid us?"

Ch'en Teng said, "Here in Hsüchou there is a scholar whose family has been intimate with the Yüans for three generations. If we can get him to write Shao in our behalf, I am certain he will aid us."

The scholar did write the letter, and it was dispatched to Yüan Shao. Reading it, he mused, "Liu Pei killed my younger brother; we owe him nothing. But with this letter in his behalf we really have to do something." He put the question of attacking Ts'ao Ts'ao to his officers and officials.

One counseled: "These wars have gone on for years, and the common folk are weary of supporting them. Our grain supplies are too low for us to mount a large force. Now is the time to announce our victory over Kung-sun Tsan to the Emperor. If they deny us access to him, we can petition, declaring that Ts'ao Ts'ao is keeping us from his presence. *Then* we can take up the sword and plant ourselves at Li Yang, enlarge our naval forces, repair and deploy our weapons, and assign crack troops to dig in along the borderland. In three years the campaign can be concluded."

But another counseled: "With the uncanny martial prowess of our brilliant patriarch Shao, whose splendid might has calmed the north, it would be no more difficult for us to bring Ts'ao Ts'ao to justice than to wave a hand. Why keep putting it off?"

Another said: "It is not 'splendid might' that determines victory. Ts'ao Ts'ao has kept civil order; his forces are steeled and seasoned. They are not an easy target, as Kung-sun Tsan's army was when you encircled it. You would be abandoning the sound strategy of formally announcing the victory to the Emperor; instead you would be raising a force with no legitimate justification. I beg you not to take this course."

Another argued: "That is wrong! How can anyone claim that we lack 'legitimate justification' for mounting an operation against Ts'ao? This is the very moment when we should not fail to seize the opening. I urge that we follow the proposal of the letter and, with Liu Pei steadfast in the highest allegiance, flush out Ts'ao Ts'ao and exterminate the criminal. This would correspond to the intent of Heaven and coincide with the inclination of the people— a genuine felicity."

The four disputed back and forth without coming to an agreement, and Yüan Shao, favoring now one, now the other, could not resolve it himself.

Only when two other trusted advisers spoke in favor of the campaign against Ts'ao Ts'ao did Shao finally agree to it and begin to coordinate his plans with Liu Pei's.

Then the adviser K'uo T'u proposed: "Because the brilliant patriarch resorts to arms in the cause of the highest allegiance, it is necessary that we spell out Ts'ao's crimes and circulate the charges in the various districts to publish his offense and secure his punishment. Thus our claim will be valid and our position lawful."

Shao agreed to this suggestion and asked Ch'en Lin to draft the indictment. In part, it states:

Ts'ao Ts'ao's grandfather, T'eng, was a palace eunuch who combined with others to perform demonic excesses. His rampant avarice was injurious to the royal prestige and lacerating to the common people. Sung, his adopted son and Ts'ao's father, wheedled his way to patronage and contrived a position for himself through bribes. By trafficking in precious metals and jades, and conveying his gratuities to the gates of the mighty, he crept into the highest public office and subverted the instruments of government. Ts'ao Ts'ao is a vexatious remnant of those parasitic eunuchs who were utterly without integrity or virtue; he has cunningly insinuated himself into the Court's confidence; he cherishes sedition and rejoices in calamity.

Yüan Shao, on behalf of this military headquarters, will bring these predators under control—sweep out these vicious usurpers. This is the sequel to the appearance of Tung Cho, who infiltrated the government and did violence to our polity. Then did we take up the sword and flourish our war drums, issuing word to the east of the realm to gather together our valiant warriors. Thus Yüan Shao came to be Ts'ao's colleague and gave him a supporting command, thinking that his aggressive capabilities might be of service to the state. But he proved ignorant and frivolous—shortsighted in strategy, hasty in advancing, capricious in retreat. Maimed and mutilated, his recruits suffered in battle time after time. Yet again Yüan Shao parceled out the finest men to him—no questions asked—to make his losses good and his strength whole. Yüan recommended him for imperial inspector in Yen, cloaking him in the tiger colors and enhancing his authority in hopes of gaining the fruit of his vengeance against Tung Cho.

But Ts'ao has now run wild with what we have provided him. By his unbridled conduct and malignant excesses he has bloodied the common people, savaged the worthy, and injured the decent. Was not Pien Jang, governor of Chiu Chiang, known across the land for his splendid talents and towering stature, his frank speech and forthright expression? Was he not honored as a man whose judgment was never swayed by craven flattery? And was he not decapitated, head piked, body hung at the city hall, wife and babes snuffed out like damped ashes? From that time the community of scholars was sore with indignation as the grievances of the people grew heavier.

Then one man thrust up his arm in revolt, and a whole province responded. Was not Ts'ao crushed near Hsü, his territory seized by the rebel Lü Pu, so that Ts'ao was left to roam the eastern fringes with nowhere to tread or hold? But Yüan Shao, affirming the principle of "strong trunk, weak branches," sanctioned no revolt by the disaffected. Again we hoisted our banner and wrapped round our mail, rolled up our setting mats and commenced the campaign. Gong and drum echo and shudder: Lü Pu's hosts melted away. Yüan Shao had plucked Ts'ao from sure

disaster and restored his position in Yen—though this was more
fortunate for Ts'ao than for the people of Yen.

Later it happened that the royal carriage was attacked in Hsü
by a band of captives. Yüan Shao was away from the capital on
a military emergency, and he sent Ts'ao to protect the young
sovereign. This became the occasion for Ts'ao to give rein to his
ambition. Like a domineering bully he took charge of the Court,
giving the customary prohibitions short shrift, demeaning the
royal house, and destroying laws and standards. The three highest offices came into his hands, and he monopolized the Court's
power. Office and bounty, punishment and mutilation were bestowed according to his whim. Those he favored were esteemed
as the five ancestors; those he detested were exterminated to the
last kinsman. Those who spoke openly were publicly executed;
those who spoke privately were secretly done away with. Official-
dom sealed its lips. Abroad, people communicated with their
eyes. The secretariat simply recorded the convenings. The ministers merely filled the bureaucratic ranks; no more.

And then Ts'ao set up new offices—"court commandant for
exhumations" and "adjutant for searching out valuables"—with
agents who broke open and poked through everything they came
by, exhuming corpses to the last bone. He held the highest
office, but he played the part of thief and murderer. He fouled
the state and injured the people, and the poison affected the living
and the dead.

Now Ts'ao holds the granary on Ao. The Yellow River barrier fortifies his position. It seems he would contest the track for
an oncoming chariot with the equipment of a mantis! Our headquarters, in possession of the sacred spirit of Han's majesty, fends
off any thrust from any quarter. Our long spears number mil-
lions, our nomad militia thousands of units. We have roused warriors the equal of past heroes and summoned the strength of
crack bowmen. We have crossed mountains and forded rivers.
Our main force has come down the Yellow River to engage
Ts'ao's vanguard, and we have descended to trip him up from
behind. His doom is certain—as sure as the sea quenches embers,
as the torch fires the kindling.

And those of Ts'ao's officers and sergeants who can fight come
from the northern provinces, Chi or Yu, or are cadres of former
units, and all chafe at their long service, yearning to go home,
tearfully gazing northward. The rest of the people of Yen and
Yü, as well as the remnants of Lü Pu's and Chang Yang's adherents, overwhelmed and hard-pressed as they are, will follow

anyone out of expedience. Each bears some wound; each has his mortal antagonist. If we return from the field, mount a high ridge, and sound the drum and fife, waving the white signal to offer an avenue of surrender—they will come apart like soil or clay, without waiting for a decision by blood and blade.

Now the House of Han is deteriorating, the social fabric is slack and torn. The Court lacks even a shred of support. The top administration is defenseless. In the region of the capital the elite are downcast, doing nothing to sustain the Court. Though loyal liegemen remain, how can they display their integrity when they are menaced by barbaric ministers?

Ts'ao controls a private army of seven hundred which surrounds the outer gates of the palace. It purports to be a round-the-clock guard, but is in reality a form of detention. Alarmed at these early signs of usurpation, we have made our move accordingly. This now is the season for the loyal to dye the ground with their gore, for ardent scholars to make their mark. Dare any fail us?

Ts'ao has forged decrees proclaiming his control and dispatched subalterns to raise troops. We fear that remote regions may wrongly heed his call for reinforcement and lead their people astray by participating in the rebellion. Those who do will see their names ruined; they will become a mockery before the world.

On this day we are advancing from four provinces—Yü, Ping, Ch'ing, and Chi. Others will respond when our letters reach them. In every region the loyalists are marshaling their forces and staking out their borders, consolidating their power to join in securing the shrines to the gods of our soil.

Who takes Ts'ao's head will be made lord of five thousand families and awarded fifty million coin. We will ask no questions of any commandant, officer, or man of Ts'ao's armies who defects. Let this be widely published through the empire, that all may know the emergency which has befallen our sacred dynasty.

Shao read the bill of indictment with great satisfaction and ordered it circulated through all regions and hung at key passes, fords, and defiles. The document reached Ts'ao at a time when he was stricken with vertigo and confined to bed. When he read it, he trembled with panic from his hair to his bones and broke into an icy sweat. His vertigo cured by the shock, he leapt out of bed to find Ts'ao Hung. "Who wrote this?" he asked. When Hung said that it was reported to be from the pen of Ch'en Lin, Ts'ao laughed. "Such literary style is going to require military strategy to follow through. However exquisite Ch'en Lin's style, what can it do for Yüan Shao's military shortcomings?" And he summoned his counselors to confer on engaging the opposition.

K'ung Jung the scholar was informed and came to Ts'ao. "Yüan Shao's power is immense," he said. "We cannot do battle with him; we can only come to terms."

But Hsün Yü said: "Yüan Shao is an ineffectual fellow. Nothing compels us to consider making peace."

K'ung Jung said: "Yüan Shao's territory is extensive and his people are hardy. His staff includes shrewd planners, loyal public servants, and generals braver than the generals of the imperial forces. His commanders are all renowned. What do you mean by calling him ineffectual?"

Hsün Yü laughed. "Shao's troops are numerous but disorderly. His loyal servant, T'ien, is rigid and insubordinate; Hsü Yü is greedy and imprudent; Shen P'ei arbitrary and unimaginative; Feng Chi resolute but ineffective. These men have little tolerance for one another and are bound to quarrel. As for those brave generals of his—are they so out of the ordinary? They will fall in a single battle. And the rest are not worth our consideration."

K'ung Jung fell silent. Ts'ao Ts'ao laughed. "They all do fit Hsün Yü's appraisal!"

Ts'ao Ts'ao decided to strike. He sent twenty legions north against Yüan Shao at Li Yang and five legions east against Liu Pei in Hsüchou.

When Liu Pei learned of the advance of Ts'ao Ts'ao's forces, he said to his adviser, Ch'en Teng, "Yüan Shao is well positioned at Li Yang but frustrated by the disharmony among his advisers. He has yet to show initiative. Ts'ao Ts'ao's whereabouts are not known. They say his personal banner is not with the force at Li Yang, but it seems to have turned up here. I wonder why."

"Ts'ao Ts'ao displays his cunning in hundreds of ways," said Ch'en Teng. "He must protect his main stronghold to the north, where he is personally in command. But he has his banner displayed here instead of there in order to deceive us. My feeling is that Ts'ao Ts'ao could not be here."

"Who will go and find out?" asked Liu Pei. Chang Fei offered, but Liu Pei would not allow it. "Your temper is too explosive, third brother," he said, and assigned three thousand men to Kuan Yü, who marched out of the city toward the enemy lines.

It was early winter. Darkening clouds formed a canopy. Light snow swirled crazily. Ts'ao Ts'ao's men braved the snow to pitch camp as Kuan Yü charged up and hailed Wang Chung, Ts'ao Ts'ao's general.

"Chancellor Ts'ao Ts'ao himself is here," cried Wang Chung. "Have you any reason not to surrender?"

"Please ask him to come out," said Kuan Yü. "I have a few things to tell him."

Wang Chung said, "Is the Chancellor likely to receive you under the circumstances?"

Kuan Yü charged. Wang Chung poised his spear to engage. Their horses crossed. Kuan Yü whipped up his horse and galloped away. Wang Chung raced after him, rounding a hillslope. Kuan Yü swung sharply around. With a single short cry, his blade dancing, he rushed Wang Chung. Unable to defend himself, Wang tried to bolt, but Kuan Yü snatched his shield straps and dragged him out of his saddle and across his own mount.

Kuan Yü took his prisoner to Liu Pei, who said: "Who are you, and what office do you hold, that you would dare counterfeit the Chancellor's colors?"

"*Would* I dare?" replied Wang Chung. "I was ordered to create a false impression as a decoy. In fact, the Chancellor is not here."

"I knew you wanted no bloodshed," said Kuan Yü aside to Liu Pei. "So I took him alive."

"I was nervous about Chang Fei's explosive temper," said Liu Pei. "He might have slain Wang Chung. There's no point in killing people like him, but they can be detained and used as a basis for negotiation."

Then Liu Pei turned to Wang Chung and said, "The Chancellor wrongly suspected that I had turned against him, and he sent you to settle accounts. But I have enjoyed the generous grace of the Chancellor and long to repay him, not to betray him. If you would speak well of me when you reach Ts'ao Ts'ao in Hsü, the capital, I would greatly appreciate the favor."

"We are deeply in your lordship's debt," said Wang Chung. "When the moment arises, we shall defend you to the Chancellor."

When Wang Chung had left, Sun Ch'ien advised Liu Pei:

"Hsüchou cannot long be held. We would be better off stationing troops at Hsiao P'ei and the town of P'i, making a 'horn-points' pincer movement against Ts'ao Ts'ao."

Liu Pei adopted the suggestion, leaving Kuan Yü to hold P'i and Sun Ch'ien to hold Hsüchou, while he went to Hsiao P'ei with Chang Fei.

The Chief Physician, Chi P'ing, Tries to Poison Ts'ao

As the conflict between Ts'ao Ts'ao and Yüan Shao loomed on the horizon, new threats to Ts'ao Ts'ao arose at Court.

After Tung Ch'eng had left Liu Pei with a parting appeal to remember the Emperor's secret decree, Ch'eng and Wang Tzu-fu constantly discussed possible strategies against Ts'ao Ts'ao, but they could develop no plan of action. It was the fifth year of the reign period titled "Establish Security."* At the primal dawn devotions, Ch'eng would see Ts'ao more ruthless and arrogant than ever, and the pressure of his indignation began to affect Ch'eng's health. The Emperor observed the decline of the Senior State Uncle and ordered the Court master physician, Chi P'ing of Lo Yang, to treat him. P'ing applied various tonics and stayed with the patient. He observed his mournful sighs, but refrained from putting any question to him.

Midway through the first month, P'ing and his patient were drinking in the evening. Ch'eng was depressed and drifted into a dream in which everyone seemed surprised when the servants announced Wang Tzu-fu and four others.

Tzu-fu: "Everything is synchronized."

Ch'eng: "Let's have the details."

Tzu-fu: "Liu Piao, governor of Ching province, has joined with Yüan Shao. They have half a million men and are hacking their way here in ten columns. And Ma T'eng has joined with Han Sui in the northwest to form a force of seven hundred thousand—now

* A.D. 200.

on its way. Ts'ao Ts'ao has mobilized down to his last man and horse, dividing his fronts to meet his enemies. The capital has been evacuated. We can raise over a thousand men by marshaling the boys and servants of our five houses: we seize the moment of the evening banquet for the mid-month festival, throw a cordon around the place, go in, and kill him. The opportunity must not be missed!"

Enthusiastic, Ch'eng calls together the men of the household. Night; the second drum. All advance. Tung Ch'eng raises his jeweled sword and strides barefoot into the banquet hall. Ts'ao is there. "Don't move, traitor," cries Ch'eng, chopping with his blade. As Ts'ao crumples in the wake of his hand, the curses continue to flow from Ch'eng even as he awakens from the empty dream.

The physician leaned forward. "So you would like to do Ts'ao in?"

Ch'eng could not reply. P'ing: "Do not be so disconcerted. I am only a physician myself, but I have never forgotten the Han. Day after day I have watched you vent these deep sighs, but could not bring myself to question it. Now fortune has shown me the actual situation through the words you spoke in your dream. Please do not try to deceive me. If there is some useful role I can play, though we suffer clanwide extermination, I shall have no regret." And he bit off the tip of a finger as his pledge.

Then Ch'eng produced from his girdle the loyalists' oath to destroy Ts'ao Ts'ao. "Now our plans have poor prospects, Liu Pei having gone his way. It is because we have no effective strategy that I developed this affliction."

P'ing: "But your concern is quite unnecessary. The traitor's life is in these hands. He suffers chronic headaches whose pain pierces to his marrow. No sooner does one come on than he calls me for treatment. When the next summons arrives, I will administer a dose that is sure to kill him. Why bother with weapons?"

Ch'eng: "If we could only succeed in this, the salvation of the sacred shrines of the Han will be to your credit."

Chi P'ing took his leave. Ch'eng suppressed his excitement and was walking to his room when he came upon a house-servant embracing a maid in a secluded corner. Angrily he had them seized and would have had them killed but for a steward who convinced him to relent. Each was given forty strokes with a stave, and the man was locked in a chilly chamber. Nursing his resentment, in the dead of night the servant forced open the metal lock and bounded over the wall, going direct to Ts'ao to inform on the conspirators. He even revealed that he had seen Chi P'ing bite off a finger tip in oath. Ts'ao had the man concealed, and Tung Ch'eng could learn only that he had escaped.

The next day Ts'ao feigned a headache and called for Chi P'ing. "A traitor meets his end," thought P'ing as he entered the room. From his bed Ts'ao ordered P'ing to prepare the drug.

P'ing: "One dose and you will be over it." He called for a vial and heated the brew there in front of Ts'ao. When it was simmering he added the poison and handed it to Ts'ao who, knowing the truth, was slow to drink.

P'ing: "Take it while it is hot. A brief sweat and it will pass." Ts'ao lifted himself and spoke: "You are versed in the Confucian texts and must be familiar with the proprieties. When the king must take medicine, the servant tastes it first. When the father, so the son. You are my most intimately trusted friend. Don't you think you should taste it before offering it?"

P'ing said: "This drug is for curing your headache, not mine; what would be the use of my tasting it?" But he realized that the truth was out and yanked Ts'ao's ear to try and pour it into him. Ts'ao forced the potion aside and it spattered on the ground, cracking the stones. Before Ts'ao could give the order, P'ing was pinned down by the guards.

Ts'ao: "You really thought I was ill, then? It was all arranged to test you, to see if you actually meant to do me harm."

P'ing was removed for interrogation, then brought back before Ts'ao in bonds and thrown on the floor. But he was impassive and showed no fear. Ts'ao: "You are supposed to be a physician. What is the justification for trying to poison me? Someone must have set you to it. If you tell, there will be clemency."

P'ing snarled: "You are a traitor who abuses our king and ensnares our government. The entire world would see you dead—not I alone."

But Ts'ao hammered at him with questions. P'ing said only: "My wish to kill you was my own. No one sent me. Now that the mission has failed, nothing remains but to die." Ts'ao had him locked away and beaten unmercifully until his skin split open and his flesh lay on him in oozing strips. Then, fearing that he would die and his testimony would be lost, Ts'ao ordered a respite.

The next day Ts'ao invited all the eminent Court officials to a banquet. Only Tung Ch'eng declined, pleading illness. Wang Tzu-fu and the other conspirators felt compelled to attend lest Ts'ao's suspicions be awakened.

The banquet was set out in Ts'ao's private apartments. Several rounds of wine had circulated when Ts'ao said: "Our feast lacks what may serve for entertainment. We do have one man, though, who may sober you all up." Twenty jailers dragged forth Chi P'ing secured in his movable stocks. Ts'ao: "You officials assembled here may not be aware that this fellow has organized an evil faction in opposition to the Court. They conspired to kill me, but today Heaven has ruined them. Please hear it in his own words."

Ts'ao had him struck, and he collapsed to the ground in a faint. When they squirted his face with water he revived, opening his eyes and grinding his teeth as he said: "Traitor! Is there a better time to kill me?"

Ts'ao: "Your co-conspirators were initially six. You made the seventh. Is that right?" P'ing redoubled his denunciation as the others involved stared helplessly, vacantly, at one another as if on a bed of needles. Ts'ao ordered beating, followed by reviving, to continue. But P'ing had no thought of seeking mercy. When he realized that P'ing would not testify, Ts'ao had him dragged off.

The assemblage dispersed. Ts'ao detained only Wang Tzu-fu and the other four for an evening banquet. They felt as if their souls would not cleave to their bodies but had no choice. Ts'ao: "I had not meant to hold you; however, there is something I would like to broach. You see, I still have not been informed as to the discussions you have been having with Tung Ch'eng."

Wang Tzu-fu: "Nothing of any importance."

Ts'ao: "What is written on the white silk roll?"

When no answer was made, Ts'ao had the servant who betrayed them brought forth.

Tzu-fu: "Well, where did you turn up?"

Servant: "Six of you, in private, together, put down your names. Can you deny it?"

Tzu-fu: "This wretched runaway became familiar with a serving girl of the Senior State Uncle's. He was punished and now slanders his master. He cannot be credited."

Ts'ao: "Chi P'ing gave me poison—if not at Tung Ch'eng's bidding, then at whose? If you own up here and now, there is still time for leniency. If you wait until the whole thing is exposed, it will be difficult to make allowances." But they insisted together that there was nothing to expose, and Ts'ao barked to his followers to remove them.

The next day Ts'ao led a delegation to Tung Ch'eng's home to inquire after his health. Ch'eng had no choice but to receive them. Ts'ao: "On what account did you not attend last night's banquet?"

Ch'eng: "I have a slight ailment that continues to trouble me. I may not go out except for an emergency."

Ts'ao: "Probably just a case of 'concern for the nation.' You are aware of the Chi P'ing affair, State Uncle? No? How could the Senior State Uncle not know? Bring him in to compare ailments with Senior State Uncle." The jailers dragged in a swearing Chi P'ing.

Ts'ao: "This man has pulled down Wang Tzu-fu and the other four—I have them already in custody. Only one remains to be apprehended. P'ing, who instructed you to drug me? Testify quickly."

P'ing: "Heaven instructed me to kill a rebel-traitor."

Ts'ao had him beaten, but his body had no skin left to be flayed. Ch'eng watched from his seat, his heart torn. Ts'ao questioned P'ing again: "You were born with ten fingers. Why do you have nine now?"

P'ing: "I chewed it off as an oath to kill a traitor."

Ts'ao called for a blade, and hacked off the other nine. "Cut off in one stroke. There's a lesson in oath taking."

P'ing: "As I have a mouth to swallow a traitor, so I have a tongue to curse one."

Ts'ao ordered his tongue cut out.

P'ing: "Stay your hand a moment. I can bear it no longer. I am resigned to testifying. Let slip these bonds." It was done. P'ing stood erect and looked in prayer toward the gates: "That I failed to rid the nation of a traitor is no more than the design of the Heavens." Then he dashed his head against the stair and died. Ts'ao gave a public order for his dismemberment. It was the fifth year of "Establish Security," A.D. 200.

From the official historian we have the following poem:

> The Han dynasty could stand no more.
> Treating the state was Chi P'ing,
> Who cast his oath to purge treason's clique,
> Who gave his life for sovereign's sage luster.
> In extremity his words were only more severe.

In the death agony his spirit lives.
We look back over a thousand autumns
To his extraordinary name:
Ten bloody dripping stumps.

Seeing that Chi P'ing was dead, Ts'ao brought the servant to confront Tung Ch'eng. "Does the State Uncle recognize this man?"

Ch'eng: "That runaway, here? He should be brought to justice at once."

Ts'ao: "He has volunteered information on the conspiracy. He is here to testify. Who dares punish him? Wang Tzu-fu and the others have already been taken. They have confessed; do you still resist and deny?" Tung Ch'eng was held while Ts'ao's followers entered his quarters. There they discovered the decree in the sash and the oath of the loyalists. Ts'ao read these through and laughed. "How can rats like these hope to get away with it?" He had Tung's entire clan seized.

Ts'ao brought the documents to his counselors and advisers and demanded that the Emperor Tributor be deposed and another enthroned.

Alas: A few columns of red ink disclose vain hopes. An oath on a scroll brings a tragic end. The fate of the Emperor is told in the following chapter.

Chi P'ing interrogated

Ts'ao Murders the High Consort; Liu Pei Flees to Yüan Shao

Having discovered the secret decree, Ts'ao proposed to set aside the Emperor Tributor and to select a man of virtue to reign in his stead. But Ch'eng Yü advised against it: "The reason my illustrious lord can make his influence felt and his commands effective throughout the kingdom is because of his devotion and service to the name of Han. Now if you rush to depose when the feudal lords remain discontented, it is sure to end in warfare."

Ts'ao agreed, contenting himself with the execution of Tung Ch'eng, the five conspirators, and their entire households—adults and children alike. All told, over seven hundred died. The spectators, whether commoners or officials, wept freely. Later a poem was written mourning Tung Ch'eng.

> A secret command via the jade sash—
> The Heavenly word goes through the barred gate.
> One day he rescued the royal progress.
> One day he received a sovereign's grace.
> Obsessed with the safekeeping of the throne,
> "Rid the traitor" stole into his dreaming soul.
> His loyal rectitude withstands a thousand ages.
> "Success" and "failure" are for whom to judge?

Another poem honored the memory of the conspirators.

> Life and loyalty pledged on a footlong silk,
> King, father, ardent to redeem.
> Mourn their sheer courage; hundreds fell,
> Whose fire-tried hearts outlast a thousand autumns.

But Ts'ao's rage was not allayed by these clanwide executions. The sister of Tung Ch'eng, the Emperor's high consort, now five months with child, was his next target. When Ts'ao entered the palace, improperly armed with a sword, the Emperor was in the rear quarters discussing the Tung Ch'eng affair with Empress Fu and the consort Tung. Without warning Ts'ao entered, all fury. The Emperor lost his composure.

Ts'ao: "Were you aware or not that Tung Ch'eng was conspiring to rebel?"

Emperor: "Tung Cho was brought to justice long ago."

Ts'ao: "I said Tung *Ch'eng*, not Tung Cho."

The Emperor quivered. "We had no knowledge of this—truly."

Ts'ao: "I suppose you have forgotten the pierced finger, the decree drawn in blood." All reply failed the Emperor as Ts'ao snapped at his lieutenants to seize the consort Tung.

Emperor: "The consort is in her fifth month. We hope the Chancellor will act compassionately."

Ts'ao: "Had Heaven not wrecked things for you, I would have been murdered. Why should I spare this woman to create a future nemesis?"

Empress Fu: "Demote her, then, to the 'cold' palace and wait until she has delivered. There will be time enough to get rid of her."

Consort Tung: "Then let me die with my corpse intact—and no exposure." Ts'ao had a white cord brought in for her to see.

Emperor: "In the world below the Nine Springs, hold no grievance against ourself."

His tears came like rain; the Empress Fu's also. But Ts'ao said curtly: "Still carrying on?" The soldiers bore her out and strangled her at the gate. Later a poem was written lamenting the consort's murder.

> Springtime of pleasure, the royal mansion,
> Grace received—only to be wronged.
> Grieve! The dragon seed aborted,
> Even as her life.
> Stately-regal imperial lord
> No way to rescue.
> Covers face, vain to watch, tears
> A welling fountain.

Thereafter Ts'ao had all the imperial clansmen by marriage excluded from the palace except by his consent.

Ts'ao said to Ch'eng Yü, his adviser: "Now Tung Ch'eng and the rest have been executed, but two of their number remain: Ma T'eng in the northwest, and Liu Pei. These two must be eliminated."

Yü: "Ma T'eng is posted at Hsi Liang, where he cannot be easily taken. Write to placate him. Don't let him become suspicious; entice him to the capital and then deal with him. Liu Pei is in Hsüchou, his forces deployed in a head-and-tail pincer formation. He cannot be underestimated, either. Not to speak of Yüan Shao, posted at Kuan Tu and ever aiming at our capital, Hsü. No sooner do we strike eastward at Liu Pei than we compel him to seek aid from Yüan Shao, who is sure to take advantage of your troops' absence from the capital. How will you meet that?"

Ts'ao: "Not exactly right. Pei is the main threat, and if we hold back till his wings are fullspread he will be extremely difficult to deal with. Shao, despite his strength, is too vexed by his problems to be decisive; he is really not worth worrying about."

Another adviser, K'uo Chia, entered the discussion. Ts'ao asked him: "We want to move east against Liu Pei, but what about Yüan Shao?"

Chia: "By nature Shao is not quick to move, and he worries about everything. His counselors are jealous of each other and present no real problems. Liu Pei has just revamped his forces and they are not yet completely loyal. If the Chancellor leads an eastern campaign, a single battle will conclude the matter."

Ts'ao: "This coincides with my own thinking." And he raised two hundred thousand men, whom he led out in five columns to subdue Liu Pei in Hsüchou.

When spies brought this information to Liu Pei, he said, "The only way to ease the pressure is to seek help from Yüan Shao." He composed a note for Sun Ch'ien to take to the provinces north of the Yellow River.

Sun Ch'ien was received by T'ien Feng, to whom he described the situation in detail and asked to be taken to Yüan Shao. Ch'ien submitted Pei's note, but Shao was agitated, his expression vexed, his clothes awry. "I am soon to die," he cried. "Of the five sons born to me, only the youngest shows true promise. Now he is afflicted with scales and sores, and his survival is uncertain. I have no heart to consider anything else."

Feng: "Ts'ao Ts'ao marches to the east against Liu Pei, leaving the capital vacant. If we take the opportunity to invade, we shall preserve the Emperor and save the populace. This is a rare and critical moment, if only my illustrious lord will shape it."

Shao: "I too recognize the supreme advantage here, but alas, I vacillate within, irresolute, in dread of some mischance."

Feng: "What is there to vacillate over?"

Shao: "Of my five sons, only this one has developed into something truly extraordinary. Should there be some unforeseen crisis, our fate is sealed." And so he resolved not to strike, but simply asked Sun Ch'ien to convey his reasons to Liu Pei with the assurance that if things went badly, he would personally see to Pei's safety.

Feng beat the ground with his staff. "To have this once-in-a-lifetime opportunity, and for the sake of a child's disease to let it slip—there is no hope for our cause. But how painfully I rue it." With broken stride and protracted sighs he went out.

Sun Ch'ien's news alarmed Liu Pei, who saw no hope until Chang Fei said: "Elder brother's anxiety is needless. Ts'ao's force comes from afar and is sure to be fatigued. If we exploit the moment of their arrival, rush ahead and storm their camp—they can be demolished."

Liu Pei: "I used to think you a mere warrior. But yours is the plan of a strategist—it tallies nicely with the logic of warfare." Chang Fei's suggestion was accepted.

Ts'ao Ts'ao led his army toward Hsiao P'ei. On the march a gale sprang up. They heard a cracking sound; one of the banners had split. Ts'ao called a conference to consider the omen, and Hsün Yü asked the direction of the wind and the colors of the broken banner. The gale had come from the southeast. The banner was horn-pointed and two-colored, blue and red. Hsün Yü announced: "It can only signify a night raid by Liu Pei." Others confirmed the omen's meaning, and Ts'ao fortified the camp accordingly.

> Pity this scion of kings: isolated, outspent,
> Staking his fortunes on a nighttime raid.
> Could he help the broken-banner sign?
> Old Man Heaven! Why let this villain off?

Chang Fei's gambit was doomed. Fei himself was routed and took refuge in the mountains. Liu Pei fled to Yüan Shao. Kuan Yü remained in Hsia P'i in charge of Liu Pei's family.

When Liu Pei arrived at Yüan Shao's stronghold, he was greeted by Yüan T'an, Shao's eldest son. Pei told him the full details of his defeat and his hopes for Shao's protection. T'an provided for him and sent a letter to his father. Yüan Shao came out of his city at Yeh thirty leagues to receive Liu Pei with full honors. Pei raised his hands, clasped in respect, disclaiming the honors even as Shao made haste to repeat them. "Our son's recent illness has caused us to fail in our duty to you, and makes us most uneasy. But now good fortune brings us together, and a lifelong expectation is fulfilled."

Liu Pei: "Isolated and in extremity, I have long desired to throw in my lot with you, though by fate or circumstance it was never accomplished. Now I am under attack by Ts'ao Ts'ao. My wife and children are lost. And I long for a general who can find a place for the warriors of the kingdom. So, undeterred by shame, hoping to receive support, and vowing to obtain revenge, I come straight to you."

Pleased, Yüan Shao treated Liu Pei with great generosity, and they resided together in the northern province of Chi.

On the night of the abortive counterattack, Ts'ao Ts'ao had seized Hsiao P'ei and attacked Hsüchou. The defenders could not hold, and Ch'en Teng surrendered the city to Ts'ao. When Hsüchou was secured Ts'ao summoned his advisers to discuss taking Hsia P'i.

Hsun Yü said: "Kuan Yü is there, keeping Pei's family safe. He will defend it to the death. If you fail to strike swiftly, Yüan Shao will take it from you."

Ts'ao: "I have long treasured Kuan Yü's military competence and personal ability. If we would win him to our own service, it is best to have someone persuade him to surrender."

K'uo Chia: "His loyalty is too strong. He would never come over. An envoy might end by losing his life."

But Chang Liao said: "I am acquainted with the man and would like to attempt it."

Ch'eng Yü: "Though you two are on familiar terms, as I read the man, no words will persuade him. I have a plan. If we hem him in first and then use Chang Liao to work on him, he will transfer his allegiance to the Chancellor."

Lord Kuan Comes
to Terms with Ts'ao Ts'ao;
Lord Kuan Rescues Ts'ao Ts'ao
at White Horse

Ch'eng Yü proposed the following: "Kuan Yü can stand off a myriad men; only some stratagem will serve to take him. Now, if we send some of the turncoats formerly under Liu Pei's command back into Hsia P'i to see Lord Kuan, they can explain that they have managed to escape, and then they can remain in the city in covert contact with us. From our side, we can draw Lord Kuan out to battle, feign defeat, and entice him to a prearranged point. Crack troops can cut off his way back. Then you can begin to negotiate with him."

Ts'ao Ts'ao accepted the advice and began the operation. A few dozen captives surrendered to Lord Kuan in Hsia P'i, and Lord Kuan received them in good faith. The next day Hsia-hou Tun spearheaded Ts'ao's attack.* Five thousand came against Kuan Yü to provoke battle, but Lord Kuan held back. Then Tun sent a man to denounce him at the foot of the wall, and Kuan Yü's fury rose. He led three thousand men out of the walls against Tun. The two forces fought over ten bouts, after which Tun wheeled his horse around and fled. Kuan Yü rode hard after him. Tun fought and ran, fought and ran. They had gone twenty leagues when Kuan Yü, fearing for Hsia P'i, raised his arm for the men to return—only to hear the peal of bombards. Left and right, squadrons checked his escape. Lord Kuan moved to force a path. From

---

* Ts'ao Ts'ao may have been a Hsia-hou by birth. See page 10 above.

two sides the ambushers massed their crossbow fire, and the shafts whizzed down like locusts. Kuan Yü could not pass. He fought until evening but found no way home, and only managed to lead his men to a mountain summit for respite.

Ts'ao's men clustered around the mountain and sealed the avenues of escape. In the distance Kuan Yü could see flames rising heavenward out of Hsia P'i, for the false defectors had quietly opened the gates to Ts'ao's men, who had set the fires only to confuse Kuan Yü. Now, seeing the flames, Lord Kuan was panicked. Again and again through the night he charged down the hill, only to be driven back by flurries of arrows. Enduring until daybreak, he marshaled his men for a breakthrough, when from nowhere he saw a single rider racing toward him. It was Chang Liao.

Lord Kuan, receiving him: "You come as an adversary, I presume?"

Liao: "No. I come in respect of our long-standing friendship." And he dismounted and threw down his weapons. The formalities performed, they sat at the summit.

Lord Kuan: "You have really come to win me over, haven't you?"

Liao: "No. You once did me the kindness of saving my brother. How could I not try to save you in return?"

Lord Kuan: "Then you have come to lend us aid!"

Liao: "Not that, either. Liu Pei's survival is in doubt, as is Chang Fei's. Yesterday Lord Ts'ao took Hsia P'i, but with no injury or threat to the soldiers or civilians. A special detail keeps guard over Liu Pei's family to spare them harm or anxiety, and I come, first of all, that you may know this."

Lord Kuan, angry: "Your talk is only to win me over. For the moment I may be cut off, but death is no more to me than a homecoming. You should leave now. I will be riding down to give battle."

Chang Liao laughed out loud: "Brother, this will only become the object of men's mockery. Dying here, you commit three offenses."

Lord Kuan: "Well then, go on and explain them to me."

Liao: "In the beginning, when you and your lord, Liu Pei, bound yourselves in fraternal allegiance, you vowed to share life or death. Now your lord has been defeated. If you die in battle and he survives to seek your aid but cannot get it, haven't you betrayed your oath? That is the first offense. Your lord's kinsmen are entrusted to you, and if you die now, the two women will have no one to depend on. That is the second offense. Your martial skill is incomparable. You are versed in the classics and the histories. If you lapse in your determination to join with your lord in upholding the House of Han, and achieve instead a commonplace valor by vainly throwing yourself onto the fire—how have you fulfilled your 'allegiance'? That is the third offense. Could I refrain from making these known to you?"

Lord Kuan mused deeply. "Well, you have explained the three offenses. What would you have me do?"

Liao: "Lord Ts'ao's troops are on four sides. If you refuse to submit, you will die. To die in vain avails nothing. Submit for now, while you seek news of Liu Pei. When you learn where he is, you may go to him immediately. This way you will preserve the two women, you will keep the Peach Garden Compact, and you will preserve your own most useful life. These are the advantages for you to consider."

Lord Kuan: "Brother, you speak of three advantages. I have three terms. If the Chancellor complies, I shall take off my arms. If not, I am content to die with the three offenses upon me."

Liao: "The Chancellor is magnanimous in his judgment. Where has he shown intolerance? I beg to hear your three terms."

Lord Kuan: "The Imperial Uncle, Liu Pei, and I have sworn to stabilize the House of Han. My surrender now is to the Emperor and not to Ts'ao Ts'ao. That is the first term. I request for my two sisters-in-law the care and support befitting an Imperial Uncle's wives. No one, however high or low his station, may be permitted to approach their gate. That is the second term. At the remotest indication of Imperial Uncle Liu's whereabouts, no matter what the distance, I shall depart forthwith. That is my third term. Deny any of the three, and I shall not surrender."

When Chang Liao relayed to Ts'ao Lord Kuan's insistence on yielding to the Emperor and not to him, Ts'ao laughed: "I am the Chancellor. I am the Han. The Han is I. This may be granted." To the second of Kuan Yü's terms, Ts'ao replied: "To the income of an Imperial Uncle I will add a like amount, thus doubling it. As to the strict prohibition of intercourse between Court and commoner, that is our common law. What doubts are there?" But at the third term Ts'ao demurred: "In that case I will be feeding him for nothing. This is difficult to grant."

Kuan Yü keeps vigil over his sisters

Liao: "Have you forgotten the saying, 'As the king treats me, so I treat the king'? Liu Pei treats Lord Kuan with gracious generosity—no more. If the Chancellor can extend an even greater largess to bind him, need we fear his defection?" Ts'ao thought Liao's words apt and accepted the three terms.

Ts'ao Ts'ao came out of the city wall to greet Lord Kuan, who dismounted and made obeisance. Ts'ao rushed forward to reciprocate. Lord Kuan: "As the general of a defeated army, I am obliged by your mercy in sparing me."

Ts'ao: "Having long esteemed your dedication and loyalty, I am favored today with a meeting which fulfills a lifelong expectation."

Lord Kuan: "Chang Liao has submitted on my behalf the three terms. I am honored by your response, and trust there will be no retraction."

Ts'ao: "Once my word has been given, there is no breach of faith."

Lord Kuan: "Should I learn of the Imperial Uncle's whereabouts I must join him, whatever the dangers or obstacles. In that event I may not have time even to take formal leave and humbly beg to receive your pardon now."

Ts'ao: "If Liu Pei still lives, you should join him. But he may have perished unnoticed in the confusion of battle. For the time being you might as well accept the situation and allow us to collect more information."

*   *   *   *

Ts'ao Ts'ao moved from the newly conquered Hsia P'i to Hsü, the capital and residence of the Emperor. Lord Kuan and his sisters-in-law made the journey too. They broke their travels at a hostel, where Ts'ao aimed to disrupt the proprieties between lord and liegeman by assigning Lord Kuan and the sisters-in-law to a single chamber.* Lord Kuan remained at attention at the door, a candle in his hand, until dawn, no trace of fatigue showing in his eyes. This enhanced Ts'ao's respect for Lord Kuan. In Hsü, Ts'ao provided suitable quarters.

Ts'ao Ts'ao conducted Lord Kuan into the presence of the Emperor, who conferred on him the title of adjutant general. The

---

* A possible allusion to the levirate, which was practiced by the Mongols but sternly proscribed by the Ming. See page 303 below.

next day Ts'ao held a major banquet, assembling the entire corps of his advisers and officers and treating Lord Kuan as a state guest. Ts'ao seated him in the upper dais and presented him with brocade silks and gold and silver utensils and vessels—all of which Lord Kuan presented in turn to his sisters-in-law. Ts'ao showed him unusual generosity, giving small banquets every third day, large ones every fifth. Ten handsome women attended Lord Kuan, but he sent them on to serve his two sisters. Every three days he would appear at the sisters' door to perform the proper formalities, and they would ask for news of the Imperial Uncle. Only when the sisters had excused him would he retire. When Ts'ao learned of this high courtesy, he inwardly honored Lord Kuan more than ever.

One day Ts'ao noticed Lord Kuan's worn-out green battle garb. He had Lord Kuan's measure taken and presented him with battle dress of the rarest brocade. Although Kuan Yü accepted it, he wore it beneath the old one so that nothing showed. Ts'ao Ts'ao teased Lord Kuan about his stinginess, but Lord Kuan said: "It is not my frugality. The old dress was a gift from Imperial Uncle Liu. When I wear it, it is as if we were together. Do you expect me to forget my elder brother's gift on account of the Chancellor's new one? That's why I wear it underneath."

Ts'ao Ts'ao expressed admiration at such fidelity, but inwardly he was troubled.

One day Lord Kuan was told that his sisters-in-law had collapsed in tears and were calling for him. Kneeling at their door, Lord Kuan heard Lady Kan: "I dreamed the Imperial Uncle was trapped in a pit. I woke and told Lady Mi, and we believe he is now beneath the Nine Springs, and so we lost our composure."

Lord Kuan: "Dreams of the night bear no credence. This comes from your excessive worry. Do not vex yourselves with such anxieties."

At this time Ts'ao had Lord Kuan called to a banquet. Ts'ao asked the reason for his anxious look, and Lord Kuan replied: "My sisters-in-law yearn for my elder brother and cry so piercingly that I cannot master my own feelings." Ts'ao smiled and tried to console him, urging him to drink. Lord Kuan became intoxicated and let his beard spread fully on his chest. "I have failed in my duty to home and country, and I have betrayed my elder brother," he said. "I live in vain."

Ts'ao: "Have you ever counted the hairs in your beard?"

Lord Kuan: "There are several hundred. In autumn I lose some. In winter I wrap it in a black silk sack lest the hairs break." Ts'ao Ts'ao had a silken sack made for Lord Kuan to protect his beard.

The next day they were received by the Emperor, who asked the purpose of the silk sack on Lord Kuan's chest. Lord Kuan: "As my beard is rather long, the Chancellor bestowed this sack on me to keep it safe." At the Emperor's request he unfurled it in the royal sanctum, and it reached below his stomach. The Emperor called him "Lord of the Magnificent Beard." And so he was known thereafter.

Once when Ts'ao was escorting Lord Kuan, he inquired: "Why is your lordship's horse so emaciated?"

Lord Kuan: "My worthless carcass has grown overweight. The horse can hardly bear me." Ts'ao had his aides bring in a horse. Its body was like fiery coal, its stature magnificent. Lord Kuan: "Isn't that Red Hare, the horse Lü Pu* once rode?" Ts'ao acknowledged it and presented the mount, completely equipped, to Lord Kuan. Kuan Yü repeatedly joined his hands and declared his gratitude.

"I sent you beautiful women, gold, rolls of silk, one after the other, and never did you condescend to nod. Now I have given you a horse and you keep bowing. Do you value a beast above humans?" Ts'ao asked.

Lord Kuan: "I know this horse. It can cover a thousand leagues in a day. If I get word of my elder brother's whereabouts, I can reach him in a single day." Ts'ao swallowed his astonishment and regretted the gift.

Later a poet wrote:

> To the wronged general
> The false minister
> Shows courtesy.
> How was he to tell
> Lord Kuan would not rebel?

Ts'ao sighed. "That is what devotion means: to serve one's lord, never forgetting the original vow!"

Hsun Yü: "But he recently told Chang Liao that he would not leave until he had performed some work of merit. If we never

* A man who betrayed his master, Tung Cho.

For the prize horse Kuan Yü expresses devout thanks

give him the opportunity to do so, it will be difficult for him to depart." This point Ts'ao approved.

*   *   *   *

Liu Pei was with Yüan Shao, who asked: "Why do you remain vexed?"

Liu Pei: "Of my two brothers I have had not a shred of news. My wife and children have fallen into Ts'ao's hands. I have neither preserved my family nor redeemed my sovereign. How can I help grieving?"

Shao: "I want to move against the capital, Hsü. The spring thaw has arrived—the ideal time for marshaling the army."

They discussed strategies for destroying Ts'ao. T'ien Feng objected: "Before, when Ts'ao attacked Liu Pei in Hsüchou and left the capital undefended, you did not respond to the opportunity. Now Hsüchou has fallen, and Ts'ao's troops are at their keenest. He cannot be lightly opposed. Why not simply hold fast here until some weakness shows itself in Ts'ao's army?"

Shao asked Liu Pei's view of T'ien Feng's conservative tactics. Pei: "Ts'ao Ts'ao is a rebel who has betrayed the sovereign. If my illustrious lord fails to bring him to justice, I fear we forfeit our great principle of allegiance in the eyes of the entire world."

"Liu Pei's position is well taken," said Shao. He told T'ien Feng, "Your sort is addicted to civil process and despises the military side of things. You would have us forfeit our integrity."

T'ien Feng bowed to the ground and knocked his head on it. "Ignore my words and you will march your army into disaster." Shao wanted him beheaded, but Liu Pei's strenuous pleas got him off with imprisonment.

> *Yüan Shao appointed Yen Liang as general of the vanguard and ordered an attack on White Horse. Kuan Yü learned of Ts'ao's preparations and offered his services, but Ts'ao declined. Then the battle began to go poorly for Ts'ao, and Ch'eng Yü proposed that Kuan Yü be used against Yen Liang.*

Ts'ao: "I fear that once Kuan Yü accomplishes something, he will leave us without hesitation."

Ch'eng Yü: "If Liu Pei is still alive, he must have joined Yüan Shao. Now if Lord Kuan destroys Yüan Shao's troops, Shao is

sure to suspect Liu Pei and kill him. Once Pei is dead, where can
Lord Kuan turn?" This satisfied Ts'ao, who sent to Lord Kuan re-
questing his help.

Raising the Blue Dragon sword, mounted on Red Hare, a few
dozen men in train, Lord Kuan rode to White Horse* to see Ts'ao
Ts'ao. Ts'ao described to him the exploits and ferocity of Yen
Liang. It was reported that Yen Liang was issuing challenges to
battle, and Ts'ao led Lord Kuan to a hilltop to observe. They sat
together, the various generals standing around, while Ts'ao
pointed to the foot of the mountain where Yen's forces were
camped, their banners and standards fresh and brilliant, spear
blades like a stretch of forest, impressive in their strict order.

Ts'ao to Lord Kuan: "Such valiant stalwarts—the men and
horse of these northerners."

Lord Kuan: "Mudhens and clay dogs to me."

Ts'ao pointed again. "Under the command canopy, with the
brocade robe and the metal shield, armed, erect on his horse—
that's Yen Liang!"

Lord Kuan glanced skeptically over the scene. "I can see Yen
Liang's head stuck on a pole for sale."

Ts'ao: "Do not underrate him."

Lord Kuan: "Little merit as I have, I beg leave to seize his
head to present to my Chancellor."

Chang Liao: "We do not make sport in the army. Be a little
less reckless."

With a thrust of energy, Lord Kuan leaped onto his horse.
Holding the Blue Dragon sword point down, he raced downhill,
his phoenix eyes round and fixed, silkworm eyebrows bristling
erect. He dashed for the opposing camp. The northern army
parted like a wake as Lord Kuan charged straight for Yen Liang.
Before Liang could identify the figure crashing toward him, the
speed of Red Hare had already brought Lord Kuan and him face
to face. Liang was too slow, and with a stroke of the sword Lord
Kuan pierced him. Before the stunned enemy, Kuan dismounted
and cut off the head, strapped it to the rear of his horse, remounted, and sped out of the camp, sword raised in warning—
all as if moving across an empty plain. Men and leaders of the
northern force were thrown into tumult, routed without having
fought. Ts'ao's troops seized their chance to strike. The dead were

* The white horse is the "positive" of the two Manichaean signs. See page
303 below.

beyond numbering. The booty in weapons and horses was enormous.

Lord Kuan reascended the mountain, to the acclaim of Ts'ao's generals, and laid the head before Ts'ao, who said: "My general is more than mortal."

Lord Kuan: "Not worth mentioning. My brother Chang Fei took the head of the chief general of an army one hundred times

Kuan Yü takes Yen Liang's head

that size." This information so impressed Ts'ao that he had his staff transcribe it on their inner garments as a warning.

*   *   *   *

Yen Liang's defeated force fled homeward, meeting Yüan Shao halfway. When Shao heard the report, he recognized the work of Liu Pei's brother, Lord Kuan, and angrily reproached Pei: "Your brother has killed our most valued commander. I am sure you were involved in this plot. What point is there in keeping you?" He had the axemen take Liu Pei out to be beheaded, but was persuaded to refrain because the identity of the warrior who had killed Yen Liang had not yet been verified.

Yüan Shao Loses Two Generals;
Lord Kuan Leaves Ts'ao Ts'ao

Ts'ao Ts'ao rewarded Kuan Yü by making him master of the Han Shou district. Kuan Yü again entered the battle, this time against Wen Ch'ou, whom Yüan Shao had sent to avenge the fallen general Yen Liang.

The report came back to Liu Pei: "It's that red-faced, long-bearded one again who has cut down Wen Ch'ou." Liu Pei dashed forward to get a look. Across the river a group of men and horses were moving back and forth as if they were flying. A banner carried the words: "Lord Kuan, Master of the Han Shou District."

Liu Pei silently thanked the heavens and the earth. "So my brother is with Ts'ao Ts'ao after all." He sought the chance to hail Lord Kuan, but a mass of Ts'ao's men intervened and he had to pull back.

An adviser said to Yüan Shao: "Once again that Kuan Yü has killed one of our generals, while Liu Pei fends us off with feigned ignorance." Shao was enraged against the "long-eared devil" and, when Liu Pei arrived, had him seized for execution. "You purposely sent your brother to destroy my top generals," he said. "How can you claim to be innocent?"

Liu Pei: "Allow me one last statement. Ts'ao Ts'ao has always been bitterly jealous of me. He knows I came with your illustrious lordship and dreads my helping you. For this reason he is sending Lord Kuan to cut down your generals—so that your lordship will blame me. Thus through your hand he would do me in."

Yüan Shao recognized the truth of these words and invited Pei to sit beside him in the main tent. Gratefully Liu Pei said: "I am indebted to your lordship's magnanimous consideration, which I can neither match nor repay. But let me have a trusted friend to carry a secret letter to Lord Kuan; he will come at once to lend his support to your lordship. Together we may execute the traitor Ts'ao and avenge Yen Liang and Wen Ch'ou. What do you say?"

Yuan Shao: "To get Lord Kuan is worth more to me than ten Yen Liangs or Wen Ch'ous."

*   *   *   *

Chang Liao went to speak to Lord Kuan for Ts'ao Ts'ao: "They say you have received news of your elder brother. I have come especially to congratulate you."

Lord Kuan: "My former lord may be alive, but I have not seen him. There is nothing to rejoice for."

Liao: "How is a blood-brother relation different from that between you and Liu Pei?"

Lord Kuan: "You and I are as friend to friend. Liu Pei and I are brothers even more than friends, liege and liege man even more than brothers. The relationships are not comparable."

Liao: "Now that he is north of the river with Yüan Shao, will you join him or not?"

Lord Kuan: "I cannot renege. Will you convey my wishes to the Chancellor?" But when Chang Liao did so, Ts'ao said: "I have a way to detain him."

Lord Kuan was mulling over the situation when an old friend was announced. But when the visitor entered, it turned out to be someone else.

"Who are you, sir?" said Lord Kuan.

"Actually, I am in the service of Yüan Shao."

Lord Kuan shooed his attendants away. "To have come here! What is your purpose?" The man produced a letter from Liu Pei.

You and I joined oaths in the peach garden, swearing to die together. Now why do you turn away, severing the bonds of grace and allegiance? It can only be that you seek some fame of merit or aspire to wealth and status that you would offer up my poor head to make your accomplishment complete. Who can write all he wishes to say? Unto death I await your instruction.

Lord Kuan: "Would I not have pursued my brother, had I but known where? Do you think I would agree to deny our long-standing oath for the sake of 'wealth and status'?"

The messenger said: "Liu Pei's anxiety to see you is most keen. If you remain true to the oath, go to him as soon as possible."

Lord Kuan: "In this life on earth, he who does not finish what he starts is no man of honor. When I came to Ts'ao it was open and aboveboard, and I can leave him no other way. Let me compose a letter and ask you to convey it to my brother. This will give me time to take my leave and deliver the women."

Messenger: "And if Ts'ao refuses, what then?"

Lord Kuan: "Then I am content to die rather than remain."

Lord Kuan's reply to Liu Pei:

> In my humble view, allegiance brooks no reservation, and loyalty is no respecter of death. In my youth I came to know the classics and to appreciate something of the social forms and proprieties. When I reflect upon the fraternal devotion of ancient models, I cannot help sighing over and over through my tears. When I was holding Hsia P'i, we had no stores and no reinforcements. My own wish was to make a swift end to myself. But what could I do—with the heavy responsibility of two sisters, could I sacrifice myself and thus neglect those entrusted to me? So I restrained myself for the while in hopes of meeting you later. Only recently have I had reliable word from you. I go immediately to bid good-bye to Lord Ts'ao in person and deliver the two sisters home to you. May God and man destroy me if I harbor any other thought. But pen and parchment cannot express the agony I feel. Humbly awaiting the time when I can bow before you, I offer this for your examination.

The messenger took the letter. Lord Kuan informed the sisters and went straight to Ts'ao's headquarters. Ts'ao knew why he was coming and had the customary sign of absence hung at the gate. Perturbed, Lord Kuan left. He ordered his own men to prepare for departure and then to await developments. He instructed the members of his household to leave all gifts from Ts'ao in place—none were to be removed. The next day he went again to headquarters; the sign of absence still hung there. Although Lord Kuan returned several times, he never succeeded in meeting Ts'ao Ts'ao. He sought out Chang Liao, but Liao pleaded illness and did not

Kuan Yü leaves Ts'ao Ts'ao

appear. Realizing that the Chancellor would not let him take leave, yet resolved to leave, he wrote his farewell to Ts'ao Ts'ao:

> In my youth I undertook to serve the Imperial Uncle, vowing to share both life and death with him. The radiant Heavens and the fertile Earth are true witnesses to these words. When I lost my command at Hsia P'i, I received your gracious consent to the three terms I asked. Now I have discovered my first lord in the army of Yüan Shao, and I think back to my past oath. To betray it is unacceptable. However ample your recent generosity, a first allegiance is hard to put out of mind. I hereby deliver this letter to announce my departure, presuming to hope that you may consider it. For whatever kindness I may yet remain in your debt, I beg you to defer it to a future time.

Transcribed and sealed, it was delivered to headquarters. All valuables were locked in the vaults. The seal of his office, master of the Han Shou district, was suspended in the hall. His two sisters-in-law mounted the carriage. Astride Red Hare, the Blue Dragon sword in hand, a small guard surrounding him, Kuan Yü pushed with menacing eye and leveled sword straight out of the city gate past the objecting gate warden. Then he fell back to the rear as the suite hastened along the highroad.

Lord Kuan Pursued

Among Ts'ao Ts'ao's generals and subordinates Ts'ai Yang alone had been antagonistic to Lord Kuan. When he learned of Lord Kuan's departure, Ts'ai wished to pursue him. Ts'ao protested: "He does not forsake his first lord, and his leaving was as aboveboard as his coming. He is a true man of honor—whom you would do well to emulate."

Ch'eng Yü said: "The Chancellor treated that man with utmost generosity, yet he left improperly. That parchment scrap of nonsense insolently sullies your prestige. His offense is great. If you set him free to return to Yüan Shao, it is adding wings to a tiger. Better to pursue and dispatch him, and have done with future troubles."

Ts'ao: "In the beginning I granted his terms. Can I break faith? He acts for his own lord. Do not pursue." And to Chang Liao, Ts'ao said: "Lord Kuan locked up the valuables and left his seal of office. Rich bribes serve not to move him, nor do dignities and emoluments deflect his purpose. We cannot esteem such men too deeply. He is still within range. I'll make one personal appeal to him—work on his feelings of fellowship. Run ahead and beg him to stop till I can escort him off properly and provide him with some money for the journey and a battle suit, that he may remember me in future times." Chang Liao rode on ahead, and Ts'ao Ts'ao followed with a few dozen cavalry.

Lord Kuan riding Red Hare could not have been overtaken were he not deliberately holding back to guard the rear. Someone behind shouted for him to slow down. He turned and saw

Chang Liao pounding toward him. "I trust you are not coming in pursuit," he said.

Chang Liao replied: "I am not. The Chancellor, in consideration of the long road ahead, wishes to see you off properly and sent me ahead to request that you delay for a moment. He has no other intent."

Lord Kuan: "Since he is bringing up armored cavalry, I expect to decide it with a battle to the death." He poised his horse on an overpass to survey their approach. When Lord Kuan came into view, Ts'ao ordered his men to show that they were unarmed, and Lord Kuan became easier.

Ts'ao: "Why do you go in such haste?"

Remaining mounted, Lord Kuan bent forward to reply: "Before leaving I submitted my account to the Chancellor. Now that my first lord is with Yüan Shao, there is no excuse for delay. Time after time I hastened to your quarters but did not succeed in speaking with you. So in all humility I wrote to announce my departure, put the valuables in the vault, and hung up my seal for restoration to the Chancellor who, I am confident, will not forget what he agreed to."

Ts'ao: "I seek the trust of all the world. Would I renege on my word? In my concern that you might run short on your journey, general, I made a point of coming to see you off with something for your expenses." He offered Kuan Yü a plate of gold.

Lord Kuan: "Time and again I have benefitted from your considerate bounty, of which much yet remains. Reserve this to reward your own officers."

Ts'ao: "This trifling recompense for your magnificent accomplishments is as one to ten thousand. Why must you decline it?"

Lord Kuan: "My paltry efforts are not worth the mention."

Ts'ao smiled. "A true liege-bound warrior before all the world. I regret that my fortune is too meager to hold you. This damask robe is a modest expression of my good will." One of Ts'ao's captains dismounted, carried the robe to Lord Kuan, and offered it to him with two hands. Cautiously Kuan Yü lifted it with the tip of his sword and draped it on his body. Reining his horse around, he expressed his thanks: "I am indebted for the Chancellor's gift. Another day we may meet again." And he departed to the north.

Kuan Yü made good his escape only after cutting down several of Ts'ao Ts'ao's checkpoint guards.

Kuan Yü cuts down Ts'ao Ts'ao's guards

Reunion

During this time Chang Fei had spent several months in the hills. Seeking news of Liu Pei, he came to the walled town of Ku. He went to the imperial offices to borrow provisions, but was refused. Angered, Fei evicted the government officials, appropriated the seals, and took possession of the town, deciding to make use of it as an expedient refuge. Sun Ch'ien, bearing Kuan Yü's orders, entered Ku to see Chang Fei.

The amenities exchanged, Sun Ch'ien spoke: "Liu Pei will be leaving Yüan Shao and will go to Ju Nan city. Lord Kuan is coming here directly from the capital with Lady Kan and Lady Mi, Liu Pei's wives. Pray go forth to welcome him." Chang Fei made no answer but armed himself at once and mounted. He led one thousand men through the north gate of Ku. Startled but afraid to question him, Sun Ch'ien followed.

Kuan Yü was overwhelmed with joy to see Chang Fei approach. He handed his sword to an aide and charged in his brother's direction. But what he saw was Chang Fei's round, menacing eyes and bristling tiger whiskers as he roared in a voice like thunder and flourished his spear with taunting thrusts. Kuan Yü was aghast and dodged away as he cried: "What is the reason for this, worthy brother? Can you have forgotten the pact in the peach garden?"

Chang Fei shouted: "Since you have revoked your allegiance, have you the face to confront me? You have betrayed our elder brother, submitted to Ts'ao, and accepted rank and title. But you've come back to get something off me! So let's settle it here, once and for all."

Kuan Yü: "Can you actually not know—how can I explain myself? Attend my two sisters-in-law, worthy brother; question them yourself."

Lady Kan: "Second brother did not know your whereabouts, so we lodged temporarily with Ts'ao Ts'ao. When we learned where first brother was, Lord Kuan faced many an ordeal to deliver us. Do not cling to your misconceptions, third brother."

Lady Mi: "Our stay in the capital was something beyond our control."

Chang Fei: "Sisters, be no more deceived by him; the loyal liege man dies before he is disgraced. What man of honor serves two lords?"

Kuan Yü: "Worthy brother, do not distort my case."

Sun Ch'ien: "Lord Kuan has come only to find you."

Chang Fei: "You speak like a fool! What good intentions can he have? He's here to capture me!"

Kuan Yü: "To do so I would need to have brought the army."

Chang Fei: "And what is that!"

Kuan Yü turned. In a haze of dust a crowd of riders was approaching. It was Ts'ao's army.

"Do you still dispute it?" said Chang Fei, threatening Kuan Yü with his spear.

Kuan Yü stayed him: "I will execute their leader to demonstrate my true thoughts."

When Kuan Yü performed this feat, Chang Fei was slowly reconciled with him.

*   *   *   *

Sun Ch'ien brought word of these developments to Liu Pei, who resolved to leave Yüan Shao. He decided to offer to go to Ching province and persuade the governor, Liu Piao, to join Yüan Shao in the war against Ts'ao Ts'ao. This would provide Pei with an opportunity for getting away.

Liu Pei went to Yüan Shao and said: "Liu Piao keeps guard over the nine districts of Ching province.* His weapons are keen,

* Chingchou, the strategic central province around which the three kingdoms will take shape.

his grain ample. We should reach agreement with him and jointly attack Ts'ao Ts'ao."

Yüan Shao: "I have tried to arrange it, but he is unwilling."

Liu Pei: "The man is my clansman. If I go to him, I know he will not rebuff us."

Yüan Shao: "If we can persuade Liu Piao, the advantage will be considerable."

Liu Pei thus made good his departure and rode to the city of Ku, where he rejoined his two brothers. He had another commander in Chao Yün and an army of some five thousand.

When Yüan Shao realized that Liu Pei would not return, he was moved to anger. But an adviser said: "Liu Pei need not concern you. Ts'ao Ts'ao is your active opponent; he must be eliminated. And Liu Piao, even though he holds the province of Ching, will not become a power. On the other hand, Sun Ts'e dominates the land below the Long River,* an area that includes six districts. His counselors and commanders are many. Ally with him to attack Ts'ao!" Yüan Shao accepted the advice and sent an emissary.

---

* The Yangtze.

Sun Ts'e Beheads Yü Chi;
Sun Ch'üan Rules the Southland

The narrative turns to the Southland, Wu, south-southeast of the Long River. Here Sun Ts'e was based, with elite troops and ample provisions. It was A.D. 199, the fourth year of the reign entitled "Establish Security," that Sun Ts'e had achieved his hegemony and presented a memorial to the Emperor detailing his victories.

Ts'ao Ts'ao recognized that Sun Ts'e's strength was great and had to admit that he was a "lion hard to vie with." So he had his cousin Ts'ao Jen's daughter given in marriage to the youngest brother of Ts'e, Sun K'uang, binding the two houses.

Sun Ts'e sought to be made chief marshal, but Ts'ao refused. In his resentment Ts'e developed a lasting ambition to surprise and conquer the capital, Hsü.

Hsü Kung, warden of a Wu command, secretly appealed to Ts'ao Ts'ao:

> Sun Ts'e is bold and ambitious. It might be appropriate for the Court to demonstrate its appreciation of him and recall him to the capital, rather than letting him remain in a remote military area where he may become a future problem.

A messenger bore the letter across the river, but the guard seized him and immediately turned him over to Ts'e, who read the letter and beheaded the messenger. Then he summoned Hsü Kung for consultation on some pretense, showed him the document, and snarled: "You would like to have me sent to the land of the dead,

I see!" And he called the officers to strangle him. Kung's family fled. Three of his retainers wished to avenge him, but despaired of finding an opportunity.

One day Sun Ts'e led some troops in a hunt. A large deer charged up, and Ts'e's horse, given his head, chased it up the mountainside. Ts'e found himself among some trees, where three men stood with spears and bows. They claimed to be deer hunters, and Ts'e was about to pass on when one of them hefted his lance and pinked Ts'e's left thigh. Ts'e desperately cut at the man with his waist sword. Suddenly the blade dropped to the ground, leaving only the handle in his hand. Another of the men had already hefted his bow into place and positioned an arrow. The shot struck Ts'e high in the cheek. Ts'e pulled the arrow out of his flesh, fitted it to his own bow, and shot back at the man, who fell as the bowstring sang. The other two forced Ts'e back with their lances as they cried: "We are Hsü Kung's retainers, come to avenge our lord!" Ts'e had no other weapon and could only fend them off with his bow as he moved away. But they would not relent; it was a struggle to the death. Ts'e had been lanced in several places, and his horse too bore wounds. But at the moment when his death agony was to begin, an aide rode up with a few men and, at Ts'e's command, hacked Hsü Kung's retainers to a pulp. Seeing his lord's bloody face and massive wounds, the aide bound him with cloth cut from his own robe and took him to safety.

Once home, Ts'e sought the healer Hua T'o, but T'o had gone to the north. Only a disciple remained in Wu, and he was summoned to cure Sun Ts'e. "These arrows were tipped with some drug, and the poison has already gone into the bone," said the disciple. "You need quiet convalescence for one hundred days before you will be out of danger. But if you let moods of anger buffet you, the damage will be hard to control."

Sun Ts'e was by nature extremely irascible, and he felt frustrated that he could not be cured that very day. He resolved to be patient, however. He had been resting for some twenty days when he heard that a messenger was back from the capital. Sun called him for questioning.

Messenger: "Ts'ao Ts'ao is quite wary of you, sovereign lord, and his staff planners are respectful and submissive—save K'uo Chia."

Ts'e: "And what does *he* have to say?"

The messenger's reluctance to reply angered Ts'e, who pressed him irritably. The messenger had to convey the facts: "K'uo Chia told Ts'ao Ts'ao that my sovereign lord was not worth his concern, that you were a lightweight, hasty and deficient in planning, a common fighting man sure to die by a scoundrel's hand."

Ts'e: "That nonentity dares to take my measure? I'll take his capital, I swear."

Without waiting for his wounds to heal, he wanted to begin planning the campaign. Chang Chao* objected: "The physician has cautioned my sovereign against moving for one hundred days. Now you propose to risk your invaluable self because of a moment's rage?"

At this point the messenger from Yüan Shao arrived with the news that his master wanted to become Wu's ally in an attack on Ts'ao Ts'ao. Ts'e was delighted and assembled his generals in an upper story of the city wall, where a banquet was prepared in honor of Yüan Shao's messenger. During the ceremonies the guests suddenly began whispering to each other and streamed out of the room. Astonished, Ts'e was told by his attendants: "The holy transcendent, Yü, has passed beneath us. The guests simply want to go out and show him honor."

Ts'e arose and looked out over his balcony at a Taoist priest cloaked in crane feathers, a staff of goosefoot wood in his hand, blocking the roadway. A group of commoners burned incense and knelt on the road in veneration. "Who is this sorcerer?" Ts'e cried angrily. "Quickly! bring him to me."

The attendants informed him: "The man's surname is Yü; he is called Chi.† He resides in the east and has traveled here bringing spells and potions which have relieved an unusual number of ailments. Far and wide he is called the 'holy transcendent.' Do not thoughtlessly abuse him."

Ts'e's rage rose and he demanded to see the man, who was bustled into Ts'e's presence. "Lunatic priest!" Ts'e exclaimed. "You dare to fan the flames of man's ignorance?"

Yü Chi: "I am but a poor priest from Lang Yeh. During the reign of the Emperor Hsün, the Obedient, I went once into the mountains to gather herbs, and found a sacred text by the spring-

---

* An important figure in the Southland's court and an advocate of submission to Ts'ao Ts'ao.
† A proponent of the "Age of Equality" and an influence on Chang Chüeh (see pages 6–7 above), Yü Chi was active early in the second century A.D. and was therefore nearly one hundred years old at this time.

head titled *The Ch'ing Ling Way to the Age of Equality.* It came in one hundred scrolls, all concerned with techniques for the cure of pain and disease. When your humble priest had obtained it, I devoted myself to spreading its influence on behalf of the gods, for the salvation of mankind. I have never accepted the slightest gift from anyone. What do you mean by 'fanning the flames of man's ignorance'?"

Ts'e: "If you accept nothing from people, where do your food and clothing come from? You actually belong to the Yellow Scarves. If we do not execute you now, you will become a problem in the future."

He snarled at his underlings to cut off Chi's head, but Chang Chao objected. "The priest has been living east of the river for dozens of years and was never guilty of any offense. You can't put him to death."

Ts'e: "These heretics I kill as a butcher kills pigs and dogs." The assembly of officials, including Yüan Shao's messenger, implored in vain; Ts'e could not be appeased. He ordered the priest imprisoned until he had decided what to do with him.

Even before Ts'e had returned to his quarters a palace attendant had notified his mother, Lady Wu, who summoned Ts'e to her private apartments. "They tell me you have thrown the saintly transcendant Yü in jail. He has worked many cures and is revered by the army and the populace alike. You may not subject him to injury."

Ts'e: "The man is a heretic who can use his arts to mislead the multitude. He has to be eliminated." His mother implored him to set the priest free. Ts'e: "Mother, you should not give credence to the absurd statements of outsiders. I will handle this in my own way."

There were vigorous protests and intercessions on the priest's behalf. Eventually Sun Ts'e agreed to spare Yü Chi if he could summon rain by prayer as proof of his spirituality.

After bathing and changing his clothes, Yü Chi bound himself under a blazing sun upon an altar. The common folk thronged the streets and choked the lanes to witness the spectacle. Yü Chi spoke to them: "I will try for three feet of sweet rain to succor the myriad masses. But in the end I shall not escape my death."

The people: "If your rain-summoning spiritual power proves itself, the sovereign lord will have to submit and honor you."

Yü Chi: "My 'vital number' is up. Unfortunately there is no escaping."

Soon Sun Ts'e himself arrived at the altar. "If no rain falls by noon, burn Yü Chi to death." And he had the kindling heaped up in anticipation. It was almost noon when wild winds mounted to the skies, and where they blew, dense clouds slowly converged from all sides.

Ts'e: "It is nearly noon, the sky is black, but there is no rain. Some wonderworker!" He had Yü Chi stretched across the kindling pile, which attendants torched on four sides. The flames licked up in the wake of the wind. A trail of black smoke appeared, rising into the empty sky—emitting a single re-echoing wail. Thunder and lightning issued together, and the rain coursed down in currents. In moments the main road became a river and the streams were overflowing with three feet of rain.

Flat upon the pyre, Yü Chi stared at the heavens and howled. The clouds withdrew, the rains were stayed; the sun reappeared. Officials and commoners steadied Yü Chi as he climbed down from the pyre, and as they took off his ropes they bowed and acknowledged their mistake.

When Sun Ts'e saw everyone bowing, knee-deep in water, he could not contain himself. "Fair weather and storms are predetermined!" he cried. "The sorcerer has simply taken advantage of a favorable accident. What are all of you doing in such a mindless uproar?" Gripping his sword, overpowering all objection, Ts'e ordered his men to behead Yü Chi on the spot. A single stroke, and Yü Chi's head dropped to the ground. A trail of bluish vapor rose away to the northeast. Ts'e ordered the corpse abused in the marketplace to censure these sins of the supernatural.

Wind and rain thrashed through the night. By dawn the corpse's head was gone. The corpse watchers reported this to Ts'e, who was ready to kill them. From nowhere a man appeared, walking slowly in front of Ts'e's house. It was Yü Chi. Ts'e, moving to hack at the apparition, fell down in a faint and had to be carried to his bedroom. He recovered shortly, and his mother, Lady Wu, came to him. "My son, you have provoked disaster by wronging this saintly transcendent."

Ts'e: "From my earliest days I accompanied my father on mili-

小霸王怒斬
于吉

Yü Chi decapitated

tary campaigns, and we cut men down like hemp stalks. There was never any 'provoking disaster.' Today we have killed a heretic precisely to put an end to a great 'disaster.' What do you mean by saying that it will bring disaster back upon us?"

His mother advised making donations to charity in order to ward off retribution, but Ts'e refused. "My life and destiny lie with Heaven. Sorcerers cannot create disasters. So there is no use in 'warding off.'" Her exhortation unavailing, Lady Wu privately arranged for good works to absolve her son in the eyes of gods and men.

That night at the second watch as Ts'e lay in his chamber, a chill gusty wind sprang up. The lamp blew out and then relit. In the shadows it cast, Ts'e saw Yü Chi standing in front of his bed. Ts'e screamed out: "My life is dedicated to destroying the supernatural and purging it from the world of men. You ghost from the shades, how dare you approach me!" He threw his sword at it as the ghost disappeared.

Lady Wu: "Confucius said that ghostly spirits can manifest their potency inexhaustibly. And he said, 'Pray ye to the spirits, dispersed above, concentrated below.' We may not doubt such things as ghostly spirits. Your murder of the good priest Yü will evoke reaction! I have already had a feast laid in the Temple of Jade Purity. Go there yourself and pray for your life. Then things may settle themselves."

Unable to refuse his mother's command, Ts'e betook himself to the temple. He burned incense at the priests' behest, but he offered no apology. The fumes rose but hung undispersed in the air, taking the form of a canopy with Yü Chi sitting erect on top of it. Spitting and cursing, Ts'e quit the sanctuary. Yü Chi appeared again perched on the sanctuary gate, where he glared down at Sun Ts'e.

Ts'e asked his followers if they saw the sorcerer's ghost, but none did. He aimed his waist sword at Yü Chi and threw it. A man was struck and fell over. When the crowd looked, it was the common soldier who had struck Yü's deathblow the day before. The blade had split open his skull, and his orifices ran blood as he died. Ts'e ordered the corpse removed and buried. As they left the temple, there was Yü Chi again, strolling into it. Claiming, "The temple harbors sorcerers," Ts'e seated himself facing it and ordered five hundred warriors to tear it down. They pulled apart the stonework of the upper rooms, but Yü Chi remained in the structure even as the stones were flung to the ground. Ts'e ordered the priests evicted, and his men set fire to the sanctuary. But where the flames sprang up, Yü Chi was visible at their heart.

Ts'e returned to his quarters; again Yü Chi stood at the portal. Instead of entering, Ts'e mustered the full triple army and camped outside the wall, calling his generals to discuss joining Yüan Shao in a two-pronged attack on Ts'ao Ts'ao. But the generals urged that he wait, for they felt that there would be sufficient time for the campaign after his health had returned. Again that night Yü Chi appeared in the camp, his hair streaming behind him. The visitation threw Ts'e into a prolonged fit of hysteria.

His mother called for him and, seeing his exhaustion, sobbed: "Your natural self is no more!"

Ts'e reached for a mirror to examine himself. His face and body were utterly wasted. "What can I do, I have become so ravaged?" he cried to his attendants.

As he spoke, Yü Chi hovered in the mirror. Ts'e struck the mirror away with a shout. His battle wounds split open as he swooned. Recovering momentarily in his bedchamber, he mourned: "I cannot live on," and summoned the adviser Chang Chao and his younger brother Sun Ch'üan to his bedside.

Ts'e adjured them: "In this period of great upheaval, the possibilities for the Southland are tremendous. Moreover, we are blessed with Chang Chao's wise ministry to my younger brother."

He took his seal and conferred it on Sun Ch'üan. "For mobilizing our people, for the split-second decision in the field of battle, for contending with the world to gain mastery—in these you are not my equal. But for employing and promoting worthy and capable men so that they give of themselves utterly to protect the Southland, I am not *your* equal. Bear always in mind the hardships and difficulties that your father and brother have suffered in founding this heritage, and be vigilant to preserve it." Ch'üan wept and bowed as he accepted the seal.

Ts'e said to his mother: "The years of my time are no more. I can no longer serve my devoted mother. I hereby transfer the seal and tassel to my brother and pray, Mother, that you may guide him at all times in serving those who have gone before."

Mother: "Your brother is yet immature and may prove unable to undertake affairs of state. Then what shall we do?"

Ts'e: "He surpasses me by ten to one and is fully capable of the highest responsibility. In the event that some internal matter confounds you, take it to Chang Chao; if some external matter confounds you, take it to Chou Yü. I only regret that Chou Yü is not here himself to accept these instructions."

Ts'e warned his brothers against discord and asked his wife, the lady Ch'iao, to honor his mother and to have her sister pass along his wishes to Chou Yü. When he closed his eyes and departed, he was twenty-six. It was in the summer of A.D. 200.

En route home, Chou Yü learned of the death of Sun Ts'e. He was wailing at the coffin when Lady Wu appeared to deliver Ts'e's final charge. Yü bowed to the ground and said: "I will perform even the labor of a beast, and pursue it to the death." Sun Ch'üan entered and said: "I trust my lord has not forgotten my dead brother's final charge." Yü touched his head to the floor. "I would strew the very ground with my liver and brains to repay his sympathetic generosity."

Ch'üan: "Now I take possession of this patrimony. By what strategy shall I preserve it?"

Yü: "It has ever been that 'He who wins men is exalted; he who fails to, vanishes.' To shape plans for the present, you must seek out high-minded, provident intellects to support you; then the Southland can be consolidated."

Ch'üan: "My late brother's last words were, 'Trust internal matters to Chang Chao, external ones to Chou Yü.' "

Yü: "Chang Chao is a worthy and accomplished scholar fit for great tasks. But I am not, and I feel reluctant to shoulder the burden confided to me. Let me recommend a man to assist you— Lu Su, a mine of strategies, a storehouse of machinations, who early lost his father and serves his mother with utmost filial piety. His family is extremely wealthy, and he has been known to distribute largess to the poor. Once when I was short of grain he put an entire granary at my disposal. He has always been inclined to swordsmanship and horseback archery. Call him to you without delay."

Ch'üan sent Yü to relay his respectful intent to Lu Su, who replied that he was already engaged.

"You recall the words 'Not only does the lord choose his man, but the man must choose his lord'?" said Chou Yü to Lu Su. "Now, general Sun Ch'üan will nurture men of merit and receive scholars well. He has given support to remarkable and extraordinary men—something all too rare. Heed no other commitment, good sir, but come east with me to Wu. This is the correct course."

Lu Su accepted his proposition, and Ch'üan received him with the greatest respect. Their commentaries and discussions continued untiringly the day long.

Once, late at night, Ch'üan said to Su: "Now the House of Han is tilting precariously and the four quarters of the empire are in turmoil and disarray. As one who has been orphaned, I take possession of the accumulated patrimony of my father and my brother and yearn to do as those ancient leaders Huan and Wen once did. My lord, what course would you advise me to pursue?"

"I would account the Han beyond recovery," replied Lu Su, "and Ts'ao Ts'ao beyond eliminating. My judgment is that for you, there is no alternative to making the Southland the firm foot of a tripod and observing the opportunities in the empire. If you can exploit the many preoccupations of the north, gouge out Huang Tsu's position, and then advance on Liu Piao in Ching province, in the end you will come to hold the Long River entirely. This done, you may establish titles—becoming king or emperor, as you wish—and aspire to empire. This was what the founder of the Han achieved."

Hearing this analysis, Ch'üan was exuberant and sent gifts to both Lu Su and Lu Su's mother. Su also recommended to Ch'üan a man of great learning, talent, and devotion: Chuko Chin of Lang Yeh, whom Ch'üan treated as a royal guest. Chin convinced Sun Ch'üan not to associate himself with Yüan Shao, but rather to adjust relations with Ts'ao Ts'ao for the time being until it was convenient to maneuver against him. And so Ch'üan sent Yüan Shao's messenger home with a letter breaking off relations.

Now, when Ts'ao Ts'ao heard that Sun Ts'e had died, he wanted to muster his forces and descend upon the Southland. But one of the civil advisers dissuaded him: "To take up arms exploiting the mourning season is more than immoral; if you fail, you will have discarded all amity and brought enmity to fruition. Rather, utilize the occasion to treat him handsomely." Ts'ao approved the advice and recommended to the Emperor that Sun Ch'üan be made general and warden of K'uei Chi. Sun Ch'üan was elated. His prestige was now felt throughout the Southland, and the people became deeply devoted to him.

Seven years passed, during which Ts'ao Ts'ao conquered Yüan Shao at Kuan Tu and forced Liu Pei to take refuge with Liu Piao in Chingchou. Then, with the successful invasion of the Wu Huan tribes beyond the northeast sections of the Great Wall, Ts'ao Ts'ao fully consolidated his hold on north China.

Lady Ts'ai Eavesdrops;
Liu Pei Vaults the River T'an

Ch'eng Yü appealed to Ts'ao: "We will return to the capital with the north firmly under control. It is time to humble the Southland."

Ts'ao smiled. "That has long been my ambition." That night he slept in the upper chambers in the eastern corner of the city of Chi chou. From the porch he looked up to observe the sky. Pointing south, he said to Hsün Yu: "There is a royal solar aura glowing there. I don't think we have much chance."

Yu: "To the Chancellor's heavenly prestige, none dares offer resistance."

As they gazed, a golden ray arose from the earth and made a path across the sky. Yu: "There must be something valuable here under the ground." Ts'ao came down from his chambers and had the beam of light traced back; there they dug into the earth.

> Astral patterns point south
> But treasures appear in the north.

At the point of the golden emanation, Ts'ao unearthed a bronze sparrow. He asked Hsün Yu what it portended, and Yu replied: "In ancient times the mother of Shun bore him after dreaming that a jade sparrow had entered her bosom. Now we have obtained this bronze sparrow—it must be a favorable sign."*

Delighted, Ts'ao ordered a tall tower built to celebrate the good omen. They broke ground and cut down trees, fired tiles and

* In this analogy Ts'ao is Shun and the Emperor Tributor is Yao, the mythic first Emperor, who yielded the throne to Shun in recognition that Shun's merit took precedence over Yao's son's birthright.

ground stones to construct the Bronze Sparrow Tower above the Chang River. The work was to take about a year.

One of Ts'ao's sons, Chih, proposed: "When you build a storeyed tower, there have to be three sites: in the middle, the tallest—the 'Bronze Sparrow'; another on the left—'Jade Dragon'; and a third on the right—'Golden Phoenix.' Then if you will make two flying bridges traversing the space between, it will be a magnificent sight."

Ts'ao: "My son's words are well spoken. In later times when the towers are completed, they may serve to give pleasure to me in my declining years."

Ts'ao Ts'ao had five sons, but Chih alone was quick-witted and clear-sighted. He was also adept at composition, and Ts'ao had always favored him. So he left Chih with his brother P'ei behind in Yeh to build the tower, while he withdrew with Yüan Shao's conquered forces, which numbered some half-million, to the capital at Hsü.

Once again he assembled his counselors to discuss a southern campaign against Liu Piao. But Hsün Yu said: "Our major force has only now returned from the northern campaign and is not ready for remobilization. If we wait half a year, recover our strength, and nourish our mettle, Liu Piao and Sun Ch'üan will fall at the first roll of the drums!" Ts'ao accepted this advice and assigned the soldiers to farming duties, where they awaited the call to action.

*   *   *   *

Since Liu Pei's arrival in Chingchou, Liu Piao had treated him with the kindest generosity. One day as the guests were gathering for a banquet, there was a report that two generals were pillaging the population of Chiang Hsia and organizing an insurrection. Piao said in alarm: "If two more rebel, it will be a disaster."

Liu Pei said: "Elder brother's anxious concern is unnecessary. Let me go there and punish them." Piao was delighted and detailed a force of thirty thousand to accompany him.

Within a day Liu Pei arrived at Chiang Hsia, and the insurgents led out their troops to give battle. Liu Pei, Kuan Yü, Chang Fei, and Chao Yün rode under their own banners. Chao Yün stepped out with his lance raised and charged the enemy line. One of the insurgent generals accepted the challenge. Within three passages at arms the rebel was pierced and dropped beneath his horse. In one motion Chao Yün seized that animal's reins and dragged it back to his own lines. The other insurgent general charged after him to recapture it, but Chang Fei stabbed him to death. The rebel host broke and dispersed. Liu Pei pacified the remaining factions, and calm returned to the counties of Chiang Hsia.

When Liu Pei returned, Liu Piao received him outside the walls and brought him into the city. At a banquet to celebrate the victory Piao, warming with the wine, said to him: "If this is a sample of your valor and skill, Chingchou will be in safe hands. Our one anxiety is the Southlanders, who may strike at any moment. And Sun Ch'üan is more than enough cause for worry."

Liu Pei: "Your younger brother has three generals who are 'more than enough' for such an assignment. Have Chang Fei patrol the southern border, Kuan Yü defend at Ku-tzu city, and Chao Yün defend at the Long River confronting Sun Ch'üan. What will remain to worry you?"

Liu Piao was delighted with the proposal. But Ts'ai Mao told his sister, Liu Piao's wife: "If Liu Pei sends his three generals to occupy those strategic points while remaining in the capital, there is bound to be trouble."

So at night Lady Ts'ai confronted Liu Piao: "They are saying that liaison is developing between Liu Pei and a number of Chingchou people. You can't afford not to take precautions. If we allow him to remain in the city, it doesn't do us any good. Why not send him elsewhere?"

Piao: "Liu Pei is a humane and benevolent man."

Lady Ts'ai: "I am afraid that others do not share your view." Piao turned thoughtful and did not reply.

The next day they went outside the city wall, and Piao saw how magnificent Liu Pei's horse was. Learning that it had been captured from the Chiang Hsia insurgents, he expressed such admiration that Liu Pei presented the animal to him. However, someone told Piao that the horse had "tear-tracks" below his eyes and white spots on his brow, that such horses are unlucky and thus endanger their riders, and that indeed, the original owner had lost his life. "My lord should not ride it."

Piao returned the horse on the pretext that Liu Pei would be going on missions at any moment. He added: "My esteemed brother has been here so long that your military talent is going to waste. Northeast of Hsiang Yang is a city called Hsin Yeh, a

The brothers establish themselves at Hsin Yeh

rather prosperous place. What do you say to taking your own force there and establishing an outpost?" Liu Pei agreed.

As he rode out of the gate, a man came up to him and said: "My lord should not be riding that horse." Pei dismounted to question him. The man continued: "Yesterday someone told Liu Piao that the horse will bring misfortune to whoever rides it.

That's why it was returned to you, my lord. How can you mount it now?"

Liu Pei said: "Deeply grateful as I am for your concern, every man has an appointed time of life, which no horse can change." To this wisdom the man deferred, and afterwards he kept in frequent touch with Liu Pei.

Liu Pei's arrival at Hsin Yeh was a boon to soldier and civilian alike, for he completely reformed the political administration. In the spring of the twelfth year of "Establish Security" (A.D. 207), Liu Pei's wife, Lady Kan, bore Liu Shan. On the night of the birth a white crane alighted on the government building, sang some forty notes, and flew into the west. During parturition, an unknown fragrance filled the room. Once Lady Kan had dreamed that she swallowed the stars of the Big Dipper and conceived as a result; hence the child's milk-name of Ah-tou or "Precious Dipper."

This was the time when Ts'ao Ts'ao was on his northern campaigns. Liu Pei returned to Chingchou to persuade Liu Piao to act. "At this moment Ts'ao has all his forces engaged, and Hsü, the capital, stands vacant and vulnerable," Pei said. "If we combine your Chingchou forces with mine to surprise the capital, we can achieve a great victory."

Piao said: "I am content to hold these nine districts of Chingchou. Why try for anything more?" Liu Pei fell silent.

Piao invited him to his private apartments to have wine. As they became mellow Piao sighed deeply, and Liu Pei asked why. Piao: "There is something on my mind about which it is rather difficult to speak plainly."

Liu Pei was about to inquire further when Lady Ts'ai emerged from behind a screen. Piao lowered his head and did not speak again. Shortly afterward they adjourned, and Liu Pei rode back to Hsin Yeh.

Winter came, and Ts'ao Ts'ao returned from his campaigns. Liu Pei despaired over Liu Piao's refusal to adopt his proposal. Unexpectedly Liu Piao sent for him, and Pei went at once. The ceremonies of greeting concluded, Piao conducted him to his private apartments for a banquet. Piao said: "We have had word that Ts'ao Ts'ao is back in Hsü with his forces, and that his position is becoming stronger every day. He cannot help wanting to take over Chingchou and Hsiang Yang. Now I regret ignoring your worthy recommendation and losing so fine an opportunity."

Liu Pei: "Now the empire is divided and torn. The shield and the spear are in evidence every day. Do you think 'opportunity' is used up? If you can rise to it in the future, then it is not worth 'regretting' yet." Piao agreed. They drank further and became mellow.

Suddenly, Piao began to weep. Pei asked the cause. Piao said: "There is something on my mind which I tried to reveal to you before, but found it inconvenient."

Liu Pei: "What is my brother's problem? If I can be of any use, death itself would not deter me."

Piao: "My earlier wife, a Ch'en, bore my first son, Ch'i. Though his character is worthy enough, he is too weak and timid to keep affairs of state on a steady course. My second wife, a Ts'ai, bore the younger son, Ts'ung, a bright and perceptive boy. If I set aside the elder and make the younger my heir, I would be going against the customary law. If I leave the elder as my heir, what can I do about the Ts'ai clan, whose members all have military control and are sure to create trouble afterwards? This is why I am wavering and cannot reach a decision."

Liu Pei: "From most ancient times, removing the elder and confirming the younger has been the road to disaster. If you are worried about the extent of the Ts'ais' power, you could pare it down a bit at a time. But you may not confirm the younger as heir because you are hopelessly in love with Lady Ts'ai." Piao fell silent.

Lady Ts'ai had been suspicious of Liu Pei from the beginning, and she would invariably eavesdrop whenever she came upon him and her husband in discussion. At this moment she was behind a screen, and she resented Pei's words bitterly.

Liu Pei himself realized that he had said more than he ought; he rose and strolled back and forth. He noticed that his hips were becoming heavy, and surreptitious tears ran from his eyes. In a few moments he resumed his place. Piao noticed his sad expression and asked about it. Liu Pei gave a profound sigh. "I never used to leave the saddle, and there was no flesh on my hips. Now it is so long since I have ridden that I am growing thick. Days and months pass me by, years come on, but my task is not being accomplished, and it grieves me."

Piao: "They say, worthy brother, that in Hsü the capital, while they brewed wine from green plums, you and Ts'ao Ts'ao judged the heroes of the age together. Ts'ao would accept none of the

renowned warriors whom you proposed; he acknowledged only
himself and you. If Ts'ao Ts'ao with all his power and influence
still did not rate himself above you, why are you concerned that
'your task is not being accomplished'?"

Liu Pei was feeling the effects of the wine and overspoke himself when he replied: "If I had a real base, these tedious sorts need
be no care indeed!" Piao listened in silence. Liu Pei realized that
he had slipped. He arose, alleging intoxication, and went back to
his shelter.

After Pei had left, Liu Piao felt discontented. Lady Ts'ai said
to him: "Just now I overheard Liu Pei's words. How contemptuous he is! It's easy enough to see that he means to take over
Chingchou. If he is not eliminated now, he is going to make
trouble." Piao made no rejoinder but simply shook his head.

Next the Ts'ais secretly summoned Ts'ai Mao for discussions.
Mao said: "Let me go to his shelter and kill him. Afterwards we
can report to our lord." This was approved.

Someone warned Liu Pei, who hastened back to Hsin
Yeh. When Ts'ai Mao arrived, Pei was already far off.

Bitter at having failed to overtake Liu Pei, Mao transcribed a
seditious poem on the wall of Pei's room and then informed Piao
that Pei had written it. The poem read:

> Too many years in vain—held and hemmed,
> Futile: to face these unvarying hills.
> What dragon is made for a pool?
> Mount the thunder and up to the sky!

When he saw these lines, Liu Piao was enraged and swore on
his sword to kill the "faithless common foot soldier." But his
anger shortly abated, and he reconsidered. "In all the time we
have spent together, I have never known him to compose poetry,"
Piao mused. "This must be the design of some outsider to estrange
us."

Therefore Liu Piao made no further move against Liu
Pei. In fact, he asked Pei to officiate in his place at the Harvest
Celebration in Hsiang Yang.

Secretly delighted to have Liu Pei under his hand again, Ts'ai
Mao had a messenger request Pei's presence in Hsiang Yang. Pei
had fled back to Hsin Yeh well aware that he had brought danger
upon himself with his careless statements. He kept his own coun-

sel, however, until suddenly the messenger arrived inviting him to attend the festival at Hsiang Yang. Sun Ch'ien said: "My sovereign lord came home yesterday so disturbed and discontented that I feared something had happened in Chingchou. Now you have this unexpected invitation, but you should not go without careful consideration."

Liu Pei confided the matter to a few intimates. Lord Kuan said: "Brother, it is only your own suspicion that you misspoke. Liu Piao is not holding it against you. And not everything the Ts'ais say is to be taken on faith. Hsiang Yang is not far from here, and if you do not go, Liu Piao *will* become suspicious." Liu Pei approved Lord Kuan's view. But Chang Fei objected: " 'No banquet is a good banquet; no conference is a good conference.' It's better to stay home."

Chao Yün said: "I will take three hundred footsoldiers and horsemen to escort you and prevent anything untoward." And it was done.

Ts'ai Mao received Liu Pei and Chao Yün outside of the walls and showed himself both modest and attentive. Then Liu Ch'i and Liu Ts'ung, Piao's two sons, led a delegation of officers and officials to greet them. Seeing the two sons made Liu Pei less wary. He was invited to the guest house, and Chao Yün set up the guard.

Liu Ch'i, the elder, spoke to Liu Pei: "My father's breathing ailment is disturbing him, and he is unable to move. But he especially wanted to ask you, Imperial Uncle, to receive the guests and to give sympathetic encouragement to the officials who guard and govern our various districts."

Liu Pei: "For myself I would never dare to undertake it, but since my brother has commanded me, I dare not refuse."

The next day it was reported that the official personnel from the forty-two circuits of the nine administrative departments had arrived and were settled in their places.

Ts'ai Mao arranged to have all escape routes cut off except for the turbulent T'an River on the west. Liu Pei allowed Chao Yün to attend a military banquet that had been contrived by Ts'ai Mao in order to draw Yün away.

Liu Pei rode to the circuit headquarters and had his horse picketed in a rear garden. The officials had assembled in the main hall. Liu Pei officiated, while the two sons sat on either side of him and the other guests were placed according to rank. In the meantime Ts'ai Mao had sealed the place as tight as an iron tub and was waiting only until the company was mellow with drink before giving the signal to strike.

It was the third round of wine. A man raised his cup and approached Liu Pei, stopped before him, and murmured with an urgent look: "Excuse yourself." Liu Pei took his meaning and went at once to the side privies. After presenting his toast, the man rushed to the rear garden to meet Liu Pei. He whispered: "Ts'ai Mao has laid plans to kill you. Outside the wall, the east, the south, and the north are sealed. You can only leave by riding west. My lord should get away immediately."

In high alarm Liu Pei untied the horse, pulled him out through the rear garden, dove into the saddle, and left for the western gate without looking for an escort. Challenged by the gatekeepers, he made no reply but laid on his whip and was out. The gatekeepers could not check him, but they reported his flight at once to Ts'ai Mao, who pursued with five hundred soldiers.

Liu Pei had crashed through the west gate and traveled only a few leagues when a great river loomed before him: the T'an, a spur of the Hsiang River, many rods broad, its waves whipping. Liu Pei rode to the edge and saw that he could not cross. He turned his horse, but in the distance he saw dust thrown up at the western wall: the pursuers would soon arrive. Thinking that his end had come, he turned his horse back to the river's edge. He looked behind him; Mao's troops were already close; at his wit's end, he charged into the current. In a few paces the horse lost his footing, soaking Pei's tunic. Belaboring the horse, he shouted: "Today you have brought me misfortune!" But the horse thrust himself upward and, advancing three rods with every surge of his body, gained the opposite bank. Liu Pei emerged from the wild water as if from cloud and mist.

> The touch of hooves cracks the glass-green sea.
> Where winds of heaven sound, he wields a golden whip.
> Faintly behind—a thousand cavalry.
> There! two dragons rear amid the waves:
> The noble hero of the west
> On the dragon-steed that saves.

Liu Pei vaults the river T'an

Liu Pei Discovers a Sage

Liu Pei was numb and intoxicated. He thought: "To have vaulted so broad a stretch has to have been Heaven's will."

On winding roads he journeyed toward Nan Chang. Riding as the sun went down, he saw a shepherd on the back of an ox, piping as he approached. "It was never my fortune to feel so carefree," sighed Liu Pei as he poised his horse and watched. The lad halted his beast and stopped playing. He seemed to recognize Liu Pei. "It must be general Liu Pei, who destroyed the Yellow Scarves!" he said.

Liu Pei was startled. "You are a youth from an obscure village. How do you know my name?"

The boy: "I usually attend my master, and when strangers come I often hear them speak of Liu Pei—over six feet, arms that hang past his knees, eyes that can see round to the ears—a hero of the age! Since the description fits, I think you must be he."

Liu Pei asked who his master was. The boy replied: "He has the double surname Ssuma; his majority name is Te-ts'ao; his formal Taoist name is Shui-ching, Master of the Water-mirror."* Liu Pei asked about the master's friends. The boy replied: "P'ang Te-kung and P'ang T'ung—both from Hsiang Yang. They are uncle and nephew."

After further discussion, Liu Pei acknowledged his identity and asked to be introduced to Water-mirror.

* Water, like the mind, reflects accurately only when calm—a Taoist theory.

Liu Pei enters the world of the hermits

The boy guided Liu Pei some two leagues to a farmstead, where they dismounted. Entering the central gate, they heard a lute playing exquisitely. Liu Pei leaned attentively to listen and asked the boy to wait before announcing him. The notes stopped, however, and the lute was struck no more.

A man came out, smiling as he said: "The cadences of the lute were distinct, low-voiced, and subdued; suddenly amid the tones a proud, assertive melody surged up. There must be some noble hero who has come to listen unobtrusively." It was the boy's master. Liu Pei saw that he had the configuration of a pine tree, the bone structure of a crane. His physique and his aura were utterly extraordinary. Flustered, Liu Pei came forward to offer a greeting; his tunic was still soaking.

Water-mirror said: "My good lord, today it was your blessing to be spared great calamity."

Liu Pei was struck speechless. Water-mirror invited him into his thatched chambers, where they sat as host and guest. Liu Pei saw written scrolls heaped on a table, pine and bamboo flourishing outside the window. The lute lay across a stone frame. The atmosphere was pure and exhilarating. Water-mirror asked why he had come.

Liu Pei: "I happened to be passing through, and thanks to the boy's guidance have succeeded in paying homage to your venerable self, for which I feel boundless appreciation."

Water-mirror smiled: "There is nothing to conceal or evade, my lord. I am certain you are here for refuge."

So Liu Pei related the incident at Hsiang Yang.

Water-mirror: "I already knew the circumstances from your attitude and expression. I have long been acquainted with your great name, illustrious sir. But what is the reason that to this day, your star has not risen?"

Liu Pei: "The road ordained for me has not been smooth; thus I have reached this point."

Water-mirror: "Not necessarily. The problem may be that you have not found the right man to second you."

Liu Pei: "I am not myself particularly capable. But for officials I have men like Sun Ch'ien, and for officers I have Kuan Yü, Chang Fei, and Chao Yün. These men are utterly loyal, and I rely on their support."

Water-mirror: "Your warriors are a match for ten thousand; it is a pity you have no one to put them to good use! Your officials are pasty-faced bookworms, not of a caliber to unravel things and reduce them to order and tide our poor age over."

Liu Pei: "Actually I have been impatient to find some neglected sage, but alas, I have yet to encounter him."

Water-mirror: "You can't have forgotten Confucius's maxim, 'In any township of ten households, one is sure to find loyalty and good faith.' What do you mean, there is no such man?"

Liu Pei: "I am dull and unobservant and would be grateful for your instruction."

Water-mirror: "You must have heard the jingle from the Chingchou–Hsiang Yang locale—

> In nine years' time, things start to waste.
> In thirteen years, there isn't a trace.
> For God's will sends things where they're due.
> And the dragon uncoils and climbs the blue.

This jingle originates from the first year of 'Establish Security.' In the eighth year Liu Piao displaced his first wife, giving rise to domestic turmoil. That is what 'things start to waste' means. As for 'there isn't a trace,' Liu Piao will shortly pass away, and his officers and officials will scatter to the four winds. 'God's will sends things where they're due,' and 'the dragon uncoils and climbs the blue,' find their echo in you, my general."

Liu Pei protested in alarm: "How dare I assume this!"

Water-mirror: "Now the most extraordinary talents of the empire are here. You should go and seek them out."

Liu Pei: "Where are these extraordinary talents? And who are they?"

Water-mirror: "Sleeping Dragon, Phoenix Chick—either of those two men would enable you to secure the empire."

Liu Pei: "And who are they?"

Rubbing his palms, Water-mirror laughed out loud. "Very well! Very well, then!" he said, and invited Liu Pei to remain the night. In the morning there would be further discussion. And he ordered the needs of man and horse to be satisfied.

*   *   *   *

Liu Pei was to spend the night in a room adjoining the thatched chamber. He lay down but could not sleep for thinking of Water-mirror's words. It grew late. He heard a man knock and enter. Water-mirror said: "Yüan-chih, what brings you?" Eavesdropping, Liu Pei sat up in bed. The man replied: "I have long heard how Liu Piao treats both the virtuous and the malicious as they deserve, and so I made a point of presenting myself to him. But I found that his reputation was false. He favored the virtuous all right, but he couldn't use them in the government; and he condemned the contemptible but couldn't get rid of them! So I took my leave by letter and came here."

Water-mirror: "You have the ability to be a king's right-hand man and should be more selective about whom you serve. Why sell yourself short by going to see Liu Piao? Especially now, when we have a heroic contender and enterprising champion right here with us. You have failed to spot him!"

The man: "What you say is correct."

Liu Pei listened with elation and surmised that the man must be Sleeping Dragon or Phoenix Chick. But though he wanted to show himself, he was afraid to appear awkward and hasty.

When the dawn came, Liu Pei went to see Water-mirror and asked who had arrived in the night. "A friend of mine," replied Water-mirror. Liu Pei asked to meet him. "He seeks to commit himself to an enlightened ruler and has already gone elsewhere," replied Water-mirror. Liu Pei asked his name. "Very well, very well, then!" replied Water-mirror.

"Sleeping Dragon, Phoenix Chick—who are these men?" pressed Liu Pei. But Water-mirror only laughed: "Very well, very well, then!"

With upraised hands clasped, Liu Pei appealed to Water-mirror to leave the mountain and join him in upholding the House of Han. But Water-mirror said: "We disengaged men in the mountain wild cannot bear employment in this evil age. There should be men ten times my superior to aid you, and you should take yourself to them."

As they were speaking, there was a commotion outside the farmstead. Chao Yün had ridden up with several hundred men. He reported that an attack on Hsin Yeh was imminent, and Liu Pei rode back with him after bidding Water-mirror good-bye. En route they met Kuan Yü and Chang Fei, and to the general astonishment, Liu Pei described his crossing of the T'an.

When they reached Hsin Yeh, Sun Ch'ien said: "We must send a letter to Piao explaining all that happened." Accordingly Liu Pei dispatched Sun Ch'ien to Chingchou.

Liu Piao summoned Ch'ien and said: "I invited Liu Pei to at-

徐庶

痛恨高賢不再逢
臨歧
泣別兩情濃
片言
卻似客雷震
能使南陽
起臥龍

辛酉

Tan Fu

tend the conference in Hsiang Yang. Why did he leave so uncere-moniously?" Sun Ch'ien presented Liu Pei's letter detailing Ts'ai Mao's attempt on his life and his escape over the T'an. Piao was enraged, summoned Mao, castigated him, and ordered him be-headed. Lady Ts'ai's tearful appeals for mercy were unavailing.

But Sun Ch'ien said: "If you kill Ts'ai Mao, I am afraid the Imperial Uncle will no longer be safe here." And Piao released Mao with further reproofs.

Piao sent his elder son, Ch'i, back with Sun Ch'ien to Liu Pei to acknowledge the offense. At Hsin Yeh Liu Pei received Ch'i and prepared a banquet. As the wine mellowed them, Ch'i began to weep, and Liu Pei asked the cause.

Ch'i: "My second mother, Lady Ts'ai, has a treacherous and conspiratorial mind, and I am without means to avoid disaster. If only my uncle would favor me with his advice."

Liu Pei urged him to remain circumspect and scrupulously filial and assured him that no calamity would result. The next day Ch'i left tearfully. Escorting him beyond the boundary, Liu Pei pointed to Red Hare and said: "If it were not for this horse, I would have been a man of the 'Springs' below." Ch'i said: "It was not the horse, my uncle, but rather your mighty good fortune." And they parted.

Back in the city, Liu Pei rode through the market and saw a man with a turban of vines and a plain cloth tunic, black straps and black footgear, crooning as he approached:

> "Heaven and Earth is topsy and turvy-o!
> The 'fire'* is going cold.
> A stately hall is coming down-o!
> It's hard for one beam to hold.
> But the hills and the valleys hold worthy men-o!
> Who long for a lord to whom to repair.
> And though that lord is seeking the men-o!
> Of me he is all unaware."

Liu Pei heard the song and thought: "This has to be one of the men that Water-mirror spoke of!" He dismounted and addressed the singer, inviting him into the county office, where Pei asked his name.

The man replied: "My surname is Tan ['single'], my given name Fu ['blessing']. I have long known, my lordship, that you are hospitable to worthy scholars, so I wished to join you, but did

* Symbol of the Han.

not dare approach too abruptly. By performing in the market-place, I sought to awaken your interest."

Liu Pei was delighted and treated him as a guest of honor. Tan Fu asked to see the horse that Liu Pei was riding, whereupon he said: "Is this not an unlucky horse? Although it is a thoroughbred, it will only bring misfortune to its master. You should not ride it."

"But he has discharged his sign!" said Liu Pei, and related how he crossed the T'an.

Fu said: "Indeed, that time the animal saved its master rather than ruining him. But in the end the horse will bring misfortune—though I have a scheme by which you can avert it."

"I would like to hear," said Liu Pei.

Fu: "If you have an enemy, give him the horse as a gift. Wait until its curse is spent upon that man, and then you can ride it without incident."

Liu Pei turned color. "Sir! you have come to me for the first time, and would advise me not to be righteous but to harm another for my own gain! Excuse me if I decline to hear such advice!"

Fu laughed and apologized: "They all said that my lord was humane and virtuous, but I was unwilling to believe it automatically. So I used this idea to test you, that's all."

Liu Pei's expression relaxed and he too rose to apologize: "My 'humane virtue' is inferior. It is for you, good master, to advise me."

Fu: "When I arrived here, I heard people in Hsin Yeh singing—

> Now that Liu Pei is our mayor,
> The people have enough and to spare.

So I can tell that my lord's humane virtue is *not* inferior."

Liu Pei honored Tan Fu with a supervisory position in the army so that he could reorganize and train the men and the horses.

* * * *

Now we speak of Ts'ao Ts'ao who, since returning to Hsü, was determined to take Chingchou. For this purpose he assigned Ts'ao Jen, Li Tien, and others to assemble thirty thousand men at Fan. This was a walled city where they could peer down tiger-like upon Chingchou and Hsiang Yang, probing and watching for strengths and weaknesses.

Two of the commandants petitioned Ts'ao Jen: "Now Liu Pei

has a force stationed at Hsin Yeh, recruiting troops and purchasing horses, accumulating fodder and storing grain. His ambitions are not petty, and you had better prepare your moves against him in good time. We two, since surrendering to the Chancellor, have nothing at all to our credit. We beg to request five thousand crack troops to take Liu Pei's head and present it to the Chancellor."

Ts'ao Jen agreed with pleasure, and the two generals, Lü K'uang and Lü Hsiang, began cutting a bloody swath toward Hsin Yeh.

Spies rushed word to Liu Pei, who consulted Tan Fu. Fu: "They must not be allowed to enter the boundaries. Send Lord Kuan out to the left to check them midway. Send Chang Fei out to the right to check their rear. You and Chao Yün should meet them head on. The enemy can be defeated."

Liu Pei adopted the proposal, and the three brothers rode out with their companies. Pei had not advanced far when he saw dust rising behind the hills. The Lüs had drawn up their forces. Each side now had positioned archers at the ends of a semicircular battle line. Liu Pei rode out under his colors and called: "Who dares to try and breach our boundary?"

One of the generals retorted: "I am chief general Lü K'uang, and I hold the Chancellor's mandate to bring you back alive!" Liu Pei sent Chao Yün forward. The two generals closed in combat, but before many passages Chao Yün had lanced Lü K'uang and put him under his horse.

Liu Pei motioned his forces to charge. Unable to withstand them, Lü Hsiang drew back and fled. But as he was retreating, the force led by Kuan Yü attacked him. After a short space of clash and slaughter, the bulk of Lü's unit was cracked. He had to seize what route he could to get away, and he had traveled less than ten leagues when another force blocked his path. Hoisting his spear, Chang Fei shouted, took his man at spearpoint, thrust him through, and overturned him under his horse. The rest of the enemy host scattered. After the battle Liu Pei withdrew to Hsin Yeh, where he gave a banquet for Tan Fu and rewarded the three contingents.

Upon hearing the reports of the battle, Ts'ao Jen was appalled. Li Tien said: "Our generals were deceived by the enemy and destroyed. Now we can only hold our units where they are while we petition the Chancellor to raise a large enough force to clean them out. That is the best strategy."

Ts'ao Jen: "Not at all! In no time we've lost two generals, and a good number of men and horse to boot. The reprisal must be swift! I don't account Hsin Yeh more than a 'bowshot' of a place—hardly worth troubling the Chancellor's army for!"

Li Tien: "Liu Pei is a champion among men. You should not underrate him."

Jen: "Why are you losing your nerve?"

Tien: "According to the rules of warfare, 'If you know the enemy and know yourself, then in a hundred engagements, a hundred victories.' It's not that I'm losing my nerve, but I am afraid that victory is uncertain."

Jen: "Perhaps it is your loyalty that is uncertain. *I* will take Liu Pei alive."

Tien: "If you go, I will guard Fan."

Jen: "If you refuse to go with me, your disloyalty is certain!"

And Li Tien had no alternative. Together they mustered twenty-five thousand soldiers, crossed the river Ch'ing, and made for Hsin Yeh.

Truly here was a case of

> Captains dishonored: corpses carted home;
> Troops raised again: to right the wrong.

Liu Pei Surprises Fan;
Tan Fu Recommends Chuko Liang

Ts'ao Jen, having mobilized local Fan troops, struck out across the river Ch'ing, meaning to trample Hsin Yeh flat.

In Hsin Yeh meanwhile, Tan Fu said to Liu Pei: "When Ts'ao Jen discovers that his two generals have been put to death, he will raise a massive army and come to do battle."

Liu Pei asked how he should respond. Tan Fu: "If they come in full force, Fan will stand vacant and vulnerable and can be captured in the interim." Liu Pei asked for specific tactics, and Tan Fu whispered certain strategies in his ear.

The outposts reported Ts'ao Jen's approach, as Tan Fu had predicted, and Liu Pei put his forces into the field against them. The opposed ranks were drawn up. Chao Yün issued the challenge to the opposing generals. Ts'ao Jen ordered Li Tien to go forth from the ranks and begin combat. They had crossed weapons some dozen times when Li Tien judged that he could not overcome Chao Yün and wheeled back to his own line. Yün charged after him, but from both wings there was a sustained firing of arrows. The two combatants held their weapons and returned to camp.

Li Tien said to Ts'ao Jen: "Their army is spirited and keen and may not be recklessly engaged. We would do better to return to Fan."

Ts'ao Jen: "You! Even before the campaign you were already wearing down our morale. And now again you betray the ranks to save yourself—a crime that merits beheading." Only the most strenuous appeals by the assembled commandants prevented him from putting Li Tien to death.

Ts'ao Jen led the front unit himself, and the next day the drums sounded the army on to Hsin Yeh. There it deployed in formation, and Jen sent a messenger to Liu Pei to ask if he recognized the particular pattern. Tan Fu, having surveyed the enemy from a hilltop, told Liu Pei: "This is the 'eight gates iron-sealed formation.' First, 'refrain'; second, 'alive'; third, 'wounded'; fourth, 'blocked'; fifth, 'high ground'; sixth, 'death'; seventh, 'panic'; and eighth, 'open up.' If you enter through 'alive,' 'high ground,' or 'open up,' things will go in your favor. If you take 'wounded,' 'panic,' or 'refrain,' you will be wounded. If you take 'blocked' or 'death,' you are lost. Now, these 'gates' are deployed in perfect order, and yet the central mainstay or axis is missing. Surprise them at 'alive' on the southeast corner, move due west and out at 'high ground,' and their ranks will be dislocated."

Liu Pei ordered his men to maintain the "horn points" of their formation and commanded Chao Yün to take five hundred men and carry out Tan Fu's recommendation. As Yün cut his way in, Ts'ao Jen retreated to the north. Instead of pursuing him, Yün broke through the west gate and swung around to the southeast again. Ts'ao Jen's army was in complete disarray. Liu Pei signaled his force to advance at full speed, and Ts'ao Jen's men retreated in total ruin. Tan Fu halted the pursuit, regathered his force, and returned.

Ts'ao Jen, now beginning to have some respect for Li Tien's views, said to him: "In Liu Pei's army there must be someone very capable, as my formations were utterly destroyed."

Li Tien: "While we are here, I am especially worried about Fan." Ts'ao Jen returned to Fan, and from the city walls he heard a volley of drums as a general rode forward and shouted: "I took Fan some time ago." Ts'ao Jen's host looked awestruck at the general: it was Kuan Yü. Jen wheeled his horse around and fled back to Ts'ao Ts'ao in Hsü. On his way he learned that the military strategist proposing plans and stipulating tactics for Pei's army was Tan Fu.

*   *   *   *

Liu Pei's victory was complete. When he entered Fan he was received by a kinsman, Liu Pi, who invited Pei to his home and feasted with him. There Pei saw a pleasing youth with dignified deportment standing to the side. He asked who it was, and Liu Pi said: "This is a nephew, K'ou Feng. He became our dependent when his parents died." Liu Pei took a great liking to him and wished to adopt him as his heir, and in appreciation Liu Pi had K'ou Feng honor Liu Pei as his father. His name was changed to Liu Feng. Liu Pei brought Liu Feng back from the feast and had him honor Kuan Yü and Chang Fei as uncles. But Kuan Yü said: "Elder brother already has a son. What use have you for another's young? Later it is bound to create confusion."

Liu Pei: "If I treat him as my son, he will serve me as his father. What 'confusion' are you talking about?" Kuan Yü was dissatisfied, but Pei turned to the problems of tactics with Tan Fu and ordered Lord Kuan to take a force of one thousand to guard Fan. Meanwhile Pei returned to Hsin Yeh.

*   *   *   *

In Hsü, the capital, Ts'ao Jen and Li Tien saw Ts'ao Ts'ao. Tearfully they prostrated themselves and confessed their offense.

"Victory and defeat," said Ts'ao Ts'ao, "are commonplaces to a military man. But I wonder who drafted the plans for Liu Pei."

When Ts'ao Jen mentioned Tan Fu's name, Ch'eng Yü identified him as Hsü Shu from Ying Ch'uan, a man whose majority name was Yüan-chih. He was an expert swordsman who became a fugitive after avenging someone who had been wronged. Tan Fu had then mended his ways and pursued his studies, often in the company of Ssuma Hui.

Ts'ao asked Ch'eng Yü to evaluate Tan Fu's ability. "Ten times mine," replied Ch'eng Yü.

Ts'ao: "It is unfortunate that worthy and capable scholars are opting for Liu Pei. Once his wings are fully formed, what then?"

Ch'eng Yü: "Although Tan Fu is with the other side, if the Chancellor is determined to employ him, there is an easy way to achieve it. He is devoted to his mother, his father having died when he was young. If his mother can be enticed here and then induced to write her son to come, Tan Fu cannot refuse."

The mother, Madam Hsü, was brought to the capital, and Ts'ao treated her royally. Ts'ao: "They say your excellent heir is actually one of the extraordinary talents of the empire. Now he is in

Hsin Yeh assisting the disobedient subject Liu Pei, traitor to the Court. That so precious a jewel has fallen into the mud is truly unfortunate! We would prevail upon you to write and call him back to the capital. I will guarantee him before the Emperor, who will reward him amply." Ts'ao ordered the instruments for writing brought to them.

The matron Hsü asked: "What manner of man is Liu Pei?"

Ts'ao: "A low-class sort, making preposterous claims to being an 'Imperial Uncle'—utterly without credibility or righteous commitment—a perfect example of 'a noble man outside, a base man inside.'"

The matron Hsü in a strident voice said: "You! what fraudulent fabrication! I have known for many many years that Liu Pei is of the royal House of Han, a man who humbles himself before scholars, who treats others with heartfelt respect, and who has a peerless reputation for humanity. Why, callow youths and grey old men, flock-tenders and wood-gatherers—all know his name. He is one of the true heroes of this age. And if my son serves him, then he has found himself the right master. As for you, though you claim the name of Chancellor of the Han, you are in reality a traitor. And when you so perversely take Liu Pei to be the 'disobedient subject' and would have my son forsake the light and elect the dark, are you without *any* shame?" She took an inkstone to strike Ts'ao Ts'ao.

In a fury, Ts'ao ordered armed guards to march the matron out and behead her. But Ch'eng Yü swiftly checked him: "The matron antagonized you *in order* to die. If you kill her you will earn yourself a vicious name even as you raise high the matron's virtue. For once she is dead, Tan Fu will be committed unto death to assist Liu Pei as a means to vengeance. You'd be better off detaining her so that the son's body will be in one place and his heart in another. That way, even if we are letting him assist Liu Pei, he will not give his utmost. Second, by keeping the woman alive, we give ourselves the means of inducing Tan Fu to come here and assist the Chancellor!"

Ts'ao agreed and spared the woman. She was detained and cared for.

Ch'eng Yü visited her regularly and, pretending that he had once sealed a pact of brotherhood with her son, attended her as his own mother. He regularly honored her with gifts which always included a personal note, and the matron would answer in her own hand. Having coaxed this sample of her script out of her, Ch'eng Yü proceeded to imitate it. Then he forged a letter and sent it to Tan Fu in Hsin Yeh. It said:

> The recent death of your younger brother has left me without kin wherever I turn. In the midst of my sorrow and isolation I never dreamed Chancellor Ts'ao would entice me to the capital, to protest your betrayal and revolt and put me in chains. My life has been spared only through Ch'eng Yü. Only if we can get you to give yourself up will my life be saved. When you read this do not forget the hardships of your parents, but come with all speed to keep intact the principle of filial piety. Afterwards we can plan at our leisure to go home and till our former gardens, lest we incur some major calamity. My life hangs by a thread, and you are my sole hope of salvation. Need I implore you further?

Tan Fu's tears rose freely within him as he went to Liu Pei to acknowledge his identity and his reasons for joining Pei. Fu: "Water-mirror took me severely to task for not recognizing my true lord; he urged me to serve you. So I made that mad song in the market to interest your lordship. I was favored with your gracious acceptance and was given grave responsibilities. But what am I to do, now that my mother has been tricked and taken by Ts'ao and threatened with harm? She has herself written to summon me, and I cannot fail her. It is not that I am loth to toil for my lordship, but having my tender mother seized is more than I can bear, and I cannot give my utmost. Permit me therefore to announce my departure, giving ourselves time to plan to meet again."

Liu Pei cried out at this. But he said: "Between the son and the mother is the kinship of ordained nature, and there is nothing that need occupy you on our account. We can wait until you have met with your mother for another opportunity to profit from your instruction." However, Liu Pei prevailed upon him to remain for the night rather than leaving at once.

Sun Ch'ien took Liu Pei aside. "This extraordinary genius has been in Hsin Yeh so long that he is thoroughly familiar with our military strengths and weaknesses. If you let him transfer his allegiance to Ts'ao Ts'ao, he will be used at the highest levels, putting us in danger. My sovereign lord should keep him at all costs. Then Ts'ao will execute the mother, and when Tan Fu finds out, he will fight even more fiercely against Ts'ao Ts'ao to avenge her."

Liu Pei: "Unacceptable; to let them kill the mother while we use the son would be inhumane. To hold him back and sever the link of son to mother is unethical. I would rather die than do it." Moved, the assembled officials all sighed.

Liu Pei invited Tan Fu to drink. But Tan Fu said: "Knowing my mother is imprisoned, I could not force the most precious potion, the most exquisite liquor down my throat."

As they parted outside the city, Liu Pei proposed a last toast: "My meager lot, my paltry destiny keep us from remaining together. I hope you will serve your new master well and achieve a reputation for meritorious work."

Shu: "Someone like me, of insignificant talent and superficial knowledge, was charged by your lordship with the gravest responsibility. Now adversity separates us midway, truly on my old mother's account. But however Ts'ao Ts'ao may compel me, I will not propose a single strategy for him to my dying day."

Liu Pei: "Once you have gone, master, Liu Pei himself will also withdraw to the mountain forest."

Fu: "When I lay plans with my lordship for the royal cause, this paltry intelligence is all I count on. Now, because of my mother, I cannot think clearly. Even were I to remain, I would be of no use. My lordship would be advised to seek elsewhere some high-minded worthy to support and assist you in conceiving your great enterprise. Consume yourself no more on my account."

Liu Pei: "None surpasses you."

Fu: "How can my useless commonplace qualities deserve such high praise?"

On the verge of parting, Tan Fu urged the generals not to follow his example of failing to finish what was begun. Liu Pei could not bear to bid farewell, and saw him off one stage further, then another stage. Finally they separated tearfully. Liu Pei poised his horse on the forest's edge to watch Tan Fu leave in agitation. Some trees blocked his view of his departing counselor, and Pei wanted them chopped down.

But at that moment Tan Fu reappeared, whipping his horse to a gallop, and Liu Pei rushed forward to meet him. Fu: "My emotions were so tangled that I forgot one thing. There is an extraordinary scholar in the area, in Lung Chung barely twenty leagues from Hsiang Yang. Your lordship should seek him out."

Liu Pei: "Dare I trouble you to request that he come for an interview?"

Fu: "The man cannot be 'sent for.' Go to him personally. If you win him, it will be like the Chou dynasty winning Lü Wang, or the Han gaining Chang Liang."

Liu Pei: "Compared with your own self, master, what are his talents and virtues?"

Fu: "Compared with someone like me? It is like comparing a dray with a pegasus, a crow with a phoenix. The man has a habit of comparing himself with Kuan Chung and Yo I,* but I think he surpasses them. For he is perhaps the one man in 'the empire who can plot the interaction of the Heavens and the Earth."

Liu Pei: "I would hear his names."

Fu: "He is from Lang Yeh. His surname is double, Chuko; his given name, Liang; his majority name, K'ung-ming. He is a descendent of Chuko Feng, military governor of the capital province. His father's given name was Kua, his majority name Tzu Kung; he was chief assistant to T'ai Shan command. He died young, leaving Liang to the care of his younger brother, Hsüan. This Hsüan was a long-standing friend of Chingchou's governor Liu Piao, which is why they went to him for protection and made their home in Hsiang Yang. After Hsüan's death, Liang tilled the farm himself with his younger brother Chuko Chün in Nan Yang. He often liked to perform the 'Liang Fu Elegies.'† Where he lived there was a range of hills known as the Recumbent Dragon Ridge, so he took the sobriquet Master Sleeping Dragon. His powers are indeed transcendent. Your lordship should visit him soon. For if he is willing to support and assist you, you need never fear that the empire cannot be stabilized."

Liu Pei: "Is he one of the two men Water-mirror mentioned to me: Sleeping Dragon or Phoenix Chick?"

Fu: "Phoenix Chick is P'ang T'ung of Hsiang Yang. Sleeping Dragon is none other than Chuko K'ung-ming."

Liu Pei: "Then these great men are before my very eyes. But for you, I should have remained blind."

A poem commemorates the moment:

> Bitter to rue: that noble worthy—never to meet again.
> At road's fork: to part, emotion both ways strong.

* Two advisers of genius who failed to bring their masters to complete sovereignty.
† The "Liang Fu Elegies" were songs of filial mourning. The reference is to K'ung-ming's early loss of his father. The Liang Fu mountain is one of the lesser elevations near Mount T'ai and is said to have been used in ceremonies of dynastic transition.

A few words dropped, like spring thunder,
Rouse the Sleeping Dragon of Nan Yang.

Having recommended K'ung-ming, Tan Fu parted from Liu Pei a second time. And Liu Pei was awakened to the meaning of Water-mirror's words. He led his assembly back to Hsin Yeh to prepare gifts to carry to K'ung-ming in Nan Yang.

*   *   *   *

Having left, Tan Fu was still affected by lingering anxiety. He feared that K'ung-ming would not leave the mountains to support Liu Pei, so he rode to see the scholar in his thatched hut. K'ung-ming asked his purpose in coming.

Fu: "My wish was to serve Liu Pei. But what choice had I, when my old mother was seized by Ts'ao and wrote summoning me? I was on the verge of leaving when I recommended you to Liu Pei. He is coming to you at once to offer his respects. I hope you will not shunt him aside, but will put at his disposal those great abilities you have always shown. What a blessing that would be!"

K'ung-ming froze. "And you mean to make me the victim of your sacrificial feast?" Saying no more, he flicked his sleeves and went in. Tan Fu retreated in embarrassment and resumed his journey.

Liu Pei Solicits
the Recluse

When Ts'ao Ts'ao learned of Tan Fu's arrival, he ordered Hsün Yü, Ch'eng Yü, and other advisers to go out and receive him. Tan Fu then entered the Chancellor's headquarters and offered his respects.

Ts'ao: "Sir, how could such a noble and enlightened scholar as you lower himself to serve a Liu Pei?"

Fu: "In my youth I got into trouble and ran away, floating through all sorts of places. By chance I came to Hsin Yeh, where I formed a strong friendship with Liu Pei. But now that my dear mother, whose maternal kindness has been my blessing, lives here, I have been overcome with a sense of my negligence."

Ts'ao: "Now, sir, you are here precisely so that you may tend and care for this honored relation at all times. I too may be able to listen to your lucid clarifications."

Fu, respectfully declining the compliment, left and rushed to see his mother. Tearfully he prostrated himself before his home. His mother said in amazement: "What brings *you* here?"

"I have been serving Liu Pei," he said. "Your letter came, and I rushed here."

The matron Hsü exploded in rage and swore as she struck the table: "You disgrace! Flitting around hither and thither for so many years! I thought you were making progress with your studies. How can someone who started well turn out so badly? At least you have read enough to know that loyalty and filial piety do not always complement each other. How could you *not* realize

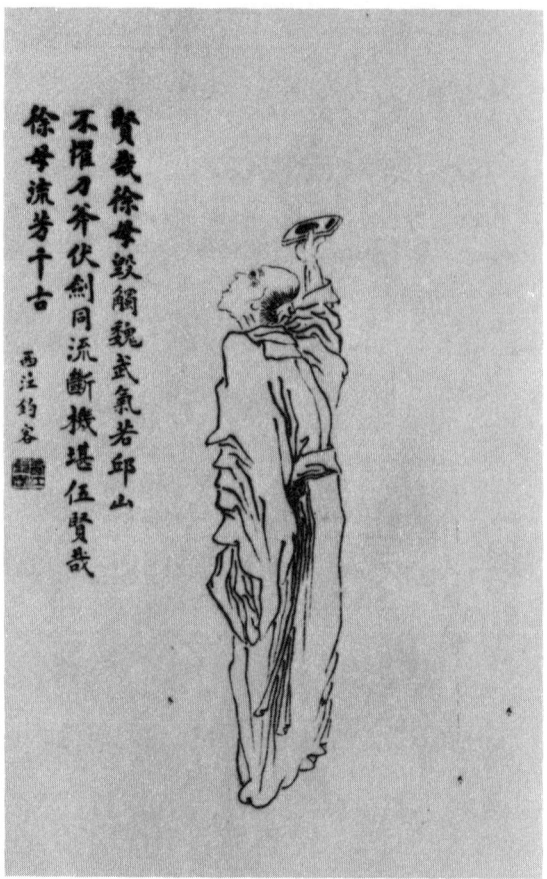

Mother Hsü

that Ts'ao Ts'ao is a traitor who has abused and ruined his sovereign? And that Liu Pei is known far and wide for his humanity and his ethics? Not only that, but once you were in the service of a Liu, the patronym of the Han, you had found yourself a proper master. But now, trusting a forged scrap of paper (which you never verified), you have abandoned the light and elected the darkness and earned yourself a contemptible name. How gross! With what kind of self-respect am I supposed to receive you, now that you have shamed the spirit of your ancestors and uselessly wasted your own life?"

She swore so furiously that Tan Fu cowered on the ground, hands clasped above his head, not daring to look up. And with that the matron wheeled around and vanished behind the screens. Moments later a handmaiden screamed: "Our mistress has hanged herself from the rafters!" Crazed, Tan Fu rushed in, but her breath had ceased.

Later someone wrote "In Praise of Mother Hsü":

> Mother Hsü's integrity
> Will savor for eternity . . .
> A model lesson for her son:
> Self-execution, martyrdom.
> An aura like a sacred hill,
> Allegiance sprung from depth of will . . .
> In life her proper designation,
> In death her proper destination:
> Mother Hsü's integrity
> Will savor for eternity.

Seeing his mother already dead, Tan Fu lay broken on the ground. Much time passed before he revived. Ts'ao Ts'ao sent a representative to the ceremonial presentations and the vigil over the body, and he personally attended the sacrificial offering. Tan Fu interred the coffin at the Southern Font of the capital, abided the mourning, and guarded the grave site. Every gift Ts'ao Ts'ao proffered he declined.

At the time, Ts'ao was considering launching his southern expedition. But he was persuaded to await the spring thaw. He then diverted water from the river Chang to make a lake, on which he began naval maneuvers in preparation for the southern expedition.*

*   *   *   *

As Liu Pei was preparing ceremonial articles for his visit to Chuko Liang (K'ung-ming) in Lung Chung, the arrival of a strange-speaking, strange-looking man with a tall hat and thick sash was announced. "Why, this must be the very Chuko K'ung-ming," Pei said, straightening his clothes to go and welcome him. But it turned out to be Ssuma Hui, the mountain recluse. Liu Pei was delighted and invited him into his private quarters. "Since leaving your transcendent presence, I have been occupied daily

---

* Unlike the southerners, who were skilled in naval operations, the northerners were accustomed to horseback and land warfare.

with military concerns and have failed to pay courteous call. But now this splendid visit gratifies my deeply felt longing and admiration."

Hui: "I had heard Tan Fu was here and came especially to see him."

Liu Pei: "Ts'ao Ts'ao has imprisoned his mother, who sent a letter recalling him to the capital."

Hui: "So he fell for Ts'ao Ts'ao's ruse! There was never any doubt about the matron Hsü's integrity, and even if Ts'ao did imprison her, she would never agree to write for her son. The letter has got to be a forgery. If Tan Fu had *not* gone, he could have saved his mother; if he went, she is doomed."

Agitated, Liu Pei asked the reason. Hui: "She lives according to the highest ethic, and would be humiliated to receive her son."

Liu Pei: "As he was leaving, he recommended Chuko Liang of Nan Yang. What do you know about him?"

Hui smiled. "If Tan Fu left, he left. But why did he have to get that other one to come out and sweat his heart's blood?"

Liu Pei: "Why do you say that, good master?"

Hui: "K'ung-ming, Tan Fu, and three men named Meng, Ts'ui, and Shih—these five close friends dedicated themselves to the cult of spiritual purity. K'ung-ming was the only one who contemplated the doctrine in its entirety. He would sit embracing his knees, intoning lengthily, and remark to the others, 'In official service any of you might advance to an inspectorate or a governorship.' But when the group asked what his own ambition was, he would only smile. He was wont to liken himself to Kuan Chung and Yo I. His ability is beyond measuring."

Liu Pei: "I wonder why the Ying Ch'uan area has produced so many great men."

Hui: "Long ago, a skilled observer of the heavens remarked that with so many stars congregated here, the place was sure to have many worthy officials."

Lord Kuan was listening also. He said: "To my knowledge Kuan Chung and Yo I are major figures of the Spring-and-Autumn and Warring States period—men whose merit overarches the realm. Is it not an exaggeration for K'ung-ming to compare himself to them?"

Hui smiled. "To my mind, he might rather be likened to Chiang Tzu-ya, who helped found the eight-hundred-year Chou dynasty, or Chang Tzu-fang, who helped the House of Han flourish for four hundred years." The company was aghast. And Hui left, refusing to be detained by Liu Pei. Gazing upward, he laughed aloud. "Sleeping Dragon has found his lord but not his time!" he said. "What a pity!" And he was gone like a gust.

The next day Liu Pei, Lord Kuan, and Chang Fei went to Lung Chung. On the hillsides men were carrying mattocks to their acres, singing:

> "The blue sky's a rounded vault,
> The planed earth a chessboard,
> Where men their 'black-and-white' divide
> In seesaw conflicts' shame and pride.

> "For the winners, peace and comfort,
> For the losers, tiring toil.
> Liang in Nan Yang lies secluded,
> Securely sleeping. 'Stay abed'!"

Liu Pei reined in and asked the farmers who had made the song. "Why, Master Sleeping Dragon," was the reply. Pei asked his whereabouts. They directed him to a thatched hut in a thin wood before the Recumbent Dragon Ridge.

Liu Pei arrived at the farmstead and knocked on the wattle gate. A youth appeared to ask who it was. "Left imperator of the Han, lord of I Ch'eng district, chief warden of Yu province, Imperial Uncle Liu Pei comes to pay his respects to your master."

Youth: "I can't remember all those names."

Liu Pei: "Just say that Liu Pei comes to pay a call."

Youth: "He went out for a bit early this morning. His movements are uncertain. I don't know where he is. We are not sure when he will return. Perhaps in three to five days, perhaps ten or more."

Disappointed, Liu Pei was persuaded by Kuan and Chang to leave his name with the youth and return home.

They had ridden several leagues when they reined in and looked back upon the scenic figuration of Lung Chung. Now the hills seemed more luxuriant and elegant than lofty, the streams more sparkling than deep, the land more smooth than spacious, the wood more lush than large. Gibbon and crane intimately associating, pine and bamboo interlaced, blue-green, shimmering—he could not take his eyes away. Suddenly a man appeared, his countenance imposing, his bearing dignified, his stature grand but simple. He wore a scarf casually around his head and a plain black tunic on his frame. With his staff of goosefoot wood he came down a mountain byroad.

Liu Pei was sure this was K'ung-ming, but it turned out to be one of K'ung-ming's friends, Ts'ui Chou-p'ing, who asked:

"Why does my general want to see K'ung-ming?"

Liu Pei: "With such great disorder in the empire, the four quarters are as unsettled as the clouds, and I would meet K'ung-ming to find the strategy to secure and stabilize the commonwealth."

Chou-p'ing smiled. "My lord, you are bent on bringing disorder to an end. But from ancient times, periods of civic order and discord have alternated quite unpredictably, the greatest good will notwithstanding. When the Supreme Ancestor slaughtered the snake and embarked on the rising that destroyed the renegade Ch'in and led to the Han, that was a transition from discord to civic order. Two hundred years later, when the era of Great Calm had lasted long, Wang Mang usurped the throne and brought us from order to disorder. Then the First Emperor of the Latter Han revived the dynasty, righting the foundations once again and bringing us out of discord to civic order. Now two hundred years more have gone by, and the population has long been secure. Again the shield and the spear are all around us. It is a moment of transition back to disorder, and things can not be abruptly brought to a conclusion. And if you would have K'ung-ming redirect the Heavens and the Earth to compensate for destiny, I'm afraid it will not be easy—a futile expense of mind and body. I'm sure you know that 'Who adapts to Heaven shall know content; who contravenes Heaven shall toil in vain,' and that 'None can deduct from the Reckoning; none can force what is fated.'"

Liu Pei: "Your words show great insight. But I am a Liu, scion of the Han, bound to right the ruling house, and cannot lay the burden on 'fate' or 'the Reckoning'."

Chou-p'ing: "A mountain rustic is unprepared to interpret the affairs of the empire. I happened to be honored with your exemplary question and so expressed myself rashly."

Liu Pei: "I am favored with your insight and instruction, but I would learn where K'ung-ming has gone."

Chou-p'ing: "I too would pay him a call, but do not know where he has gone."

Liu Pei: "Would you be interested in coming back to our poor county seat?"

Chou-p'ing: "My uncultured nature has grown too fond of leisure's freedom to give thought to merit's fame. There will be time for us to meet again."

The man left with a long salutation, and Liu Pei rode on with Lord Kuan and Chang Fei, who remarked: "Again we did not manage to pay our call and bumped into this rotten Confucian instead. Too much idle talk!"

"That is how men in seclusion express themselves," replied Liu Pei.

Soon the three men returned to Lung Chung, again looking for K'ung-ming. They found instead a youth who said:

"I am not he. I am his younger brother, Chuko Chün. There are three of us: the eldest, Chuko Chin, is in the Southland serving Sun Ch'üan; K'ung-ming is the middle brother."

Liu Pei: "Is Sleeping Dragon at home?"

Chün: "Yesterday he and Ts'ui Chou-p'ing were making plans to go off rambling."

Pei: "Do you know where?"

Chün: "They might have piloted a small craft down the lakes and rivers, or paid a call on some Buddhist or Taoist on a mountain, or gone looking for a friend in the back villages, or decided to entertain themselves with lutes and chess in some cavern den. He comes and goes quite unpredictably, and I have no idea where."

Liu Pei: "How meager my lot! Twice I have missed this excellent man!"

Chün: "Sit awhile and let me offer you tea."

Chang Fei: "The master is not here. Let us be going."

But having come so far again, Liu Pei wished to stay. He asked Chün: "They say your esteemed elder brother is a past master of military science and regularly studies the subject. Can you tell me more about it?"

When Chün said he knew nothing, Chang Fei spoke: "Better not to ask further. Look how severe the wind and snow. Better to go back now." But Liu Pei dismissed it, and Chün said: "My brother is not here, and I should not detain you military men for so long. But there will be time soon for me to return your courtesy."

Liu Pei: "I would never dream of imposing on you to travel. In a few days I should be coming again. Only I would borrow some paper for a letter to leave your elder brother—an expression of the intense earnestness of my wish." The letter read:

> Long have I, Pei, enthusiastically revered your honored name, and twice have I come to present myself, only to return, having failed to meet you, to my keenest disappointment. I remain humbly mindful that as a remote kinsman of the royal Han Court, I have lavishly enjoyed prestige and position. But when my thoughts turn to the rude displacement at Court, our laws and customs crumbling and swept aside as countless contenders subvert the state and vicious factions abuse the sovereign, my heart breaks, my gall splits. For whatever sincerity we may have to rectify and deliver the Han, perishes for want of strategy. I idolize your humane compassion, your ethic of loyalty. If in your greatness of spirit you would unfold your mighty talents and apply your grand tactics, the empire and the sacred grain shrines would be doubly blessed. I am forwarding this to inform you that after providing again for ceremonial purification, I shall importune your most honored presence, respectfully offering my poor simple sincerity. With all my hopes for your discerning consideration.

Liu Pei submitted the letter and took his leave, reiterating his intentions. Suddenly a youth waved from beyond the fence. "The master is coming!" Liu Pei looked at a small bridge. A man with a winter headdress and fox furs came through the descending snow. He sang:

> "Night long, north wind chill,
>   Tinged clouds massed a myriad leagues.
>   Everlasting space: the capering snow—
>   The changeless land is what it never was.
>
> "Look into the vastness of sky.
>   Could it be a jade dragon melee?
>   Scales strewn every which way
>   Quickly filling the hollow zone.
>
> "Aback a mule, across a bridge,
>   Sighing, alone,
>   At the plumtrees' skeleton."

Liu Pei was certain that this was Sleeping Dragon and dismounted to extend his courtesy: "Master, it is hard for you to brave the bitter cold, and we have been long expecting you." Startled, the man climbed off of his mule and returned the courtesy. Chuko Chün came up and said: "This is not Sleeping Dragon; it is his father-in-law."

Liu Pei: "I happened to hear your chant. It was most elevated and poignant."

"I was examining the 'Liang Fu Odes' in my son-in-law's home. I recalled one stanza. As I crossed the bridge I noticed the plum trees by the fence. It moved me to recite. I never thought an honored guest would hear me."

Liu Pei: "Have you seen your esteemed son-in-law?"

"In fact I am coming to see him."

And so Liu Pei took his leave, remounted and headed home. Wind and snow grew fiercer. Uncertainty and sadness overcame him.

Back in Hsin Yeh, time crept past until it was another spring. Then he ordered the diviners to cast for a propitious time to visit K'ung-ming on Recumbent Dragon Ridge. Lord Kuan and Chang Fei were displeased and presented their objections together.

> The highest worth has yet to bow the warrior's will.
> He crooks the knee and makes his fighters skeptical.

K'ung-ming
Fixes the Course of War;
Sun Ch'üan Destroys Huang Tsu

In spite of his failures, Liu Pei wished to pay another call at Lung Chung. Lord Kuan said: "Two times, brother, you went and respectfully presented yourself. Such courtesy is indulgence. I am beginning to think that K'ung-ming has a false reputation and no real learning. That is why he avoids you and won't show himself. Why are you so captivated by this man?"

Liu Pei: "Not 'captivated.' Long ago the patriarch of Ch'i tried to see the Recluse of the East Boundary and returned five times before he gained a meeting. This is a magnificent authority we are trying to contact. How much more effort should we make!"

Chang Fei: "Dear brother, I think you misjudge him. I would rate him a village bumpkin! What makes him a 'magnificent authority'? Spare yourself the trip. If he refuses to come, it only takes a bit of rope to bring him here!"

Liu Pei scowled. "I suppose you never heard of king Wen, founder of the Chou, presenting himself to Chiang Tzu-ya! If king Wen himself could show a wise man such respect, what allows you such utter discourtesy? Lord Kuan and I will go together; you may stay here."

Fei: "Since my two elder brothers are going, I cannot stay behind."

Liu Pei: "If you come, then, there must be no failures of etiquette."

Fei agreed, and the three rode to Lung Chung. Approaching the cottage on foot, they met Chuko Chün, who told them his

Liu Pei visits K'ung-ming

brother had returned and could be seen, and with that sauntered away.

Liu Pei: "This time our gamble has paid off."

Chang Fei: "How disrespectful! Would it have hurt him to bring us to the farmstead? Why did he just make off?"

Liu Pei: "He has his own business. You want to use force on him?"

When they arrived, the lad told them that K'ung-ming was sleeping. Liu Pei had his two companions wait outside.

Liu Pei watched K'ung-ming sleep, face up, on a couch in the cottage; he stood below, arms folded. A while passed, but the master had not awakened. Seeing no movement, Lord Kuan and Chang Fei came in and found Liu Pei standing in attendance as before. In great anger Chang Fei said to Lord Kuan: "What insolent negligence! Our brother stands below in attendance, and he pretends to sleep peacefully on! Let me go out and torch the rear and see whether that gets him up or not!" Lord Kuan calmed his junior down, and Pei sent them out to continue waiting. Soon after, K'ung-ming awoke and hummed a song:

> "When all's a dream, who would first awake?
> But from our common life we learn:
> Indoors, spring's simple sleep suffices;
> But outside, summer ripens time."

K'ung-ming stopped, turned to the lad, and asked: "Any visitors from the world of men?"

The lad: "Imperial Uncle Liu is here and has been waiting."

K'ung-ming arose and said: "Why didn't you report it sooner? I still need time to change my clothes." He hurried out, and it was another while before he reappeared, clothes and cap correct, to greet Liu Pei.

K'ung-ming appeared to Liu Pei a man of medium height, face like gleaming jade, a kind of turban wound on his head, crane plumes on his body—he had the buoyant air of a spiritual transcendent.

Liu Pei made a deep gesture of reverence: "This poor unexceptional fellow, distant scion of the House of Han, has long felt your mighty name, master, reverberate in his ears like thunder. Twice before have I presented myself but, failing to gain audience, set my worthless name on a letter. I never learned whether it was brought to your discerning attention."

K'ung-ming: "This unsophisticated person of Nan Yang, unresponsive and indolent by nature, is indebted to the general for the trouble he has taken to travel our way, and is overcome with compunction."

After further civilities, tea was served and the conversation continued. K'ung-ming: "I could see in the intent of your letter your deep compassion for the people and the commonwealth. But I fear that my years are too few, my talents too sparse, and that you are mistaken in seeking my help."

Liu Pei: "How could the words of Ssuma Hui and Tan Fu be empty talk? I only hope you will not reject me as crude and without worth but will vouchsafe your edifying instruction."

K'ung-ming: "They are two of the noblest scholars of our age. I am no more than a common tiller of the soil. What business have I to speak of the empire? Ssuma Hui and Tan Fu have made a preposterous recommendation. What can it avail you to seek a rough stone and leave a precious jewel?"

Liu Pei: "How can a man of your capacity to bring order to the age waste himself among groves and springs? I beg you to keep in mind the world of the living and agree to enlighten me, that I may be free of ignorance and folly."

K'ung-ming laughed. "I would learn your aspiration, general."

Liu Pei dismissed everyone who was present, moved his seat beside K'ung-ming's, and declared: "The House of Han teeters on ruin. Unscrupulous subjects have stolen the mandate of rule. I failed to recognize my limitations and tried to extend the great principle of allegiance throughout the empire. But my knowledge is superficial and my methods fall short. I have made no progress so far. But if you, master, would relieve my ignorance and ease our difficulties, the blessing would be truly ten-thousand-fold!"

K'ung-ming: "Since the time of Tung Cho's sedition, numerous aggressive and enterprising magnates have appeared. Ts'ao Ts'ao could overcome a Yüan Shao though his strength was inferior to Shao's, thanks to wise planning and a favorable occasion. Now Ts'ao holds sway over a population of four million. He uses his grip on the Son of Heaven to enjoin the feudal barons. There is no way you can cross spearpoints with him. Sun Ch'üan has had a firm hold on the Southland for three generations now. Their territory is difficult of access and the people are devoted to Ch'üan. They can be used for rear support, but they are not a strategic objective.

"Chingchou commands the Han and Mien Rivers to the north. It has the full benefit of the great lakes to the south. Eastward it links up with the Southland. Westward it offers access to the Riverlands. Here is the place to wage war; unless you dominate it, you will have no secure defense. And this is the very place that Heaven seems to be furnishing you with, general. Can you have second thoughts? The Riverlands are inaccessible and naturally fortified. Their fertile wildlands extend thousands of leagues—a realm that is Heaven's treasure house. Han's Supreme Ancestor based himself on them to consummate his imperial endeavor. The Riverlands' governor, Liu Chang, is benighted and feeble, and though the people are loyal and the realm is rich, he does not know how to keep and care for them. Men of insight and capability yearn for enlightened rule.

"Now, general, you are a scion of the imperial house, known across the land for allegiance in good faith, a man who keeps the contenders in hand and thirsts for men of merit. If you sit astride the two territories of Chingchou and the Riverlands, guard their formidable defenses, come to terms with the various Jung tribes on the west, placate the I and Yüeh to the south, form a diplomatic alliance with Sun Ch'üan, and conduct a program of reform in your own territory, then you may wait until the situation develops to the point when you can have one of your chief generals drive from Chingchou north through my home district toward the old eastern capital [Loyang]. Meanwhile you yourself can lead a Riverlands army onto the 'riverways of Ch'in' [Kuan Chung, the western heartlands, whose capital was Ch'ang An].* And won't the good common folk 'basket food and jug beverages' to welcome you, my general! Truly thus can your great endeavor be consummated and the House of Han revived! This is how I would shape strategy. It only remains for you to consider it."

K'ung-ming had a map hung up, and continued: "These are the fifty-four territories in the Riverlands region. To achieve hegemony, let Ts'ao Ts'ao assay the Heaven-sent occasions from the north; let Sun Ch'üan assay his positional advantages from the south; while you, my general, assay the possibilities for political combination.

"The first step is to take Chingchou and make it your home base. Then proceed to take the Riverlands and lay the foundation

* Giving Liu Pei a grip on the two political centers of north China. Ch'ang An was the capital of the Former Han, Lo Yang of the Latter Han (see map, p. 284).

撥亂扶危主 殷勤受託孤 英才過管樂 妙策勝孫吳 傳二幽師表 堂堂八陣圖 如公全盛德 應嘆古今無

清溪釣徒 題

K'ung-ming

for achieving your third of the triangle of power. And then you may make the high central plains to the north your objective."

Hearing this proposition, Liu Pei came up off his mat and folded his hands in respectful gratitude. "Master, you have opened the thicket that barred my way and made me feel as if clouds and mists had parted and I had gained blue sky. The only thing is that Liu Piao of Chingchou and Liu Chang of the Riverlands are both primary kinsmen of the royal house. How could I bear to seize what is theirs?"

K'ung-ming: "At night I watch the configurations of the Heavens. Liu Piao will not be long among the living. Liu Chang is not a ruler of any endeavor. In time he will transfer his allegiance to you."

Liu Pei pressed his head to the floor in respectful acknowledgement. And by this single interview K'ung-ming showed that he perceived the tripartite empire without ever having left his cottage—truly an incomparable man in any generation!

Liu Pei appealed to K'ung-ming: "Though my name is inconsiderable and my virtue meager, I beg that you not spurn my crudeness and commonness. Come out from these mountains to lend us your aid, and I will listen obediently to your enlightening instruction."

K'ung-ming: "I have long been content with my plow and mattock and feel reluctant to respond to the age. I cannot accept your command."

Liu Pei wept. "If you remain here, master, what of the living?" His tears wet his tunic sleeves and soaked his front. K'ung-ming saw that his intent was entirely sincere and said: "Then, general, if you will not spurn me, I am willing to emulate the toil of a beast of burden."

Elated, Liu Pei called in Lord Kuan and Chang Fei. They offered their gifts, which K'ung-ming adamantly declined until Liu Pei assured him: "This is not a ceremony of petition but a humble expression of personal feeling."

They all remained overnight on the farmstead. The next day Chuko Chün returned, and K'ung-ming left him with final instructions: "I have accepted the kind generosity of Imperial Uncle Liu's triple solicitation. It is inexcusable not to go. Remain at your labors and do not let our acres run to seed, until I have succeeded, when I shall return to obscurity."

A wistful poem was written in later times:

> About to soar, he fain would homebound walk.
> The task fulfilled, the parting words remembered in vain.
> For Liu Pei pleaded and pleaded again.
> Star falls—fall wind—the last campaign.

When they returned to Hsin Yeh, Liu Pei and K'ung-ming dined at the same table and slept on the same platform. They spent the days discussing the events of the empire. K'ung-ming observed: "Ts'ao Ts'ao made the Hsüan Wu Lake in Chi to train for naval warfare. That must mean he intends to invade the Southland. We ought to send someone under cover to cross the river and mark the lay of the land." And it was done.

*   *   *   *

Now we speak of Sun Ch'üan, who after the death of Sun Ts'e consolidated his hold on the Southland and carried on the patrimony founded by his father and brother. He brought into his government scholars of merit and opened wide the doors to guests from other regions.

In the seventh year of "Establish Security" (A.D. 202) Ts'ao Ts'ao, having broken Yüan Shao, sent a representative to the Southland demanding that they send a son for the imperial processions. Ch'üan marked time and made no decision. His mother, Lady Wu, summoned Chang Chao and Chou Yü for consultation.

Chang Chao: "Ts'ao's attempt to have us send a son to Court is an old device for controlling the feudal barons. But if we do not obey, I am afraid there is a very definite danger of his raising an army to subdue the Southland."

Chou Yü: "General, you are the inheritor of a task your father and brother began. You have brought together the populations of six districts. Your army is elite; your grain supplies are ample; your generals and officers are responsive to your command. What pressure are you under to send hostages to anyone? Once they hold a hostage you can not help forming an alliance with Ts'ao Ts'ao. If he then has any command or summons, you cannot avoid responding. That makes you subject to another's control. It is best not to send but to cautiously observe how things develop while you prepare a sound defense."

Lady Wu: "Chou Yü is correct."

Ch'üan accepted the recommendation, cordially dismissed Ts'ao's representative, and refused to send a son. After that Ts'ao Ts'ao was determined to reduce the Southland. But the northern lands remained unquiet, and there was no intermission for a southern campaign.

In the eleventh month of the following year, Sun Ch'üan attacked Huang Tsu. They fought in the Long River (the Yangtze), and Tsu's forces were defeated completely. But the winds were unfavorable, and so Sun Ch'üan called his forces home.

*   *   *   *

In the twelfth year, A.D. 207, Lady Wu spoke her final charge to Sun Ch'üan: "You are to serve Chou Yü and Chang Chao with neither lapse nor negligence, as if you were formally in their charge. My younger sister and I were given together to your father in marriage. Thus she is your mother as well. Serve her as you would serve me. But care for her considerately, too, and make a suitable match for her." With these words she passed away. Sun Ch'üan wailed in grief and fulfilled the ceremonies of the cortege and the interment.

> Liu Piao's general, Huang Tsu, held Hsia K'ou, a point east of Chingchou where the Yangtze humps north and meets the eastern terminus of the Hsiang River. Hsia K'ou is the critical pass through into Chiang Hsia, the zone under the hump, geographically in the orbit of the Southland but strategically important to Liu Piao and Ts'ao Ts'ao as well.

> Sun Ch'üan was unable to decide whether to resume operations against Huang Tsu at once or to wait (as Chang Chao urged) until the mourning period for his mother had ended. Chou Yü, his naval director, insisted on the urgency of the operation and prevailed.

> Sun Ch'üan's general Lü Meng, called the Queller of the North, was an advocate of a forward policy in the Chiang Hsia region. He introduced a defector from Huang Tsu named Kan Ning.

Sun Ch'üan to Kan Ning: "Your coming wins our good will. There can be no thinking of old grudges; be assured of that. We only hope you will show us the way to destroy Huang Tsu."

Sun Ch'üan attacks Huang Tsu

Kan Ning: "The holy services of the Han are daily endangered. Ts'ao Ts'ao's Chancellorship must end in a usurpation, and Ching-chou is a place he must strive for. Liu Piao does not provide for the future, and his sons are clumsy knaves who could never further what he has established. My lord, you should make this territory your objective in good time—before Ts'ao Ts'ao does! Huang Tsu should be taken first. He is old and apathetic, absorbed in his commercial dealings. He infringes upon his officials and exacts much from the populace; there is widespread disaffection. His fighting equipment is in disrepair, and his army has no discipline. If you attack, he will fall. And then sound the drum and march west. Hold the Ch'u pass and aim for the Riverlands. Your hegemony can be achieved."

Sun Ch'üan: "This is an invaluable assessment."

Liu Ch'i Seeks
K'ung-ming's Aid;
The Military Director's Debut

Lü Meng and Kan Ning persuaded Sun Ch'üan to attack Huang Tsu, and the expedition succeeded. But Sun Ch'üan decided not to hold the ground gained; instead he retreated, to prepare for Liu Piao's retaliation.

The narrative divides, and we return to Liu Pei, who received the following intelligence: The Southland has struck. Huang Tsu is dead. The Southlanders are digging in at Chai Sang.*

Liu Pei was consulting with K'ung-ming over the new developments when Liu Piao summoned him. K'ung-ming: "He will be asking your participation in formulating a strategy for revenge. I should be with you so that we can observe the possibilities of the situation, for I have a strategy of my own. First you must apologize for the incident at Hsiang Yang when you fled the banquet. If Piao enjoins you to make a punitive expedition against the south, you must under no circumstances agree. Simply say that you need time to go back to Hsin Yeh and get your forces in condition."

Liu Pei and K'ung-ming were received by Liu Piao. Liu Pei offered his apologies for his flight from the banquet, and Liu Piao said: "I know that you were in mortal danger. At the time, I was prepared to behead Ts'ai Mao on the spot as satisfaction to you. But so many appealed for him that we have provisionally forgiven him. Will my worthy brother kindly not take offense?"

* "Enclosed Mulberries," a town slightly east downriver from Chiang Hsia. An important forward position for Sun's forces.

Liu Pei: "It was not general Ts'ai's doing. I think the plot was hatched by his subordinates, that's all."

Piao: "Now we have lost our hold on Chiang Hsia, and Huang Tsu has met his death. Therefore I have asked you to come to take part in planning the retaliation."

Liu Pei: "Huang Tsu was a violent personality, incapable of using men. That's how he brought on this catastrophe. Now, if we raise an army for a southern expedition, suppose Ts'ao Ts'ao comes from the north. What then?"

Piao: "My years are many and my ailments multiply. I cannot handle affairs. Worthy brother, if you will come to assist me, when I pass away you will be the ruler of Chingchou."

Liu Pei: "Elder brother, how can you say such words? Can you imagine that I would presume to undertake so heavy a responsibility?"

K'ung-ming eyed Liu Pei, who said: "We must allow time to think of a sound strategy." And he excused himself and returned to his lodgings.

K'ung-ming: "My lord, he was ready to consign Chingchou to you. Why did you rebuff him?"

Liu Pei: "Piao has treated me with consummate grace and etiquette. To exploit his moment of peril to seize his estate would be too cruel."

K'ung-ming sighed. "A truly humane and compassionate lord!"

During this discussion one of Liu Piao's sons, Liu Ch'i, came to call. Tearfully Ch'i importuned: "My stepmother can not tolerate me. My very life may be ended in a matter of days. I look to my uncle to rescue me, for pity's sake."

Liu Pei: "This is a family matter, nephew, which you may not bring to me."

K'ung-ming smiled faintly, and Liu Pei turned to him. But he said: "This is a family matter with which I would not dare to become acquainted."

Later as Liu Pei escorted the lad out, he whispered to him: "Tomorrow I will have K'ung-ming return your kind call, and you may thus and so"—And he described a ruse to obtain K'ung-ming's advice, adding, "I am sure he will have some ingenious suggestions."

The next day Liu Pei put off all obligations, claiming a stomach ailment, and entrusted K'ung-ming with the courtesy call to his nephew. K'ung-ming consented and was led into Ch'i's private apartments.

Ch'i: "My stepmother has no use for me. Master, favor me with a word to relieve my plight."

K'ung-ming: "I am here as a state guest. There are no grounds on which I may meddle in a matter among kinfolk. If it were known, the harm would be considerable." He rose to leave.

Ch'i: "Having favored me with your illuminating regard, why must you leave me now perfunctorily?" He led K'ung-ming to a private chamber, where he continued: "My stepmother has no use for me. I implore you for a word that will help me."

K'ung-ming: "I may not give counsel in such matters." Again he attempted to leave.

Ch'i: "Master, if you will not speak, there is nothing more to say. But why would you leave so precipitously?" K'ung-ming returned to his place, and Ch'i resumed: "I have an old text that I would like you to examine." He led K'ung-ming to a small attic, where he repeated: "My stepmother has no use for me. My life is a matter of days. Can you so cruelly deny me a single word of help?"

K'ung-ming arose angrily and tried to leave the attic, only to find that the ladder had been removed. Ch'i: "I am seeking your advice for a sound strategy. Does your fear that it will leak out make you reluctant to speak? Now then, we are between the Heavens and the Earth. What comes from your mouth can only go into my ear. You may therefore grant me your advice, or I must end my life before your eyes." And he drew his sword.

K'ung-ming checked him. "There does exist a good device. You must remember the incident involving Shen Sheng and Ch'ung Erh? The former remained home and perished. The latter sought his fortune and found safety. Huang Tsu has just been destroyed, and Chiang Hsia has no one to guard and defend it. Why not petition your father for a defensive force to hold Chiang Hsia, as a way of avoiding disaster?"

Ch'i thanked him with clasped hands and ordered the ladder brought. K'ung-ming returned to Liu Pei, whom he told about the disposition of Liu Ch'i's problem. Liu Pei was delighted.

When Liu Piao received Ch'i's petition, he was undecided and consulted Liu Pei. Pei said: "Chiang Hsia is a crucial spot. You certainly cannot let just anybody defend it; one of your own sons

K'ung-ming advises Liu Ch'i

is precisely what is called for. Then he can deal with problems to the southeast while I deal with those to the northwest."

Piao: "They are saying that Ts'ao Ts'ao made an artificial lake to train his navy. That means he intends to campaign against the south. Our defense must be prepared."

Liu Pei: "We already know this. Do not be too anxious, brother."

Liu Pei returned to Hsin Yeh, and Liu Piao assigned Liu Ch'i three thousand soldiers to secure Chiang Hsia.

* * * *

It was at this time that Ts'ao Ts'ao terminated the duties of the three state ministers and attached their functions to his own office.

He created certain subordinate offices among which one, the "office of documents," was occupied by Ssuma Yi. Ts'ao thus had a full complement of documentary and propaganda services.

Ts'ao Ts'ao gathered his generals to discuss the campaign against the south. Hsia-hou Tun proposed: "We have heard that Liu Pei is in Hsin Yeh, where he is steadily developing his fighting men. He will be a serious problem in the future and should be our first objective."

Ts'ao Ts'ao ordered Tun to take charge of a hundred-thousand-man force to approach and fix their sights on Hsin Yeh. But Hsün Yü objected: "Liu Pei is a mighty contender, and now that he has acquired K'ung-ming as military director, he cannot be recklessly confronted."

Tun: "Liu Pei is a mouse that won't escape me."

Tan Fu said: "General, do not underestimate Liu Pei. Now that he has K'ung-ming's support, he is like a tiger with wings."

Ts'ao asked who K'ung-ming was, and Tan Fu identified him.

Ts'ao: "How does he compare with you?"

Fu: "There is no comparison. I am a firefly; he is the full-risen moon."

Tun: "That is absurd. To me K'ung-ming is a straw reed. What is there to fear? If in a single engagement I fail to capture Liu Pei and take this K'ung-ming alive, I am prepared to offer my head to the Chancellor."

Ts'ao: "Then bring me an early report of victory and allay my distress." And Tun began the campaign.

* * * *

It may be mentioned that Liu Pei's ritual acknowledgement of K'ung-ming as his master caused the two brothers Lord Kuan and Chang Fei no little distress. They said to Liu Pei: "K'ung-ming is so young, not yet thirty. How much ability and knowledge can he have? Brother, your treatment of him is more than what is called for—even before you have put him to the test." But Liu Pei ended the matter by saying, "K'ung-ming is to me as water is to a fish."

One day a man presented Liu Pei with a yak tail, which Pei wound into a headdress. When K'ung-ming saw it, he said very formally: "My illustrious lord is not keeping to his long-range commitments if this is all he devotes himself to!"

Liu Pei tossed the headdress to the ground and said: "I was only killing time to forget my troubles."

K'ung-ming: "My illustrious lord, in your own estimation how do you compare with Ts'ao Ts'ao?"

Liu Pei: "I fall short."

K'ung-ming: "Your host numbers but a few thousand. Suppose Ts'ao's army appears. How will you deal with it?"

Liu Pei: "That is the very problem that has been consuming me. But I have not found a good plan."

K'ung-ming: "You had better rally a militia as quickly as possible. I will train them myself in anticipation of the enemy." So Liu Pei sent the call among the people of Hsin Yeh. Three thousand answered, whom K'ung-ming instructed intensively in the principles of formations.

Then word came that a force of a hundred thousand, led by Hsia-hou Tun, was scything its way toward Hsin Yeh. Chang Fei said to Kuan Yü: "Let's have K'ung-ming go forward to deal with them and be done with it." As they spoke, Liu Pei summoned them to ask their advice. "How about sending the 'water'?" they replied.

Liu Pei: "For brains I depend on K'ung-ming; for courage on you two. They can not be interchanged." The two brothers went out.

Liu Pei called K'ung-ming, who said: "I am concerned lest Chang Fei and Kuan Yü refuse to accept my verbal orders. If you wish me to serve as your military executive, I beg to borrow your sword and seal." When Liu Pei had turned these over to him, K'ung-ming assembled the military commanders. Chang Fei said to Kuan Yü: "We might as well go, if only to see how he sorts things out."

K'ung-ming enjoined the commanders: "Ts'ao Ts'ao's army marches south for Po Wang. To their left, the Yü hills. To their right, the An forest. These can be used to hide men and horse in ambush. Let Kuan Yü take a thousand fighters and hide in the Yü hills. When the enemy reaches you, let them pass without opposition. Their equipment and food supplies will be in the rear. But only when you see fire on the southern front should you unleash your men to strike; then burn out their grain and fodder. Let Chang Fei hide in the An forest. When he sees the fire, he should head for the old supply depot at Po Wang and burn it. Kuan P'ing and Liu Feng are to take five hundred men and flammable materials to the hills around Po Wang itself. When the enemy forces return, put the hills right to the torch."

K'ung-ming also called on Chao Yün to lead the front corps— but in order to lose, not win. Finally Liu Pei was to bring up the rear. "All must act according to plan. There must be no slips," he ended by saying.

Lord Kuan said. "We are all to go forth and engage, but we have not had the chance to review your own role as military director."

K'ung-ming said: "I am simply going to remain and guard our base."

Chang Fei guffawed: "We all go to the slaughter while you sit at home—perfectly content and self-possessed!"

K'ung-ming: "Here are the sword and seal. Whosoever violates my order is dead."

Liu Pei said to his brothers: "Can you be unaware that 'Plans evolved within the tent determine victory a thousand leagues away'? You must not violate the orders, my brothers."

Chang Fei smiled coldly and left. Lord Kuan said: "We may as well see whether his idea works or not. Then there will be time enough to confront him." And he left too.

The commandants, unclear about K'ung-ming's overall strategy, remained doubtful and unsure, though they obeyed. K'ung-ming said to Liu Pei: "My lord, take your troops and station them at the foot of the Po Wang Mountains. By tomorrow evening the enemy will have arrived. When they do, abandon camp. At the fire signal, turn back on them and charge. I will guard our city. Have victory celebrations and the certificates of achievement made ready." When K'ung-ming's orchestration was complete, Liu Pei was also doubtful and unsure.

*   *   *   *

When Ts'ao Ts'ao's commanders, Hsia-hou Tun and Yü Chin, neared Po Wang, they assigned half of their crack troops to the front corps and half to guard the stores. It was fall, and the great autumn wind was gradually picking up. As infantry and cavalry rushed ahead, dust began to fly. Tun deployed his forces and asked the guide where they were.

The guide: "Ahead are the Po Wang hillsides; behind is the Lo River mouth." Tun came out of the ranks to scan the horizon: a force of cavalry was approaching. Tun laughed aloud. "Before the Chancellor himself Tan Fu extolled K'ung-ming as a divine figure," he said. "But look how he uses his troops! To send such a puny force against us is like sending dogs and sheep against tigers and panthers. I boasted before the Chancellor that I would take Liu Pei and K'ung-ming alive. I will make good my words."

Chao Yün, who had been instructed to feign defeat, led out his cavalry. Tun: "You follow Liu Pei like a bereft soul following a ghost." Yün gave his horse its head and rode into combat. The two fighters closed. After several passages Yün retreated, and Tun chased him some ten leagues. Yün turned and fought, then retreated again. An officer raced up to warn Tun that he was being drawn into an ambush, but Tun ignored him and pressed on to the Po Wang hillsides.

With a roar of the catapults Liu Pei led his troops pounding toward Tun. As they engaged, Tun said to the man who had warned him: "Is this your ambush? If we don't reach Hsin Yeh tonight, I swear not to halt the army!" And he thrust forward, Liu Pei and Chao Yün both retreating before him.

The sky was already darkening. Thick clouds stretched across it. There was no moon. The day winds had risen; the night winds grew stronger. Tun was intent on charging for the kill. His commanders, Yü Chin and Li Tien, reached a narrow point where dry reeds crowded the roadway from both sides. Li Tien said to Yü Chin: "If you hold the enemy in contempt, you will fail. To the south the roads narrow; streams and hills press close on them. The foliage is dense and tangled. What if they use fire?"

Yü Chin agreed, but by the time they reached Hsia-hou Tun and he realized the necessity or calling a halt, they could already hear the hissing of fire rising in a crescendo as arms of flame began to reach up. Then the dry reeds hugging the roadway were alight. In moments, all sides in all directions were howling with flame as the wind whipped up. Ts'ao's infantry and cavalry trampled each other, and the toll was incalculable. Chao Yün pressed the slaughter. Braving the smoke, Hsia-hou Tun broke through the fires and fled. The remaining elements of Ts'ao's broken force stumbled into the ambushes, to be destroyed by Lord Kuan and Chang Fei. Arms littered the wilds, and the streams ran red.

Chang Fei and Lord Kuan dismounted and bowed in acknowledgement before K'ung-ming's carriage. The spoils were brought home to Hsin Yeh. K'ung-ming said: "Nonetheless, Ts'ao Ts'ao will bring a major force down on us. But I think I know how to withstand him."

The Ts'ais Surrender Chingchou to Ts'ao Ts'ao; Liu Pei Leads His People Across the River

When Liu Pei asked how to repel Ts'ao, K'ung-ming said: "Hsin Yeh is a small township and cannot long maintain us. The rumor is that Liu Piao's illness is critical and worsening. This is the time to take Chingchou and secure ourselves while we improve our chances of driving Ts'ao Ts'ao back."

Liu Pei: "That makes good sense, but how can I intrigue against the man who has favored me with kindness?"

K'ung-ming: "If you do not, what will your regret avail?"

Liu Pei: "I would die before I could do something so disloyal."

K'ung-ming: "We will have time to speak of this again."

> *Ts'ao named Liu Pei and Sun Ch'üan as his principal enemies and ordered an army of half a million raised to sweep the south.*

> *On his deathbed, Liu Piao asked Liu Pei to administer Chingchou. Liu Pei declined but agreed to serve as Liu Ch'i's guardian. Piao named Ch'i as his successor and Liu Pei as his regent. The Ts'ai clan, backers of Piao's other son, Ts'ung, sealed the palace gates in their displeasure.*

At this time Liu Ch'i was in Chiang Hsia, where K'ung-ming had advised him to go. When he learned that Liu Piao's disease was critical, he came to Chingchou only to find Ts'ai Mao barring the gates.

Mao: "As an ordinary son* of the patriarch, you were commissioned to maintain order and guard over Chiang Hsia. You have abandoned your duties without authority. What will you do if the soldiers of the Southland come? If I admit you to the sovereign patriarch it will annoy him and aggravate his disease, and that would be unfilial. You should return to Chiang Hsia at once." Liu Ch'i stood outside the gates and, after a spell of lamentation, sadly returned to Chiang Hsia. Liu Piao's condition continued to deteriorate. At last, despairing of Ch'i's coming, he gave several loud groans and passed away.

> The Yüans held the Yellow River north,
> And Liu Piao the middle Yangtze.
> Till women's rule dragged their houses down
> And without a trace they were gone.

With Liu Piao dead, Lady Ts'ai and Ts'ai Mao forged a will appointing the second son, Liu Ts'ung, as heir. Then they commenced the mourning and announced the funeral. Liu Ts'ung, who was just fourteen but rather shrewd, said to the assembly: "My father has departed this world. My elder brother Ch'i is presently in Chiang Hsia. And my uncle Liu Pei is in Hsin Yeh. You all have instated me as sovereign. But what if my brother and my uncle raise an army to challenge my deed? How shall we explain ourselves?"

Before the assembly could reply, an assistant stepped forward. "The patriarchal son's point is well taken. We must abandon the course you have chosen. Dispatch a letter of mourning to Chiang Hsia inviting the first son to be the sovereign; then follow up by ordering Liu Pei to share the administrative duties. This way, to the north we can withstand Ts'ao Ts'ao; to the south we can repulse Sun Ch'üan. It is a plan that provides for all contingencies."

Ts'ai Mao reviled him: "And who are you that dares with seditious expression to contravene the last will of the sovereign patriarch?"

The assistant: "You have used various factional conspiracies to declare a false will, depose the senior, and instate the junior. You have delivered our nine districts to the hands of the Ts'ais for all to see. If our late lord's ghost is present, he will wreak disaster upon you." Ts'ai Mao ordered him removed and beheaded. And the man's curses ended only with his life.

* By a wife other than Lady Ts'ai, the principal wife.

The Ts'ais assumed military control of the capital, sending Lady Ts'ai and her son, Ts'ung, to Hsiang Yang. But no sooner did they arrive than news also came of Ts'ao's approaching army.

A secretary said to Liu Ts'ung: "And the approach of Ts'ao's army is not our only danger. The elder son is in Chiang Hsia and Liu Pei is in Hsin Yeh—and both have yet to be informed of the funeral. If they raise a force to challenge us, Chingchou is in mortal danger. But I have a plan that will make our population as secure as Mount T'ai and at the same time preserve your sovereign name and office."

Ts'ung: "Where could such a plan come from?"

The secretary: "Your best option is to present the nine divisions of the Chingchou–Hsiang Yang district to Ts'ao Ts'ao, who will not fail to treat you generously, my lord."

Ts'ung shrilled back: "What does that mean? Orphaned, I accept the estate established by our late king. Now before my possession is firm, am I simply to relinquish it to someone else?"

Another follower advised Ts'ung: "The choice between rebellion and submission must be made in broad perspective. The disproportion between your forces and Ts'ao's cannot be altered. Ts'ao Ts'ao's southern campaigns and his northern expeditions are undertaken in the name of the imperial Court. My sovereign, in repulsing him you win no name for obedience. Moreover, you are newly instated. Problems abroad have not been stilled, and those at home begin to stir. Our people, hearing of Ts'ao's approach, are chilled to the gall before they have seen battle. How can you make a stand with frightened men?"

These and other arguments slowly melted Ts'ung's resistance. When his mother, Lady Ts'ai, confirmed the advisers' judgment, he sent a letter of surrender to Ts'ao Ts'ao. But Lord Kuan intercepted the messenger, and the letter was brought to Liu Pei. Piao's other son, Ch'i, the rightful heir, had sent a representative to Liu Pei. Seeing Ts'ung's letter of surrender, Ch'i's spokesman said:

"If such is the case, my lord, you should hasten to Hsiang Yang, where Ts'ung is, on the pretext of observing the death watch for Liu Piao. Lure Liu Ts'ung out to receive you, seize him, and exterminate his faction. And then Chingchou will revert to you, my lord."

K'ung-ming: "This is a correct position. You should accept it."

Liu Pei sobbed: "As the end approached, my brother Piao entrusted his sons to me. If I should seize his son and lay hands on his land, how shall I face my brother again when I am dead beneath the Nine Springs?"

K'ung-ming: "If you do *not* do it, how do you propose to resist Ts'ao Ts'ao, whose troops are at Yüan even now?"

Liu Pei: "Let us rather retreat to Fan to avoid them."

Liu Ch'i's emissary was sent back to Chiang Hsia with word to prepare for battle. Announcements were posted at the four gates of Hsin Yeh: "Without regard to age or sex, let all who are willing to follow us proceed directly to Fan city." Arrangements were made to move the populace across the river, and officials were sent ahead to the new city.

> *Liu Pei moved his people to Fan, lacing the vacated city of Hsin Yeh with fire traps. Ts'ao's army occupied Hsin Yeh only to be driven out by the fires. Their escape route led across a stream that Liu Pei had dammed, and Kuan Yü released the waters, killing more of Ts'ao's men.*

> *Ts'ao laid siege to Fan. Liu Pei and K'ung-ming decided to move again to the city Hsiang Yang, where Liu Ts'ung had gone.*

The proclamation was made throughout the city of Fan: "Ts'ao's army is about to arrive. This single city cannot long defend itself. Those of the people who would follow with us must cross the river in a group." The people of the two cities, Hsin Yeh and Fan, spoke in their assemblage: "All of us will follow our Lord even to the death." And that day the pilgrimage commenced, amid tears and howling. They steadied the old and dragged along the young, led on the men and escorted the women—a rolling sea of people crossing the river, the sound of their cries continuing from both shores.

Surveying the scene from a boat, Liu Pei was profoundly shaken. "If we have made these good people suffer this hardship for our sake—what have I lived for!" He attempted to throw himself into the river but was restrained by those around him. All who heard him were pierced with grief. Liu Pei waited until the last of the refugees had been carried across before he remounted.

They marched to Hsiang Yang, only to be greeted by a great arc of banners and a moat whose border was webbed with sharpened sticks.

Liu Pei: "Liu Ts'ung, my worthy nephew, we seek aid for these good people and have no other intent. You may open your gates to us." Liu Ts'ung was too afraid to appear, but Ts'ai Mao ordered the archers to fire on the people massed at the walls.

Liu Pei could not expose his people to the conflict. He retreated to another city.

Liu Pei: "In trying to preserve my people I only injure them. We will not enter Hsiang Yang."

K'ung-ming: "Chiang Ling is a strategic point of Chingchou. Why not settle in there?"

Liu Pei: "That is exactly my thought." And they led the throng away from Hsiang Yang and on to Chiang Ling. In the commotion, many people from Hsiang Yang slipped out and joined Liu Pei.

More than one hundred thousand, soldiers and commoners, thousands of carts and carriages, and innumerable burden bearers came together in the procession. They passed Liu Piao's grave site, where Liu Pei led his generals in a mass devotion. With shaken voice he declared: "Your junior brother, to his shame, wanting in virtue and lacking in talent, has failed the heavy charge you confided. The fault lies with me alone and does not touch these good people. I look to your splendid spiritual force to grant succor to the people of Chingchou." Neither soldier nor civilian could contain his feelings.

When news came that Ts'ao Ts'ao had taken Fan, Liu Pei's generals said: "Chiang Ling is a strategic location which will enable us to resist and defend. But we have such a mass of people on our hands that we barely cover ten leagues a day. Who knows when we can make Chiang Ling? If Ts'ao's army gets to us, how can we engage and oppose them? Wouldn't it be more to our advantage to part from these people for now, and go on ahead ourselves?"

Liu Pei replied emotionally: "Any undertaking must be based on the people. Since they believe in me, would I abandon them?"

His remarks became known, and all were moved. And the procession lumbered ahead. Since Ts'ao Ts'ao was soon to catch up, K'ung-ming had Liu Pei send to Liu Ch'i for help.

*   *   *   *

From Fan, Ts'ao sent to Hsiang Yang to summon Liu Ts'ung, but Ts'ung was afraid. Ts'ai Mao implored him to go, but someone else informed Ts'ung privately: "Your generals have already submitted. Liu Pei is gone. Ts'ao will be flaccid and unready. Assemble a surprise attack force, position them at the key junctions, and strike—Ts'ao himself can be taken. Then your influence will be felt across the empire, and though the north-central plain is broad, you could bring it under control by issuing proclamations. This is an opportunity rarely met. Do not let it slip."

Liu Ts'ung reported the suggestion to Ts'ai Mao, who repudiated it as ignorance of the mandate of heaven. But the one who had made the proposal rejoined: "Thief of a nation, what would I not give to chew your live flesh!" Others stepped in to still the quarrel.

Ts'ai Mao went to Fan to see Ts'ao Ts'ao, whom he approached with fawning and pandering.

Ts'ao Ts'ao: "What are Chingchou's resources in men, horses, coin, and grain?"

Mao: "Fifty thousand horse, one hundred and fifty thousand foot, and eighty thousand marines; most of the coin and grain are in Chiang Ling, the rest is in various places; there is enough to supply us for a year."

Ts'ao: "How about the warships? And who is the naval commander?"

Mao: "All told, seven thousand ships. I myself am in command."

Ts'ao then conferred military titles and a command upon Ts'ai Mao and added: "For Liu Ts'ung, this compliant son of Liu Piao, I will memorialize the Emperor to endow in perpetuity his rule of Chingchou." Ts'ao explained privately to his own followers that these steps were taken only because he needed Ts'ai Mao's knowledge of naval warfare. Afterwards there would be a different disposition.

Liu Ts'ung was most grateful for Ts'ao Ts'ao's generous treatment of Ts'ai Mao. But when Ts'ao Ts'ao appointed

Ts'ung himself to the northern region of Ch'ing, he was reluctant to go.

Ts'ao insisted that Ts'ung accept the appointment, however, and the youth could only proceed north with his mother, accompanied by a single loyal commandant, Wang Wei. His other officers returned after seeing him to the river.

Ts'ao summoned his general Yü Chin and instructed him to pursue Liu Ts'ung and his mother and put them to death. Yü Chin, arresting them, cried: "I hold the Chancellor's command to slay you both, mother and son. Lower your heads without delay." Lady Ts'ai held the boy in her arms and cried out as the soldiers of Yü Chin set to work, but all were killed. Ts'ao also searched for K'ung-ming's family in Lung Chung, but they had long since been moved and concealed by K'ung-ming.

* * * *

Ts'ao Ts'ao's spies reported that Liu Pei was making a scant ten leagues a day. Ts'ao ordered five thousand of his best mailed cavalry to overtake them in twenty-four hours, while he advanced with the main army.

Liu Pei now was at the head of more than a hundred thousand commoners and a cavalry of three thousand, all jostling together as they moved slowly toward Chiang Ling. K'ung-ming: "We have had no word from Lord Kuan since he went to see Liu Ch'i in Chiang Hsia. I wonder what the outcome was."

Liu Pei: "Is it possible to trouble my military director himself to take the trip down? Ch'i will be mindful of the advice you once gave him, and if he sees you in person things are bound to go smoothly."

K'ung-ming left, and Liu Pei marched on accompanied by his civil advisers. Just then a violent gale scooped up the dust in front of the horses and sent it skyward, blotting out the red sun. Liu Pei exclaimed: "What sign is this?"

Chien Yung, who had some insight into the permutations of the yin and the yang as presaged by climatic change took an unobtrusive augury and said: "This foreshadows great ill fortune, which should strike this night. My sovereign patriarch, abandon these people with all speed and be gone."

Liu Pei: "These good people have followed us this far even from Hsin Yeh. How could I bear to abandon them?"

Chien Yung: "My lord, if sentiment forbids you to depart, disaster is not far away."

Liu Pei: "What territory lies ahead?"

Those around replied: "The city of Tang Yang, where the Highland Mountain stands."

Liu Pei ordered camp to be pitched at the mountain.

It was autumn's end. Chill winds pierced men's bones. As the fallow darkness came on, clamoring voices spread through the wilderness. Late in the night, at the fourth watch, the encamped multitude began to hear it—out of the northwest, the shouts of men that shook the ground as they came. Liu Pei leaped to his horse and led two thousand of his cavalry to meet them. But Ts'ao's force had the advantage of surprise; there could be no effective opposition. Liu Pei, fighting to the death, had reached his mortal extremity when Chang Fei cut an escape route for him. Liu Pei fled until dawn. Only a few hundred cavalry remained with him. Nor did any know where he had gone. Liu Pei lamented: "One hundred thousand living souls, who out of their affection for us have met with these woes. We know nothing of the fate of our generals, our elderly, our young. A man would have to be made of clay or wood not to grieve."

Then word of Chao Yün's defection was brought. Liu Pei: "His ties with me are long-standing. How could he turn against us?" Chang Fei: "He sees that our position is lost and our strength spent, and he probably looks to Ts'ao for wealth and station, that's all."

Liu Pei: "Chao Yün has stayed with us through the worst of our tribulations. His will is like hard stone. Wealth and station are not what would move him," Unconvinced, Chang Fei went off to find out for himself.

During Ts'ao Ts'ao's raid, Chao Yün had lit into the enemy troops, slaughtering them recklessly until daybreak. Then he searched in vain for Liu Pei as well as for the members of Pei's family. He thought: "My lord confided to my personal care both Lady Mi and Lady Kan, together with the young lord Ah Tou. Now they are scattered among the fighting hosts, and I cannot in self-respect look on my lord's face. It is better to be killed in battle while I am at least trying to locate his loved ones." With only some thirty or forty on horseback behind him, Chao Yün charged into the tangle of armies. Mingled with them were the commoners of the two cities Hsin Yeh and Hsiang Yang. The cries of the people shook heaven and moved earth as they fled, pierced by arrows, lanced by spears, abandoning sons and daughters. Who could tell their numbers?

Chao Yün came upon a man lying wounded in the grass who said that Lady Mi and Lady Kan had abandoned their carriage and were proceeding on foot with Ah Tou.

Liu Pei flees to Hsia K'ou

Chao Yün found Lady Kan and turned her over to Chang Fei. Then he resumed the search for Lady Mi and the child.

Chao Yün searched hectically and at last found them in a house-wall gutted by fire: Lady Mi holding Ah Tou, squatting beside a dry well, keening. Chao Yün dismounted and knelt before her. Lady Mi: "To see you, general, means Ah Tou's salvation. I hope you will have compassion for his father who, through the hazards of half a lifetime, has but this bit of bone and blood that is his own. Guard the boy and let him see his father's face, and I can die without remorse."

Chao Yün: "Your trials are my offense. There is nothing to be said. Please take the horse. I will proceed on foot and see you through the encircling troops."

Lady Mi: "You cannot! You cannot spare your horse. The boy's life is entirely in your trust. I bear many wounds, and my death would not be worth regretting. Take him and go, for truly I cannot, and you must not compound the wrong." Refusing Chao Yün's repeated appeals, she left the child on the ground and rolled herself over into the dry well.

Chao Yün realized that the woman was dead. He pushed over the wall to cover the well; then he loosened his armor straps and placed the child inside the gleaming plate guarding his breast. And in this way the child was restored to Liu Pei.

K'ung-ming and Kuan Yü returned from their mission to Liu Piao's first son, Liu Ch'i, who brought reinforcements from Chiang Hsia and generously offered his city to Liu Pei. At this time Ts'ao Ts'ao was consolidating his position in Ching-chou.

Sun Ch'üan's Overture to Liu Pei

Ts'ao Ts'ao took counsel with his generals. "Liu Pei has found refuge with Liu Ch'i in Chiang Hsia, and I am afraid it will increase our difficulties if he forms an alliance with the Southland. What plan would serve to destroy him?"

Hsün Yu: "Now that our might is widely felt, send to the Southland inviting Sun Ch'üan to join you in a hunting party at Chiang Hsia. Together make Liu Pei your prey, divide Chingchou, and seal an everlasting amity. Sun Ch'üan will agree to it all out of alarm and uncertainty, and then our plans will carry."

At the same time, Ts'ao Ts'ao sent land and sea units down the Yangtze toward the Southland.

*   *   *   *

Sun Ch'üan had stationed his forces at Chai Sang when word of Ts'ao's gains was received. Consultations for the south's defense began at once.

The adviser Lu Su said: "Chingchou lies adjacent to our state. Its rivers and mountains afford formidable security. Its elite and its commoners are energetic and prosperous. If we can seize and hold it, we will have the resources for imperial rule. Liu Piao is newly dead, Liu Pei newly defeated. Let me carry your mandate to the obsequies in Chiang Hsia and use the occasion to convince Liu Pei that he should encourage Piao's military leadership to join us against Ts'ao Ts'ao. If it pleases Liu Pei to accept, our great endeavor will be consummated." Sun Ch'üan adopted the suggestion and sent Lu Su to Chiang Hsia.

In Chiang Hsia, Liu Pei took counsel with K'ung-ming and Liu Ch'i. K'ung-ming: "Ts'ao Ts'ao's power is growing so that it is almost more than we can withstand. Our best option is to throw in our lot with Sun Ch'üan in the Southland, since he can serve as rear support. If north and south hold each other at bay, why should we not find our advantage between them?"

Liu Pei: "The Southland is so rich in men and material goods that they are bound to have long-range ambitions. How would they be willing to accommodate us?"

K'ung-ming smiled. "Ts'ao is leading a million-man host, perched like a tiger on the Chiang and Han Rivers. How could the Southland not send men to gather information about his strengths and weaknesses? If someone comes to us, let me take a little sail downriver. Trust to my three inches of limber tongue to persuade him of the appetite that north and south have for one another. If the southern armies prevail, we join with them to settle Ts'ao Ts'ao and retake Chingchou. If the northern armies prevail, we have a chance to exploit the situation and take the Southland."

Liu Pei: "Your theory is profound. But how do we get a Southlander to come?"

That very moment, Lu Su was announced. K'ung-ming laughed and asked Liu Ch'i: "When Sun Ts'e, Ch'üan's father, died, did Chingchou send anyone to the funeral service?"

Ch'i: "The deepest enmity was between us. How could we be exchanging representatives at ceremonies of celebration or condolence?"

K'ung-ming: "Then it is for no obsequies that Lu Su comes, but to sound out the military situation. My lord, if he questions you concerning Ts'ao Ts'ao's movements, plead ignorance. If he persists, suggest that he ask me."

When all ceremonial formalities were performed, Liu Ch'i arranged a meeting between Lu Su and Liu Pei.

Lu Su: "Long has the Imperial Uncle's great name been known to me, though I have lacked occasion to pay you homage. Fortunately we meet today, a satisfaction for which I am truly grateful. They say you have joined battle with Ts'ao Ts'ao, and I presume you know his strengths and weaknesses, so I would make bold to ask the approximate number of his forces."

Liu Pei: "My forces are insignificant, my generals few. No sooner do we hear of his approach than we make off." But when Lu Su pressed him for details, he arranged a meeting with K'ung-ming, to whom Lu Su said: "Your talent and your virtue have ever been the objects of my esteem, master. Now that fortune enables us to meet, I would learn the perils of the present situation."

K'ung-ming: "Ts'ao Ts'ao's treacherous devices are entirely known to us. But our strength, alas, falls short, and therefore we have to avoid him."

Su: "Will you remain here, then?"

K'ung-ming: "My master has an old friend, Wu Ch'en, to whose care he will entrust himself."

Lu Su: "Wu Ch'en has too little grain and too few men to protect himself, not to speak of another."

K'ung-ming: "Yet it will do for a while until we can make other plans."

Lu Su: "General Sun Ch'üan holds the six Southland districts in a steel grip. His soldiers are keen, his grain ample. He shows the utmost respect to men of worth, the utmost courtesy to men of parts. Heroes from all around the Yangtze flock to him. Now, in planning for your lord, what could be better than to send a man you trust to the Southland to engage an alliance and jointly project the great endeavor?"

K'ung-ming: "Liu Pei and general Sun have no relationship. I fear your persuasion is in vain. Nor is there any one to send."

Lu Su: "My master, your brother is an adviser for the Southland. Every day he looks forward to receiving you. Incompetent as I am, I beg to accompany you to see general Sun for mutual discussions."

Liu Pei feigned disinterest, relenting when K'ung-ming alleged the urgency of the situation. K'ung-ming bid Liu Pei and Liu Ch'i goodbye and set out by boat for Chai Sang.

K'ung-ming's Verbal Warfare

Sailing toward Chai Sang, K'ung-ming and Lu Su reviewed the situation. Lu Su: "But when you see general Sun, it is imperative that you not speak too candidly of the size of Ts'ao Ts'ao's army or the extent of his leadership."

K'ung-ming: "It is not necessary, Su, for you to keep reminding me. I will make my own replies."

Sun Ch'üan's officers and officials were already in plenary session to consider Ts'ao Ts'ao's proposal when word of Lu Su's return came. Su was speedily summoned to the gathering and questioned about his mission. Then Sun Ch'üan showed him Ts'ao's letter, which read:

> With trepidation I have lately taken upon myself the imperial decree, accepting its exhortation to strike down state criminals. Our banners tilted southward. Liu Ts'ung bound his hands. The populace of Chingchou sensed the direction of events and tamely transferred its allegiance to us. One million hardy warriors are in my command, and a thousand able generals. I wish to join with you, general Sun, for a hunting expedition in Chiang Hsia to cooperate in striking Liu Pei down. Sharing his territory, we may seal an everlasting amity. If it is our good fortune that you will join us, rather than looking on from afar, favor us with a speedy reply.

Lu Su said to Sun Ch'üan: "My sovereign patriarch, what is your most honored view?"

Sun Ch'üan: "We have yet to reach a final decision."

Chang Chao spoke. "No resistance to Ts'ao Ts'ao, who commands a million men and assumes the imperial name, has been successful. Moreover, the major advantage at your disposal was the Yangtze—until Ts'ao Ts'ao took Chingchou. Now he shares with us the Long River's defensive benefits. He cannot be opposed, and in my poor estimation, we would do better with the total security which submission affords."

Though many seconded this position, Sun Ch'üan murmured to himself. He did not speak, however, but rose to step outside. Lu Su followed him. Ch'üan seized his hands: "But what do *you* look for, my friend?"

Lu Su: "What they all say, my general, how deeply they wrong you! It is true that ordinary men may submit, but you may not submit."

Ch'üan: "How do you mean?"

Su: "For someone in my position, to submit means going home to my own community. Eventually I will regain some official status. But if you submit, where can you go? To a minor estate? to a single carriage? to a single mount? to a handful of followers? And what of your claim to royalty? Your advisers all consider themselves. You must not heed them. It is time for you to make a master plan for yourself."

Ch'üan sighed. "All their counsel is wide of my aspiration. Your notion of a 'master plan' is precisely my thinking. Heaven has favored me with you! But now Ts'ao Ts'ao possesses Yüan Shao's legions and the troops of Chingchou as well. It looks as if there is no way we can resist."

Lu Su: "From Chiang Hsia I have brought Chuko Chin's younger brother, K'ung-ming. Patriarch, ask him about the strengths and weaknesses of the enemy."

A preliminary meeting with Sun Ch'üan's cabinet was arranged. Lu Su brought K'ung-ming, after reminding him again not to mention the size of Ts'ao Ts'ao's force.

The civilities performed all around, Chang Chao opened the questioning. "I am an official of small consequence, who has long heard that from the security of Lung Chung you compare yourself to Kuan Chung and Yo I. Is there any truth to it?"

K'ung-ming: "I have found some slight basis for comparison."

Chang Chao: "They say that Liu Pei solicited you three times from that thatched hut and felt so favored to get you that he compared it to a fish gaining water and dreamed of rolling up

K'ung-ming's verbal warfare

Chingchou in the palm of his hand. Only we wake up to find that it belongs to Ts'ao Ts'ao. We are anxious for the opportunity to evaluate your conception of the situation."

K'ung-ming knew that Chang Chao was Sun Ch'üan's chief adviser, the man he had to confound or there was no hope of convincing Ch'üan himself. So he replied: "Oh, in my view, taking the territory would have been as easy as turning over the palm. But my lord, Liu Pei, conducts himself in a humane and ethical way. He could not bear to steal a kinsman's estate and vigorously declined it. The adolescent Liu Ts'ung, taken in by insidious counsel, secretly surrendered himself and as a result was devoured by Ts'ao Ts'ao. My sovereign is stationed at Chiang Hsia and has some worthwhile prospects of his own which it is not necessary to mention here."

Chang Chao: "Then, master, your word is at variance with your deed. For the men you are wont to compare yourself to led their lords to sovereignty in their time—and so set the empire to rights. But you, master, were in your thatched hut, playfully indifferent as the breeze and the moon, or else profoundly absorbed in your meditations. But after you entered Liu Pei's service, we expected you to promote the welfare of the living souls of the realm and to root out and exterminate sedition and treason. Before Liu Pei obtained your services, he was scrambling all over, holding onto any walled and moated town he could get. Now that he has you, people are looking up to him. Even children are saying that the striped tiger is growing wings, and that we will be witness to the restoration of the Han and the elimination of the Ts'aos. Old public servants of the Court, recluses from the mountain forests rub their eyes in expectation, imagining that the salvation of the people, the deliverance of the empire is coming in their time.

"One can only wonder why, since you committed yourself to Liu Pei, everything has gone wrong. The moment Ts'ao Ts'ao's armies appeared, the shields were flung down, the spears cast aside, and he scurried where he sensed safety, unable either to fulfill his obligations to Liu Piao and secure his populace, or to sustain Liu Ts'ung in the defense of his land. After that, Liu Pei quit Hsin Yeh, fled Fan, lost Tang Yang, and bolted to Hsia K'ou for refuge. But no one will have him! So we see that Liu Pei was better off before you came. Is that what Kuan Chung and Yo I were like? Kindly forgive my simple frankness."

K'ung-ming smiled through closed lips. Then he spoke: "The

great roc ranges a myriad leagues. Can the common world of fowls appreciate its ambition? When a man is gravely ill, he must be fed weak gruel and medicated with mild tonics until his internal state is readjusted and balanced, and his condition gradually stabilizes. Only then can meat be added to his diet and powerful drugs used to cure him. Thus is the root of the disease eradicated, and the man's health regained. If you do not wait until breath and pulse are calm and steady but precipitously use powerful drugs with an overwhelming taste, such an attempt to preserve health is sure to fail.

"When my lord suffered defeat at Ju Nan, he threw himself on Liu Piao's mercy. He had less than a thousand men and no generals save Lord Kuan, Chang Fei, and Chao Yün. At this point he was virtually crippled. Hsin Yeh was a small town away in the mountains, with few people and scant grain. It was no more than a temporary refuge. Could he really stay there and defend it? Yet look how, with poor weapons, vulnerable city walls, untrained forces, and day-to-day shortages of grain, we burned Ts'ao out at Po Wang and flooded him at White River, putting Hsia-hou Tun and Ts'ao Jen into panic and dismay. I am not sure that Kuan Chung and Yo I surpassed us in warfare. As for Liu Ts'ung's surrender to Ts'ao Ts'ao, the truth is that Liu Pei knew nothing of it. Nor could he bear to exploit the confusion and steal a kinsman's estate. This is indeed great humanity and devotion to ethical duty. In the case of the Tang Yang defeat, Liu Pei saw that he had several hundred thousand devoted subjects—old and young all in the procession—whom he could not leave to their fate. Though making but ten leagues a day, he did not think of running ahead and capturing Chiang Ling but was content to suffer the defeat with the people, another instance of his humanity and ethics.

"The few cannot oppose the many, and victory or defeat is the common fate of soldiers. The founder of the Han was often defeated by Hsiang Yü, but was not his final victory due to Han Hsin's sound strategy? Han Hsin, who in his long service had no impressive record of victories! For the grand strategy of the commonwealth, the security of our national altars, truly there is a master plan. It is a plan utterly different from those of your boasting rhetoricians, whose empty reputations overawe people, who have no peer in armchair debate and standing discussions, but who cannot approach the crisis and respond to its rapid development. What a farce to amuse the world!"

To this discourse Chang Chao could make no reply. But another rose to the challenge. "Ts'ao Ts'ao has one hundred legions and one thousand commanders, prancing like dragons, glaring like tigers. They could swallow Chiang Hsia with ease. What are you going to do about it?"

K'ung-ming: "Ts'ao Ts'ao took Yüan Shao's soldiers who were clustered like ants, and stole Liu Piao's host who converged thick as crows. But even his million are not worth worrying about."

The reply: "Your forces were ruined at Tang Yang. Your plans came to naught at Hsia K'ou. You are looking for any scrap of help you can find, and yet you say 'Don't worry.' This is boastful deceit."

K'ung-ming: "How can Liu Pei hold off a million murderous men with a few thousand troops dedicated to humanity and justice? We retired to Hsia K'ou to bide our time. In the Southland the men are well trained and the grain is plentiful. The Yangtze is a natural defense, and yet, giving no thought to the disgrace and mockery of it, you would have your lord crook his knee and submit to a traitor. As I judge it, Liu Pei is not one to fear the charlatan Ts'ao." His critic made no reply.

Another rose to ask: "Are you not emulating those seductive diplomats of times past, Chang I and Su Ch'in, in an effort to prevail upon our country to serve your own ends?"

K'ung-ming: "You take them for mere rhetoricians and forget that they were men of distinguished achievement holding the highest state office, men who gave counsel that enlightened and fortified their governments. They were hardly like those who cringe before the mighty and victimize the weak, cowering at the sword's blade. You honorable gentlemen, hearing that Ts'ao Ts'ao had issued certain deceptive statements, urged surrender with craven dispatch. Are you the ones to mock Chang I and Su Ch'in?" The man fell silent.

Another asked: "K'ung-ming, what is your view of Ts'ao Ts'ao?"

K'ung-ming: "A traitor to the Han. Do you need to ask?"

The man: "You are in error, sir. In the passage of the calendar of Han to this day, its Heaven-ordained number comes to term. Already Ts'ao Ts'ao has possession of two-thirds of the empire, and all men tender him allegiance. Liu Pei refuses to recognize the season of history, and in forcing the issue is like the egg dashed against the rock."

K'ung-ming responded stridently: "How can you offer arguments that negate both king and father? In man's short life between Heaven and Earth, loyalty and filial love are the foundation of personal integrity. Since, sir, you are a subject of the Han, when you see a man who disavows his duty as a subject, you should vow to join in his extermination, for such is a true subject's obligation. Ts'ao Ts'ao, who profited in office under the Han, unmindful of his debt, bore within him a seditious usurper's heart, to the common indignation. When you tender him allegiance on the ground of 'Heaven-ordained number,' you deny king and father and are not worth talking to. I pray you, do not speak again."

Another from the council picked up the argument. "Though Ts'ao Ts'ao enjoins the nobles through coercion of the Emperor, yet he is a descendant of the great Prime Minister Ts'ao Shen. Though Liu Pei claims descent from King Ching, it has never actually been verified. As far as one can tell, he is a mere mat-weaver, a sandal merchant, hardly a worthy contender with Ts'ao Ts'ao!"

K'ung-ming: "If Ts'ao Ts'ao is the descendant of the great Prime Minister Ts'ao, then for all these generations the Ts'aos have been the subjects of the Han. Now for a Ts'ao to monopolize power and recklessly wield it, deceiving and abusing prince and father, is more than the negation of the king; it is the nullification of the sacred ancestor. This makes Ts'ao more than a seditious subject to the Han; it makes him a traitorous son to Ts'ao! Liu Pei has the full dignity of the imperial scion; he is a man whom the present Emperor granted recognized status in accordance with the official genealogy. Why do you say there is no 'verification'? Consider further that Kao Tsu, the first Emperor, began his career as a precinct magistrate and in the end took possession of the empire. What is there to be ashamed of in mat-weaving or sandal selling? Your puerile point of view makes you an unworthy participant in the discussions of distinguished scholars."

K'ung-ming had confounded the Southland's political elite in debate. Lu Su now brought him to private audience with Sun Ch'üan.

On the way K'ung-ming encountered his elder brother, Chuko Chin. K'ung-ming saluted him ceremonially, and Chin said: "Worthy younger brother, why have you not come to see me since your arrival in the Southland?"

K'ung-ming: "As I am in the service of Liu Pei, it is reasonable and proper that my public duties take precedence. I cannot attend to private ones until they have been concluded. I beg forgiveness."

*　　　*　　　*　　　*

Lu Su led K'ung-ming to see Sun Ch'üan and stood beside him as he conveyed Liu Pei's intentions. K'ung-ming stole a glance at Sun Ch'üan, an imposing presence with greenish eyes and dark red beard. He thought: "His appearance is striking. He can be incited but not won over by argument. But I cannot do it until he questions me."

When the tea service was completed, Sun Ch'üan said: "Lu Su has so often mentioned your talents, and now that we have the good fortune to meet you, I make bold to seek the benefit of your teaching."

K'ung-ming: "This incompetent one lacks any learning and could only embarrass your enlightened questions."

Ch'üan: "You were recently in Hsin Yeh assisting Liu Pei in strategic decisions for the war with Ts'ao Ts'ao. You must have profound knowledge of Ts'ao's military position."

K'ung-ming: "Liu Pei's forces are paltry, his generals scarce. On top of that, Hsin Yeh was small and nearly without grain. How could he hold off Ts'ao Ts'ao?"

Ch'üan: "How many men does Ts'ao Ts'ao have?"

K'ung-ming: "Mounted, foot, and naval, all told—over one million."

Ch'üan: "That has to be a trick!"

K'ung-ming: "No trick. He already had two hundred thousand men when he took over Yenchou. He vanquished Yüan Shao and added five or six hundred thousand. He has recently recruited three or four hundred thousand from the north central plains. And now he has gained another two or three hundred thousand from Chingchou. It adds up to no less than one and a half million. I said 'one million' for fear of scaring off your warriors."

From the side Lu Su listened stunned and pale, eyeing K'ung-ming, who pretended not to notice. Ch'üan: "And his military leaders? How many are they?"

K'ung-ming: "He has well-informed, inventive advisers and hardened, seasoned commanders; they may well number one or two thousand, or more."

Ch'üan: "Now that he has quelled the Chingchou region, has he further ambitions?"

K'ung-ming: "As of now, he has camped all along the Yangtze. If his ambition is not to take the Southland, I cannot imagine what other territory he has in mind."

Ch'üan: "If their intention is to swallow and assimilate us, must we fight, or not? I beg your judgment on this."

K'ung-ming: "I do have something to say about it, but I am afraid you will be reluctant to listen."

Ch'üan: "I would hear your esteemed judgment."

K'ung-ming: "The realm has been in turmoil for many years. That is why you roused the Southland and Liu Pei rallied his hosts south of the Han River to contest the empire with Ts'ao Ts'ao. Now Ts'ao has surmounted his greatest difficulties, and things are somewhat settled down. With his fresh triumph in Chingchou, Ts'ao overawes and shakes the entire realm. Whatever contenders there are lack the base for waging war. That is why Liu Pei made good his removal to this area. I would urge you to weigh your strength and come to a decision: If you can contend for mastery with the north, then break quickly with Ts'ao Ts'ao. If you cannot, why not follow your advisers' judgment? Lay down your arms, hang up your shields, and submit to his rule."

Before Sun Ch'üan could reply, K'ung-ming continued: "You have let it be known that you may favor submitting, but I know you are torn. If you do not take action when the situation is so precarious, disaster may be expected at any moment."

Ch'üan: "If all you say is accurate, why has not Liu Pei submitted to Ts'ao Ts'ao?"

K'ung-ming: "Even T'ien Heng of old, the stalwart loyalist, held fast to his integrity and refused to shame himself. Liu Pei is a royal scion, renowned in his time, a standard of universal admiration. If his endeavors fail, it is Heaven's doing. How could he put himself in a position of subjugation?"

His composure breaking, Sun Ch'üan swept his robes about him and left the room. The assembly dispersed, snickering. Lu Su berated K'ung-ming: "My sovereign's temper is too liberal, fortunately, to censure you publicly, but you have demeaned him by your words."

K'ung-ming tilted his head and laughed. "Why should he be so unforbearing? I have my own plan for destroying Ts'ao Ts'ao. But he did not ask me, so I did not mention it."

Lu Su: "If you actually have a sound strategy, I will ask my lord to seek your instruction."

K'ung-ming: "To me Ts'ao's host is like a crowd of ants, that I can scatter by raising my hand."

Lu Su then talked with Sun Ch'üan, whose anger had not subsided. Ch'üan: "His insolence is insufferable."

Lu Su: "I have rebuked him for this. But he chided me and said you were 'touchy.' He was reluctant to speak precipitously of his strategy for destroying Ts'ao Ts'ao. Why did you not solicit it?"

Sun Ch'üan's consternation passed, and he softened. "So he had a strategy all along. That's why he was inciting me with those statements. I was deceived by appearances for the moment and nearly spoiled everything."

Sun Ch'üan and Lu Su received K'ung-ming once again. Apologies were exchanged and wine circulated.

Ch'üan: "Ts'ao Ts'ao's lifelong enemies were Lü Pu, Liu Piao, Yüan Shao, Yüan Shu, Liu Pei, and myself. But all those contenders are no more except for Liu Pei and me. I cannot have our whole Southland subject to another's control. My plan is firm. Save Liu Pei, none can oppose Ts'ao Ts'ao. But after his fresh defeats how can he assume such tasks?"

K'ung-ming: "Though Liu Pei was recently defeated, Lord Kuan commands ten thousand elite troops, and Liu Ch'i's fighters from Chiang Hsia number no less. Ts'ao Ts'ao's host is exhausted, having come so far. In their recent pursuit of Liu Pei, their light cavalry was covering three hundred leagues in twenty-four hours. This is a case of 'When the arrow's spent, it cannot break fine silk.' Consider too that the northerners are unused to naval warfare, and that the officers and men from Chingchou follow Ts'ao by compulsion, not voluntarily. General, if you can unite hand and mind with Liu Pei, the destruction of Ts'ao's army can be guaranteed. And when he returns north, the combined strength of Chingchou and the Southland will form an independent tripodleg of power. The delicate balance between defeat and victory rests with this day. And it is yours to shape."

Ch'üan was exhilarated. "Hearing you, master, is like breaking out of a thicket and into a clearing. My mind is made up. I have no further doubts. The deliberations on raising an army to combine with Liu Pei in destroying Ts'ao Ts'ao shall begin this very day."

When Chang Chao learned of it, he said to the counselors: "He has sprung K'ung-ming's trap," and he rushed to see Sun Ch'üan. "We have heard, sovereign patriarch, that you mean to challenge Ts'ao Ts'ao. How do you think you measure up against Yüan Shao, whom Ts'ao conquered with a roll of the drums when his forces were still relatively weak? How much less may you recklessly oppose him when he has one million men at his command on a southern expedition? Listen to K'ung-ming and undertake this ridiculous mobilization, and you will be 'carrying kindling to put out the fire.' "

Sun Ch'üan lowered his head as Ku Yung supported Chang Chao: "It is because Liu Pei suffered defeat at Ts'ao Ts'ao's hands that he wants to borrow our forces to drive him back. Why be used by him, my lord?"

The opponents of the mobilization left, and Lu Su re-entered to argue in favor of it.

Sun Ch'üan dismissed everyone and retired to ponder his dilemma, with some of the military leaders advocating war and all of the civil officials advocating submission.

Lady Wu spoke to him: "What so troubles you that you forsake both food and sleep?"

Ch'üan: "Ts'ao Ts'ao is camped on the Yangtze, intent on subduing the Southland. We have put the question to our civilian and military advisers. Some would capitulate and some would wage war. If we risk the battle, I fear our fewer numbers can not stand against their greater. If we risk submission, I fear that Ts'ao Ts'ao will not accommodate our terms."

Lady Wu: "Have you forgotten my elder sister's dying words?"

K'ung-ming
Incites Chou Yü

"When an internal matter cannot be resolved, consult Chang Chao. When an external matter cannot be resolved, consult Chou Yü," said Lady Wu, recalling to Sun Ch'üan her elder sister's advice from the deathbed.

When Sun Ch'üan's summons came, Chou Yü was already on his way, for he had learned of Ts'ao Ts'ao's advance. Lu Su went ahead to brief him. "Contain your anxiety," he told Su. "I have my own view of this, but you must get K'ung-ming here for a meeting." Lu Su left to find him.

Chou Yü was about to rest after his journey when a group led by Chang Chao was announced. Chou Yü went straight to the reception chamber and seated himself punctiliously. The amenities concluded, Chang Chao spoke: "You have been informed how things stand with us?"

Yü: "Not yet."

Chao: "Ts'ao commands a million-man host camped on the river. Yesterday he summoned our sovereign patriarch to join his hunting party at Chiang Hsia. Though he means to gobble us up, what form it will take is not yet clear. We have been urging the patriarch to submit in hopes of sparing the Southland the catastrophe of invasion. Who would have thought Lu Su would bring Liu Pei's military director, K'ung-ming, down from Chiang Hsia? He has his own scores to settle and will make a point of riling the patriarch with his all too convincing arguments. Lu Su for his part clings to illusions and does not wake up. And so it is you we are counting on to settle things once for all."

Yü: "You have a consensus among you, gentlemen?"

Chao: "We have conferred and do concur."

Yü: "Such has been my own wish for some time. I beg you all to return. Early tomorrow I am to present myself before the patriarch. And then the debate will be settled accordingly."

Chao and his delegation excused themselves and left.

Soon Ch'eng P'u, representing the military faction, came to see Chou Yü. P'u: "Have you heard that soon the Southland must lose its independence and be annexed to another power?"

Yü: "I have not been so informed."

P'u: "We have followed the Suns in the founding and development of this estate through battles great and small. Only now have we come into the full possession of the towns and waterworks of our six districts. What a shameful deed if the patriarch should heed the counsel of those who would surrender. We prefer death to disgrace, and we hope you will convince the patriarch to muster the troops in a cause to which we dedicate our utmost."

Yü: "Is there consensus among you, generals?"

One of them arose and struck his palm to his temple, swearing, "Let my head roll before I submit." The group echoed the oath.

Yü: "To decide the issue by combat is precisely what I desire. How could I acquiesce in surrender? I beg you, return, and after I meet with the patriarch the debate will be settled accordingly."

No sooner had the war faction left than a party of civil officers led by Chuko Chin came to call. Chuko Chin: "My younger brother, K'ung-ming, brings word that Liu Pei seeks to join with us in operations against Ts'ao Ts'ao. But our civil and military authorities remain locked in debate. Since my own brother comes as Liu Pei's representative, I stayed out of the discussions, biding my time until you came to settle the question."

Yü: "What is your own assessment?"

Chin: "Submission gains an easy security. The outcome of battle is hard to guarantee."

Yü: "I will have some proposals to offer. Join us tomorrow at the patriarch's chambers, where we shall settle it."

As Chuko Chin retired, another party was announced, led by Lü Meng and Kan Ning. Some insisted on surrender, some were determined to fight. When the group departed, bearing the same answer as the others, a cold smile remained on Chou Yü's face.

That evening Lu Su brought K'ung-ming to pay his respects. Chou Yü came forth to the gate to escort them in. Lu Su: "Ts'ao has launched an offensive against the Southland, and between the two courses, war or peace, our sovereign patriarch cannot decide. In this matter he is yours entirely. And I would inquire what your own view is."

Chou Yü: "Ts'ao Ts'ao acts in the name of the Son of Heaven. His host cannot be withstood. And with the growth of his influence he cannot easily be engaged. If we fight, defeat is certain. If we surrender, security is cheaply bought. I have formed my opinion. Tomorrow before the patriarch I shall advocate sending a representative to convey our submission."

Lu Su was appalled. "But this is most misguided! The estate we have founded now spans three generations. How can we consign it to strangers overnight? The dying words of the patriarch's mother were to entrust external matters to you. And now, at the very moment we must look to you to preserve the state, to serve as our dependable Mount T'ai—what will become of us if you follow the counsel of cowards?"

Yü: "The living souls in our six districts are more than can be numbered. If we bring upon them the disasters of war they will lay their grievance to us. That is why I have formed a plan to sue for peace. Nothing remains to be said."

Su: "Not so! Not so! With a general of your mettle and the sure defensibility of the land, Ts'ao is far from assured of fulfilling his ambitions."

The two men argued round and round while K'ung-ming looked on immobile, smiling with sangfroid. "What makes you smile so disdainfully?" said Chou Yü.

K'ung-ming: "What but your antagonist, Lu Su, who refuses to recognize the exigencies of the occasion."

Su: "What do you mean, perversely to mock me for 'refusing to recognize the exigencies of the occasion'?"

K'ung-ming: "My brother, Chin, has made up his mind in favor of submission, as seems perfectly reasonable."

Chou Yü: "Any scholar who understands the exigencies of the times—and K'ung-ming is surely one—must be of the same mind."

"Then even you can argue this way?" said Lu Su to K'ung-ming.

K'ung-ming: "Ts'ao is a master of warfare, whom none in the empire dares engage. Those who did, Lü Pu, Yüan Shao, Yüan Shu, and Liu Piao, have been annihilated, and there are no others —save Liu Pei, who has refused to 'recognize the exigencies of the occasion' and contends with Ts'ao for mastery. But now he stands alone in Chiang Hsia, where his very survival is in question. The plan you have formed to submit to Ts'ao ensures the safety of your kinfolk and provides for maintaining your wealth and status. And if the sacrificial services are to be removed elsewhere, why—ascribe it to the mandate of Heaven. Need we burden our memories with these things?"

Lu Su was moved to wrath: "What! You would see our sovereign crook his knees and endure disgrace before a treasonous rogue?"

K'ung-ming: "I *have* thought of another possibility that might well spare us the 'leading over our flocks and bearing over our wine jars; transferring our lands and tendering the seal of state.' You would not even need to cross the river yourself, but merely to send a solitary representative to escort two persons to the opposite shore. If Ts'ao Ts'ao can get hold of these two, his million-fold host will unhook their shields, furl their banners, and retire."

Chou Yü: "And with what two persons do you propose to effect this reversal?"

K'ung-ming: "For the Southland to part with these two persons may be likened to an oak shedding a leaf, a granary diminished by a grain of wheat. Yet if he gets them, Ts'ao will depart content."

Chou Yü: "Well, what two persons?"

K'ung-ming: "When I was in residence at Lung Chung, I heard that Ts'ao was building a new tower on the banks of the Chang. It was called the Bronze Sparrow Tower—an absolutely magnificent edifice! Elegant! They searched far and wide for beautiful women to fill the chambers (for Ts'ao is basically of the type inclined to wantonness). Well, Ts'ao had known for some time that in the Southland the two daughters of the patriarch Ch'iao were beauties whose faces would amaze the world of nature, abash the very blossoms, and outshine the moon. And Ts'ao vowed, 'My first desire is to sweep and calm the realm to consummate the imperial endeavor. My second is to possess the two daughters Ch'iao of the Southland and install them in my tower to pleasure my late years. Then, even death would bring no regret.' Ts'ao may lead his million-fold host to menace the Southland, but in reality it is for the sake of these two women. General, seek out the patriarch Ch'iao, procure his girls with gold, and dispatch someone to deliver them to Ts'ao. When he has them, his satisfied wish guarantees the retreat. Why not act at once?"

Chou Yü: "Can you verify Ts'ao's desire to possess these two women?"

K'ung-ming: "He once commissioned his youngest son, Chih, to compose the 'Bronze Sparrow Tower Ode,' in which he declared his fitness for sovereignty and his vow to wive Ch'iao's daughters."

Chou Yü: "Can you recall it?"

K'ung-ming: "Infatuated with its florid elegance, I presumed to commit it to memory."

Chou Yü: "May I request a recitation?"

K'ung-ming then recited:

> Resplendent Queen attending rapture's transport,
> Mounting the tiered tower for pleasure's consummation,
> Surveying the Palace's unfolding prospects,
> Which your royal virtue surrounds.
> Sky-piercing gates erected,
> Double pylons touch the Crystalline,
> Splendid observatory raised to midair,
> Linked lofty chambers over the western capital,
> Overlooking the ever-flowing Chang,
> Whose gardens promise increasing glories.
> And raised high along: twin towers—
> Left, Jade Dragon; Right, Gold Phoenix,
> To keep the Southland's daughters Ch'iao,
> For their pleasure, morning-evening.
> Look down! on the capital's spacious elegance.
> Birdlike, we peer through shimmer of rose-cloud,
> Gratified by the confluence of many talents,
> And by auguring dreams of greater power.
> Look up! the gentle solemnity of spring!
> Hear! heart-forlorn cries of a myriad birds!
> The empyrean stretches over what already stands
> As we seek a twin fulfillment for our House.
> Casting benevolent influence wide through the realm,
> Winning all homage for the capital.
> Even the splendor of earlier kings
> Pales beside this sagely glory.
> Divine Grace! So excellent!
> Compassion, generosity cast abroad.
> Uphold the sovereign House
> That the four quarters may know content.
> Our king is measured even as the Heavens and the Earth,
> He resembles the radiance of sun and moon.
> Ever honor-nobled without limit,

Immortal as the sky's sovereign star,
Driving the dragon banners round the imperial circuit,
Reining the phoenix chariot round the realm,
His clement influence touches the kingdom's corners.
Prize offerings to him heap high—the people prosper.
May this tower stand ever firm
For pleasures without end and for all time.

When K'ung-ming's performance was done, Chou Yü started from his seat and pointed north: "Traitor! Rogue that abuses us beyond enduring."

K'ung-ming arose, swift to check him: "Of old, when the Hunnish Khan encroached our border, the Emperor of Han would grant him a princess to forge amity through kinship. Can we not now spare two female commoners?"

Chou Yü: "There is something you are not aware of. The elder daughter of the patriarch Ch'iao was the first wife of Sun Ts'e, the sovereign patriarch's elder brother. The younger daughter is my own wife."

K'ung-ming looked astonished. "Truly, I did not know it. I have blundered unforgivably, dreadfully. It is a capital offense!"

Chou Yü: "Ts'ao, old traitor, you and I cannot share footing on this earth. So I swear."

K'ung-ming: "The situation requires cautious deliberation lest our actions entail regret."

Chou Yü: "I hold our late sovereign's solemn trust. Surrender to Ts'ao cannot be justified. What I said just before was indeed only to test you. Since I left the Po Yang lake, my one thought has been to take up arms against the north. The executioner's axe upon my neck could not alter this resolve. May I hope for your stout aid, that we may together smite the traitor Ts'ao?"

K'ung-ming: "If you favor me by accepting my service, I would emulate the toil of the ox and stand ready and attentive to your offensive strategy."

Chou Yü: "Tomorrow I present myself to the patriarch to debate the mustering of troops."

K'ung-ming and Lu Su departed their separate ways.

The morning of the next day, Sun Ch'üan ascended the hall of assembly. To his left were the civil officials led by Chang Chao and Ku Yung; to his right, the military led by Ch'eng P'u and Huang Kai. Chou Yü entered and, the amenities concluded, spoke:

"They say that Ts'ao Ts'ao is stationed on the river Han and that his letter has arrived here. I wonder, patriarch, what your own honorable wishes are in this matter?"

Sun Ch'üan passed the letter to Chou Yü, who smiled. "To approach us so derisively, the rogue must imagine that we have no men worthy of the name in the Southland!"

Ch'üan: "What is your own view, my lord?"

Yü: "Has the patriarch discussed it thoroughly with the officers and officials?"

Ch'üan: "For days on end. Some advocate submission and some war. Because I have not yet reached a final decision, I appeal to you to resolve it once for all."

Yü: "Who are those urging submission?"

Ch'üan mentioned Chang Chao who, when questioned, reiterated his arguments, closing: "It is better to submit for now and go on to plot future tactics."

Chou Yü replied: "Such is the convoluted judgment of pedants! Now, in the third generation since the founding of the Southland, how could we bear to throw it all away overnight?"

Ch'üan: "So then, what is your grand strategy to be based on?"

Chou Yü: "Posing as Chancellor of the Han, Ts'ao is in fact a traitor. But you, General, with a god's martial skill and your father's and your brother's estate under you, have possession of the Southland. Your troops are keen, your grain stores ample. This is the right moment to give yourself scope in the empire and dispel cruelty and violence for the sake of home and country. How futile to submit to the traitor! Furthermore, Ts'ao, by coming here, has broken the most sacred rules of military science. His north is still untamed, and while Ma T'eng and Han Sui threaten his rear, he takes too long on his southern campaign. That's the first sacred rule. His troops are unused to naval warfare, yet Ts'ao has put by his saddle steeds and takes to his boats to strive with our mariners. That's the second sacred rule. Now the height of winter is upon us, and the horses lack food. That's the third sacred rule. He has driven the northmen far afield to the rivers and lakes —unfamiliar terrain where disease is rife. That's the fourth sacred rule. And so, however numerous his men, they will be defeated. This is the day that you will take Ts'ao Ts'ao captive. I appeal to you for a few thousand crack troops to proceed to Hsia K'ou and destroy them!"

Sun Ch'üan arose, his eyes flashing: "Long, too long, has he sought to remove the Han and establish his own house. Of those whom he had to be wary of, none remains save us. I, this solitary orphan, and a traitor—one of us must fall. That is my oath. Friend, your voice for war meets my own thought. You must have come to me through Heaven!"

Chou Yü: "As your servant I would resolve upon a bloody course of war. I shrink from no extremity but that I fear, General, you remain undecided."

Ch'üan drew his sword and sheared off a corner of a table. "Whoso speaks again for submission will be dealt with so." Then he gave the sword to Chou Yü and appointed him chief commandant. Ch'eng P'u and Lu Su were made his assistants.

Now that the debate was settled, Chou Yü summoned K'ung-ming to ask his advice.

K'ung-ming: "His conviction remains unsteady, and thus we may not determine the strategy."

Chou Yü: "What do you mean, 'His conviction remains unsteady'?"

K'ung-ming: "At heart he still shrinks before the size of Ts'ao's army, convinced that the few cannot withstand the many. You will have to make him perfectly confident on this point before our great endeavor can be fulfilled." Chou Yü went back to Sun Ch'üan, who confessed his anxiety over the numerical imbalance.

Chou Yü: "It is on this very point that I have come to reconcile you." Speaking with eloquence, Chou Yü succeeded in dispelling his sovereign's doubts. However, he observed inwardly: "K'ung-ming divined my lord's state of mind so early that his strategy too will be superior to mine. In the long run his brilliance bodes danger, and we might do well to kill him now." He confided his thoughts to Lu Su.

As the armies of Ts'ao Ts'ao and Sun Ch'üan moved into position, the rivalry between Chou Yü and K'ung-ming became volatile—a sign of the fragility of the alliance between Liu Pei and Sun Ch'üan. For both sought to possess Chingchou, Ts'ao Ts'ao's present base.

Sun Ch'üan summoned Liu Pei to the Southland intending, over Lu Su's objections, to assassinate him. But Sun was intimidated by Kuan Yü and failed to give the signal, and Liu Pei returned to Chingchou.

During Liu Pei's brief visit to the Southland, K'ung-

ming arranged to have Chao Yün sail downriver and pick him up near the South Screen Mountains on the twentieth day of the eleventh month. "When the south wind comes up," K'ungming said, "I shall return."

Spies and counterspies moved between the northern and the southern battle lines. Ts'ao Ts'ao sent an old friend of Chou Yü's south to gather intelligence. Chou Yü planted false information with him concerning the loyalty of Ts'ai Mao, Ts'ao Ts'ao's Chingchou naval commander. The ruse succeeded. The friend returned to Ts'ao Ts'ao and transmitted the fatal information. Ts'ao Ts'ao executed Ts'ai Mao and thus left himself deficient in naval leadership.

K'ung-ming
Borrows Some Arrows

Chou Yü sent Lu Su to K'ung-ming to see if he had detected the subterfuge by which Ts'ai Mao was eliminated.

Lu Su: "Day after day I am taken up with military concerns and miss your good advice."

K'ung-ming: "Rather, I am the tardy one, having yet to convey my felicitations to the chief commandant Chou Yü!"

Lu Su: "What felicitations?"

"Why, for that very thing he sent you to ask whether I knew." The color left Lu Su's face. "But where did you learn of it, master?"

K'ung-ming: "The subterfuge was good enough to fool the messenger. As for Ts'ao Ts'ao, though he was hoodwinked this time, he will realize it quickly enough—except that he won't admit the mistake, that's all. But with the naval adviser dead the Southland has no major worry, so congratulations are certainly in order! But I hope you won't mention to Chou Yü that I knew about this beforehand, lest he become jealous and seek to do me harm."

Lu Su agreed, but could not help telling the whole truth to Chou Yü, who said in alarm: "We absolutely cannot let this man stay. I am determined to kill him."

Lu Su: "If you do, you will be the mockery of Ts'ao Ts'ao."

Chou Yü: "No, I can do it openly and legitimately. Wait and see."

The next day in the assembly of generals, Chou Yü asked

—

K'ung-ming: "When we engage Ts'ao Ts'ao in battle, crossing arms on the river routes, what weapon should be our first choice?"

K'ung-ming: "On the Yangtze, the bow and arrow."

Chou Yü: "Precisely. But we happen to be short of arrows. Dare I trouble you, master, to take responsibility for the production of one hundred thousand shafts? This is a public service which you would favor me by not declining."

K'ung-ming: "Whatever you assign I will strive to achieve. Dare I ask by what time you will require them?"

Chou Yü: "Can you finish in ten days?"

K'ung-ming: "Ts'ao's army will arrive any moment. If we wait ten days, it will spoil everything."

Chou Yü: "How many days do you estimate you need, master?"

K'ung-ming: "It will take only three before I can respectfully deliver the arrows."

Chou Yü: "There is no room for levity in the army."

K'ung-ming: "Dare I trifle with the chief commander? I beg to submit my oath in writing. Then if I fail to finish in three days, I deserve the maximum punishment."

This elated Chou Yü, who accepted the document.

K'ung-ming: "On the third day from tomorrow, send five hundred small craft to the river to transport the arrows."

After K'ung-ming left, Chou Yü said to Lu Su: "I will have the artisans delay things intentionally, just to be sure that he misses the appointed time. But go to him and bring me back information."

Lu Su went to K'ung-ming, who said: "I *did* tell you not to speak of this to Chou Yü. He is determined to kill me. I never dreamed you would refuse to cover for me. And now today he actually pulled this thing on me! How am I supposed to produce one hundred thousand arrows in three days? You're the only one who can save me."

Lu Su: "You brought this on yourself. How could I save you?"

K'ung-ming: "I need you to lend me twenty vessels, with a crew of thirty for each. On the boats I want curtains of black cloth to conceal at least a thousand bales of straw that should be lined up on both sides. But you must not let Chou Yü know about it this time, or my plan will fail." And Lu Su obliged him, and even held his tongue.

The boats were ready, but neither on the first day nor on the second did K'ung-ming make any move. On the third day he secretly sent for Lu Su: "I called you especially to go with me to get the arrows." And linking the vessels with long ropes, they set out for the north shore and Ts'ao Ts'ao's fleet.

That night tremendous fogs rolled over the heavens, and the river mists were impenetrable. People could not see their companions who were directly in front of them. K'ung-ming urged his boats on.

From the ode "Great Mists Overhanging the Yangtze":

> Everywhere the fog, stock still:
> Not even a cartload can be spotted.
> All-obscuring grey vastness,
> Massive, without horizon.
> Whales hurtle over waves, and
> Dragons plunge and spew up mist.
> East they lose the shore at Chai Sang,
> South the mountains of Hsia K'ou.
> Are we returning to the state without form—
> To undivided Heaven and Earth?

At the fifth watch the boats were already nearing Ts'ao Ts'ao's river stations. K'ung-ming had the vessels lined up in single file, their prows pointed west. Then the crews began to volley with their drums and roar with their voices.

Lu Su was alarmed: "What do you propose if Ts'ao's men make a coordinated sally?"

K'ung-ming smiled: "I would be very surprised if Ts'ao Ts'ao dared plunge into this heavy a fog. Let us attend to the wine and take our pleasure. When the fog breaks we will return."

In his encampment, Ts'ao Ts'ao listened to the drumming and shouting. His new naval advisers rushed back and forth with bulletins. Ts'ao sent down an order: "The fog is so heavy it obscures the river. Enemy forces have arrived from nowhere. There must be an ambush. Our men must make absolutely no reckless movements. But let the archers fire upon the enemy at random." The naval advisers, fearing that the forces of the Southland were about to breach the camp, ordered the firing to commence. Soon over ten thousand men were concentrating their fire toward the center of the river, and the arrows came down like rain. K'ung-ming ordered the boats to reverse direction and press closer to the shore to take the arrows, while the crews continued their drumming and shouting.

K'ung-ming borrows some arrows

When the sun rose high, dispersing the fog, K'ung-ming ordered the boats to rush homeward. The grass bales in gunnysacks bristled with arrow shafts. And K'ung-ming had each crew shout its thanks to the Chancellor for the arrows as it passed. By the time the reports reached Ts'ao Ts'ao, the light craft borne on swift currents were beyond overtaking, and Ts'ao Ts'ao was left with the agony of having played the fool.

K'ung-ming said to Lu Su: "Each boat has some five or six thousand arrows. So without costing the Southland the slightest effort, we have gained over one hundred thousand arrows, which tomorrow we can return to Ts'ao's troops—to their decided discomfort."

Lu Su: "You are supernatural! How did you know there would be such a fog today?"

K'ung-ming: "A military commander must be versed in the patterns of the Heavens, must recognize the advantages of the terrain, must appreciate the odd chance, must understand the changes of the weather, must examine the maps of the formations, must be clear about the disposition of the troops—otherwise he is a mediocrity! Three days ago I calculated today's fog. That's why I took a chance on the three-day limit. Chou Yü gave me ten days, but neither materials nor workmen, and plainly meant for my flagrant offense to kill me. But my fate is linked to Heaven. How could Chou Yü succeed?" When Chou Yü received Lu Su's report, he was amazed and resigned. "I cannot begin to approach his uncanny machinations and subtle calculations!"

When K'ung-ming came to Chou Yü, he was received with cordial admiration. "Master, we must defer to your superhuman powers of calculation."

K'ung-ming: "A petty subterfuge of common cunning, not worth your compliments."

Chou Yü: "Yesterday my sovereign urged us to advance. But I still lack the unexpected stratagem that wins the battle. I appeal for your instruction."

K'ung-ming: "I am a run-of-the-mill mediocrity. What kind of surprise are you looking for?"

Chou Yü: "Yesterday I surveyed Ts'ao's naval stations. They are the epitome of strict order, all according to the book, invulnerable to any routine attack. I have one idea, but—"

K'ung-ming: "Refrain from speaking for a moment. We'll each write on our palms to see whether we agree or not." Each wrote, masking his word. They opened their hands together and laughed: the word was *fire*.

> *Exasperated by the loss of the arrows, unnerved by his vulnerability on the water, Ts'ao Ts'ao sent a trusted friend to the Southland to gain information.*
>
> *At Chou Yü's direction, the unemployed military strategist P'ang T'ung (another name of Phoenix Chick) succeeded in persuading Ts'ao's friend that he was disaffected and willing to serve Ts'ao Ts'ao. Knowing how eager Ts'ao was for guidance in naval warfare, the friend arranged for P'ang T'ung to be introduced to Ts'ao Ts'ao and for Ts'ao Ts'ao to receive another "defector," Huang Kai.*

P'ang T'ung's Advice

Ts'ao Ts'ao said to P'ang T'ung: "Chou Yü is immature; he counts on his ability, but wrongs the populace and rejects sound strategy. Your fame has long been known to me, and now that we enjoy your favorable regard, I hope you will not deny me advice and instruction."

P'ang T'ung: "People have always said that your use of military forces sets the standard, but I would like to check over the features of your deployment."

Ts'ao Ts'ao took P'ang T'ung to a hilltop. As they looked over the scene, P'ang T'ung said: "Alongside a mountain, backed up against a forest, lookouts front and back, gates of exit and entry, indirect courses of advance or retreat—even if the ancient masters of the art of war were reborn, they could not surpass it!"

Ts'ao Ts'ao: "Master, you should not praise me so profusely. I still look to you for improvement."

Again P'ang T'ung cast his eyes south over the naval stations. There were twenty-four breaks in the shore and in each, rammers and warboats were laid out like a city wall, within which clustered small craft. For passage there were channels, and everything proceeded in good order. P'ang T'ung smiled. "Chancellor, if your use of forces is like this, your reputation has not preceded you for nothing!" And P'ang T'ung pointed across the river and cried: "Chou, Chou my friend! Now comes the time; you are doomed."

Immensely pleased, Ts'ao returned to camp and invited P'ang T'ung into his tent to share his wine and tell tales of military machinations. P'ang T'ung spoke with profundity and defended his points heroically, fluent in all his responses. Ts'ao felt his admiration and respect deepen and treated his guest with diligent hospitality.

Feigning intoxication, P'ang T'ung said: "I am wondering if there are good medical services for the troops. There is much illness among the sailors, and good physicians are needed to cure them."

The truth was that at the time Ts'ao's men, unable to adjust to the southern latitude, all were seized with nausea and vomiting, and many had died. Ts'ao had been preoccupied with the problem. T'ung continued: "Your methods for training a navy are superb—only, unfortunately, something is missing." Ts'ao Ts'ao importuned him until T'ung replied: "There is a way to free the sailors of their ailments and make them steady and capable of success." Ts'ao was delighted and eager to learn.

P'ang T'ung continued: "On the great river the tide swells and recedes. The wind and the waves never cease. These northern troops, unaccustomed to shipboard, suffer from the pitching and rolling. This is the cause of their ailment. Reorganize your small and large vessels so that they are marshaled in groups of thirty or fifty and linked fast with iron chains, stem to stem and stern to stern. Then if wide planks are laid so that horses as well as men can cross from ship to ship, however rough the waves or steep the tides there need be no further concern."

Ts'ao Ts'ao came off his mat and expressed his gratitude on his knees. "Master, if it were not for your sound strategy I could never destroy the Southland." And Ts'ao Ts'ao ordered the suggestion implemented, to the great relief of officers and men.

P'ang T'ung offered to return to the Southland and arrange for more defections. Ts'ao Ts'ao granted him safe passage and protection for his family. But as T'ung was about to embark, he saw a man on the shore in the tunic of a Taoist priest who detained him, saying:

"Your audacity is remarkable! Kan Tse delivers the false letter announcing Huang Kai's defection, and now you submit the plan for linking the boats—your only concern being that the flames might not consume everything! Such insidious mischief may be enough to take in Ts'ao Ts'ao, but it won't work on me!" And P'ang T'ung's heart quailed as his cloud-soul escaped upward and his earth-spirit departed from him in fear.

The
Celebration on the Yangtze;
Ts'ao's Ode

The speaker turned out to be Tan Fu, and when P'ang T'ung recognized his old friend he became calm. "If you expose the plans, it entails misfortune for the good common folk of the Southland's eighty-one districts."

Tan Fu: "And what of the lives and fate of the eighty-three legions over here?"

P'ang T'ung: "You mean to expose me, then?"

Tan Fu: "I am grateful for Imperial Uncle Liu's generous kindness and have always hoped to repay it. Ts'ao Ts'ao sent my mother to her death, and I promised I would never frame strategy for him. How could I expose my brother's very respectable plan? The thing is, I am a part of Ts'ao's forces, and when they are destroyed, the jewel won't be distinguished from the rock. How do I avoid disaster? You must suggest some device to save me, and I will sew up my lips and remove myself."

P'ang T'ung spoke a few phrases into Tan Fu's ear.

Tan Fu caused rumors of threats to Ts'ao Ts'ao's hold on the north to circulate. Then he managed to have himself appointed to guard a key northwestern pass.

After dispatching Tan Fu to the north, Ts'ao Ts'ao's mind was easier. He rode to the shoreline to review the stations in turn. He boarded one of the large ships and planted in its center a banner marked "Commander in Chief." On both sides the naval stations stretched out, and aboard every ship a thousand bowmen lay in wait. Ts'ao Ts'ao stood on deck. It was late in A.D. 208, the fifteenth day of the eleventh month of the thirteenth year of "Establish Security." The weather was clear and bright, the wind calm, the waves still. Ts'ao ordered a feast laid for the generals on the ship's deck. The complexion of the heavens reflected the advancing night as the moon climbed up over the eastern mountains and beamed down like the incandescent sun. The Yangtze lay slack, like a bolt of white silk unrolled.

Aboard the ship, surrounded by several hundred men fully dressed and armed, the officers and officials seated in order, Ts'ao looked at the picturesque South Screen Mountains. To the east he could see the boundary of Chai Sang; west, he contemplated the stretch of the Yangtze; south, he gazed at Mount Fan; north, he peered into the Black Forests. Wherever he turned the view stretched into infinity, gladdening his heart. He spoke to the assembly: "Since first we raised this loyalist force to join with the ruling family in dispelling evil and purging injustice, I have sworn to sweep clean the realm and, by paring and whittling, bring calm to the empire. The Southland is where we have yet to make gains. Today I possess a million heroic fighters. And relying on such as you to apply our commands, need we fear for our success? When we receive the submission of the Southland and the empire is at peace, we shall share with you the enjoyments of wealth and station to celebrate that 'Day of Great Peace.'" The generals expressed their appreciation and reiterated their commitment.

Warmed with wine, Ts'ao continued: "Liu Pei, K'ung-ming: you have not taken the measure of your ant-like strength but attempted to shake Mount T'ai. How foolish!" To his generals he said: "Now I am fifty-four. If we take the Southland I shall have my humble wish. Long ago I made an agreement with the patriarch Ch'iao, knowing that his two daughters would be national beauties. I never dreamed Sun Ts'e and Chou Yü would take them to wife. Recently I built the Bronze Sparrow Towers upon the river Chang. If I win the Southland I will take these women to wife and install them in the towers to pleasure my declining years. Thus my wishes will be satisfied." Falling silent, he smiled.

Suddenly they heard a raven cawing as it flew southward. Ts'ao said: "Why does the raven cry in the night?"

Those around him replied: "It supposes the brilliance of the moon to be the dawn. That is why it has left its tree and cries."

Ts'ao laughed again. Already drunk, he set his spear in the prow of the boat and offered wine to the river. He said: "I wielded this weapon when I smashed the Yellow Scarves, when I took Lü Pu, when I eliminated Yüan Shu, when I took possession of Yüan Shao's forces, when I penetrated to the northern outposts, and when I struck out eastward toward Korea, crisscrossing the empire. In all these endeavors my spear has never betrayed me. And now I face a prospect that fills me with high ardor of the soul. I shall compose a song, and you must join me.

"Cup to cup calls for song.
Man's life—how long?
A morning's dew? Alas!
Many a day is done—

"But bear a noble spirit
Against all haunting sorrows,
Sorrows naught allays,
Save the cup, since ancient days.

"'Green, green the youth,
Long my longing heart.'
On the king's cause
Brood without pause.

"'Loo! Halloo!' sing deer
And nibble the plain.
We have honored guests
For string and reed to cheer.

"The moon beckons afar.
Who can cull it?
And sorrow within,
What can annul it?

"Now all come their ways,
Bear hardship to join us.
Long absent ones share our feast,
Where old favor is well remembered.

"Moon swells, stars fade.
The raven flies south,
And circles a tree
That lends no shade.

"The mountain no height eschews,
The sea no deep,
Nor did the earnest Duke of Chou*
An empire's trust refuse."

* The Duke of Chou is the historic model of the loyal regent.

Ts'ao Ts'ao's recitation

As the assembly took up the singing amid general enjoyment, a man stepped forward and said: "At this juncture of confrontation for our armies, when the generals and officers must apply their commands, for what reason do you utter such ominous words?"

Ts'ao looked at him. The speaker was Liu Fu, a man long in Ts'ao Ts'ao's service and with many achievements to his credit. Ts'ao leveled his spear and asked: "What was ominous about my words?"

Liu Fu: "The stars fading as the moon brightens, the raven winging south, circling the tree three times but finding no branch —these are ominous words."

Ts'ao: "You dare to wreck our delight and enthusiasm?" With a single heave of his spear, Ts'ao Ts'ao pierced Liu Fu. He was dead. The assembly was aghast; the banquet was dismissed. When he recovered the next day, Ts'ao was wracked with remorse, and he told the son who came to claim the body that Liu Fu would be interred with the highest honors.

A few days later the naval commanders announced that the linkage of the boats was completed and the invasion could commence. The central unit flew yellow banners, the forward unit red, the rear black, the left blue, and the right white. The drums thundered through the camps, the gates parted, and Ts'ao Ts'ao's navy came forth.

The wind gusted sharply out of the northwest. The ships let out their sails, thrusting and beating upon wave and billows, yet steady as if on flat ground. On board the northmen, bounding and vaulting to display their courage, thrust their spears and plied their swords. The various units maintained ranks as small craft monitored their discipline.

Ts'ao stood in the commander's tower and surveyed the performance, immensely pleased, thinking he had found the secret of certain victory. He ordered an interim dropping of the sails, and all ships returned to the camps in good order.

Ts'ao said to his advisers: "Had divine decree not come to our aid, could we have had Phoenix Chick's ingenious plan? With iron bonds linking the ships, we can actually cross the river as if we were walking on land."

Ch'eng Yü said: "The ships are bound fast. Though they are level and stable, if the enemy attacks with fire it will be hard to escape. This must be prepared for."

Ts'ao laughed loudly. "Though you are provident, still there are things you cannot see. Any attack with fire must rely upon the force of the wind, and now at winter's depth there are only north winds and west winds. How could there be a south or an east wind? Our position is northwest, theirs all on the southern shore. If they use fire it will actually burn out their own troops. What have we to fear? Were it mid-autumn or early spring, I would have provided against fire long ago."

The generals bowed respectfully. "Your superior insight outstrips the rest of us."

Ts'ao Ts'ao: "Our hosts from the four northern regions were inexperienced as naval fighters. If not for this device, how could they have negotiated the treacherous Yangtze?"

K'ung-ming
Supplicates the Wind;
Chou Yü Unleashes the Fire

From a mountaintop Chou Yü pondered the scene. Suddenly he turned, toppled, and began to spit blood. He lost consciousness, and the general staff was thrown into confusion.

Lu Su went to see K'ung-ming. "This is a blessing for Ts'ao Ts'ao, a catastrophe for the Southland."

K'ung-ming laughed. "Such an illness even I could cure!" And he went with Lu Su to see Chou Yü.

Lu Su: "Commander, how is your condition?"

Chou Yü: "My insides feel unsettled and tender, and the spells return from time to time."

Lu Su: "What medicines have you been taking?"

Chou Yü: "I reject everything. I can't keep medicine down."

Lu Su: "I have just seen K'ung-ming. He says he can cure you. He is outside now. Do you mind if he troubles you with his remedy?" Chou Yü invited him in.

K'ung-ming: "It is many days since we met, but I never imagined that your precious health was failing."

Chou Yü: "For man, 'The morning's fortune may come to grief by evening.' There are no guarantees."

K'ung-ming smiled. "And the winds and clouds of the heavens are beyond man's ken. Who can anticipate them?"

At these words Chou Yü lost his color and made a low murmuring noise. K'ung-ming continued: "Commander, do you seem to feel aggravation gathering inside you?" Chou Yü nodded. K'ung-ming: "You must take a cooling tonic to dispel it."

Chou Yü: "I have, to no effect."

K'ung-ming: "First you must regulate the vital ethers. When the vital ethers are flowing smoothly in the proper direction, then in the course of your respiration you will naturally become whole."

Chou Yü, sensing that K'ung-ming must know his unspoken thought, teased him by saying: "To get the vital ethers flowing in the proper direction, what medicine would you recommend?"

K'ung-ming smiled. "I have a prescription to facilitate this." Taking pen and paper and waving away the attendants, he wrote:

> To break Ts'ao's back
> We need fire to attack
> Everything is set, but
> The east wind we lack!

He handed the note to Chou Yü, saying: "This is the source of the capital commander's illness!"

Chou Yü was shocked and thought: "He is truly supernatural. He realized my problem at once. I'll simply have to tell him the truth."

Chou Yü smiled. "Since you already know, what medicine shall we use to cure it? The situation is moving swiftly to a crisis, and I look for your timely advice."

K'ung-ming: "Though I myself have no talent, I once met an extraordinary man who handed on to me divine texts for tracking the numerology of the heavens. These could be used to call forth the winds and rains. When the capital commander wants a southeast wind, he should erect a tower, the Platform of the Seven Stars, on the South Screen Mountains. It should be nine feet high, with three levels, and surrounded by one hundred and twenty men holding the banners. On the platform I will perform the devices to borrow three days' and three nights' southeast winds to assist you in your operations. What do you say?"

Chou Yü: "Never mind three days' and three nights' wind! With one night's gales our endeavor could be consummated. But the crisis before us brooks no delay."

K'ung-ming: "On the twentieth day of the eleventh month— for that is the first day of the cycle—we will make an offering to the wind. By the twenty-second day, the winds will have died away."

Chou Yü was elated and ordered work on the tower begun.

Built with the ruddy earth of the southeast, it consisted of three three-foot tiers rising from an area of over one hundred square cubits.

On the lowest tier were twenty-eight flags representing the heavenly mansions. Along the eastern face were blue flags: the two Virginis, Librae, the three Scorpii, and Sagittarii—arrayed in the shape of the Sky-blue Dragon. Along the northern side, seven black flags: the second Sagittarii, Capricorn, the three Aquarii, and the two Pegasi—made in the form of the Mystic War-dancer. On the western side, seven white flags: Andromedae, the two Arietis, the two Tauri, and the two Orionis—in the menacing crouch of the White Tiger. On the southern side, seven red flags: Geminorum, Cancri, the three Hydrae, Crateris, and Corvi—making the outline of the Vermilion Sparrow.

The second tier was encompassed by sixty-four yellow flags, one for each set of oracular lines in the *Book of Changes*. On the top tier, four men with headdresses, black tunics loose-hanging, wide sashes emblematic of the phoenix, vermilion shoes, and squared kilts. At front left, one man held a long pole, fledged at the tip with chicken feathers to catch any sign of the wind. At right front K'ung-ming put a man with a long pole, the banner of the seven fixed stars fastened to the top to show the character of the wind. At left rear, a man with a prize sword; at right rear, a man with an incense burner.

On the twentieth day of the eleventh month, K'ung-ming performed the ablutions and fast and assumed the sacred vestments of a priest of the Tao. Barefoot, hair flowing behind, he came before the platform. He sent Lu Su back to the camp and told him not to be surprised if his prayers drew no response. Then he ordered the guard to observe strict order and silence.

K'ung-ming ascended with deliberate steps, marked that all stations were set, lit the incense, and poured water into a vessel. Then he stared up at the heavens and began a silent incantation. He descended and reascended three times, but there was no sign of a southeast wind.

Chou Yü, awaiting developments in his tent, kept Sun Ch'üan informed. Huang Kai, the counterfeit defector whom Ts'ao Ts'ao expected to sail across, had prepared twenty torch-ships, their prows studded with large nailheads. Within the ships were stacks of reeds and dry brambles, drenched with fish oil, overspread with an inflammable compound of sulfur and saltpeter, and all covered

K'ung-ming supplicates the wind

over with black cloth. At the prows, the notched banner of the Blue Dragon; at the stern, light craft.

Everyone watched the sky intently as evening drew on, but the heavens held clear and no wind stirred. Chou Yü said to Lu Su: "How absurd are K'ung-ming's claims! There can be no east wind in this season." But toward the third watch, they heard from nowhere the echoing voice of the wind. The pennons and banners began to loll to and fro, and when Chou Yü came out to look, the ribbons were actually fluttering northwest. Within moments a stiff gale was coming up out of the southeast.

In consternation, Chou Yü said: "This man has snatched some method from the creative force of heaven and earth, some unfathomable technic from the world of departed spirits. If we fail to do away with him, he will be the root of the Southland's downfall. He should be gotten rid of as soon as possible to prevent future ruin." Chou Yü called for two generals to take one hundred men to the Altar of the Seven Fixed Stars and behead K'ung-ming. They set out downriver against the southeast wind.

When the generals arrived, K'ung-ming was already well upriver, bound for his rendezvous with Chao Yün.

One general hailed K'ung-ming across the water: "Do not depart, director; the capital commander Chou Yü has a request to make."

K'ung-ming stood smiling in the stern of the craft. "Report back to your commander. Tell him to use his forces carefully. I am returning to Liu Pei for now, but there will be time for us to meet again."

The general: "Pray stop a moment. I have something urgent to say."

K'ung-ming: "I expected that Chou Yü would be unable to accept me. You can only be here to do me injury. But I arranged beforehand for Chao Yün to meet me, and you had best not pursue!"

But the general saw that K'ung-ming's craft had no sail, and, disregarding everything, pressed ahead. Then Chao Yün stood up in the stern of the boat and cried: "I am Chao Tzu-lung of Ch'ang Shan and bear commands to receive the military director. What do you mean by pursuing us? It would only take an arrow to cut you down, and thus openly throw away our two houses' amity. But I would like to give you a demonstration of marksmanship!" Chao Yün fitted his arrow and shot away the sail cord, causing the sail to drop into the water and the boat to spin sideways. K'ung-ming raised his sail and proceeded west.

K'ung-ming was welcomed back by Liu Pei. At once the military director assigned positions to Liu Pei's commanders

*so that they could take Ts'ao's retreating forces. Chao Yün,
Chang Fei, and others were dispatched.*

Then K'ung-ming arose and said to Liu Ch'i, son of the departed patriarch Liu Piao: "The region within sight of Wu Ch'ang
is absolutely crucial. I would have you return there at once with
your own men and deploy them at the shore points. Some fugitives
from Ts'ao's defeat are bound to come, and you will be there to
seize them. But do not leave the city walls without cause."

Liu Ch'i took his leave of K'ung-ming and Liu Pei. Then K'ung-
ming spoke to his lord: "Sovereign patriarch, station your men in
Fan K'ou. Find some high vantage point for observation, and
tonight we can sit and watch Chou Yü achieve great merit."

All the while Lord Kuan was waiting at their side, but K'ung-
ming spared him not even a glance. Unable to endure it, Lord
Kuan cried out: "My poor self has followed in elder brother's
wake through the long campaigns of war for more years than can
be told, and I have never fallen behind. Today we close with a
great enemy, but the military director has no assignment for me.
What is his intent?"

K'ung-ming smiled. "Do not take offense. It was my desire to
trouble you to hold an absolutely crucial gorge. Forgive me, but
something deterred me, and I was reluctant to ask."

Lord Kuan: "What deterred you? I would like an explanation
here and now."

K'ung-ming: "Once Ts'ao Ts'ao treated you most generously.
And you are bound somehow to repay him. When his army is
defeated, Ts'ao will take the Hua Jung trail. If we order you
there, I am certain you will let him pass. That is why I was
reluctant to ask you."

Lord Kuan: "You are so mistrustful! It is all too true that he
treated me most attentively, but I repaid him when I beheaded
the generals Yen Liang and Wen Ch'ou and when I broke the
siege at White Horse. And if I run into him today, I would hardly
just release him."

K'ung-ming: "But if you should release him, then what?"

Lord Kuan: "I would have military law applied to my misdeed."

K'ung-ming: "Well then, put it in writing here and now."

Lord Kuan did so, saying: "And if Ts'ao Ts'ao does not take
that route?"

K'ung-ming: "I'll give *you* a formal statement that he will."
This satisfied Lord Kuan completely. K'ung-ming continued: "But
refrain from showing any mercy."

When Lord Kuan had left for the Hua Jung trail, Liu Pei said:
"His sense of obligation is very strong. If Ts'ao Ts'ao actually takes
that route, I am afraid my brother will let him pass when it comes
to it."

K'ung-ming: "Last night I surveyed the celestial formations.
Ts'ao is not to meet his doom. But to have Lord Kuan preserve
a bit of human sympathy is rather a pretty touch, after all."

*Word of the imminent arrival of the expected South-
land defector, Huang Kai, reached Ts'ao Ts'ao in the form of a
letter.*

The text read: "Chou Yü has held me under the tightest guard,
and so I have had no means to get away. Recently we had a new
grain shipment, and I have been put on as escort. Opportunity
has presented itself. I will find a way to cut down one of our
eminent commanders and present his head with my submission.
Tonight at the second watch, look for a boat with the Blue Dragon
notched banner—that will be the grain boats."

Delighted, Ts'ao and his generals watched for the arrival of
Huang Kai's ships.

Wearing only a breastplate, his hand gripping a sharp sword,
Huang Kai was on the third boat. On his banner, four large characters: "Van Guard Huang Kai." Riding the favorable wind all
day, he set his sights for the Red Cliffs. By now the east wind was
in full motion. Waves and whitecaps surged tumultously. Ts'ao
Ts'ao scanned the river and looked up to the moon. Its reflections
flickered over the waters, making the river seem like a silvered
serpent with a myriad gleaming scales turning and sporting in the
waves. Ts'ao faced the wind and smiled, thinking he would achieve
his ambition. Suddenly an officer shouted: "South of here, the
river is serried with sails riding in on the wind!" As Ts'ao strained
his eyes southward, the report came: "They are all flying the Blue
Dragon notched banner. Among them a giant banner: 'Van Guard
Huang Kai.'"

Ts'ao smiled. "This defection is Heaven-sent to us." But as the
boats approached, Ch'eng Yü warned: "It is a ruse. Do not let
them near the camps."

Ts'ao: "How do you know?"

Ch'eng Yü: "If they carried grain, they would lie low and steady in the water. But the boats coming on are so light they are practically skimming—and with the force of this southeast wind, you cannot evade such a trap."

Then the truth dawned on Ts'ao, and he ordered Wen P'ing to go out and stop them. "By the Chancellor's mighty authority," P'ing called out, "the ships from the south are to approach no further but to remain in mid-river. Take down your sails at once!"

But as he spoke an arrow sang, and P'ing was felled. There was commotion on P'ing's ships, and they fled back to the shore.

The ships from the south were now only two leagues from Ts'ao's stations. Huang Kai motioned the first line of the onrushing Southland ships to be torched. The fire was sped by the might of the wind, and the boats came on like arrows in flight until smoke and flame screened off the sky. Twenty fiery ships rammed into the naval stations. Within moments Ts'ao's ships caught fire and, locked in place by their chains, could not flee. Catapults sounded from across the river, and the fiery ships came on from all sides. The face of the water could scarcely be seen as the flames chased the wind, a piercing current of red that seemed to flow up to the heavens and through the earth.

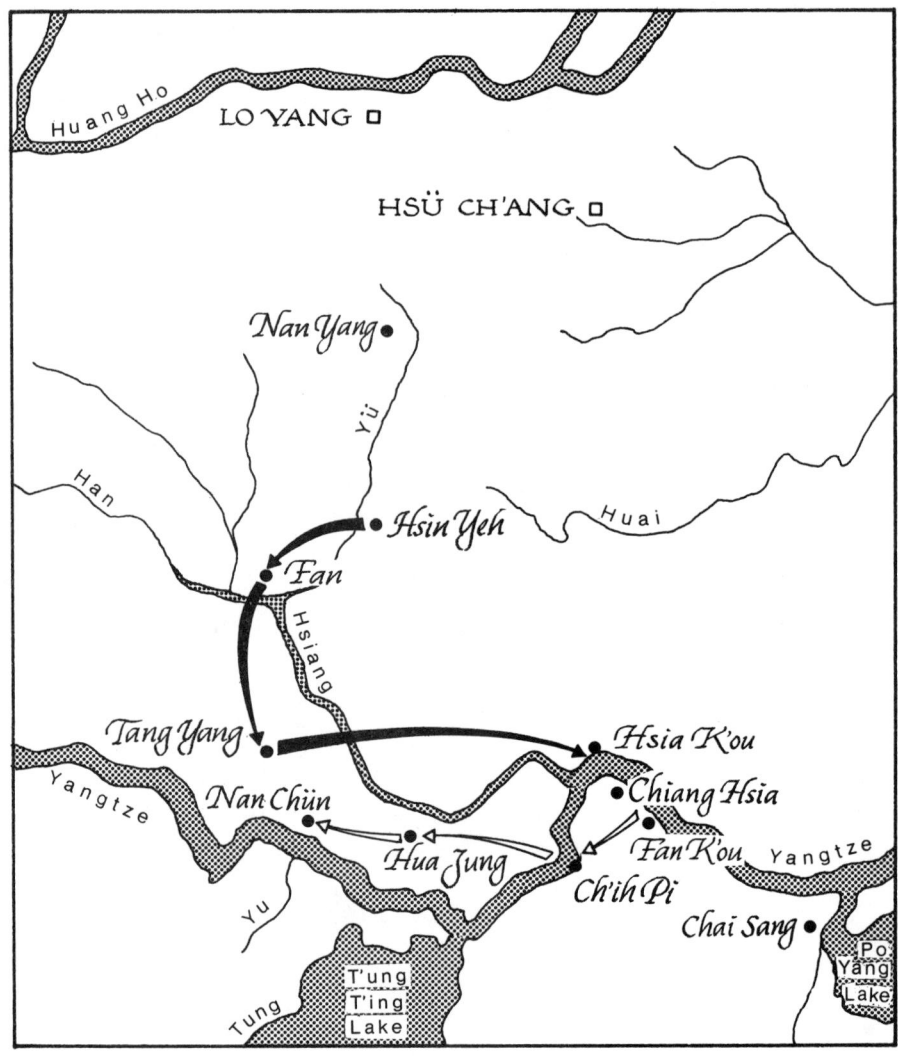

Liu Pei's flight from Ts'ao Ts'ao and the battle at the Red Cliffs.
The dark arrows trace Liu Pei's flight, which ended in Hsia K'ou.
At Fan K'ou he joined the Southland forces (white arrows) to
attack Ch'ih Pi (Red Cliffs), defeating Ts'ao Ts'ao, who fled to
Hua Jung. There Kuan Yü released Ts'ao Ts'ao. In the confusion
of battle K'ung-ming seized Nan Chün, a key stronghold of
Chingchou.

As Predicted, Lord Kuan
Obliges Ts'ao Ts'ao

Routed at sea, Ts'ao Ts'ao fled overland. Units dispatched by K'ung-ming as well as troops of the Southland harassed him.

Ts'ao's men were famished and without supplies. The majority had fallen. Ts'ao roared for the men and horses to trudge ahead. The dead were beyond numbering, and the sound of howls and cries on the trails did not cease.

Angry, Ts'ao said: "Life and death go according to fate. What need is there for cries? Whoever cries out again will be executed." They passed a treacherous junction. The road began to flatten out. Looking behind, Ts'ao saw he was left with a mere three hundred mounted followers, utterly without shields and mail and all out of formation. They protested that the horses were spent and had to rest. Ts'ao replied: "We must push on to Chingchou, and there you will have time enough to rest."

Another few leagues, and Ts'ao Ts'ao laughed aloud. "They all said Chou Yü and K'ung-ming were such shrewd tacticians. But as I see it, neither is especially capable: now, if they had thought to set a battalion in ambush here, we would have to surrender without a fight!"

That moment the explosion came. Five hundred men, swords crossed, were positioned on both sides. At their head, raising the Blue Dragon blade, astride Red Hare—Lord Kuan, checking Ts'ao's advance. Ts'ao's men felt their souls desert them and their courage die. The horses' fatigue made a last stand impossible.

Ch'eng Yü said: "Lord Kuan is known to disdain the high and forbear with the humble. He would molest the mighty but never persecute the weak. He is without duplicity and has ever demonstrated his good faith and integrity. In times past, Chancellor, you showed him great kindness, and now if you would appeal to him personally we could get out of these difficulties."

Ts'ao agreed and directed his horse forward. Bowing, he addressed Lord Kuan. "You have been well, I trust, general, since your departure?"

Lord Kuan bowed in return. "I am bearing orders from the military director and have been awaiting you, Chancellor, for some time."

Ts'ao: "The army is defeated, and the situation is critical. Having reached this point, I have no way out. But I trust, general, you will give due weight to the mercy you once enjoyed."

Lord Kuan: "Though I have benefitted from your ample kindness, I fulfilled the debt when I destroyed two enemy generals and relieved the siege at White Horse. In the present situation I could not set aside public duty for personal considerations."

Ts'ao: "You still recall, do you not, how you slew five of my generals when you left my service? A real man gives the greatest weight to good faith and integrity. You have a profound understanding of the *Spring and Autumn* and must be familiar with the story of the apprentice who pursued his instructor in marksmanship only to release him, unwilling to use the man's own teachings to destroy him."

And Lord Kuan, whose sense of obligation was as palpable as a mountain, could not put Ts'ao Ts'ao's many obliging kindnesses or the thought of the slain generals from his mind. Despite himself, he felt moved. Also, seeing Ts'ao's men distracted and on the verge of tears, Lord Kuan softened inside. He wheeled his mount and ordered his troops to fan out, clearly signaling his intent to let Ts'ao Ts'ao through.

When Ts'ao saw Red Hare turn away, he and his followers bolted past, and when Lord Kuan came back they were gone.

> *Ts'ao Ts'ao returned to his capital Hsü. He left his chief generals, Ts'ao Jen and Hsia-hou Tun, in charge of his strongholds in Chingchou.*

When Kuan Yü released Ts'ao Ts'ao and was leading his men home, the other commanders assigned by K'ung-ming had already

Kuan Yü releases Ts'ao Ts'ao

returned to Hsia K'ou with their booty of horses, grain, and equipment. Only Lord Kuan returned empty-handed to Liu Pei, having taken neither man nor mount. K'ung-ming was in the midst of congratulating Liu Pei when Lord Kuan's return was reported.

K'ung-ming rushed from his place and, bearing the cup of congratulation, went forth to meet him. "It is time to rejoice, my general, in your epoch-making achievement—ridding the empire of a monstrous evil. It might have been more suitable to come out on the road to greet and congratulate you."

Lord Kuan was silent. K'ung-ming: "General, can it be that you are displeased because we did not come to greet you?" K'ung-ming turned on the attendants. "Why did you not report his approach earlier?"

Lord Kuan: "I come only to request the punishment."

K'ung-ming: "You do not mean to tell me that Ts'ao Ts'ao did not take the Hua Jung trail?"

Lord Kuan: "He did come that way, in fact, but I was so inept that he got away from me."

K'ung-ming: "What generals and officers did you seize?"

Lord Kuan: "None."

K'ung-ming: "That means that you were mindful of Ts'ao Ts'ao's past generosity and purposefully released him. But since we have the formal documents, we shall not fail to apply the law." K'ung-ming barked for his guards to execute him. But Liu Pei intervened: "That day when we three brothers bound ourselves to public service, we swore to share life or death. Now Kuan Yü has broken the law, but I cannot bear to go against our former covenant. I hope you will suspend the rule this time and record his fault—but let his merits compensate for his offense."

With that, K'ung-ming pardoned Lord Kuan.

These events took place in A.D. 208.

K'ung-ming
Vexes Chou Yü

Chou Yü rewarded his troops and planned to move into the Chingchou area. Liu Pei sent Sun Ch'ien to congratulate Chou Yü.

Sun Ch'ien: "My lord Liu Pei has commanded me to express his respectful gratitude for your great might, and to tender these poor courtesies."

Chou Yü: "Where is Liu Pei?"

Sun Ch'ien: "As far as I know, he has transferred his troops into positions at the mouth of the Yu River."

Startled, Chou Yü asked: "Is K'ung-ming there too?"

Sun Ch'ien: "Both K'ung-ming and my lord are there."

Chou Yü: "Then please return at once, and I shall go there myself to express our gratitude."

After Sun Ch'ien had left, Lu Su said to Chou Yü: "Why on earth did you lose your composure?"

Chou Yü: "If Liu Pei is positioned on the Yu River, he must be thinking of taking Nan Chün, the key to Chingchou. *We* are the ones who expended so many men and horse, who consumed so much coin and grain, that now Nan Chün is ready to fall into our hands. But if they harbor such ruthless ambition as to intercept our prize, they'll have to reckon with the fact that I am still alive."

Lu Su: "What strategy could force them back?"

Chou Yü: "I'm going to talk to them myself. If we agree, fine; if not, I'm not waiting for them to take Nan Chün. I'll finish off Liu Pei first."

Lu Su: "I should join you." With three thousand light cavalry the two men headed for Liu Pei's camp on the Yu River.

When Sun Ch'ien told them that the Southland commander was on his way, Liu Pei asked K'ung-ming: "What is his purpose in coming?"

K'ung-ming smiled. "Hardly for paltry courtesies. He is coming on account of Nan Chün."

Liu Pei: "If he has many troops, how can we meet him?" K'ung-ming suggested certain replies that could be made to Chou Yü. Then he ordered the warships arrayed on the river and the land forces along the shore.

When Chou Yü arrived, he was disquieted by the strength and vigor of Liu Pei's military position. He was well received by Liu Pei and K'ung-ming, and a banquet was laid. As the wine was passing, Chou Yü said: "Liu Pei, in moving your forces here, are we to understand that you intend to take Nan Chün?"

Liu Pei: "We heard that you wished to take it and came to lend our assistance. If you should not take it, of course, I shall."

Chou Yü smiled. "We in the Southland have long wished to assimilate the area, and now that Nan Chün already lies in our grasp, how could we not take it?"

Liu Pei: "The outcome of any engagement is hard to foretell. Before returning north, Ts'ao Ts'ao left Ts'ao Jen to defend Nan Chün and other points in Chingchou. There are sure to be some surprises for us, not to speak of Ts'ao Jen's unchallengeable bravery. I was only wondering if the commander would be able to take Nan Chün."

Chou Yü: "In the event that we fail, you are welcome to try."

Liu Pei: "Lu Su and K'ung-ming are there as witnesses. Do not go back on your word, commander."

Lu Su hemmed and hawed without answering. But Chou Yü said. "When a man of honor gives his word, there is no taking back."

K'ung-ming: "Your position, commander, is certainly fair-minded. Let the Southland go to take Nan Chün first. If you do not subdue it, my sovereign will try. What objection can there be?"

After Lu Su and Chou Yü had departed, Liu Pei said to K'ung-ming: "All the same, those replies that you had me make just then seem unjustified now that I think it over. I am isolated and destitute, without a place to set my foot. I sought Nan Chün as an expedient refuge. If Chou Yü takes it, with its walls and moat, for the Southland, where am I supposed to go?"

K'ung-ming laughed. "Remember when I tried to get you to take Chingchou, my sovereign, and you ignored me? But today you yearn for it."

Liu Pei: "Then it was Liu Piao's land; I could not bear to take it. Now that it is Ts'ao Ts'ao's, I am justified."

K'ung-ming: "Never mind fretting and worrying, my lord. Even if Chou Yü decimates the place, before long I will have you sitting in power within its walls." And so they held the position on the river Yu and made no move.

K'ung-ming Cunningly
Puts Lu Su Off

What looked simple to Chou Yü proved less so. Chou Yü was wounded in the attack on Nan Chün. He stayed within his camp and lured Ts'ao Jen into a night raid. During the fighting, however, Chao Yün took Nan Chün for Liu Pei. Then Liu Pei's generals occupied other key cities of Chingchou.

Unable to master his vexation, Chou Yü said to Lu Su: "I am going to assemble an army, decide the question of supremacy with Liu Pei and K'ung-ming, and so recover my cities. You must favor me with your assistance."

Lu Su: "Impossible. Just when we have Ts'ao Ts'ao at bay, and the outcome is undecided, and when you have not yet subdued Ho Fei—if we start to devour each other and Ts'ao Ts'ao exploits this weakness, the situation will become critical. What's more, Liu Pei and Ts'ao Ts'ao have an old friendship of some depth. If we press him too hard and he tenders the city to Ts'ao Ts'ao and joins him in attacking us, what will you do then? Let me go to Liu Pei myself and see if I can reason with him. If not, there will be time enough to call up the troops."

Lu Su went directly to Nan Chün, only to learn that Liu Pei was already in the city of Chingchou, capital of Chingchou province. When he arrived, he saw the strict order of the pennons and banners and the splendid appearance of the military. Secretly he admired K'ung-ming.

Lu Su was admitted and treated as an honored guest. He said

to K'ung-ming: "My sovereign, the lord of the Southland, and Chou Yü, his commander, have instructed me to make an emphatic representation of their views to the Imperial Uncle. Ts'ao led a million-man host, claiming he would subdue the Southland. But in reality he came to settle the score with the Imperial Uncle. It has been our good fortune to slaughter and drive back Ts'ao's army. The Imperial Uncle has been saved, and the nine districts of Chingchou ought in all right to belong to the Southland. But the Imperial Uncle has used a subterfuge to seize and hold the area, so that we have spent coin, grain, men, and horses in vain while the Imperial Uncle safely reaps the advantage. I doubt that this is consonant with accepted principles."

K'ung-ming: "Lu Su, on what grounds does a high-minded and enlightened scholar like yourself make such statements? It is commonly agreed that 'Things belong to their owners.' Chingchou's nine districts are not the Southland's territory but rather the estate and heritage of Liu Piao, and my lord, as everyone knows, is his younger brother. Though Liu Piao himself is dead, his son is still alive. For an uncle to support a nephew in taking Chingchou—what can there be to object to?"

Lu Su: "If in fact the patriarchal son, Liu Ch'i, were holding the territory, it would be defensible. But he is at Chiang Hsia; obviously he is not here."

K'ung-ming: "Would you care to see the patriarch's son?" He motioned to the attendants. And before Lu Su's very eyes, steadied by two supporters, Liu Ch'i came out from behind a screen and spoke to Lu Su. "My ill health prevents me from performing the proper courtesies; please forgive my offense."

Lu Su swallowed his amazement and kept silence for some time. Then he said: "But if the patriarchal son were not alive, what then?"

K'ung-ming: "He lives day to day under our care. When he dies, there will be something to negotiate."

Lu Su: "When he dies, the territory must be returned to the Southland."

K'ung-ming: "I think your position is correct." Then a banquet was prepared to fete Lu Su.

When Lu Su returned with the news to his own camp, Chou Yü said: "Liu Ch'i is in the prime of his youth. How is he going to die for us? And when do we get Chingchou back?"

Lu Su: "Commander, rest assured that the responsibility is

mine alone. I will see to it that Chingchou is restored to the Southland."

Chou Yü: "You have some special knowledge?"

Lu Su: "Anyone could see how dissipated in wine and sex Liu Ch'i is; disease has penetrated his vitals. His face looks feeble and wasted; his breath is labored; he spits blood. The man could not live beyond six months. At that time I will go to claim Chingchou, and Liu Pei should have no grounds whatsoever to put me off."

At this point Sun Ch'üan ordered Chou Yü to attack Ho Fei, and the Chingchou question was left in abeyance. Liu Pei installed Liu Ch'i as governor and proceeded to consolidate his position in Chingchou.

The Struggle in the West;
Liu Pei Moves to the Riverlands

Within the year Liu Ch'i died, and Lu Su returned to Chingchou to claim the land for Sun Ch'üan. Unable to stall further, K'ung-ming laid before Lu Su the next phase of his strategy.

K'ung-ming: "Let us borrow Chingchou as our base for the time being until we are able to acquire another territorial complex. Then we will return it. What do you think of the proposition?"

Lu Su: "What territory do you plan to take over before returning Chingchou?"

K'ung-ming: "It would be premature, would it not, to set our sights on the north. But in the Riverlands to the west, Liu Chang is weak and incompetent. My lord concentrates his hopes there, and if we succeed we shall return what is yours."

The Chingchou-Southland alliance was fortified by the marriage of a daughter of Sun Ch'üan's to Liu Pei, whom Sun Ch'üan officially designated governor of Chingchou.

Ts'ao Ts'ao secured his western flank by defeating Ma T'eng, one of the original "girdle oath" conspirators who swore to support the Emperor and destroy Ts'ao Ts'ao. This advance brought Ts'ao within striking range of Han Chung, the buffer region between Ts'ao and the Riverlands of the west, object of K'ung-ming's long-range designs.

When Ts'ao Ts'ao defeated Ma T'eng, exposing the buffer Han Chung, the leaders of Han Chung began to think of

retreating into the Riverlands. Alarmed, Liu Chang, Prince of
the Riverlands, sent Chang Sung to Ts'ao's capital, Hsü, to seek
aid.

Having arrived in Hsü, Chang Sung was shown the parade of
the Tiger Guards. Ts'ao pointed to five thousand strutting troops
arrayed on the training field, helmets and armor fresh and brilliant,
their tunics glorious. Gong and drum shook the sky. Poleaxe and
spear gleamed in the sun; men on horses pranced against the
horizon.

Sung glanced sidelong at the pageant. After a while Ts'ao summoned Sung and gestured outward. "Have you ever seen such
splendidly valiant heroes in your Riverlands?"

Sung: "No. We have never seen such military force in our
homeland. We govern ourselves by humanity and justice only."

Ts'ao Ts'ao's countenance altered as he regarded Sung, but
Sung felt no alarm. Ts'ao: "We take this 'River-rat' class for straw
reeds! Where our army goes, it conquers. What it attacks, it takes.
Those who go with us live. Those who go against us die. You
know this?"

Sung: "That the Chancellor conquers and captures wherever he
directs his forces has always been common knowledge, as when
you met Chou Yü at the Red Cliffs and Lord Kuan at the Hua
Jung Pass, showing you are without rival in the empire."

Ts'ao was inflamed. "What servile Confucian dares bring up my
shortcomings?" Ts'ao Ts'ao ordered Sung executed, relenting only
when he was advised: "Though Sung deserves to die, he has come
bearing tribute from the remote Riverlands. If we kill him, we
risk losing the confidence of men from afar." Chang Sung was
drummed out of Ts'ao Ts'ao's presence.

At his lodgings Sung was preparing to return to the Riverlands,
when it struck him: "Basically I was trying to offer the provinces
and military districts of the Riverlands to Ts'ao Ts'ao, since I
never expected him to be so insolent. When I was before my lord,
Liu Chang, I gave some pretty big assurances, and now to go home
empty-handed with nothing to show must earn me the mockery of
my countrymen. They say that Liu Pei of Chingchou has a great
reputation for humanity and justice. Why not make a side trip
over to him before returning, to get an idea of what he is like?
There's little danger I'll be unduly influenced."

Liu Pei received Chang Sung personally, flanked by K'ung-ming and P'ang T'ung, or Phoenix Chick, who had recently become Pei's second adviser.

Liu Pei: "Your most excellent reputation has long been known to us; it resounds like the thunder. How we rue the distance that clouds and mountains impose, preventing us from profiting by your advice. They say you are homebound to your capital, and we have come here especially to greet you. If you would only agree to come to our poor province to break your journey and gratify our earnest hopes, truly it would be a ten-thousand-fold blessing."

Delighted, Chang Sung entered the city with them. Ceremonies were exchanged and a banquet was laid. But throughout the repast Liu Pei confined himself to commonplace conversation, studiously avoiding any reference to the western Riverlands.

Chang Sung tried to stir him up. "How many districts do you still hold in Chingchou, Imperial Uncle?"

K'ung-ming smiled. "Chingchou is only on loan to us from the Southland, and they are always sending someone to reclaim it. However, my lord is somewhat more secure here by dispensation, now that he is a son-in-law of the Southland."

Chang Sung: "And are the Southlanders dissatisfied, despite their six districts and eighty-one regions, the wealth of the state, and the vigor of the population?"

P'ang T'ung: "Our lord is the Imperial Uncle of Han, but he has never taken possession of a piece of territory like those grubbing traitors to the Han who depend on forced seizures."

Liu Pei: "Refrain from such statements, gentlemen; what virtue have I for much ambition?"

Chang Sung: "I disagree. Enlightened patriarch, you are a royal kinsman whose humanity and rectitude pervade the realm. Do not speak of 'the possession of some piece of territory' when it is not beyond expectation that you may occupy the imperial throne as representative of the legitimate line."

Liu Pei joined his hands in a gesture of denial. "Good sir, you far overestimate whatever I may deserve."

And there the matter lay during three days of ceremonies. At the parting banquet, Liu Pei toasted Chang Sung. "We are deeply in your debt for consenting to pass three days with us. The time to take leave of one another has come, and I wonder when I may again have the benefit of your counsel."

Liu Pei freely shed tears, and Chang Sung was inwardly moved to urge the Riverlands on him. "I too have often dreamed I would one day serve you, and I have rued the lack of occasion. As I survey Chingchou, I see that to the east you have Sun Ch'üan— always ravenous—and to the north Ts'ao Ts'ao—with a monstrous appetite. So this place can hardly have any enduring appeal for you."

Liu Pei: "I know it all too well, but I have had nowhere to tread in safety."

Sung: "The province of Yi, the Riverlands, is protected by formidable ranges. Its fertile territory extends for thousands of leagues, the people are diligent, and the state is wealthy. The wise and capable officials have long held your virtue in high regard. If you will rouse your populace here to make the long trek west, the hegemony can be achieved and the House of Han restored."

Liu Pei: "How could I undertake such a thing? The governor of Yi Chou, Liu Chang, is a royal kinsman like myself, and his favor has long been dispensed throughout his territory. What third party could upset things?"

Sung: "I am not one to sell my sovereign for the sake of glory. But having met with so enlightened a lord, I must bare my innermost thoughts: Liu Chang, though he is in possession of Yi Chou, is endowed with so ignorant and irresolute a nature that he ignores the worthy and neglects the competent. Add to that the threat from Han Chung in the north. People's confidence is shaken, and their thoughts turn to gaining an enlightened lord. This excursion of mine was for the sole purpose of making an offer to Ts'ao Ts'ao. I never expected that this perverse traitor would so indulge his vainglory; he is overbearing to the worthy and offensive to the learned. For these very reasons I made a point of coming to see you. My enlightened lord, first take the west Riverlands as a base. Thereafter you can scheme against the Han Chung buffer, incorporate the central plains of the north, and set the dynasty to rights. Thus will your fame pass into history and your merits surpass all rivals. If you should actually be inclined to take over the Riverlands, I am willing to engage in the most arduous labor to coordinate matters from within. But I would not anticipate your esteemed decision."

Liu Pei: "I am deeply touched by your concern. Alas—Liu Chang and I have the same ancestor, and if I attack him I would be reviled and repudiated universally."

Sung: "A man of noble ambition adjusts to his age. You may spare no effort to establish your worth and your estate. Apply the whip and assume the lead! If you do not take Yi Chou, there are others who will—and it will be too late for regrets."

Liu Pei: "They say the roads are so tortuous there that wherever you go, carriage and horse cannot ride abreast. Even if I wanted to take it, what strategy would work?"

Producing maps from his sleeve, Sung said: "I am so moved by my lord's ample virtue that I would present these. A single glance will easily apprise you of the road system of the Riverlands."

Liu Pei unrolled one slightly and examined it. The geographic details were fully spelled out: length and breadth of roads, strategic intersections, repositories of coin and grain.

Giving further assurances of his support, Chang Sung took leave. When he returned to the Riverlands, he confided the developments to his two collaborators, Fa Cheng and Meng Ta.

The next day Chang Sung spoke to his sovereign, Liu Chang. "Ts'ao has proved to be a traitor who seeks to usurp the empire. He was utterly deaf to my proposals and already of a mind to take the Riverlands."

Liu Chang: "If that is his intention, what remedy have we?"

Sung: "I have a plan guaranteed to prevent Ts'ao Ts'ao or Chang Lu of Han Chung from violating our borders. The Imperial Uncle, Liu Pei in Chingchou, is a kinsman of the royal house and has a potential for accomplishment: after all, he broke Ts'ao Ts'ao's spirit at the Red Cliffs. My lord, have a representative effect an alliance, and let Liu Pei be your support from the outside."

Huang Ch'üan, however, raised violent objections. "If you heed Chang Sung, my lord, your forty-one provinces and districts will pass to another. Considering Liu Pei's reputation, his advisers, and his military staff, if you call him here to serve in a subordinate command, do you really think he will accept such lowly service? And if you treat him as a guest, why, one state cannot tolerate two sovereigns. Chang Sung has just come through Chingchou and must have conspired with Liu Pei. Execute Chang Sung, break off with Liu Pei, and the Riverlands will enjoy unlimited good fortune. To drive back Ts'ao Ts'ao and Chang Lu, seal the borders and close the passes, deepen your moats and elevate your ramparts, until the threat blows over."

Liu Chang rejected the strategy as too weak to meet the danger posed by Ts'ao Ts'ao, but another adviser seconded it. "If Chang

Lu attacks, it's still an external complaint. If Liu Pei comes in, it would be an intestinal affliction. Think of his legendary treachery: first he served Ts'ao Ts'ao, then he plotted Ts'ao's destruction; next he joined up with Sun Ch'üan only to steal Chingchou. Can you coexist with such duplicity? If you summon him, it is the end of the Riverlands."

Liu Chang dismissed him. "Cease your subversive recital. He is a kinsman; would he steal my estate?" And he sent Fa Cheng with a written proposal to Liu Pei for joint defense.

After the formal ceremonies on Fa Cheng's arrival in Chingchou, Liu Pei took him aside. "Having long admired your virtue, of which Chang Sung spoke much, I shall be ever gratified to listen to your advice."

Fa Cheng: "A minor official from the Riverlands is hardly worth notice. But they say horses whinnied when they met the master trainer Po Lo, and a man will give his life for a lord who appreciates him. Have you thought further on Chang Sung's proposal?"

Liu Pei: "My life spent in exile has never been free of woe and discontent. I am often reminded of the little wren that keeps for itself a cozy spot and the cunning hare that provides three escape holes. And man should not? It is not that I would not have your overabundant land, but I cannot bring myself to conspire against my clansman."

Fa Cheng: "The Riverlands are a natural storehouse. But a sovereign who cannot keep control cannot last. Liu Chang has proved unable to give office to good men, and his patrimony is doomed to be lost to someone else. Today, general, he is offering it to you of his own accord. Don't make the mistake of passing it up, like the hunter who leaves the prey to another. But if you are willing, I shall do my utmost."

Liu Pei: "Much yet remains to be discussed."

Liu Pei was alone, pondering, when P'ang T'ung, his second adviser, approached him. "It is a foolish man who fails to resolve a matter that demands resolving. My sovereign has a superior intelligence. Why so many doubts? Our present situation confounds our ambitions, but the Riverlands offer the wherewithal for a great endeavor. If Chang Sung and Fa Cheng are going to help us from within, that is a godsend. Why should you have doubts?"

Liu Pei: "The man who is my antithesis, who struggles against me as fire struggles against water, is Ts'ao Ts'ao. Where his means are hasty, mine are temperate; where his are violent, mine are humane; where his are cunning, mine are true-hearted. By maintaining my opposition to Ts'ao, my cause may succeed. If now for a small advantage I were to forfeit men's trust and allegiance, I could not bear to do it."

P'ang T'ung smiled. "My sovereign lord, what you are saying accords well enough with sacred universal principles. But in a time of division and subversion, when men strive for power by waging war, there is no single course. If you cling to accustomed principle, you will not be able to proceed at all. Rather, you should opt for flexibility. You know, to incorporate the feeble and attack the incompetent, to take power untowardly but to hold it traditionally—this was the way of the great conqueror kings of the past, T'ang and Wu. When things are settled, if you make amends righteously while enriching the land and shaping it into a great power, what 'trust' will you have betrayed? Remember that if you do not take power today, another will. Give it your most mature consideration, my lord."

Liu Pei said as if perplexed: "Your memorable words shall be engraved within me." Then he consulted with K'ung-ming about raising a force to move west.

K'ung-ming told him that Chingchou could not be left undefended, and so Liu Pei assigned Lord Kuan, Chang Fei, and K'ung-ming himself to remain in Chingchou while he and P'ang T'ung, the Phoenix Chick, proceeded to the Riverlands.

Liu Pei was royally received by Liu Chang, governor of the Riverlands. Multitudes lined the road hailing the newcomer. But conflict between Liu Pei and Liu Chang was brewing.

Sleeping Dragon Wails
for Phoenix Chick

K'ung-ming was in Chingchou, and on the Seventh Evening Festival he assembled all the officers for an evening banquet to hear of Liu Pei's successes in the Riverlands. Suddenly a star, due west, the size of a Dipper star, plunged through the heavens, shedding its brilliance. K'ung-ming lost his composure and in distress pitched his wine bowl to the ground. He covered his face as he cried "Alas!" And to the questions of the perplexed assembly, he said: "Some time ago I calculated that when the North Dipper* appeared in the west this year, it would bode ill for our armed forces. I had already made it known in writing to our sovereign lord that the Heavenly Dog was going against our army, and that Venus was on the verge of the city Lo. I urged precautions against any misfortune, but who would have imagined that the star would plunge to earth in the west this evening! Phoenix Chick is doomed to relinquish his life—and my lord has lost a man who is like one of his limbs."

The assembly was shocked but disbelieving. K'ung-ming insisted that confirmation would come within days, and everyone dispersed before the banquet was concluded.

Several days later the report arrived of P'ang T'ung's death in battle on the seventh day of the seventh month—the evening of the starfall. K'ung-ming resolved to return to Liu Pei.

* Deaths are marked by the North Dipper, births by the South. Cf. chapter 69 of Chinese text.

Kuan Yü assumes full authority in Chingchou

Lord Kuan: "If you leave, military director, who will stand guard here? Chingchou is a crucial base; such a step is serious."

K'ung-ming: "Although this letter from Liu Pei does not say specifically, I think I know his mind. He has entrusted Chingchou to me with instructions to assign functions according to capability. Under the circumstances, I shall forward my recommendation that the responsibility be given to Lord Kuan who, mindful of the bond created by the Peach Garden Oath, will give his utmost to it."

Lord Kuan could not decline, and gallantly consented.

K'ung-ming ordered a banquet prepared for tendering the seals of office. At the appointed moment Lord Kuan extended both hands to receive them. K'ung-ming held up the seals: "Everything must rest with you now, general."

Lord Kuan: "When a man assumes a heavy task, he does not set it down unless he dies." But the mention of death made K'ung-ming apprehensive, and he would have put off the transfer of authority had he not already spoken.

K'ung-ming: "If Ts'ao Ts'ao attacks, how will you meet it?"

Lord Kuan: "I will repel him vigorously."

K'ung-ming: "And what if Ts'ao Ts'ao and Sun Ch'üan coordinate an attack?"

Lord Kuan: "I will divide my army and repel both."

K'ung-ming: "That would be too dangerous for Chingchou. I have eight words of advice which, if you commit them to memory, my general, will keep Chingchou intact."

Lord Kuan: "What eight words?"

K'ung-ming: "North—repel Ts'ao Ts'ao. East—conciliate Sun Ch'üan."

Lord Kuan: "The military director's words are engraved within me." And the seals were transferred.

Liu Pei Becomes
Governor of the Riverlands

The conflict between Liu Pei and Liu Chang erupted into civil war, but Liu Chang was quickly outmaneuvered.

Liu Chang said: "That I was blind is futile to regret now. There is no alternative to submitting to Liu Pei and sparing the people of this city."

A loyal adviser replied: "We have more than three legions within the city, and coin and grain to support us for a year. What's the good of simply surrendering?"

Liu Chang: "My father and I have governed the Riverlands for more than twenty years without conferring any favor, material or spiritual, upon the people. In three years' warfare they have consigned flesh and blood to the fields, and it is my own fault. What content could I enjoy? Better to submit and protect the people."

The next day Liu Chang personally presented the instruments of state to Liu Pei. Liu Pei came forth from his camp to receive Liu Chang. He held Liu Chang's hands and, weeping, said: "Circumstances have compelled this. It is not that I do not practice a humane ethic." Together they went back into the camp.

When Liu Pei entered the capital, the common folk greeted him at the gates with flowers and candles.

K'ung-ming said: "Now the Riverlands are secured. But two kings cannot be tolerated. Have Liu Chang escorted to Ching-chou."

"We should not send him off so far when we have only just gained the land," replied Liu Pei.

K'ung-ming: "He lost his estate by excessive weakness. My lord, if you approach matters indecisively, with a womanish virtue, this place will be hard to hold for long." And Liu Pei accepted the advice.

At this time Liu Pei handsomely rewarded the officers and officials of the preceding reign who had submitted to him—some sixty in all. And all were elevated in position. K'ung-ming, Kuan Yü, Chang Fei, Chao Yün, and others were confirmed in their titles. All the commanders were duly rewarded. Oxen and horses were slaughtered to feast the soldiers, and the granaries were opened to relieve the populace. There was general rejoicing.

After the land was fully under control, Liu Pei wished to award the choicest fields and homesteads around the capital to his officials. But Chao Yün objected, arguing: Military disaster has befallen these people again and again. The deserted fields and homesteads should revert to the local people and not be appropriated for your personal bounty." Liu Pei was pleased with Chao Yün's advice and followed it faithfully.

To K'ung-ming he assigned the framing of the laws for governing the state. The penal code was made heavy and strict to compensate for the feebleness and favoritism of the former administration.

The triangular balance of power of the three kingdoms now came into being. Having supplanted Liu Chang as governor of the Riverlands, Liu Pei began to build the base for extended conquest as the struggle between Ts'ao Ts'ao and Sun Ch'üan reached an equilibrium. The limits of the Southland were revealed: it could defend but not conquer.

For Ts'ao Ts'ao the struggle with Sun Ch'üan was primarily military, the struggle with Liu Pei primarily political, because Liu Pei challenged not only territory but legitimacy. As Liu Pei's power grew in the Riverlands, Ts'ao Ts'ao halted his southern campaigns to consolidate his political position in the north. He proclaimed himself Prince of Wei and established his hereditary succession in A.D. 214—a move that portended usurpation of the Emperor's seat.

Others, among them the "girdle oath" conspirators, called for Liu Pei's aid in an attempt at a coup against Ts'ao

Ts'ao in support of the nominal Han Emperor Tributor. The plot was exposed and suppressed in heavy fighting in the capital before Liu Pei could participate.

Ts'ao Ts'ao turned to face his nemesis, Liu Pei, by launching several attacks. But control of Han Chung, the buffer between the north and the Riverlands, was won by Liu Pei.

Liu Pei Becomes
Prince of Han Chung;
Lord Kuan Thrusts North

When Ts'ao Ts'ao drew his troops back to Hsieh gorge, K'ung-ming gauged that he had given up the Han Chung region and sent some dozen columns of fighters to worry the retreating army. Ts'ao Ts'ao could not hold any position for long, and having been wounded as well, withdrew in great haste. Throughout his entire army the men's mettle was fading, their morale spent.

As Liu Pei consolidated his hold in the region, the populace was well secured and the army richly rewarded. There was general satisfaction.

Now the military leaders would have liked to elevate Liu Pei to imperial dignity, but they were reluctant to broach the matter directly. Instead they petitioned the military director, K'ung-ming, who said: "This has long been my intention also." K'ung-ming brought a group led by Fa Cheng to see Liu Pei.

K'ung-ming: "Ts'ao Ts'ao has so aggrandized his power that the people lack a rightful sovereign, but you, sovereign patriarch, are celebrated for humanity and justice. Now that you have come into full possession of the Riverlands, you might well respond to the indications of Heaven and concur with the wishes of mankind in assuming the imperial throne. Thus rightfully and justifiably you could bring the traitor to justice. This brooks no delay, and so we appeal to you to select an auspicious time."

But Liu Pei was taken aback. "You are quite mistaken, military director. I may be of the royal house, but I am a subject. If I do this, it will be an act of opposition to the dynasty."

K'ung-ming: "Not quite! At present the empire perishes of its divisions. Contenders arise one after the other to protect one region or another, while throughout the realm virtuous and talented men who faced death in the service of the sovereign long to clamber onto a dragon, to attach themselves to a phoenix, to establish their merit and their fame. But now, my lord, if you diffidently and disdainfully cling to a narrow loyalty, you risk failing the expectations of the people. Please consider it carefully."

Liu Pei: "If you are asking me to occupy the imperial dignity unlawfully, then I must refuse. But let us continue to consider what plans would be to our advantage."

Various military leaders said: "If you refuse, patriarch, the commitment of the people will slacken."

K'ung-ming: "The sovereign patriarch has always made integrity his foundation and was always reluctant simply to proclaim the imperial title. But now that you hold Chingchou and the Riverlands, you might become Prince of Han Chung."

Liu Pei: "Though you all would honor me as Prince, without the Emperor's explicit edict, this is usurpation."

K'ung-ming: "For now it is permissible to take the liberty of departing from the norm. First assume the title; then memorialize the Emperor. It will still be in good time."

Liu Pei could only accede, and in the seventh month of the year A.D. 219, he was instated as the Prince of Han Chung. His son Shan was established as heir.

When the panoply of ceremonies was concluded, Liu Pei composed a memorial and had it taken to the Emperor in the capital, Hsü. In part, the text read:

> With but the talents of a useful subject I undertook the responsibilities of a ranking general. Exercising overall command of an armed force, I bore your writ abroad. But I failed to remove the resistance of the renegades and stabilize the royal house. Too long have I retarded the influence of your majesty's sage teaching, so that within the six corners of the universe things have failed to rise from their nadir. It torments me so that I am like a man in the agony of ostracism.
>
> Thirty years ago Tung Cho contrived an avenue for sedition, and from that time a multitude of evils has overrun and ravaged the realm. But, confident in your majesty's sage virtue and awe-inspiring presence, many a loyal subject has answered. Sometimes the people have risen up to bring traitors to justice; some-

times divine punishment has come down. Violence and rebellion have been nipped, and our problems are gradually being resolved.

Only Ts'ao Ts'ao has yet to be removed and his head piked up on the walls. He has first encroached on state power and then usurped it, indulging his desires in an acme of disorder. There was a time when I conspired with Tung Ch'eng, general of chariots and cavalry, to bring Ts'ao to justice. But at the critical moment there was a failure of security, and Tung Ch'eng fell into a trap. I was thrown on my own without any base, my loyal commitment unfulfilled.

And so in the end Ts'ao Ts'ao's utter vice and extreme trespass got their way. The sovereign mother, the High Consort, was mutilated and slain, the glorious heir poisoned to death. However we might have formed organizations with the purpose of demonstrating our strength, we were too weak to resort to war, and the years passed without issue. Always in dread of being undone ourselves, we wrongly turned from our obligation to the nation.

Emperors and kings succeed by inheritance, a principle that has never been set aside. The Chou dynasty, reflecting the two eras before, established the multifarious Chi clan and trusted to the sturdy support of the two states Chin and Cheng.

Then the founder of the Han, Kao Tsu (the Supreme Ancestor), arose like a dragon and established the brothers and the sons of the kings in their due dignity. He inaugurated the nine princedoms and terminated the various branches of the Lü clan, thus securing the royal Liu clan.

And now Ts'ao Ts'ao, condemning the straight and corrupting the true, actually multiplies his henchmen, secretly intending to bring on the catastrophe. The usurpation is already manifest, and with the royal house diminished and the imperial clan without position, I have readjusted the ancient forms and fallen back on the temporary expedient of serving as minister of defense, Prince-Patriarch of Han Chung.

I think both of title—station high and favor rich—and of duty—deeply conscious of a grave task. I breathe in trepidation as one at a precipice. I am bound to give my all and deliver on my sincerity, rouse and energize the armed forces, coordinate and lead the multitude of the loyal toward the end of bringing peace to our sacred grain shrines. With respectful diligence I commend this memorial to your attention.

When the memorial reached the capital of Hsü, Ts'ao Ts'ao had already learned of Liu Pei's moves. "Little sandal-weaver! You presume too far! I vow to annihilate you!" cried Ts'ao Ts'ao, and ordered a general mobilization for a march into the Riverlands. One man, however, stepped out of the ranks to object. "Do not, my Prince, for the sake of a moment's anger, engage the Emperor in remote campaigns. There is a way to bring about Liu Pei's ruin in the Riverlands without the least military effort; and when the strength of his forces is exhausted, all you will need is a single campaign to crush him."

Ts'ao regarded the man. It was Ssuma Yi. Ts'ao asked amiably: "What is your esteemed view?"

Ssuma Yi: "Sun Ch'üan of the Southland gave his daughter to wive Liu Pei, only to seize the occasion to steal her back again. Liu Pei holds Chingchou and refuses to return it. Between the two is mortal enmity. Now is the time to send a man of persuasive powers bearing documents to try to convince Sun Ch'üan to mobilize and capture Chingchou. That would compel Liu Pei to send his forces to rescue it, at which time your majesty could mobilize to capture the river Han. Liu Pei's head and tail will not be coordinated, and his situation will be precarious." It was so ordered.

When Ts'ao's representative Man Ch'ung arrived in the Southland, Chang Chao advanced the following to Sun Ch'üan: "There is after all no real enmity between Wei and the Southland. In the past we gave credence to K'ung-ming's persuasive propositions, with the result that military campaigns between us and the north have not ceased, to the detriment of the living souls in both states. Now this representative can only be coming to talk peace. He should be greeted with the fullest courtesy."

Sun Ch'üan approved, and the representative's proposal was as expected: "Between the Southland and Wei there has never been enmity. The divisions we have suffered are all because of Liu Pei. The Prince of Wei has sent me here to work out an agreement whereby you, general, will attack and take over Chingchou while he brings his army up to Han Chung, so that we can strike from both ends. After Liu Pei is destroyed, we can divide the territories and vow a mutual peace."

When Sun Ch'üan took counsel with his advisers, Ku Yung said: "Although their plan is self-serving, yet there is reason in it. Let us send the messenger back with our agreement to coordinate against Liu Pei, but at the same time send an agent over the river to probe their movements."

But Chuko Chin suggested: "Lord Kuan has a daughter who is

still young and has not been given in marriage. I would like to go there and seek her hand for your heir. If Lord Kuan consents, then we confer with him at once regarding our common effort to destroy Ts'ao Ts'ao. Otherwise we help Ts'ao take Chingchou."

Sun Ch'üan approved, and Chuko Chin presented himself before Lord Kuan: "I come for one particular purpose—to bind our two houses' amity. My lord, Sun Ch'üan, has a son, a youth of high intelligence. And I understand you have a daughter, whose hand I have come especially to seek. If our two houses knit this amity and join forces against Ts'ao, it will be magnificent. I beg you to consider it, my lord."

But Lord Kuan responded explosively. "My tiger lass married off to a mongrel? But for your brother, I'd have cut off your head by now. Speak no more." Lord Kuan called for his aides, who drove Chuko Chin scurrying off, hands round his head.

When he returned to the Southland Chuko Chin could not conceal what had happened. In anger Sun Ch'üan exclaimed: "Barbarian!" and summoned Chang Chao and others at once to consult on the strategy for taking Chingchou. It was agreed that Ts'ao Ts'ao should be asked to have Ts'ao Jen move south from his position in Fan to draw Lord Kuan's forces away from the city of Chingchou.

*   *   *   *

Liu Pei, Prince of Han Chung, having seen to the defense of the Riverlands, began to store grain, manufacture weapons, and create communications networks with a view to capturing the heartland of the north. Spies brought word of the new alliance between Ts'ao Ts'ao and the Southland, and Liu Pei urgently called on K'ung-ming for advice.

K'ung-ming: "This plan of Ts'ao Ts'ao's was not at all unexpected, but the Southland has more than enough advisers of its own. They are bound to ask Ts'ao Ts'ao to have Ts'ao Jen make the first move."

Liu Pei: "If so, then what?"

K'ung-ming: "Send a messenger to announce Lord Kuan's new office. Have Lord Kuan take the initiative and capture Fan. That will chill the enemy's gall and make them disintegrate readily."

The Prince of Han Chung was elated, but when his representative arrived in Chingchou and delivered the announcement and

Kuan Yü refuses the marriage

Kuan Yü appointed one of the five tiger generals

command, Lord Kuan asked: "With what rank am I to be invested?"

The representative of Liu Pei replied: "Head of the five tiger generals."

Lord Kuan asked: "What five tiger generals?"

The representative: "Yourself, Chang Fei, Chao Yün, Ma Ch'ao, and Huang Chung. These are the five."

Lord Kuan grew angry. "Chang Fei is my younger brother, and Ma Ch'ao is renowned. Chao Yün has followed my elder brother for so long that he is as good as my brother. For such men to rank alongside me is admissible; but who is Huang Chung, that he dares rise to my level? What hero teams up with a common soldier?"

And so Lord Kuan refused the seal.

Liu Pei's representative smiled. "You are making a mistake, general. When the Han was founded, Hsiao Ho and Ts'ao Shen participated with the Supreme Ancestor in the establishment of the dynasty. No man was closer to him than those two, and yet Han Hsin, a general defecting from the enemy, was honored as a king, a higher position than that of Hsiao Ho and Ts'ao Shen. Yet no complaint was heard. Now, though the Prince of Han Chung has invested the five tiger generals, with you there is the commitment of elder and younger brother, and he regards you as one with him. You two are indeed one and the same. How could you be classed with any other? You have received generous favor of him and should share with him content and discontent, blessing and misfortune, without niggling over status and titles! Give this your mature consideration, I beg you."

Lord Kuan realized his mistake and saluted the representative with clasped hands. "My ignorance, but for your advice, might have ruined the whole endeavor." He received the seal with both hands.

The next day the representative produced the royal communication ordering the capture of Fan, a key base of Ts'ao's forces, held by Ts'ao Jen. It was a crucial point in north-south military exchanges in the central China region between the Yellow and Yangtze Rivers.

The day of the campaign, Lord Kuan was napping after performing sacrifices before his great banner inscribed "Commander-in-Chief." From nowhere a black, bull-sized boar charged into the tent and bit Lord Kuan's leg. In anger Lord Kuan snatched his sword and killed it. Its squealing sounded like tearing cloth. In another instant Lord Kuan was awake; it had been only a dream. But deep inside his leg he felt pain. Troubled by the dream, he mentioned it to his son, Kuan P'ing, who said: "The boar is, after all, a symbol of the dragon. Its coming to your feet implies a sudden rise in your fortunes. There is no need for you to be troubled as if it were a warning."

When Lord Kuan assembled his officers and told them of the sign in his dream, some interpreted it as auspicious, but others did not. Lord Kuan said: "When a hero approaches sixty, he confronts death without anxiety." At that moment a royal communication from the Prince of Han Chung arrived designating him vanguard general, conferring the seal and the axe to signal his authority, and making him supervisor of all affairs in the territories of Chingchou. When Lord Kuan had accepted the commission, the officers respectfully congratulated him: "This shows that the boar is the token of the dragon." Lord Kuan's confidence was restored, and he set out.

Kuan Yü seized the city of Hsiang Yang, slightly south of the target city, Fan.

One of Lord Kuan's officers said to him: "You have subdued Hsiang Yang, which will cause Ts'ao's army to suffer loss of morale. But Lü Meng of the Southland is posted at Lu K'ou, and Lü Meng has ever had the ambition to take Chingchou. What if they make a direct move against Chingchou?"

Lord Kuan: "It has occurred to me too. You could go and take care of it. Pick out some high hills twenty or thirty leagues apart on the river's edge and set up signal-flare stations. Have fifty men guard each one. If the Southland's army comes by night, light the flares; if they come by day, raise smoke. I will go myself to counterattack."

Siege at Fan

Kuan Yü dammed up the rain-swollen Hsiang River. As the waterline rose, he opened the dams, catching the armies of Wei in low terrain and making good his boast to turn Ts'ao's army into "fishes and turtles."

Lord Kuan's men took to their warboats, utilizing the floods that continued high, and headed north for Fan. Around the besieged city white breakers surged against the horizon, and the increasing pressure of the waters relentlessly undermined the city walls. The entire population worked ceaselessly with earth and brick to shore them up.

All Ts'ao's military leaders were stricken with fear and came to Ts'ao Jen in panic. "The crisis is beyond relieving!" they cried. "Let us forsake this place at night before the enemy arrives. We can save ourselves, even if we lose the city."

Ts'ao Jen was about to withdraw when Man Ch'ung, the man who had represented Ts'ao Ts'ao in the mission to the Southland, objected. "It is a mistake. Among these mountains the floods come on in a flash, but never remain for long. They are sure to recede in less than ten days' time. Even though he has not begun the assault, Lord Kuan has already sent a unit to Chia Hsia, which shows that he cannot advance at will because he fears we will ambush him from behind. If we abandon the city of Fan today, nothing south of the Yellow River will remain in the possession of our country. I urge you to maintain the defense of this point for the sake of our security."

Ts'ao Jen expressed his gratitude. "If not for your advice, I could have ruined our endeavor!"

Ts'ao Jen assembled his leaders and vowed: "I bear the mandate of the prince of Wei to guard this city. Whosoever mentions abandoning the city dies." And the leaders swore to hold to the death.

One day Lord Kuan went himself to the north gate of the city. Astride his horse, he flourished a whip and challenged the enemy. "What a bunch of rats! Surrender while there is time. You have nothing to wait for." As he spoke, Ts'ao Jen noticed that he was wearing only his breastplate and that from the side his green tunic was exposed. He hurriedly summoned five hundred bowmen, who fired together. As Lord Kuan wheeled to escape, his right upper arm caught an arrow, and he dropped from his horse.

> Amid the flood, seven armies quailed.
> From the wall, a single shot, a leader felled.

Hua T'o Cures Lord Kuan's Arm;
The Mariners of Wu
Cross the River

Lord Kuan's son, Kuan P'ing, rescued his father on the field of battle and brought him back to camp. But the arrowhead had been poisoned; ulceration had already invaded the bone, and the arm was greenish and swollen, impossible to move. P'ing suggested to the leaders: "If my father loses the arm, how will he give battle? Better to pull back to Chingchou for now and take care of it." But when the leaders told Lord Kuan of this suggestion, he said: "The capture of Fan is within our very grasp. And once it has been taken, we can reach Ts'ao's capital of Hsü with a hard forced march. Then we can flush him out and destroy him; the House of Han will be secured. I cannot ruin this enterprise for the sake of a minor wound. Don't sap the morale of the troops!" P'ing retired silently.

Lord Kuan would not retreat, and the wound would not heal. His attendants were searching for a physician when one arrived unexpectedly by boat from the Southland. It turned out to be Hua T'o, who had heard of Lord Kuan's wound and come to cure it. When Hua T'o was invited to examine the arm, he said: "There is aconite infiltrating the bone. If it's not cured soon, the arm is lost. I do know how to save it, but I am afraid you would shrink from the treatment."

Lord Kuan: "To me, death is a homecoming. I will not shrink."

The physician: "We will have to set up a post with a loop nailed to the top, in some quiet room. I must ask you to put your arm through the loop and let us tie it. Then we will cover your face. I will cut through to the bone with a razor and scrape the poison off the bone. After the wound is dressed and sewn up, you will not have any problem. But I am afraid you will shrink."

Lord Kuan: "If that's all, it's nothing. You won't even need the post and loop!"

After a few rounds of wine, Lord Kuan began a game of chess with a comrade as he extended his arm straight out and instructed the doctor to begin. An attendant held a basin under the arm to catch the blood. The doctor parted the flesh until the bone showed: it was already coated with green. The knife made a thin, grating sound as it scraped the surface, until everyone present blanched and covered his face. But Lord Kuan continued to eat and drink, making comments about the chess positions—altogether without a sign of pain.

When the operation was finished, Lord Kuan said: "The arm is as flexible as ever. There is no pain at all. Master, you are a supernatural physician."

Hua T'o ordered Lord Kuan to remain quiet for one hundred days. After the ceremonial banquet he departed, refusing payment.

Kuan Yü's threat to the city of Fan decided Ts'ao Ts'ao to prepare to move his capital, Hsü, northward. Again it was the military adviser Ssuma Yi who dissuaded him with a counterproposal: to try once more to join with Sun Ch'üan in making a coordinated attack on Chingchou. Ts'ao Ts'ao agreed and again made this proposal to the Southland leader. But Sun Ch'üan was inclined rather to attack the province of Hsü, east of Ts'ao Ts'ao's positions of strength. However, Sun Ch'üan's commander, Lü Meng, urged:

"True, Ts'ao Ts'ao has no time to look to his east. The province Hsü is lightly guarded, and I am sure you could conquer it, but the terrain favors the army rather than the navy. Even if you took it, you would have trouble defending it. First vanquish Chingchou, and when you have secured the whole of the Yangtze, you will be in a position to develop other advantageous plans."

Sun Ch'üan agreed. But when Lü Meng learned of the signal-flare stations that Kuan Yü had erected along the river and of the fitness of Kuan Yü's forces, he despaired of achiev-

ing what he had urged Sun Ch'üan to undertake. Lü Meng hid
from his lord under cover of illness.

Another military commander, Lu Hsün, said to Sun Ch'üan:
"Lü Meng's illness is not real; it is put on."

Sun Ch'üan: "If you think so, you may go and see."

Lu Hsün went to the naval camp at Lu K'ou and saw Lü Meng,
whose face indeed showed no sign of illness. Lu Hsün said to him:
"I have been instructed by the lord of Wu, Sun Ch'üan, to inquire
most respectfully into what has given discomfort to your esteemed
self."

Lü Meng: "Some unforeseen disorder afflicts this miserable
parcel of flesh—hardly worth troubling yourself to inquire after."

Lu Hsün: "Our lord, Sun Ch'üan, has entrusted a heavy responsibility to you. But instead of seizing the time to act, you
vainly nurse this melancholia. Why?"

Lü Meng made no reply, and after a pause Lu Hsün continued:
"I would be so foolish as to proffer a little prescription that should
remedy your disorder, general. However, I am not certain it is
applicable."

Lü Meng solicited the advice, and Lu Hsün proceeded: "Your
disorder is due to the magnificent marshaling of Lord Kuan's army
and the flare warning system along the river. But I have a plan to
keep the guardians of the flare stations from raising the signal and
to bring the armies of Chingchou to surrender tamely. Would that
suit you?"

In desperate gratitude Lü Meng said: "You speak as if you
could see into my vitals. I would learn your worthy plan."

Lu Hsün: "Lord Kuan counts too much on his heroic valor and
assumes that he has no equal. Only you cause him any concern.
General, take this opportunity to resign your office, pleading ill
health. Yield your command here at Lu K'ou to someone else,
someone whom we will instruct to acclaim and exalt Lord Kuan
with self-deprecatory phrases in order to make him even more
arrogant. Then he will be sure to pull back from the city of
Chingchou and concentrate on Fan. If he leaves Chingchou unprepared, we will gain control of it with a minimum of effort."

Lü Meng agreed to the ruse and arranged with Sun
Ch'üan to have Lu Hsün appointed in his place.

When Lu Hsün assumed the new command at Lu K'ou, he drew up a letter to Lord Kuan and sent it by messenger, together with champion horses, marvelous damasks, wine goblets, and other treasures.

When the letter announcing the change of command at Lu K'ou arrived, Lord Kuan was recuperating from his wound. Lord Kuan commented: "It seems rather shortsighted of Sun Ch'üan to appoint a mere boy as general."

The messenger: "General Lu presents this letter and these ceremonial gifts not only to wish you well, my lord, but with an earnest desire for accord and amity between your house and Sun Ch'üan's. I pray your indulgence in accepting them."

Lord Kuan examined the letter, whose language was the ultimate in self-deprecation and prudence. When he had perused it, Lord Kuan looked up and laughed loudly, ordered his men to receive the gifts, and sent the messenger back. The messenger reported to Lu Hsün: "Lord Kuan was appreciative and delighted. He will not be giving further thought to the Southland."

Sun Ch'üan, after verifying Lord Kuan's intention to attack Fan, put Lü Meng in command of the offensive against Lord Kuan's southern position in Chingchou. Lü Meng called together a force of thirty thousand men and eighty light craft. He disguised a number of mariners as merchants and put them on deck to navigate the ships. Concealed in the hulls were crack troops. Seven generals and their forces were immediately behind; the rest stayed with Sun Ch'üan as a rescue force. A letter was dispatched to Ts'ao Ts'ao telling him to raid Lord Kuan's rear troops, and when a report of these steps reached Lu Hsün, the sailors in merchants' dress began their mission. They steered their light craft to the Hsün Yang River, moving at full speed day and night until they hit the north shore.

When challenged by the soldiers at the signal-flare stations, the Southlanders replied: "We are all merchants from afar. On the river the wind blocked our course, and we took refuge here." And they offered gifts to the station guards, who took their word and permitted them to anchor along the shore.

Toward the second watch, the troops hidden in the boats emerged in a body, seizing and binding the station guards. At a silent signal the troops in all eighty boats appeared, captured the soldiers at the key signal stations, and hustled them back to the boats. Not one escaped. Then the Southlanders struck out for Chingchou in unimpaired secrecy.

As they approached the city, Lü Meng used fair words to placate the men he had captured by the river, and with various generous gifts got them to bribe their way past the city gates and to start fires as a signal once they were inside. Lü Meng led the advance team, and when they reached the city, the gatekeepers recognized their own men and thus opened at their call. A united shout arose from the crowd of soldiers, and just inside the gates they set the signal fires. The Southlanders rushed in and took the city by surprise. Lü Meng decreed: "If any soldier kills one man or takes one article without good reason, he will be dealt with by strict military law." Municipal administrators were told to continue in their current duties. Lord Kuan's family was placed under arrest, and a report was sent to Sun Ch'üan.

In a short while the cities of Kung An and Nan Chün were also captured.

Public Duty
and Personal Honor

News of the Southland's successes reached Ts'ao Ts'ao, who assigned Hsü Huang to join battle with Kuan Yü and relieve his key city of Fan.

Word of Hsü Huang's approach was brought, and Lord Kuan called for his horse. Kuan P'ing: "You cannot engage the enemy, Father, while your strength is still impaired."

Lord Kuan: "I have known Hsü Huang for a long, long time, and I am fully aware of what he can and cannot do. If he does not pull back, I will take the initiative and kill him. It will put the generals of Wei on their guard." And Lord Kuan emerged vigorously, appointed with short sword and saber, striking fear into all who saw him. He called out his challenge: "Hsü Huang, where are you!"

Where banners parted at the gate of the northmen's camp, Hsü Huang came forth. He bowed deeply. "My lord, since we parted, many years have fled. Who would have thought your hair would turn so white! Yet well and fondly do I remember the lusty years of our companionship, when I gained much of your tutelage. My appreciation is undying. Today the effect of your triumphs is felt throughout the land. It makes an old friend sigh in admiration. Here fortune grants us a meeting, and long-suffered yearnings are appeased."

Lord Kuan: "The bond of friendship between us is deep indeed —something I share with no other. Why, then, have you today driven my son so utterly to the limit?"

Kuan Yü and Hsü Huang

Hsü Huang turned to the commanders behind him and cried out in a cruel, grinding voice: "Ten thousand in gold to the man who takes his head!"

Lord Kuan was astounded: "My friend, why do you say this?"

Hsü Huang: "Today I am in the service of home and country. I am not the one to set public duty aside for personal sentiment."

And so saying, he took on Lord Kuan in direct combat, his poleaxe whirling.

> *After some eighty bouts, Kuan Yü was called back to his forces. Ts'ao Jen emerged from the besieged city of Fan and, together with Hsü Huang, routed Kuan Yü's Chingchou army.*
> *Kuan Yü learned of Lü Meng's stratagem and of the loss of the major cities behind him. Trapped between the armies of Wei and Wu, he wrote Lü Meng to try and revive the alliance.*

In the city of Chingchou Lü Meng had issued orders that the families of the warriors accompanying Lord Kuan, whatever part of the territory they might be in, were to be shielded from the troops of the Southland and suitably provided for. The families were grateful and kept to their walls.

On delivery of Lord Kuan's appeal, Lü Meng told the representative: "When I concluded an accord with general Kuan, it was a personal matter. Today I act under orders from the sovereign. I am not my own master and must trouble you to report back to the general and convey my view as amicably as you can."

Lü Meng ordered a banquet for the messenger and escorted him to the post station, where the families of Lord Kuan's warriors surrounded him for news. Some pressed letters on him, some gave him spoken messages, all to the effect that the households were sound and well cared for.

When the messenger brought back these tidings, Lord Kuan was moved to rage. "Treacherous, treasonous tricks! But I will be revenged, for I will kill him while I live, or die doing it." He pushed the messenger out roughly, and the man was quickly surrounded by warriors seeking news of their families. As they learned of the security and comfort of their loved ones and the pains Lü Meng had taken to be considerate, the warriors felt grateful and began to lose their will to fight. On the march many deserted, until Lord Kuan had only three hundred followers.

> *Kuan Yü's comrade, Liao Hua, tried to recruit local allies. Failing, he set out for Ch'eng Tu, capital of the Riverlands.*

> *Isolated, backed into a single fortress, Kuan Yü received Chuko Chin.*

Chuko Chin: "At the command of my lord, Sun Ch'üan, I come to appeal to you. The ancient saying runs, 'The man who can recognize the facts of a situation is a paragon of men.' The nine districts of Chingchou no longer belong to you. You are reduced to this single paltry city, bereft of resources within or allies without. If you do not fall in the morning, you will in the evening. Therefore take this advice: come over and make your peace with the lord of the Southland. You will be restored to your position in Chingchou and your family will be preserved. Favor this suggestion, my lord, with your fullest consideration."

His expression all rectitude, Lord Kuan replied: "I am but a warrior. By my lord's favor I am his hands and feet. I cannot betray my allegiance and throw in my lot with the enemy. If these walls fail, what is left to me is death. Jade may break, but its whiteness cannot be changed. Bamboo can be scorched, but its joints cannot be obliterated. The man may fall, but his name comes down through history. You have said too much; I urge you to withdraw. My wish is to decide all with Sun Ch'üan in a battle to the death."

Chuko Chin: "My lord, Sun Ch'üan wants to form an alliance with you, based on marriage, so that we may join forces in the larger struggle to destroy Tsa'o Ts'ao and uphold the House of Han. We harbor no other ambition. Why must you cling so to such misconceptions, my lord?"

Before Chuko Chin could finish, P'ing, Lord Kuan's son, had pulled his sword and was making for Chuko Chin. Lord Kuan stopped him. "His younger brother, K'ung-ming, is in the Riverlands serving as your uncle's right-hand man. If you kill him, fraternal feelings will be destroyed." And so Lord Kuan ordered Chuko Chin driven away. Chin rode back, his face suffused with humiliation, to apprise Sun Ch'üan: "Lord Kuan is adamant. No one can persuade him."

Sun Ch'üan: "A model of loyalty. What is our next step?"

Lord Kuan
Manifests a Divine Presence;
Ts'ao Ts'ao Feels
the Force of His Soul

Sun Ch'üan had Kuan Yü captured and brought before him.

Sun Ch'üan: "Out of long-standing admiration for your splendid virtues, I sought to work out a liaison through marriage. Why did you spurn the offer? You have ever clung to the view that you are without peer in the empire. How has it come about that today you are my prisoner? Will you, general, submit to us today, or not?"

But Lord Kuan damned him in a rasping voice: "My blue-eyed boy! My red-whiskered rodent! I bound my allegiance to Imperial Uncle Liu in the peach garden, where we swore as one to uphold the House of Han. What would I be doing in the ranks of traitors such as you in revolt against the Han? Now that I have fallen to your treacherous devices, death alone remains. There is nothing more to say."

Sun Ch'üan turned to his assembled officers: "Lord Kuan is one of the valiant champions of our time, a man I cherish deeply. I propose that we treat him with the utmost courtesy to encourage him to come over to us."

But one replied: "It will not work. That time when Ts'ao Ts'ao had him, the Chancellor made him master of the Han Shou district, granted him titles, and feasted him—every third day a minor

Kuan Yü defeated

banquet, every fifth day a major banquet. Whenever he got on his horse, Ts'ao handed him gold. When he got down from his horse, Ts'ao handed him silver. With such kindnesses Ts'ao failed to hold him, and wound up having his guards and generals beheaded as Lord Kuan left. Today Ts'ao is on the verge of shifting his capital to avoid the thrust of Lord Kuan's offensive. My sovereign lord, Kuan Yü is our captive, and if you do not do away with him immediately I fear the consequences."

Sun Ch'üan pondered for some time until he admitted the truth

of this analysis. And thus Lord Kuan and his son P'ing were
beheaded in the twelfth month of the twenty-fourth year of
"Establish Security," A.D. 220. Lord Kuan was fifty-eight years
of age.

*   *   *   *

But the vapor from Lord Kuan's soul remained whole and intact, floating attenuated until it came to rest on the Mountain of
Jade Springs in the county of Tang Yang in Chingchou province.
On the mountain lived an elderly monk whose Buddha-name was
P'u Ching ("universal equilibrium"). Scudding across the realm
of men, he had come to the mountain and, seeing its luminous
character and bountiful waters, had woven a little thatched shelter
for himself. Each day he would seat himself for meditation and
commune with the process of nature. All he kept beside him was
a single young traveling companion to turn up food for survival.

That night the moon glowed pale, and the wind blew cool and
fresh. Sometime after the third watch, as P'u Ching was sitting
mute, a man called out from the empty space: "Return my head."
P'u Ching scrutinized the air. A man was riding the steed Red
Hare and brandishing the Blue Dragon sword. Two men were in
his train, one pale, one swarthy. Together they alighted from a
cloudtop onto the summit of the Mountain of Jade Springs. P'u
Ching realized that it was Lord Kuan, and striking his door with
a deer-tail brush, said: "Lord Kuan, where are you?" Lord
Kuan's florescent cloud-soul seemed to comprehend instantly as
it dismounted and dropped on the wind before the monk's hut.
It spoke with interlocked hands. "Who are you, master? I would
know your Buddha-title."

"I am P'u Ching. We met once before; could you have forgotten?"

Lord Kuan: "My gratitude for the help you once gave me is
engraved in my memory. I have met my doom and left my life, and
appeal to you now for the redeeming counsel that will point me
out of the darkness of my wandering."

P'u Ching: "Times past are not present truth. Refrain from all
judgments. Outcomes depend on former causes. The two admit
of no discrepancy. Now you cry out for your head, having met
your death at the hands of Lü Meng. From whom shall Ts'ao
Ts'ao's guards and generals whom you killed seek their heads?"

Kuan Yü joins the gods

In a flash Lord Kuan realized the truth, and bowing his head in submission to the law of the Buddha, he departed. Thereafter he frequently manifested his divine presence on the Jade Springs Mountain to afford protection to the common people. And the local dwellers built a temple out of gratitude and made offerings there each season.

*　　　*　　　*　　　*

Now that Lord Kuan was dead, Sun Ch'üan consolidated his hold on all the territories of Chingchou province. At a banquet in Lü Meng's honor, Sun Ch'üan said: "After long frustration, our easy acquisition of Chingchou is owing to the meritorius work of Lü Meng. At an earlier time, Chou Yü, a man of exceptional prowess, defeated Ts'ao Ts'ao at the Red Cliffs. Alas, he died prematurely. Lu Su replaced him, and in his very first interview with me touched upon a grand imperial strategy for the Southland, the first great boon to us. And when Ts'ao Ts'ao descended upon us and I was universally counseled to surrender, Lu Su alone urged me to call in Chou Yü, to go against the tide and counterattack. This was the second boon. The only fault I have to find with Lu Su is that he talked me into tolerating Liu Pei in Chingchou. But today it is Lü Meng who worked out the strategy for retaking Chingchou, and thus he excels the other two by far."

Sun Ch'üan personally poured the ceremonial wine and presented it to Lü Meng. Receiving it, Lü was about to drink when he dashed the cup to the ground instead and seized Sun Ch'üan with one hand. "Blue-eyed boy! Red-whiskered rodent! Have you forgotten me? Or not?" The assemblage was aghast. As someone moved to stop him, Meng knocked Sun Ch'üan to the ground and with long strides came to the throne and seated himself upon it. His eyebrows arched vertically, his eyes grew round and prominent as he bellowed: "I have crisscrossed the empire for thirty-odd years since defeating the Yellow Scarves, only to have your treacherous trap sprung on me. But if I have failed to taste your flesh in life, I shall give your soul no peace in death—for I am Lord Kuan Yü, master of the Han Shou district!"

Fear-stricken, Sun Ch'üan led the assemblage in offering obeisance. Lü Meng collapsed on the ground, blood ran out of his seven orifices, and he died. There was general terror, and thereafter Sun Ch'üan was tormented with fear over the execution of Lord Kuan.

Chang Chao was summoned by Sun Ch'üan and told him: "My lord, when you put Lord Kuan and his son to death, you brought the Southland to the verge of disaster. For when the man bound himself to Liu Pei through the Peach Garden Oath, it was to live and die as one. Today Liu Pei controls the whole of the Riverlands. Add to that the cunning of K'ung-ming and the valor of Chang Fei, Chao Yün, and the other generals. When Liu Pei learns of Lord Kuan's death, he will mobilize the whole state and do his utmost for revenge—a threat the Southland iş going to find difficult to meet."

Sun Ch'üan faltered as he said: "It seems I have miscalculated. So then, what do we do about it?"

Chang Chao: "Ts'ao Ts'ao has command of a million men. His glance scours the northern heartland like a tiger's. However urgently Liu Pei would have his revenge, he must come to terms with Ts'ao Ts'ao. The Southland will hardly survive if those two combine their forces for an invasion. So you would be well advised to initiate the first move: send someone to deliver Lord Kuan's head to Ts'ao Ts'ao to make it plain to Liu Pei that it was all at Ts'ao's direction. His animosity will thus be redirected to Ts'ao Ts'ao. The armies of the Riverlands will turn on Wei, while we observe the fortunes of both and from the neutral vantage seize our opportunity."

Sun Ch'üan agreed, and the head was sent in a wooden box to Ts'ao Ts'ao, who exclaimed delightedly: "With Lord Kuan dead I shall spend my nights secure indeed."

But someone else said: "This is actually a device for transferring disaster away from the Southland." It was Ssuma Yi. Ts'ao demanded an explanation. Ssuma Yi replied: "At the time when Liu Pei, Chang Fei, and Lord Kuan bound themselves in allegiance by the Peach Garden Oath, they swore to share both life and death. Now, having put Lord Kuan to death, the Southland fears the brothers' reprisal. That is why his head has been presented to your majesty: to make Liu Pei shift his hatred and attack us instead of them, while they plan to seize the advantage of their middle position."

Ts'ao Ts'ao: "What you say is correct. But how do we get out of it?"

Ssuma Yi: "It is not difficult at all. Let your majesty take Lord Kuan's head, and to represent the rest of the body, carve a torso of fragrant wood to fit it for burial according to the ceremonies due a high minister. When Liu Pei learns of it, his hatred for Sun Ch'üan will deepen and he will give his all to the southern expedition. Then *we* can sit back and watch developments: if the Riverlands are winning, we attack the Southland; if the Southland is winning, we attack the Riverlands. Once either falls, the other cannot last."

Ts'ao was entranced with the scheme and called in the messenger from the South. The wooden box was presented. Ts'ao Ts'ao opened it and saw Lord Kuan's face, just as it had been in life. Ts'ao smiled. "You have been well, I trust, general, since we parted?" Before Ts'ao could finish, the mouth opened, the eyes moved, and the hair and beard stood up like quills. Ts'ao fell in a faint, reviving only after a long spell. He said to his officers: "General Kuan is no mortal." The messenger from the South told him how Lord Kuan's powers had entered into Lü Meng and reviled Sun Ch'üan. This increased Ts'ao's fear. He adopted Ssuma Yi's advice and buried the head and a wooden corpse with full royal honors outside the south gate of Lo Yang. All the officers and officials were told to tend the body, while Ts'ao personally made offerings. The Southland's envoy was sent home to report.

*   *   *   *

In both the eastern and western sections of the Riverlands the population had settled down, the state was prosperous, and the harvests were large. Suddenly a report came from Chingchou that the Southland was seeking a state marriage with Lord Kuan and that Lord Kuan had vigorously rejected it.

K'ung-ming: "Chingchou will fall. Lord Kuan must be recalled and someone sent to replace him." As they were speaking, more reports streamed in, telling how Lord Kuan had flooded seven armies at Fan and set up an impenetrable net of signal stations along the river. The reports eased Liu Pei's worries.

One day, however, Pei was seized with trembling. Walking or sitting, he could find no peace. At night, unable to sleep, he sat in his inner chamber reading by candlelight. Feeling his senses darken and lose their focus, he fell asleep against the table. A chilly gust sprang up inside the room. The candle lamp fell dark and then rekindled. Liu Pei raised his head and saw a man's form standing by the lamp. Pei called to him, but he made no reply. Puzzled, Pei arose to examine him: it was Lord Kuan, moving back and forth evasively beside the lamp.

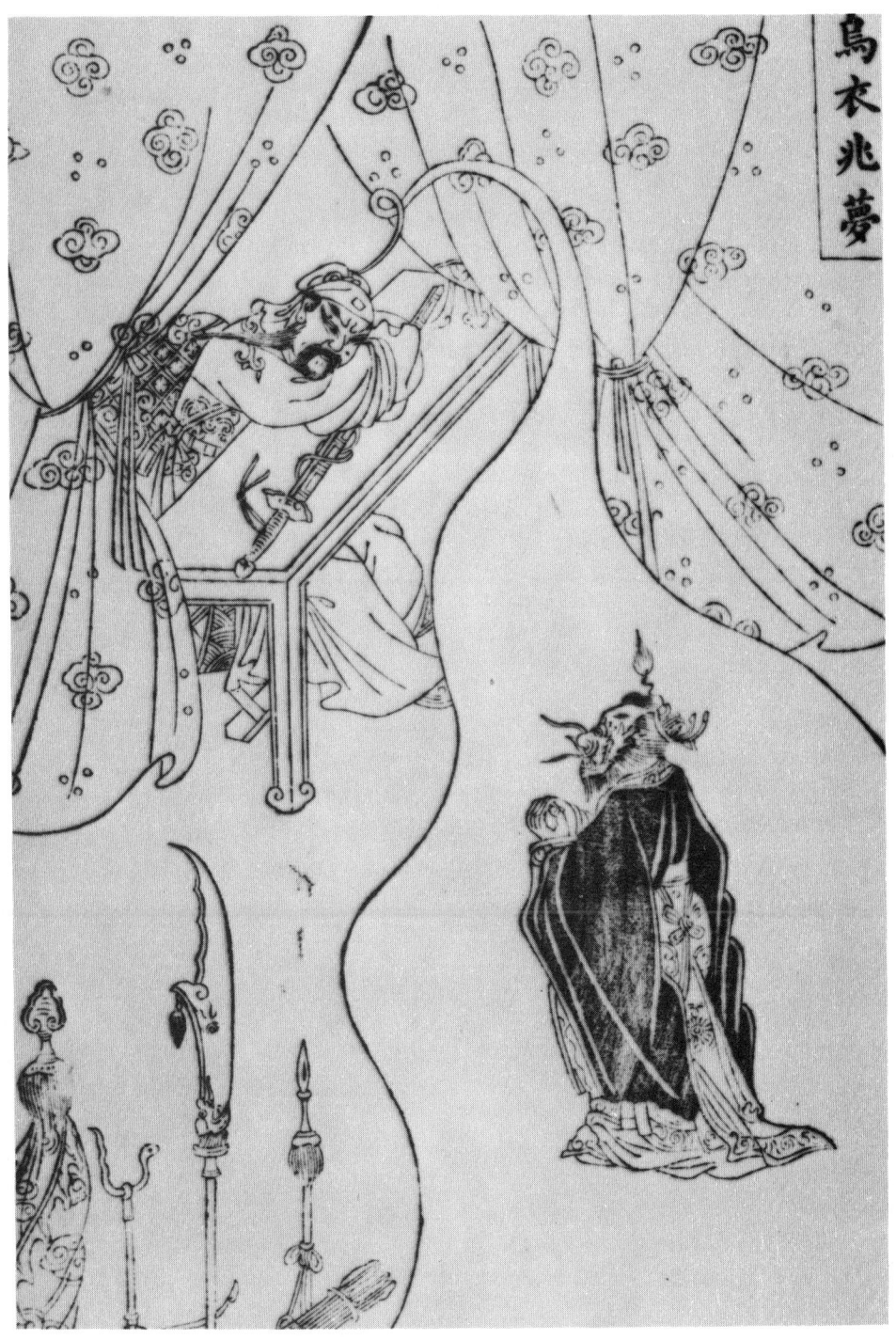

Kuan Yü's spirit appears to Liu Pei

Liu Pei: "Good brother, you have been well since we parted? You must have some serious reason for coming here in the dead of night. You and I in sympathy are one flesh. Why do you avoid me?"

Lord Kuan appealed through his sobs: "I beg my brother: Raise an army; erase my humiliation." So saying, he was no more, as the chilly gust swept by. Waking, Liu Pei called for K'ung-ming, who sought to soothe him. But before long, reports of the catastrophe in Chingchou began to come in, telling of Lord Kuan's rectitude in death. Liu Pei fell unconscious to the ground.

> Thinking of their vow to die as one,
> Can he bear to let him die alone?

Liu Pei's Oath;
Sun Ch'üan's Declaration

Five times Liu Pei fell from grief that day. For three days, refusing all food and drink, he howled out his pain until his cries brought flecks of blood to his tear-soaked robes. K'ung-ming pressed him to desist, but he said: "Neither this sun nor this moon shall I share with the Southland: so I swear."

K'ung-ming: "They say the Southland has presented Lord Kuan's head to Ts'ao Ts'ao, who has interred him with royal ceremony."

Liu Pei: "What does it mean?"

K'ung-ming: "It means that the Southland is trying to shift the doom of the Peach Garden Oath to Ts'ao Ts'ao—who, however, sees through the scheme and buries Lord Kuan royally, so that your revenge may fall on the Southland."

Liu Pei: "Then must we bare our weapons now and visit that vengeance there, where it will erase our humiliation."

"We must *not* do so," objected K'ung-ming, "for the south would have us embroiled in the north as the north would have us in the south, each evolving its schemes and awaiting an opening. Your majesty needs to *withhold* his forces and for now, simply prescribe the mourning for Lord Kuan. When the accord between north and south breaks down, we will have our opportunity." Liu Pei ordered the mourning commenced.

*　　　*　　　*　　　*

Lord Kuan was interred, but he continued to appear in Ts'ao Ts'ao's chambers at night. Ts'ao put the matter to his officials, who said: "Your supplementary palace in Lo Yang has ancient rooms with many vengeful ghosts. You must build a new residence."

An architect presented a plan for a nine-room mansion and directed Ts'ao Ts'ao to the shrine of the Vaulting Dragon. There stood a giant pear tree, which was to supply timber for the roof beam.

Elated, Ts'ao Ts'ao sent workmen to cut it down. But they could not penetrate it with saws or unseal it with axes. In disbelief Ts'ao Ts'ao led several hundred men to the shrine to inspect the tree, which soared up and spread out a leafy canopy that seemed to reach to the Milky Way.* Ts'ao ordered the men to cut it down. Some local elders came forward to object. "The tree is already several hundred years old," they said, "and a spirit has always occupied its crown. It should not be cut."

Ts'ao Ts'ao: "In all my time, everyone has feared me from the Emperor himself to the common man. What vengeful spirit here dares challenge my wishes?" He struck at the tree with his sword. There was a metallic sound; then blood splashed over Ts'ao, who threw his sword to the ground and rode home in hysteria.

That night he could not sleep. A figure came into his room and, pointing at him, said: "I am the spirit of the tree. Building the new mansion signals your intent to usurp the dynasty. But to strike at a sacred tree? I know your number is told, and I come to take your life."

Ts'ao awoke, his head seared with pain. Physicians were sought, but none could bring relief. The Court officials were depressed.

Then the physician Hua T'o arrived. But Ts'ao, reminded of Chi P'ing, grew suspicious and jailed him. Hua T'o died there, in Ts'ao's prison.

Ts'ao Ts'ao's condition worsened after he had killed Hua T'o, and he was depressed over his problems with the Southland and the Riverlands.

A letter from Sun Ch'üan was brought: "I, your subject, Sun Ch'üan, would commit my allegiance to your sovereignty, having long recognized Heaven's mandate to you, and humbly anticipat-

---

* In ancient China fallen dynasties had their sacred tree roofed over to cut off communication with the heavens.

ing the timely rectification of the imperial throne. If you would dispatch your generals to dislodge and exterminate Liu Pei, I should forthwith lead my entire court in tendering our lands in loyal submission."

Ts'ao laughed aloud and showed the note to his courtiers: "This simpleton wants to seat me upon the stove!"

But a number of the courtiers responded: "The House of Han has long been declining, while your majesty's merits and virtues mount ever higher. All living souls look up to you. Here Sun Ch'üan declares his allegiance—a human reflection of the divine, different signs with corresponding statements. So should you respond to Heaven and accord with men and quickly rectify the dynastic throne."

Ts'ao laughed: "Many years have I served the Han, and though some merit or virtue of mine may have benefitted the people. Yet as my rank advanced to Prince of Wei, my name and station reached their peak. What further dare I dream of? But if somehow the mandate of Heaven should come to rest with me, I would remain loyal to the Emperor, as did King Wen of the Chou."

Ssuma Yi: "Since Sun Ch'üan declares his allegiance, your majesty could confer rank on him with instructions that *he* resist Liu Pei." Ts'ao Ts'ao adopted the suggestion.

*   *   *   *

One night toward the third watch, Ts'ao felt his head and eyes begin to swim as he lay in his chambers. Something sounded like cloth tearing. To Ts'ao's amazement, there before him were the murdered queen, Lady Fu, the two royal sons, Tung Ch'eng, and others. Smeared with blood, they stood amid the autumn clouds and called for his life in muted voices. Ts'ao jerked his sword free and sliced at the empty air. Then there was a crash: the southwest corner of the building had fallen in. Ts'ao collapsed and was rushed to safety by his attendants.

The next night Ts'ao could hear the incessant howls of human voices. At dawn he assembled his counselors and said: "Throughout the campaigns of thirty years I have never given credence to the monstrous or the abnormal. But today, why this?"

The counselors replied: "Your majesty should command a Taoist priest to prepare the holy fires to ward off evil."

But Ts'ao sighed: "As the sage Confucius said: 'When you give offense to Heaven, to whom can you pray?' My mandate is exhausted, and I am beyond rescue." He did not allow the sacred fires to be lit.

By morning Ts'ao could feel his breathing violent and parched, and he could not identify forms. He called in his advisers, including Ssuma Yi.

Ts'ao Ts'ao: "Thirty years have I traversed the empire, and all manner of heroes have I annihilated. There remain but Sun Ch'üan of the Southland and Liu Pei of the western riverlands to be removed. But now my health is too frail for me to have further dealings with you. The time has come to entrust an heir to you. My eldest, Ang, son of Lady Liu, died in battle. Of my other four sons by Lady Pien—P'ei, Chang, Chih, and Hsiung—my favorite has always been Chih, the third. But I did not nominate him because he is superficial and somewhat lacking in sincerity, as well as overindulgent in wine. Only the eldest, P'ei, is unfailingly generous, cordial, and scrupulous—fit, therefore, to succeed to my estate. I hope you will give him all support and assistance."

He ordered seventy-two decoy tombs, lest anyone eventually discover his grave and excavate it. At the age of sixty-six he expired, in the first month of spring, the twenty-fifth year of "Establish Security," A.D. 220.

Two Emperors

On behalf of Ts'ao P'ei, the new Prince of Wei, Hua Hsin presented himself at the head of a delegation of officers and officials before the Han Emperor Tributor. Hua Hsin: "Reverently we may observe that from the time the Prince of Wei was established, his virtue spread throughout the land. Even in ancient times, none surpassed him. The assembly of the Court has consulted collectively and determines that the sacrifices of the Han have come to their end. It is expected that your majesty will emulate the ancient sages Yao and Shun by taking the mountains, rivers, and national shrines and relinquishing them ceremonially to the present Prince of Wei, Ts'ao P'ei. This coincides with the will of Heaven and the mind of men, and shall enable your majesty to secure the blessings of untroubled leisure, a boon to your ancestral clan and the living souls of the realm. The conclusion has been reached, and I come especially to appeal to you."

The Emperor listened with shocked fear, making no statement. Then, eyeing the officials, he began to sob. "I think back to the time when the Supreme Ancestor slew the serpent and led the rebellion that quelled Ch'in and erased Ch'u. Thus he founded the Han, and control of this estate has been handed down through the Liu for four hundred years. Though I have small talent, I have ever been without fault or offense. How could I bear to abandon my ancestral estate without cause? Have your discussions reopened on a more public-spirited basis."

Hua Hsin then produced two astrologers, who argued: "Since

the accession of the Prince of Wei, the unicorn has descended, the phoenix has manifested itself, the yellow dragon has appeared, prize grains grow luxuriantly, and the sweet dew has come down. Thus do the Heavens give sign and token that the Wei shall replace the Han.

"Lately have those who monitor the divine configurations observed the flaming star of Han passing its prime, and your majesty's own imperial star dimming. Meanwhile the signs for the Wei, as we probe the skies and search the earth, outnumber all telling. Moreover, there are corresponding riddles in word to indicate that the Han will abdicate to Wei in Hsü, the capital. I entreat your majesty to examine it yourself."

The Emperor: "Your augury, your graphic riddles—hollow, preposterous tricks! Would you have me set the dynasty aside on such grounds?"

Another rejoined: "From most ancient times all that flourishes must eventually be set aside; what prospers must eventually decline. Has there ever been an imperishable state or family? The House of Han has devolved for four hundred years, finally upon your majesty himself. Now its fortune and its number are spent. You should retire quickly, without delay or hesitation, lest something untoward develop."

Aggrieved, the Emperor went to his private chambers, while the Court adjourned contemptuously.

The next day the Emperor refused to appear. Armed, Ts'ao Hung and Ts'ao Hsiu went into his chambers and requested his presence. The Empress Ts'ao, daughter of Ts'ao Ts'ao, cried out: "You really are nothing but seditious traitors, angling for gain, concocting renegade schemes. My father's merit set the standard for the realm, and his authority was felt throughout the empire. Yet never did he covet the hallowed instruments of supreme power, while my good brother, who has hardly succeeded to his station, boldly yearns to supplant the Han. But the august and luminous Heaven shall refuse his sacrifices!" So saying, she wept utterly and left as the attendants lost their composure.

Ts'ao Hung and Ts'ao Hsiu strenuously urged the Emperor to attend the Court session, and he could not resist.

Hua Hsin proposed: "Let your majesty be guided by our discussions of yesterday, lest we incur some awful catastrophe."

The Emperor wept and said: "You have all long enjoyed rich recompense as servants of the Han. Among you are many sons and grandsons of renowned servants. Can you bear to commit this act of insubordination?"

Hua Hsin said stridently: "All the empire knows that your majesty lacks the 'great blessing' Heaven vouchsafes the ruler of men; this lack is the very reason for the upheaval of the realm. But for Ts'ao Ts'ao, there was more than one man who would have put your majesty to the sword. But still you refuse to acknowledge his merciful concern and, it seems, would rather induce a general assault upon your imperial self."

The Emperor was appalled and rose, making a sweeping motion with his sleeves. Hua Hsin advanced upon him intrepidly, laid hands on the sacred dragon-tunic, and spoke, his face unrecognizable: "Agreed? Or not? Which? Speak!"

The Emperor trembled and could not respond. Ts'ao Hung and Ts'ao Hsiu drew their swords and called for the keeper of the insignia. Ts'ao Hung forced the signet from him and had the keeper executed even as he protested.

The Emperor trembled uncontrollably. Around the base of his throne all he could see were hundreds of armed men of Wei. Tearfully the Emperor spoke to the assemblage: "Here we would solemnly transfer the empire to the Prince of Wei. Kindly spare what breath remains to me, that I may live out my years."

An imperial document to effect the transfer was drawn up and presented to Ts'ao P'ei. But he ceremonially declined to accept it. He likewise declined a second offer by the Emperor.

Ts'ao P'ei: "Although we have two imperial dicta, I fear the world in after times will not exonerate me of usurpation." Therefore a platform was erected upon which the public ceremony of transference would be enacted.

At the appointed time, the Emperor Tributor of the Han invited the Prince of Wei, Ts'ao P'ei, to ascend the platform and accept the throne. At the foot of the platform were some four hundred officers and officials and thirty legions of troops. Hands joined, the Emperor personally proffered the jade signet to Ts'ao P'ei, who received it. Then the multitude around the platform knelt to hear the declaration of transmission:

"Be it known to you, O Prince of Wei, that in ancient times Yao solemnly relinquished his throne to Shun, and Shun thereby committed it to Yü, the queller of the flood. For the mandate of Heaven does not abide in constancy but finds its home where virtue is.

"Now the vital principle of the dynasty is failing. Our generations have lost their proper sequence. When the succession reached our own person, in the spreading gloom of great upheaval a multitude of evils ran unchecked against the laws, and havoc was all within our sphere.

"Thanks to the supernatural military prowess of the martial prince Ts'ao Ts'ao, who retrieved our empire from rebellions in all directions, an enclave in the northern heartlands was kept clear for the security and stability of the ancestral sanctum. But how could I alone give the leadership and direction for the nine levels of nobility to enjoy tangible bounty?

"Prince of Wei, now that you have honorably succeeded into your line, all glory to your virtue in rekindling the mighty tradition of our founding kings, in reflecting the vast splendor of your late father. Their august spirit-souls send down tokens. Men and gods attest it. Mightily dedicate yourself to the task for which I make this exemplary devise of our realm."

The ceremony completed, they changed the title of the era to "Commencement of the Yellow." The state was called Mighty Wei. A general amnesty was declared, and Ts'ao Ts'ao was given the posthumous title of Great Ancestor, August Martial Emperor. The former Emperor was sent to Shan Yang with the title of patriarch. The palace was moved from Hsü to Lo Yang.

*　　　　*　　　　*　　　　*

For some time these developments had been reported to Liu Pei, Prince of Han Chung.

Overcoming Liu Pei's scruples, K'ung-ming convinced him to declare himself Emperor of the Han.

At the inauguration, the Prince of Han Chung was invited to ascend the platform and carry out the sacrifices as the following text was read:

"I, Pei, the August Emperor, resolve manifestly to announce to the August Heaven and the Fruitful Earth: the Han have held the empire for time beyond limit, with but one instance of usurpation, when the August Emperor Kuang Wu made his fury felt, executed the traitor, and restored our sacred shrines.

"More recently Ts'ao Ts'ao committed atrocities through his control of the army. He mutilated and murdered the sovereign genetrix. His crimes and evils mounted to the skies. His son P'ei now gives free rein to noxious treason, unlawfully seizing the sacred instruments of the state.

"The whole of our civil and military staffs maintain that with the services of the Han lapsed and voided, it is proper for me, Pei, to resume them and, as heir to our founders, personally carry out Heaven's retribution.

"Fearful lest my virtue prove unequal to the station, I have taken counsel among the common people and the chieftains around our borders. All agree that the mandate of Heaven must be heeded, the ancestral estate may not remain overthrown, the state may not be without a sovereign. Wherever we turn, the acclaim is for myself, Pei.

"Yet do I tremble before that clear mandate; yet do I fear the estate of the Han may come to ruin. With due caution have I selected an auspicious day to ascend the platform and in sacrificial ceremony announce our acceptance of the royal signet, that our presence may bring solace throughout the realm.

"May the gods relish the offerings of the family, and ever accommodate our rituals."

When the reading was done, K'ung-ming led the assembly in tendering the jade signet to the Prince of Han Chung, who thrice declined, but finally accepted it amid the choruses of the assembly. They changed the reign title to "Manifest Arms." The consort, Lady Wu, was made august genetrix. The eldest son, Liu Shan, was made heir apparent. K'ung-ming was appointed Prime Minister. There was a general amnesty, and the people of the Riverlands rejoiced.

The next day in full Court the Emperor delivered his first dictum: "With Lord Kuan and Chang Fei we bound our allegiance, swearing to live or die as one. Alas! My second brother, Lord Kuan, met his doom at the hands of Sun Ch'üan of the Southland. Unless we take revenge upon this enemy, the covenant is betrayed. Therefore we intend full mobilization for war against the south: to take alive the renegade traitor, to erase our humiliation."

But before he had done, someone stepped out from the ranks and threw himself at the Emperor's feet: "No!" he cried.

Chao Yün Opposes
His Lord's Campaign;
Chang Fei Meets His Doom

Chao Yün spoke against the expedition: "Ts'ao Ts'ao is the traitor, not Sun Ch'üan. Ts'ao P'ei has seized the Han state, to the common indignation of god and man. Let your majesty first make the land within the passes* your target. Station your men along the upper Wei River to bring these noxious renegades to justice. And then the loyal scholars and officers east of the passes will bundle their grain and spur their horses to welcome the royal host. But if you neglect the Wei dynasty to attack the Southland, once your forces are engaged they cannot be abruptly recalled. May your majesty consider this carefully."

Liu Pei, the Emperor, said: "Sun Ch'üan put our young brother to death. And many hold with me this implacable enmity. Until I gnaw his flesh and crush his clan, our humiliation is not effaced. Why would you stand in my way?"

Chao Yün: "Enmity against the Han traitors is a matter of public duty. Enmity for the sake of a brother is a personal matter. I urge you to give priority to the empire."

The Emperor replied: "If I should fail to revenge my brother, were I come to come into possession of these ten thousand leagues of mountains and rivers—it would make an unworthy prize." And he ignored Chao Yün's opposition. The armies were mobilized, and Chang Fei in Lang Chung was appointed general of the chariots and cavalry.

* Adjacent to Han Chung—a great natural enclave and the key to controlling the north. This was the region that the Supreme Ancestor, founder of the Han, first took in order to establish his imperial claim.

Chang Fei was in Lang Chung when the news of Lord Kuan's fate came. Through the day he howled and wept until his shirt was damp with blood. The wine he took to ease his mind only enraged him further, so that whoever crossed him was flogged immediately. A good number died from beating.

Every day he would stare into the south, gnashing his teeth in the fury of humiliation, venting cries of anguish.

The messenger from the Emperor arrived to confer the new generalship on Chang Fei.

Chang Fei: "My will to revenge my brother's murder is deep as the sea. Why have there been no appeals for mobilization in the temple and in the Court?"

The messenger: "The majority urge that Wei be annihilated before we take up arms against the Southland."

Fei cried out, angrily: "What words! We three brothers took oath to live and die as one. The second has passed from us before his time; shall I enjoy wealth and station without him? Take me to the Emperor himself. I shall serve in the vanguard, and under the banner of mourning take up arms against the south and bring the traitor home to sacrifice to my second brother, thus fulfilling the covenant." And Chang Fei headed back to the capital of the Riverlands with the messenger.

K'ung-ming was protesting the Emperor's decision to lead the invasion of the south: "Your majesty has mounted this treasured throne. If it is your purpose to strike out northward against the traitors to the Han, to extend throughout the empire the great principle of allegiance, then you should personally take command of the whole army. But if you merely intend to attack the south, it is sufficient to have a ranking general take command. What need is there to strain your sacred war chariot?"

In view of K'ung-ming's strenuous objections, the Emperor was developing reservations about his invasion plans, when Chang Fei's arrival was announced. The general prostrated himself before the Emperor and then, hugging his feet, began to cry. The Emperor cried also, and Chang Fei said: "Today you reign and the Peach Garden Oath is already forgotten! Why will you not revenge my brother?"

The Emperor: "My officials oppose it. I cannot act rashly."

Chang Fei: "What do others know of our past covenant? If you will not go, let me give myself to revenge our brother. Should I fail, I shall be content to die and see you no more."

The Emperor: "Then we will go together to attack the south and erase our humiliation."

Later the Emperor admonished Chang Fei, saying, "You have always turned violent after wine, beaten your yeoman, and then reassigned them in your personal guard. That is a good way to destroy yourself. Hereafter, make an effort to be tolerant and understanding." Chang Fei respectfully took his leave and was gone.

A scholar-official, Ch'in Mi, protested the Emperor's course too violently and was condemned to die. K'ung-ming wrote in his defense:

The treachery of the Southland led to the disaster at Chingchou. We lost our leading star; our pillar of Heaven was broken. But however keen our grief, however unforgettable, we must also remember that the crime of displacing the sacred dynastic vessels arose through Ts'ao Ts'ao. The degradation of the holy offerings of the Liu was not Sun Ch'üan's fault. And I would presume to say that if the traitors of the Wei are removed, then the Southland will tamely submit. I implore you to accept the precious advice of Ch'in Mi and take care for the strength of our armies. There are other worthwhile strategies that will bring great good fortune to our shrines and to our realm.

But the Emperor threw the petition to the ground and said: "We are resolved. Let there be no further opposition." And it was decided to commence the expedition in the seventh month of the prime year in the reign "Manifest Arms," A.D. 221.

Chang Fei returned to his camp in Lang Chung, where he alloted but three days to prepare white banners and white mail that his armies might set forth against the Southland in colors of mourning. The next day two secondary leaders entered his tent to report that the time period had to be extended to arrange for the mourning colors.

Chang Fei became enraged. "My vengeance will brook no delay. The shame is that we can't reach the traitor's borders tomorrow. And you dare contravene my order!" He shrieked for them to be bound to a tree and lashed on the back fifty times. Then he pointed at them menacingly. "Everything is to be ready tomorrow! If you fail, I'll make an example with your heads."

And one said to the other: "We've taken our punishment for today. Can we succeed in that we're ordered to do? The man's nature is violent as fire. If we do not finish by tomorrow, we will be put to death."

To this the other replied: "Better we him than he us! unless we are fated to die, he'll be drunk on his couch."

That night Chang Fei was anxious and restless; he drank for relief until he fell into a stupor inside his tent. At the first watch the two men whom Chang Fei had flogged stole into his tent on the pretext of delivering secret information. They approached the

Liu Pei attacks the south

foot of the bed. As was his habit, Chang Fei was sleeping with eyes wide open, his beard bristling. The assassins stood paralyzed. Then they heard the breath roar in his nostrils like thunder, took courage, and cut him to death with their knives. He was fifty-five years old.

Meanwhile the Emperor issued the commands. Wu Pan was placed in the vanguard. The sons of Lord Kuan and Chang Fei escorted the Emperor's chariot. By land and water they advanced, double columns of horsemen and war junks—a vast tide bearing down on the Southland.

*   *   *   *

Chang Fei's assassins carried the head to Sun Ch'üan, who accepted the two men and then addressed his officials. "Liu Pei has assumed the imperial throne; seventy crack legions are under his command. How can such vast might be dealt with?"

The officials paled and stared at one another helplessly. Then Chuko Chin stepped forth. "Long have I enjoyed my prince's bounty without having answered for it. I wish, disregarding personal safety, to meet with the sovereign of the Riverlands to persuade him of the dangers, and to help our two states to that mutual amity upon which we may jointly scourge the crimes of Ts'ao P'ei." Sun Ch'üan dispatched Chuko Chin as his representative to persuade the Emperor to halt his armies.

But Chuko Chin failed to revive the Southland–Riverlands alliance. Sun Ch'üan submitted to Ts'ao P'ei and accepted rank under Wei, but Ts'ao P'ei offered no aid. The armies of the Riverlands pressed eastward and scored early victories.

Lu Hsün Takes Command

Throughout the Southland Liu Pei was held in awe, and Sun Ch'üan felt his courage fail. At an assembly someone proposed: "The men whom the sovereign of the Riverlands holds in hatred —all those involved in the death of Lord Kuan—are dead and gone. Only the two assassins of Chang Fei are with us here. Perhaps the armies of the Riverlands can be persuaded to withdraw if we return the assassins together with Chang Fei's head, transfer Chingchou to them, and propose a truce and the restoration of former affections toward the common end of destroying the Wei."

Sun Ch'üan approved, and a delegation was sent. Liu Pei accepted the head, and the assassins were hacked to pieces and offered to Chang Fei in sacrifice.

But Liu Pei's passion to destroy the Southland did not abate. Ma Liang said: "The objects of your revenge have been destroyed. The humiliation may be considered erased. A high officer of the south has come to restore Chingchou and seal everlasting amity in the common cause against Wei. With trepidation he awaits your sage directive."

Liu Pei: "Sun Ch'üan is the man I grind my teeth for. To revive the alliance with him would mean betraying the covenant with my two brothers. First we destroy the Southland, and Wei comes next."

Word of Liu Pei's determination was brought to Sun Ch'üan who, in despair, turned for help to Lu Hsün, the young commander who had contrived the defeat of Kuan Yü. Sun Ch'üan appointed Lu commander-in-chief, with full authority over military affairs.

Sun Ch'üan's choice for commander-in-chief amazed two of his generals, Chou T'ai and Han Tang, who said: "Why would our lord give general command to an apprentice?" And when Lu Hsün arrived at the front, the men could not accept him. When he presided within the tent he was given only grudging respect.

Lu Hsün: "By sovereign authority I am empowered to command our forces for the destruction of the Riverlands. This army has an inflexible law which all of you, my lords, are obliged to observe. If there are violations, there can be no exceptions, no sympathy. Do not occasion yourselves future regret."

The men remained silent as Chou T'ai spoke: "At this moment the sovereign's nephew, Sun Huan, general to secure the east, is trapped at I Ling without food or relief. It is our earnest request, general Lu, that you provide us with a sound strategy for extricating Sun Huan to restore our sovereign's peace of mind."

Lu Hsün: "It is to be assumed that Sun Huan maintains his firm grip on morale. He can certainly hold his position, and a rescue will not be required. Once we have broken the Riverlands, Sun Huan's troops will be able to get out easily."

The men retired with barely concealed contempt. Han Tang said to Chou T'ai: "To have appointed this little pedant to the high command! The Southland is finished! You saw that performance?" Chou T'ai: "I wasn't speaking seriously, just to test him— but he had no plan at all. And he's supposed to be able to destroy the Riverlands?"

The following day Lu Hsün issued orders to the various generals to remain behind their defenses, to seal the passes, and to forbid confrontation with the enemy. The men were contemptuous of his caution and refused to maintain strict defense, and they renewed their complaints: "We are warriors seasoned in many campaigns, our lives on the line. Now our sovereign has placed you in command to drive back the forces of the Riverlands. Shouldn't you have settled on a strategy by now, deployed the men and horse, and set in motion the various expeditionary forces with a view to our great cause, instead of merely ordering a strict defense and refraining from battle? Will an act of God kill our enemies?

We are men keen for combat. Would you risk depressing our fighting spirit?"

Lu Hsün responded: "I may be a mere student. But when the sovereign entrusted this charge to me, he took the measure of my worth, my fitness to bear it. You shall make no adventurous move, and all who violate my command die." Murmuring indignantly, the men retired.

Liu Pei arrayed his forces in a seven-hundred-league line of forty camps stretching back to the entry to his territory. The flags and banners darkened the sun by day; the radiance of the camp-fires enkindled the sky by night. When word of Lu Hsün's strategy was brought to Liu Pei, he angrily ordered an advance. But Ma Liang objected: "Lu Hsün is no less capable than Chou Yü was. Do not take him on lightly."

Liu Pei: "I have grown old waging war; am I no match for this babe in arms?" Liu Pei personally led the vanguard in assaulting the Southland's several strongholds.

When Lu Hsün learned of Liu Pei's advance, he raced to the front, fearful lest Han Tang, the commander, make some ill-advised move. From a hilltop Han Tang was surveying the River-lands army, which spread over the hills and filled the wilds as it rolled on. Throughout the army a profusion of yellow umbrellas could be seen. Han Tang welcomed Lu Hsün. Horse to horse, they viewed the spectacle.

Han Tang, pointing, said, "Liu Pei has to be among them somewhere, and I mean to strike him down."

But Lu Hsün said: "Since the armies of Liu Pei began to descend eastward upon the Southland, they have enjoyed a string of victories, ten or more. Their mettle is at its keenest. So for now, we can do no more than maintain ourselves on the high ground and defend the strategic junctures. We must not go forth, for if we do we shall fail. You must drive this point home to the officers and publicize the strategy among the men. Thus we may watch the developments. At the moment the enemy troops have charged into the wilderness of the plains, and they are quite satisfied with themselves. But if we hold back and do not appear, they cannot force battle. They will have to move into the groves of the hills for relief from the heat, and that is when we should be able to overcome them with some surprise maneuver."

Han Tang said that he agreed, but in fact he remained unconvinced. Liu Pei instructed his forward units to incite battle with endless abuse and insults. Lu Hsün, however, ordered all provocation ignored and permitted no engagements. He personally went from stronghold to stronghold placating his lieutenants and enforcing strict defense.

Seeing the Southland forces refraining from battle, Liu Pei raged within. Ma Liang said to him: "Lu Hsün has a deep-laid strategy. Your majesty has come so far to do battle, from spring and on through summer. The reason they stay back is that they are waiting for some break in the situation. You must look into this."

Liu Pei: "They have *what* strategy? They are afraid of us, that's all. With the defeats they've had lately, they are not likely to be showing themselves again."

But Liu Pei's forces were camped in the raw heat of the blazing sun, and there were petitions to move the men into the hill groves near to the streams and creeks. Then when fall arrived, they could advance with redoubled vigor. And so the stations were moved into the shade.

Ma Liang said to Liu Pei: "If our men have to move and the enemy springs on us, we will be hard put."

Liu Pei: "I have instructed Wu Pan to take a legion of our least seasoned troops to encamp on the plains before the positions of the Southlanders. And I myself have chosen eight thousand crack troops and set them in ambush among the hills and gullies. When Lu Hsün realizes that we have shifted our fortifications, he will seize the moment to strike. We will have Wu Pan feign defeat, and when they give pursuit I will charge in and cut off their return. Then our little friend can be taken!"

Liu Pei's advisers unanimously acclaimed the plan, but Ma Liang said: "I have heard of late that K'ung-ming has been checking the strongholds against any penetration by the armies of Wei. Why don't you make up a sketch of these various shifts of our positions and take it to the Prime Minister for his opinion?"

Liu Pei: "I am not so ignorant of military tactics that I need to go and consult with the Prime Minister."

Ma Liang: "There is an old saying that 'Comprehensive consultation results in clarity; one-sided consultation results in blindness.' I am confident you will give thought to this."

Liu Pei: "Then, my friend, go yourself to the various forts and prepare the maps to take to K'ung-ming. If anything is wrong, bring word quickly." And Ma Liang set off.

The two Southland generals Chou T'ai and Han Tang soon learned of Liu Pei's moves and reported them to Lu Hsün. They urged him even more vehemently to attack.

Lu Hsün Burns the Camps;
K'ung-ming Sets the
Eightfold Maze

Lu Hsün scanned the field, testing the air with his whip. "A lethal aura seems to hang over the hills and ravines; an ambush may be waiting. That could be why they left those wretched troops right on the plains—to lure us out. I forbid anyone to go forth!"

The men took him for a coward. The next day Wu Pan led the Riverland decoys directly before the Southland's strongholds, where they swaggered and taunted. Slipping out of their armor, they even lolled unclothed. Lu Hsün smiled and stayed firm. "You men trust the courage of hot passion and have yet to learn the subtleties of the art of war," he said. "In three days' time it will be clear to you that this was a deception."

Commander Hsü Sheng: "In three days' time they will have finished the transfer, and you will be unable to attack."

Lu Hsün: "Precisely what I am waiting for." The commanders retired contemptuously. But in three days, the camp royal of the Riverlands emerged from ambush and crossed the plain, the lord of the Riverlands in their midst. And when the soldiers of the Southland saw it, the gall, seat of man's courage, was cleft within them.

Lu Hsün: "This is why I could not permit an attack. Now that they have emerged, we shall destroy them within ten days."

The commanders said: "The time to destroy the Riverlands was at the beginning. Now they have a network of camps stretching over five hundred leagues, vigorously defended these seven to eight months so that the danger points are well fortified. How *can* you destroy them?"

Lu Hsün: "My lords, you are ignorant of the arts of warfare. Liu Pei is a ferocious hero, and in planning he is even more cunning than ferocious. When he first concentrated his forces, his leadership was perfectly focused. But now they have held their positions too long without getting anything at all off us. Their armies are worn down and their thinking is obstructed. This is the moment for us to take them." And the commanders were reluctantly won over.

When Ts'ao P'ei learned of the deployment of the Riverlands' armies, he threw back his head and laughed. "Liu Pei is done for. No one could fend off the enemy with his camps strung out like that. And to pitch camp on level ground with heavy underbrush, where you are more or less bottled in, is a major violation of the rules of warfare. Look for news of his defeat at Lu Hsün's hands within ten days. Hsün should be moving ahead in full force to take the Riverlands itself. With the Southland's troops so far afield, their own state will be undefended. Under color of assisting them, we shall send down three units, which will make short work of them." And preparations were begun for the invasion.

*   *   *   *

Ma Liang reached the Riverlands and presented K'ung-ming with the sketches of Liu Pei's positions. K'ung-ming finished examining the documents and brought his hand down hard on his writing table as he cried in anguish: "Who advised our lord to pitch camp this way? Whoever did it should be executed!"

Ma Liang: "It was entirely the doing of our lord himself."

K'ung-ming: "Then the cycle of the Han draws to its close. If he is attacked with fire, he cannot be saved; nor can such a string of forts throw back the enemy. The end is not far off, and now we see why Lu Hsün holds so strictly back and does not show himself. You must rush to the Son of Heaven and have him change the positions. They cannot be left like this."

Ma Liang: "And if the Southland has already overwhelmed them?"

K'ung-ming: "They cannot pursue. The capital is safe, for they have Ts'ao P'ei to worry about from behind. If things go badly with our Emperor, he should find safety in Pai Ti [city of the

White Emperor]. When I came back into the Riverlands, I left
ten legions in ambush there at Fishbelly Holm."

Ma Liang was amazed. "I have been through the Fishbelly any
number of times and never saw a single soldier. What is the point
of saying such things to me?"

K'ung-ming: "You will find out later. Don't trouble yourself
any more." Ma Liang headed back to the front, and K'ung-ming
made preparations for the rescue.

*   *   *   *

Lu Hsün observed that the troops of the Riverlands were beginning to flag and were becoming negligent about their defenses.
Deciding that the period of confinement was over, he sent out a
decoy force which the Riverlands guards forced back easily. His
fighters reported: "They are too strong for us to defeat, and we
have lost men and leaders in vain."

Lu Hsün: "I have a plan, though it would never fool K'ung-
ming. But by Heaven's favor the man is not here, and this helps
us to victory."

He gathered his leaders and issued his orders: "Chu Jan is to
lead a force up the river route tomorrow afternoon when the
southeast wind becomes active. Load your boats with rushes and
hay and proceed according to plan. Han Tang attacks the north
shore, Chou T'ai the south shore. In addition to spear and sword,
everyone is to carry tinder and a bundle of rushes with saltpeter
and sulfur inside. Move on the enemy together. When you get to
their camps, use your torches according to the winds. They have
forty encampments; fire every other one. Carry dry provisions, and
do not relent for a moment until you have taken Liu Pei."

Late afternoon, the first watch. The southeast wind whips up.
A fire breaks out at a post to the left of the Emperor's camp. The
winds intensify; the fires speed. The trees catch. And the howling
is like an earthquake. The men bolt from their posts at the imperial
camp as the guards within the camp trample each other. The dead
are beyond numbering. From behind, the Southlanders—who
knows how many?—bear down for the kill. The lord of the Riverlands takes to his horse and flees to Feng Hsi, but his camp is
already an inferno. North and south of the river the glare is
powerful as the sun. Feng Hsi dashes to his horse and leads away
a few score cavalry, only to meet the murderous advance of Hsü

Liu Pei defeated at Hsiao T'ing

Sheng of the Southland. The lord of the Riverlands wheels round and rides to the west. Hsü Sheng passes Feng Hsi by and strikes out after the Emperor, who is panicked. Another Southland general blocks his way; he is trapped on four sides. Then a thunderous shout: Chang Pao, son of Chang Fei, breaks through, plucks the Emperor from the trap, and leads him to a hilltop. The tumult wells up from below. Lu Hsün's massive contingents of men and horse surround the hill. The lord of the Riverlands looks out across the raging wilderness, heaps of the dead clogging the river.

The following day the Southlanders set fires around the hill. Liu Pei's troops scurried away in disorder, leaving him in extremity. Then through the glare of the blaze, a group of men cut its way through to the hilltop. The leader was Kuan Hsing, son of Lord Kuan. "The flames press closer; we must move on," he said. "My lord, make haste to Pai Ti, where we can again regroup our forces." And they moved out.

*   *   *   *

Lu Hsün led his triumphant forces in pursuit of Liu Pei. Moving westward, he stopped short of the Kuei Pass. From the looming mountains and the river at their base a lethal miasma seemed to arise. Turning, he said to his followers: "There must be an ambush ahead. The armies must not advance." But the scouts that he dispatched brought back no word of an ambush.

Lu Hsün would not believe them. Dismounting, he climbed a hill and scanned the terrain. The same sensation of danger stole over him. He ordered a minute investigation, which turned up no man, no horse; only eighty or ninety chaotic rockpiles. He asked a resident: "Who made these piles, and why does an aura of death seem to come up from them?"

The man replied: "This is Fishbelly Holm. When K'ung-ming returned to the west, he sent troops here to arrange these rock formations on the sandflat. Since then a kind of cloud-like effluvium seems to emanate from their interiors."

Lu Hsün led a few score of cavalry to examine the rocks. From a hill slope all he could see were four fronts divided into eight planes each, with gates and doors. Lu Hsün smiled. "This is a device to perplex us. What use is it?" He rode down from the slope directly into the formation to inspect it. A subordinate said: "The sun is setting. We should return." But when Lu Hsün tried to get out, violent winds came up from nowhere. Instantly, streams of sand and rock covered the sky and the ground, until all he could see were monstrous rocks sawing the air, jagged like swordblades, and the relentless sand and mounting earth heaping upon itself like mountains. The voice of the river rumbled and rolled like the sound of war drums.

Liu Pei flees to Pai Ti

Lu Hsün was terrified: "I have sprung K'ung-ming's trap!" Frantic to return, he found no way out. An old man appeared in front of Lu Hsün's horse: "Do you desire to leave, general?" Lu Hsün: "You must lead us out."

The old man made a spurring motion with his stave and slowly proceeded to cut across the formations. Without the slightest difficulty he escorted them back to the hill slope they had come from. "Who are you?" asked Lu Hsün.

"I am the father of K'ung-ming's wife. When my son-in-law passed here on his way west, he deployed these rock formations and called them the Eightfold Maze. There are eight interconnecting gateways named according to an arcane formula: Desist,

The Eightfold Maze of K'ung-ming

Survive, Injure, Confound, Exhibit, Perish, Fear, and Liberate. Every day in every time-period, the gates are transformed with no point of reference, like a legion of crack soldiers. As K'ungming was leaving, he said to me, 'The time will come when a chief general of the Southland will wander in the maze among these ramparts. No one should help him get out.' From the cliffs I saw you go in by the gate marked 'Perish' and judged that you would be entrapped out of ignorance of the system. But all my life I have been on the kindly side. I could not bear for you to get swallowed up in here, so I took the trouble to take you out of the gate Survive."

Lu Hsün: "Good Sir, have you mastered this system of formations?"

"No," he replied. "The transformations never end; they cannot be mastered."

Shaken, Lu Hsün returned to his camp, acknowledging K'ungming's superiority. He gave the order to retreat. His seconds protested: "Liu Pei's army is ruined; his power is exhausted. We have him backed into a single walled town, and this is the very moment to attack. Why retire because of some rock formations?"

Lu Hsün: "I have no fear of those formations. But my guess is that Ts'ao P'ei, lord of Wei, is no less crafty than his father was. And if he knows we are pursuing the army of the Riverlands, he will attack our undefended homelands." And they withdrew even as news of the threat from Ts'ao P'ei began to arrive.

> Deeds to vault a thrice-torn realm,
> Fame at peak with the eightfold maze
> Of steadfast stones in the river's run,
> Monument to his rue
> That his king had choked on Wu!

> Tu Fu

Liu Pei Dies

The Southland overcame the strain of the campaign against the Riverlands and managed to meet and drive back the invaders of Wei. Ts'ao P'ei retired to his capital, Lo Yang.

Ma Liang returned from K'ung-ming to find the Riverlands defeated and the Emperor in sanctuary in Pai Ti, guarded by Chao Yün. The Emperor sighed. "Had I heeded my Prime Minister in good time, today's defeat would not have come about. How am I going to return to the capital and face the assembly of the Court?" He transmitted his wish to remain in Pai Ti and to rename his quarters the Palace of Enduring Peace. He grieved inconsolably over the loss of his commanders.

In the palace the Emperor suffered from an illness that kept him confined. His health deteriorated steadily. By the fourth month of the third year of "Manifest Arms," the Emperor could feel the disease penetrate his limbs. Keening over his brothers aggravated the symptoms. His eyes suffered spots and blackouts. From irritability with his attendants, he gave them a surly discharge and lay back on his couch in solitude. A chill, gloomy wind sprang up. The candle darkened, then flared. Two men stood in the circle of shadow. The Emperor spoke impatiently: "I thought I dismissed you, to give my troubled thoughts a moment's calm. What brings you here again?" But they ignored his cranky dismissal. The

Emperor arose to examine them, and one was Lord Kuan, one Chang Fei. "Then you are still alive!" the Emperor cried.

Lord Kuan: "We are ghosts, not men. The supernal sovereigns recognized that in our lifetimes we never forsook our good faith or our allegiance, and so conferred spiritual existence on us. The time is not far off when we shall be reunited."

The Emperor clawed at them, emitting a cry, then awoke with a spasm. The two were gone. The Emperor sighed, saying: "My time will be short in the world of men." He sent to Ch'eng, the capital, for K'ung-ming.

K'ung-ming arrived at the Palace of Enduring Peace and saw that the Emperor was critical. He knelt at the couch in a state of confusion. The Emperor: "It was only through you, Prime Minister, that the imperial quest was brought to fulfillment. How were you to know that I would prove so shallow and unsophisticated as to reject your advice and bring upon us this defeat? Persistent remorse becomes disease, and my death is in the offing. My heir is an inconsequential weakling and should not be entrusted with any issue of moment." His tears covered his face.

K'ung-ming, also in tears: "Your majesty must preserve his dragon-form to fulfill the hopes of the empire."

The Emperor: "What is your estimate of the talents of Ma Su?"

K'ung-ming: "Indeed, the man is one of the splendid talents of the age."

The Emperor: "You are wrong. In my estimation, the claims exceed the actuality. Give him no important assignment. Take careful note of this, Prime Minister."

The Emperor summoned his officials to his chambers and transcribed his testament. He handed it to K'ung-ming and spoke with a sigh: "The sage said, 'The note of a dying bird is doleful; the word of a dying man is sage.' Midway in our undertaking we must part, and I would trouble you with the care and guidance of the heir." The king brushed his eyes with one hand and took K'ung-ming's hand in the other. "I am ready to die, but I have something heartfelt to say, something I have long kept back. Your talents are ten times Ts'ao P'ei's, and I know you will be able to secure and preserve the kingdom and in the end establish our cause. If my successor proves worthy of support, then support him. If he proves unqualified, take the kingship of the Riverlands yourself!"

Sweat broke out over K'ung-ming's body. Agitatedly he pros-

Liu Pei entrusts his heir to K'ung-ming

trated himself: "Could I do otherwise than drain the strength of my limbs to fulfill the discipline of persevering loyalty whose sequel is but death?" He knocked his forehead to the ground until the blood ran.

The Emperor called his sons to the bedside and charged them

to serve K'ung-ming as they had served their father. K'ung-ming: "Though I strewed the ground with my liver and my brains, I could never fulfill my obligations to your grace."

The Emperor then spoke his charge to the assembly of the Court. When he was done, he was no more. It was the fourth month of the third year of "Manifest Arms," A.D. 223.

Epilogue

When K'ung-ming had received Liu Pei in his cottage and set forth his plan for the restoration of the Han, he had envisioned two avenues of attack against the north: a central thrust through Chingchou to take the eastern capital, Lo Yang, and a flanking attack up through the Riverlands and hooking down from the northwest to take the western capital, Ch'ang An, in the land within the passes. The success of this plan depended on the alliance with the Southland. Liu Pei's defeat by the Southland had ended the alliance for all offensive purposes. However, intermittent conflict between the north and the Southland continued giving K'ung-ming a measure of protection against the north and some latitude for maneuvering. He decided to try an invasion by the single flanking avenue through the Riverlands. He won early successes, camping in the Ch'i Mountains and reaching as far as the river Wei.

But K'ung-ming's endeavors were being undermined by the new Emperor of the Riverlands, Liu Shan, who did not inherit his father's dynastic ambition. So K'ung-ming presented his arguments to the throne:

I am a man of humble origin, who tilled his fields in Nan Yang, lucky to keep body and soul together in an age of turmoil, unwilling to make a name among the competing lords. Your father, the late king, unmindful of my low estate, demeaned himself to

K'ung-ming's petition to Liu Shan

come to my cottage three times and solicit help, confiding his cause to me. Stirred by his mission, I offered him all my energies. Soon after, at the nadir of his fortunes, I assumed command over his ruined forces in a time of peril and ordeal. Now twenty-one years have passed.

The late king appreciated my conscientious diligence and at the moment of his passing entrusted to me the conduct of his cause, a charge that made me brood lest I fail his trust and impair his lustrous virtue. That is why I crossed the River Lu south into the uncultivated lands of the Man tribe. Now that area is consolidated and our military condition is good. It is time to rouse our armies and lead them north to settle the central heartlands. Thus I would give the utmost of my limited powers to rid the realm of unscrupulous evil, restore the house of Han, and return to the traditional capital, both serving the late king and fulfilling my duty to your majesty.

Let your majesty entrust this endeavor to me. If I fail, subject me to correction and declare it to the living soul of the late king. Your majesty should take due counsel, consulting to arrive at a proper course. Discriminate and accept only the most judicious opinions, remaining deeply mindful of your father's bequeathed decree. Overwhelmed by the favor received from you, knowing that I face distant separation from your majesty, I write amid my tears, unwitting of my words.

The king perused the petition and spoke: "Honored Prime Minister, on the southern campaign against the Man you made your way through hardships and obstacles in a remote land. You have barely returned to the capital and had the chance to settle down. To continue with the northern campaign may overtax your spirits and your faculties."

K'ung-ming replied: "Since receiving from the late king the heavy charge of your care, I have never permitted myself the least negligence. Now that the south is pacified and we are free of domestic uncertainty, if we fail to take the moment to bring the traitors to justice, will there be a future time to do so?"

The astrologer stepped forward to present his view: "I have been observing the formations in the Heavens these nights. In the north no aura of prospering has matured, and the sparkle of the stars is doubly bright. You yourself, Prime Minister, know well the patterns of the Heavens. Why persist in your course?"

K'ung-ming replied: "The course of the Heavens is ever in transformation and therefore uncertain. We must not cling too tightly to such things. I am going to station our forces in Han Chung and consider fully the prospects before taking action."

Overriding all objections, K'ung-ming obtained the imperial charge and summoned the military leaders to hear the command.

K'ung-ming's successes took him to the western reaches
of the river Wei, which, further east, becomes the southern

boundary of the vital land within the passes in which the western capital, Ch'ang An, is situated. Ts'ao Jui (who replaced Ts'ao P'ei as Emperor in the north) called upon Ssuma Yi to lead his army.

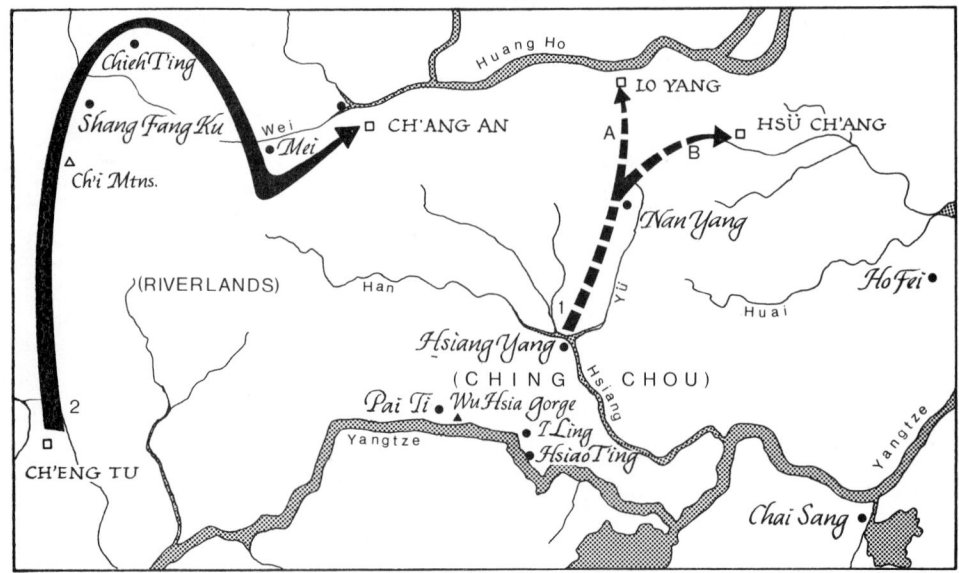

K'ung-ming's projected northern expedition. The original plan called for a two-pronged attack on the key cities Ch'ang An and Lo Yang. Liu Pei's misconceived invasion of the Southland ended in disaster at Hsiao T'ing; he fled to **Pai Ti**. With the alliance broken, the two-pronged invasion could never again be mounted. The broken arrows show the campaign that was never carried out. At the end K'ung-ming had to rely on a single invasion route through the Ch'i Mountains: his objective, Ch'ang An.

The western boundary of Chingchou was Wu Hsia gorge, the eastern boundary, Chai Sang. The northern boundary was Nan Yang at the end of the Han, but Ts'ao controlled Fan just north of Hsiang Yang, Chingchou's effective northern boundary point.

Ts'ao Ts'ao's over-all key defense points were: to the west, the Ch'i mountains; to the south, Fan; and to the east, Ho Fei.

Ma Su Loses Chieh T'ing; K'ung-ming Drives Off Ssuma Yi with a Zither

The Emperor of the Wei, Ts'ao Jui, sent Ssuma Yi to the west with twenty legions to meet the threat from the Riverlands. Ssuma Yi said to the vanguard commander: "K'ung-ming has always been cautious and meticulous. He never acts out of desperation. If I were in his position, I would make straight for Ch'ang An from the south, through the Tzu-wu gorge, saving much time. But he, while hardly at a loss for surprises, is so fearful of a slip that he is reluctant to take the risk. He is bound to come from the west through the Hsieh gorge to take the city of Mei. I have ordered the army to defend the city but on no account to give battle. West of the mountains, there is a road by the area called Chieh T'ing. It is the throat of Han Chung. To surprise Mei he must proceed from there; therefore you and I will go direct to Chieh T'ing and take it. When K'ung-ming learns that we have cut his main avenue, the lifeline of his food supply, he will take refuge in Han Chung without delay. If he turns back, I will surprise him in the byroads. If not, I will seal the roads all around, and when he has gone a month without supplies he is bound to fall captive to me!"

K'ung-ming realized that Ssuma Yi, installed in Ch'ang An and already probing beyond the passes, would try to take Chieh T'ing. K'ung-ming's call for a volunteer to hold the point was answered by Ma Su.

K'ung-ming said: "Chieh T'ing does not look like much, but

it is actually of the utmost consequence. If anything goes wrong there, the whole army is lost. I know how well versed you are in tactics, but you must take care, for the lack of walls or natural defenses makes the place extremely difficult to defend."

Ma Su replied: "I have familiarized myself with military texts since my youth. I am really fairly knowledgeable in the art of war. I doubt that I could not hold one Chieh T'ing."

K'ung-ming: "Ssuma Yi is no run-of-the-mill general. His vanguard leader is a distinguished commander. You may not be able to stand them off."

Ma Su: "Don't worry about Ssuma Yi or his vanguard leader. The Emperor himself can appear; it won't fluster me. And if I do fail, put my family to the sword with me." And Ma Su repeated the oath in writing.

K'ung-ming then summoned Wang P'ing and said: "You have always been a man of meticulous care. That is why I entrust this crucial task to you. Join Ma Su and guard Chieh T'ing vigilantly. Camp at the interception points so that the enemy cannot pass through. When you have laid out the positions, get a sketch back to me. If we hold the point, it will be a vital contribution to the capture of Ch'ang An. But take care, take care!"

Still uneasy, K'ung-ming added other support units.

Then he called Chao Yün and said: "Ssuma Yi is in command of the armies of Wei, and we have a new situation. Take a unit out from the Ch'i gorge as a decoy. If you run into enemy troops, engage and disengage at random to keep them nervous. I will lead the main army myself through the Hsieh gorge and take Mei directly. From there, Ch'ang An should fall."

Ma Su and Wang P'ing reached Chieh T'ing and examined the lay of the land. Ma Su smiled. "What could have made the Prime Minister so anxious? The Wei are hardly likely to be coming to a place so secluded in such mountainous terrain."

"Nonetheless," replied Wang P'ing, "we should pitch camp at this juncture of five roads. Set up a barrier of pickets for a protracted resistance."

Ma Su: "There's no point to pitching camp in the middle of the road. We have this hill off to the side. Here on the ground none of our flanks links easily with another. And the vegetation extends quite far. But Heaven seems to have provided us with the ideal vantage: we should camp on the hilltop."

Wang P'ing: "If we hold the road and erect blockades, ten

legions could not pass. If we move to the hill and they storm our positions, and surround us, there is no way we can hold out."

Ma Su: "That's such an adolescent way of looking at it. *The Art of War* says, 'Command the height, command the situation.' If the enemy comes, not a shield goes back!"

Wang P'ing had to be satisfied with taking a small force to hold the road while Ma Su stationed the main army on the hilltop. Several sketch maps were sent back to K'ung-ming.

When Ssuma Yi learned that Chieh T'ing had already been defended, he sighed. "K'ung-ming is more like a god than a mortal. I am not his equal."

But his second son, Chao, laughed. "Don't let your will to win fail you. I would judge the place easy enough to take. I surveyed the positions myself. There are no pickets in the road—their troops are all on the hill."

Ssuma Yi was elated. "Then Heaven hands us the victory."

Meanwhile, Ma Su ordered his men: "If they come, the moment you see the flag signal on the summit, fall upon them from all sides."

Ssuma Yi ordered one unit to neutralize Wang P'ing's road-block and led two columns to surround the hill. First he cut off the water conduits, intending to strike when confusion overwhelmed the soldiers of the Riverlands.

Ma Su looked down. All he could see was the army of the north swarming over the hills and filling the wilds, flags and ranks in perfect order. The men of the Riverlands lost their courage and were afraid to descend.

The hill was sealed for twelve hours. There was no water and no way to prepare food. Discipline broke down. One group surrendered, but Ma Su refused to give in. Ssuma Yi had fires set on the nearby hills. Confusion increased. Realizing that he could defend no longer, Ma Su drove his remnant force to a last descent and made his way out to the west.

K'ung-ming soon learned of the catastrophe at Chieh T'ing. He ordered a retreat into Han Chung. In the city of Hsi he was directing the complex retreat when, well before the expected time, emergency reports arrived telling of a massive force of fifteen legions, led by Ssuma Yi, swarming toward Hsi. K'ung-ming had not even a ranking general with him, only a cadre of officials and officers and twenty-five hundred troops.

There was panic among the cadre as K'ung-ming climbed the

wall to scout the horizon. Dust was billowing up to the skies. Two columns of northmen were bearing murderously down on Hsi. K'ung-ming ordered all flags and banners put away. The commanders of the watchtowers were cautioned, on their lives, against any unauthorized movements or audible conversation. Then K'ung-ming had the main gates thrown open and twenty men stationed at each to sweep and damp down the roadway. They were to appear oblivious when the northerners arrived. K'ung-ming decked himself in crane feathers, wound a white wrap on his head and, followed by two lads and carrying a zither, braced himself upon the city wall. Incense burned as he struck up the instrument.

When Ssuma Yi's forward units came within sight of the scene that K'ung-ming had contrived, they were afraid to advance. Incredulous, Ssuma Yi ordered a halt and raced to the front. There indeed was K'ung-ming, seated on the upper wall, appearing palpably amused as he strummed his zither amid the incense. The lad to the left held his sword; the lad to the right the yak-tail. In and around the gates, twenty-odd villagers concentrated on their sweeping as if no one were near.

Ssuma Yi viewed the scene with skepticism, but he immediately ordered a general about-face and retreated north to the mountain roads. His second son, Ssuma Chao, said: "You can be sure we have caught K'ung-ming without his forces, and that explains this exhibition. Why are we retreating, Father?"

"K'ung-ming is a man of meticulous caution," replied Ssuma Yi. "He never takes reckless chances. These gates are an invitation to an ambush. If we advance, we spring the trap. You young men do not know of such things. We should pull back without delay."

When he saw the northmen moving back, K'ung-ming rubbed his hands slowly and smiled. The cadre in the city were dumbfounded to see how the sight of K'ung-ming put to flight a mighty general and his fifteen legions.

K'ung-ming explained. "He paid heed to my lifelong reputation for caution. When he saw how things were, he suspected an ambush. But I was not taking a risk, actually; there was simply no alternative. Now he will be heading out the mountain roads to the north, where I have already placed forces to greet him."

The cadre said: "Prime Minister, neither gods nor demons could fathom your machinations. *We* would have abandoned the city."

K'ung-ming: "With twenty-five hundred men we would hardly have been able to get far enough to avoid capture." Then he clapped and grinned: "But if I were Ssuma Yi, I'd never have pulled away." Then he continued the retreat into Han Chung.

Despite his personal feeling, K'ung-ming ordered Ma Su executed and demoted himself to the rank of general. Oppo-

K'ung-ming drives off Ssuma Yi with his zither

sition at Court to K'ung-ming's forward policy increased, necessitating a purge of the peace faction before the campaigns could resume. In the summer of A.D. *229 K'ung-ming was established again in the Ch'i Mountains. It was the sixth expedition.*

The Last Campaign

K'ung-ming ordered the soldiers of the Riverlands to mingle with the populace of the Wei and work the fields. There was one soldier to every two peasants, yet the Riverlanders did not encroach on the peasants, who remained content in their occupations.

Ssuma Yi's first son, Shih, reported this to his father. "The Riverlanders have been making off with a good part of our grain. And now they have told their men to intersperse their militia colonies among our own people along the banks of the Wei.* Such long-range operations could become an enormous problem for our government. Father, is it not time to settle things with K'ung-ming once for all?"

But the strategy of the northerners was a waiting one. They knew that K'ung-ming was on his sixth expedition and could not forever override the reluctance of the second Emperor, Liu Shan, to wage war. And they knew that his food-supply problems had led him to start colonies of militia-farmers.

To whet the northmen's appetite for an engagement, K'ung-ming allowed them minor victories. One day, after capturing a few of the Riverlanders, Ssuma Yi asked: "Where is K'ung-ming now?"

His adherents who had questioned the prisoners replied: "He is no longer in the Ch'i Mountains. He has moved about ten

* The river Wei, not the name of the northern dynasty.

leagues west of the Shang Fang gorge and settled himself behind
a defense perimeter. Every day provisions are brought in and
stored."

Ssuma Yi: "Tomorrow you are to coordinate an attack on their
main camp in the Ch'i Mountains. I will bring up the reserves.
When they see us strike, all their camps will come to the rescue.
Then I will turn back upon the Shang Fang and burn their provisions."

From a hilltop K'ung-ming was observing the contingents of
the Wei and guessed their destination. He gave orders that if
Ssuma Yi appeared personally, the Wei camps were to be plun-
dered and the south bank of the river seized.

As the forces of the Wei descended on the camp, the Riverlanders charged away amid great clamor, as if seeking relief.
Ssuma Yi saw the rescue he had anticipated and, leading his two
sons and the central units, turned round and dashed to Shang
Fang for the kill.

But Wei Yen, K'ung-ming's general, was already at the mouth
of the Shang Fang and greeted Ssuma Yi with dancing sword. Yi
poised his spear and closed with him. After three passes, Wei Yen
wheeled and fled. Yi charged after. Seeing Wei Yen by himself
with a scanty company, Yi pursued single-mindedly, his sons at
his sides. Wei Yen drew his company deep into the gorge. Yi
pursued to the entry. His scouts reported no ambush, only a few
grass-matted dwellings on the hilltop.

"That's where the grain is," said Ssuma Yi.

They drove ahead into the Shang Fang. Ssuma Yi noticed that
the hilltop dwellings were of dry brambles and that Wei Yen had
disappeared. But even as he became conscious of his suspicions,
there was a clamor and quaking as wheels of fire came rolling
down the hill, sealing the exit with a wall of flame. Then burning
arrows rained down, and explosions erupted in the earth.

Too panicked to move, Ssuma Yi dismounted and embraced
his sons. "This is our end," he cried.

But in that moment a furious gale began blowing, and a dense
black atmosphere filled up the sky. A single splitting peal of
thunder announced the rainstorm. It came down in torrents, putting out the fires all over the gorge, stifling the earth-mines, and
rendering all explosive weapons useless.

Ssuma Yi and his sons broke out of the trap and retreated to the north shore of the river, having found the south shore already taken. But the Riverland forces had decimated the Wei army.

K'ung-ming had been watching Ssuma Yi enter the Shang Fang and face the inferno that followed. But when he saw the rains pour out of the heavens, he sighed: "The planning lies with man, the issue with Heaven. No one can force it."

Ssuma Yi reverted strictly to his policy of withholding from all engagements. So K'ung-ming packed a scarf and a silk dress in a large box and had it delivered to Ssuma Yi. The accompanying note read:

> Since you assumed command of the northern hordes, you seem unwilling to shoulder your armor, take up your weapon, and settle who is the hero and who the hen. You appear content to seclude yourself in your earthen nest—exactly like a woman—avoiding the blade and the arrow. So I have sent you these things which, if you cannot do battle, you should receive with due humility. But if you retain some sense of self-respect, and still have a man's bosom, send them back and set the date.

Ssuma Yi smiled through his rage and replied, "K'ung-ming considers me a woman?" simply accepting the gift and treating the bearer generously.

"Tell me something about your master—how he sleeps and eats," Ssuma Yi said to the bearer. "Is his work going efficiently, or is he overburdened?"

The bearer: "My master rises too early and retires too late. He oversees all serious offenses himself. He takes but a few handfuls of food each day."

Ssuma Yi said: "He eats too little and does too much. Can he last?"

The bearer returned to K'ung-ming with a full account. Sadly, K'ung-ming remarked: "How well he knows me."

An aide commented: "Prime Minister, personally attending even to minor affairs is exhausting you. The strain must tell. What Ssuma Yi said is really no overstatement."

Tears showed in K'ung-ming's eyes. "I am aware of this. But I have charge of the child-king from our late king, and I fear no one is so committed as I."

Some began to weep. K'ung-ming felt his spirits and his faculties disquieted. The commanders became reluctant to advance.

Among the northmen, the commanders were so incensed over K'ung-ming's gift that Ssuma Yi had to send for an imperial writ to reinforce his decision not to give battle.

One night K'ung-ming felt his mind clouding over. He dragged himself out of his tent to observe the constellations. But there was little reassurance in the stars. "My life has come to its twilight," he remarked to his second, Chiang Wei. "I see the alien star in the Great Bear doubly bright, but the host star dimmed. The

K'ung-ming prays

supporting stars are also weaker. If the aspect of the Heavens is like this, my fate is uncertain."

Chiang Wei said: "Can you not reclaim it through prayer?"

"I always offer my prayers," said K'ung-ming, "but one never knows Heaven's wish. Bring forty-nine warriors, each with black dress and a black flag. Let them form a circle around my tent. I will remain within and address my prayers to the Northern Dipper. If my master lamp stays lit for seven days, I may gain a year. If it goes out, I am bound to my mortality. Keep all nonessential persons out of the tent. A few youths can provide my necessaries."

It was the eighth month, mid-autumn. The Milky Way was glowing, constant and clear like a finely differentiated mist of jewels. The flags hung motionless. The night alarms were stilled.

K'ung-ming offered his prayer: "Born into an age of troubles, I would have been content to live out my time among the groves and streams, but for the favor of the late king, who placed the prince in my charge and committed me to toil in the service of our cause, as the ox toils, or the horse. I did not think my master star would start to fail, that my days would draw to a close. In reverence, bowed in hope of mercy, I address the vast vault of Heaven, asking that my humble fate may somehow recommend itself and be prolonged, to help restore an order that once was, and to carry on the sacred service of the Han. I would not petition the gods without good reason, but for the conviction of my heart."

K'ung-ming then stretched himself out within his tent to await the dawn. The next day he could manage his affairs, but kept spitting blood. By day he presided over the military deliberations; by night he tracked the Dipper and the Bear.

Ssuma Yi held tight to his defenses. One night while observing the constellations, he said: "I see the master star has lost its position. K'ung-ming must be ill. He will die before long. Take one thousand men to probe their positions. If the Riverlanders seem involved in any kind of trouble and do not engage you, it means K'ung-ming is ill, and we should seize the occasion to strike."

K'ung-ming had been praying for six nights. The master lamp burned brightly. K'ung-ming's spirits rose. Suddenly there was an uproar outside. Before K'ung-ming could send to inquire, Wei Yen dashed into the tent to report the arrival of the northmen. In his haste he kicked over the master lamp, and it went out.

The Star Plunges Downward;
K'ung-ming Is Heaven-bound;
His Wooden Idol Awes Ssuma Yi

"It is not his fault," said K'ung-ming. "My destiny has reached its limit." Bringing up blood freely, K'ung-ming lay on his couch and said to Wei Yen, "Ssuma Yi has guessed. He sent those men to probe our positions. Go out and meet them." Wei Yen engaged the northmen and drove them back.

K'ung-ming said to his first general, Chiang Wei: "My commitment was to recover the north and revive the Han. But man is helpless before the purposes of Heaven. If I am not dead by dawn, I shall be by evening. This text in twenty-four chapters is my life's work. Among my generals only you are fit to receive it. Do not slight it, I pray you." Receiving it, Chiang Wei wept.

K'ung-ming continued: "Here is a blueprint for the repeating crossbow we were never able to put into action. Try to manufacture some, according to the sketches. As for the roads leading into the Riverlands, there is no need to be anxious, except for the Yin P'ing pass which, though treacherously steep, is almost certain to be lost."

Then he called his men to him and said: "After my death, Wei Yen will not remain loyal. When the time comes, open this bag to find out who is to execute him."

The king's envoy arrived. K'ung-ming said to him: "It is my misfortune to perish midway in my journey. I set aside the unfulfilled cause of home and country, and the fault is mine. The lords must support the Emperor with absolute loyalty. The institutions of our state must not be altered. The men I have appointed must not be lightly set aside. My military techniques have been given to Chiang Wei, who is capable of sustaining my purposes to the fullest extent. My life enters its twilight. I shall submit my testament to our king, the Son of Heaven."

K'ung-ming tried to inspect the camp perimeter, but when he felt the autumn wind in his face, the cold took his very bones. "No more to overlook the battlelines, to scourge the enemy? These blue-grey skies stretch to infinity. What are the limits of events on earth?"

Then he prepared the testament:

Life and death are man's mortal lot. None can evade his preordained number. As death approaches, let me speak my unquestioning loyalty. I am by nature a simple, awkward man, whose life-span crossed with a time of troubles. I was entrusted with the seals of command and came to wield sole military authority. I mobilized the northward expedition but gained no success. What more is there to expect from a man fatally ill whose remaining life is a matter of days? Not to have brought to its conclusion my service to your majesty is a draft of remorse I shall drink without end. I appeal to your majesty to remain pure in heart and free of wrongful desires. Discipline yourself; cherish the people. Fulfill your filial duty to the late king. Extend humane favor within your realm. Raise the obscure and unacknowledged, promote the competent and the worthy. Reject the unscrupulous and depraved. Keep wholesome our mores and morale.

When the transcript was completed, K'ung-ming issued strict orders: "After I am dead there must be no mourning. Put the corpse in a large, dragon-figured coffin. Place seven grains of rice in my mouth, a single lamp at my feet. Everything must be kept peaceful and normal. Any outcry must be strictly prevented, or the master star may fall. My cloud-soul will rise to hold it in place. It will puzzle Ssuma Yi to see the master star in position. Let our rear camps evacuate first. Then pull slowly back, unit by unit. If Ssuma Yi gives chase, reverse your formations and face them. Take the wooden likeness of me that I had carved, and set it in the chariot with a proper guard. Ssuma Yi will see it and flee."

That night K'ung-ming was observing the North Dipper. He indicated one star. "That is my master star," he said. Those around him looked up. The star was dull and flickered as if it would fall. K'ung-ming pointed at it with his sword and uttered a chant. Then he rushed back to the tent and fainted. He would not respond to questions, and shortly was no more. Autumn, the twenty-third day of the eighth month, the twelfth year of "Establish Restoration," A.D. 234. K'ung-ming was dead at fifty-four. That night the moon dimmed gently as K'ung-ming came home.

Ssuma Yi was watching the skies. He saw a large reddish star with emanations coursing from the northeast to the southwest, the sacred corner of the universe. It dove toward the camps of the Riverlands, lurched three times, and then reascended. All around, a low murmuring could be heard. Frightened and yet elated, he exclaimed: "K'ung-ming is dead!" He ordered a large force to move on the enemy camps, but as he went through the gates, uncertainties overtook him. "K'ung-ming is master of so many ruses," he mused. "Perhaps he is feigning death because he sees how long we have avoided an engagement. I may spring his trap if I attack." Ssuma Yi turned around and sent out a forward patrol.

The patrol brought back word of the evacuation, and Ssuma Yi said: "He is dead indeed. Then we must pursue without delay." But when he reached the camps of the Riverlands, he found no one. Ssuma Yi continued to press forward until he could see the army of the Riverlands not far in the distance. Without warning, explosions sounded behind the hills, and the earth began to shake. The men of the Riverlands turned to meet him. Through the trees he glimpsed a giant banner bearing the title "K'ung-ming, Prime Minister of the Han." Close behind was a four-wheeled chariot attended by ranking generals. Upon it was K'ung-ming, seated punctiliously, wearing his turban, feathered fan, crane plumes, and black ribbons. Yi was aghast. "K'ung-ming still lives," he said. "And I have stumbled into a stronghold." He turned to flee, but Chiang Wei checked him. "You have fallen into the Prime Minister's trap," he cried. The northmen felt soul and body divide, and, throwing arms and armor to the ground, comrade trampled comrade in the flight to safety. To this day a common saying has survived: "A dead K'ung-ming can drive off a live Ssuma."

Several days later, when the Riverlanders were safely away, Ssuma Yi learned that the retreating troops had hoisted the white flags of mourning and grieved till the ground shook. Then he knew that the K'ung-ming in the chariot was a wooden idol.

The death of K'ung-ming ended the imperial ambitions
of the Riverlands. Within a single generation the weakling king,

son of Liu Pei, surrendered to the Wei. When the Ssuma clan deposed the Ts'ao clan to found the Chin dynasty in A.D. *265, they set out to unify the realm and in 280 won the allegiance of the Southland. Almost one hundred years had passed since the great uprising of the Yellow Scarves in 184. But the reign of the Chin was not to last. By* A.D. *317 the dynasty was driven south, and non-Chinese dynasties dominated the north for nearly three centuries.*

A NOTE ON THE TIMES
OF LO KUAN-CHUNG

Seven centuries ago the Mongols annihilated the fragile Sung dynasty and began the three dark generations of their rule in China, 1280–1367. They held the northern heartland and dominated the native Chinese with especial cruelty, using non-Chinese central Asians as overseers. Parts of the northern agricultural economy were devastated; acres were turned into hunting parks or pasture. In the south, where there was resistance, the treatment of Chinese peasants was even harsher. By the middle of the fourteenth century, resistance to the Mongols was organized by a number of religious sects. Secret societies and rebel groups such as the White Lotus, the White Cloud, the Manichaeans, the Maitreya Buddhists, and others fought the Mongols, sometimes under the banner of Sung restoration, sometimes for egalitarian ideals summarized in the utopian leveling slogan "T'ai P'ing," or "Great Equality," that goes back to the late years of the Han dynasty.

Toward the end of the struggle, the anti-Mongol forces formed the army of the Red Scarves. In 1355, a Manichaean group proclaimed the first year of a restored Sung dynasty under the reign title Dragon-and-Phoenix. From this group emerged the future founder of the Ming dynasty, Chu Yüan-chang, under whom the eastern branch of the Red Scarves army chased the Mongols beyond the great wall. In 1368, Chu Yüan-chang assumed the imperial throne, turned his back on restoring the Sung, and proclaimed the Ming dynasty (*ming*, "light," denoting "Manichaean" in Chinese as well as being a traditional Confucian term for "enlightenment").

The Ming Emperor called his reign Hung Wu, Mighty Floodtide of Arms. In the course of its thirty years, the Emperor, guided by Confucian officials and scholars, consciously and publicly built the Ming state system on the model of the first reign of the Han dynasty. Heretical sects like the Manichaeans, the White Cloud, and others were suppressed and proscribed, though far from eliminated. Generous land grants were made to dispossessed owners and some peasants during the first twenty years of the Hung Wu period. By and large, the great mass movements of the late Mongol period were contained by the new Confucian orthodoxy.

This effective reconstitution of the internal social order enabled the Ming to keep the still aggressive Mongols at bay—and the ferocious Tamerlane in nominal submission. From his base in Samarkand, crossroads of Central Asia, Tamerlane sought to restore the Mongol world, but though he imprisoned Chinese envoys on one occasion (1385–86) China was spared invasion by his death.

This was the world of our author, Lo Kuan-chung (ca. 1330–ca. 1400). *Three Kingdoms* was probably written late in its author's life and thus toward the end of the reign of the first Ming Emperor. The question is, Why did the author turn to the Han, an era eleven hundred years past, for the subject of his epic?

* * * *

After Liu Pei failed to restore the Han, there ensued four centuries of divided empire and unstable, short-lived dynasties until reunification under the Sui and T'ang. During those four centuries the national pride was humbled, and it seemed to many that a civilization had been eclipsed. The grandeur of the Han was no more, and even as it remained a model of achievement to all future dynasties, its disintegration stood as a warning.

Men's memories of the Han were still warm when the primary record, *The Records of the Three Kingdoms*, was compiled by the historian Ch'en Shou in A.D. 297. One hundred and thirty years later, P'ei Sung-chih supplemented the record with voluminous notes and anecdotes. These two official documents constitute the foundation upon which Lo Kuan-chung based his epic narrative. But if Lo drew on official accounts for his facts, he drew on the popular tradition of recitation and dramatic performance for the themes and spirit of his work.

Long before the Mongol conquest, northern China had been dominated by a series of non-Chinese conquerors. In 1127, the Sung dynasty was driven to the South; the Chinese would not again rule their North until the Ming. During these centuries a lively popular tradition, a veritable cultural counteroffensive, developed around the fall of the Han and the formation of the three kingdoms. Liu Pei, who had sought to restore the Han from the south, came to symbolize Chinese resistance to foreign invasion of the northern homeland and the determination to recover it. There are accounts dating even before 1127 that tell of public distress at the fate of Liu Pei and of popular animosity toward Ts'ao Ts'ao. It is this popular tradition that Lo Kuan-chung's *Three Kingdoms* brings to a sophisticated culmination.

At first glance, it seems plausible to regard *Three Kingdoms* as a celebration of Chu Yüan-chang, founder and first Emperor of the Ming dynasty, the man who brought Liu Pei's cause to fulfillment. This seems especially apt because of the effort Chu Yüan-chang made to identify himself with the first Han Emperor.* Then, too, Chu Yüan-chang, Liu Pei, and the first Han Emperor all rose from poverty and obscurity amid a multitude of conflicting contenders for power, none of whom could be emperor *de jure*. And so each forged for himself anew what the Chinese call *te*, or "virtue," the ultimate source of political authority.

Nonetheless, to write of the decline of China's greatest dynasty during the first reign of the exuberant, optimistic Ming strikes a troubling note. Do warnings lie under the obvious acclaim?

Certain crude pre-Ming versions of *Three Kingdoms* present the fall and partition of the Han as retribution for the purge of generals and advisers that the founder of the Han, the Supreme Ancestor, had conducted a few years after assuming power. The Ming Emperor conducted a similar purge midway through his reign. To be sure, the surviving editions of Lo's *Three Kingdoms* contain no such interpretations, but even the earliest postdates Lo's death by nearly a century, well after the massive historical revisionism of the Yung Lo era (1403–1425).

---

* Sung resistance would have been a difficult subject for the historian in view of Chu Yüan-chang's unscrupulous conduct toward the Sung restorationists to whom he owed his rise to power. He is said to have murdered the leader of the group.

Another indication of the complexity of the author's intentions is the use of Manichaean symbols in the opening chapter. When Liu Pei forms a brotherhood (itself a secret society rite) with two strangers, Kuan Yü and Chang Fei, the three seal their vow to serve the nation by sacrificing a black bull and a white horse. This vivid scene is preserved in the 1591 and 1644 illustrated editions, although later (Ch'ing) editions omit the animals. The sacrifice is not part of the early official record, but it is one that was often performed by heretical sects, notably the Manichaean, and probably symbolized the war of the light against the dark that is characteristic of that religion. The use of the rite by the three heroes suggests both their heretical background and their ambiguous fates, a suggestion the action bears out in its own ways. As the first Ming reign drew to a close such reminders of the Emperor's origins could have been delicately haunting.

The animals reappear at strategic points in the narrative and, in particular, point up the ambiguity of Kuan Yü's intentions. The white horse is the positive symbol of the brotherhood. It echoes the term "ming" graphically and suggests clarity and frankness. It is at White Horse (Pai Ma) that Kuan Yü satisfies his debt to Ts'ao Ts'ao by killing two enemy generals (Yen Liang and Wen Ch'ou) before leaving the advantages of high favor to rejoin his lord, Liu Pei, and an uncertain fate.

When Kuan Yü is about to meet his doom, he dreams that a black, bull-sized boar is biting his leg. The black bull symbolizes the negative side of the brotherhood, Kuan Yü's wish to rule Chingchou for his own ends rather than serve his brother's cause with unquestioning loyalty. However, the boar biting his leg suggests even darker themes. The allusion is to a story in the *Tso Chuan** that tells of fraternal betrayal through adultery, evoking the Chinese abhorrence of the levirate, a practice for which the Ming condemned the Mongols and which Ming statutes severely proscribed. The entire scene stands in stark contrast to the earlier episode in which Kuan Yü, evading Ts'ao Ts'ao's attempt to lodge him with Liu Pei's sisters, stands guard through the night at their door, a white candle in his hand. That is the popular image of Lord Kuan, the model of rectitude the Chinese revere.

On the narrative level, Kuan Yü's fate is tragic, his conduct in releasing Ts'ao Ts'ao magnanimous to a fault. Yet with character-

* Huan 18, Chuang 8.

istic complexity, the author does not exclude the possibility that Kuan Yü had calculations of his own. At the end Kuan Yü's magnanimity turns to arrogance. On the symbolic level the worst suspicions are reinforced, and K'ung-ming's reservations about the brotherhood are vindicated. The ago-old conflict in Chinese society between filial and fraternal love, vertical and lateral succession, is thus re-examined.

THE CHAPTERS OF THIS TRANSLATION
AND THEIR EQUIVALENTS
IN THE CHINESE ORIGINAL

INDEX

Hsiang Yü (pre-Han general), 157

Hsiao Ho (early Han general), 227

Hsiao P'ei (town), 36, 47–8

Hsieh, 12–13. *See also* Tributor

Hsieh gorge, 220, 284, 286

Hsien, 3 *n. See also* Tributor

Hsin Yeh (city), 85–9, 99–104, 127, 131, 135, 140–3, 156–7

Hsü (capital city), 13, 16, 28 *n.*, 46, 53, 57, 72, 87, 256

Hsü, Madam (mother of Tan Fu), 105–13

Hsü Huang (general under Ts'ao Ts'ao), 236–8

Hsü Kung (warden in Wu), 72–3

Hsü Sheng (commander under Sun Ch'üan), 268–71

Hsü Shu, 105. *See also* Tan Fu

Hsü Yü (adviser to Yüan Shao), 34

Hsüan-te, 4. *See also* Liu Pei

Hsüan Wu Lake, 127

Hsüchou (province), 28–9, 31–32, 34, 36, 46, 48, 57, 232

Hsün the Obedient (Emperor), 74

Hsün Yang River, 234

Hsün Yü (adviser to Ts'ao Ts'ao), 14, 34, 47–8, 55, 83, 111, 135, 150

Hua Hsin (representative of Ts'ao P'ei), 253–5

Hua Jung trail, 193–4, 197–200

Hua T'o (physician), 73, 231–2, 250

Huai Nan (city), 26

Huan (ancient leader), 81

Huang Ch'üan (adviser to Liu Chang), 211

Huang Chung (general under Liu Pei), 227

Huang Kai (spy for Liu Pei), 169, 178, 180, 190, 194–5

Huang Tsu (general under Liu Pei), 81, 128–32

Hung Wu (Ming era), 301

I Ling (place), 264

I tribes, 124

Imperial Uncle, 14. *See also* Liu Pei

Interlocutor (Han Emperor; father of Tributor), 3–4, 12

Ju Nan (city), 69

Jung tribes, 124

Kan, Lady (wife of Liu Pei), 50–51, 54, 63, 69–70, 87, 147–9

Kan Ning (defector to Sun Ch'üan), 128, 130–1, 165

Kan Tse (messenger to Ts'ao Ts'ao), 180

Kao Tsu (Supreme Ancestor; first Han Emperor), 19–20, 22, 116, 124, 159, 222, 227, 253, 258 *n.*, 302

Korea, 184

K'ou Feng, 105. *See also* Liu Feng

Ku (town), 69, 71

Ku-tzu (city), 85

Ku Yung (adviser to Sun Ch'üan), 163, 169, 223

Kuan Chung (scholar-adviser), 109, 114, 154, 156–7

Kuan Chung region, 124

Kuan Hsing (son of Kuan Yü), 272

Kuan, Lord. *See* Kuan Yü

Kuan P'ing (son of Kuan Yü), 137, 228, 231, 236, 239, 242

About the Translator

Moss Roberts is Professor of Chinese at New York University and Director of the East Asian Studies Program. He received his Ph.D. from Columbia University and also did advanced work in the Oriental Languages Department at Berkeley. He is the author of several articles on Chinese philosophy and philology, as well as of an extended study of funding in the China field, "The Structure and Direction of Contemporary China Studies," which was published in the *Bulletin of Concerned Asia Scholars* in 1971.